SHIELD BREAKER

SHIELD BREAKER

THE WOLF OF KINGS
BOOK TWO

Richard Cullen

An Aries Book

First published in the UK in 2022 by Head of Zeus Ltd
This paperback edition first published in 2022 by Head of Zeus Ltd,
part of Bloomsbury Publishing Plc

9 7 5 3 1 2 4 6 8

A catalogue record for this book is available from the British Library.

ISBN (PB): 9781801102070
ISBN (E): 9781801102063

Cover design: Mark Swan

Typeset by Siliconchips Services Ltd UK

Printed and bound in Great Britain by
CPI Group (UK) Ltd, Croydon CRO 4YY

Head of Zeus Ltd
First Floor East
5–8 Hardwick Street
London ECIR 4RG

WWW.HEADOFZEUS.COM

We have experienced the truth of this prophecy, for England has become the habitation of outsiders and the dominion of foreigners. Today, no Englishman is earl, bishop, or abbott, and newcomers gnaw away at the riches and very innards of England; nor is there any hope for an end of this misery.

— William of Malmesbury,
Gesta Regum Anglorum

Place Names

Alba – Scotland
Ánslo – Oslo
Banesberie – Banbury
Berchastede – Berkhamsted
Berencestra – Bicester
Berewyke – Barwick-in-Elmet
Bledone – Bleadon
Bretagne – Brittany
Brygstow – Bristol
Cantocheheve – Quantoxhead
Cornualge – Cornwall
Dublin
Dunheved – Launceston
Dun Holm – Durham
Dunster
Efor – Yorkshire
Éire – Ireland
Exonia – Exeter
Glestingaburg – Glastonbury
Grimeshou – Grimesthorpe
Hagenesse – Hackness
Haxebi – Haxby

Hereford
Laoighse – Portlaoise
Lintone – Linton
Ludenburgh – London
Middeltun – Middleton
Oleslec – Ulleskelf
Scóine – Scone
Segerston Heugh – Sacriston
Sumersete – Somerset
Waruic – Warwick
Wiltescire – Wiltshire
Yorke – York

Prologue

He would have been a king, but the crown was torn away from his grasp before he had a chance to touch its gilded edge. Edgar had stood as proudly as he was able when the witan elected him their monarch. Thegns and magnates had roared their approval, but he knew it was all for show. They had chosen him aright, but only for his youth and naivety. He would have been a puppet on the throne, a tool for the wielding of other men. Little more than a year on, and the one they called Aetheling was naïve no longer.

His ship had sailed north along the coast, then down the firth to the river that cut a path to this notorious seat of power in Alba. As it cruised to the jetty he could only feel the ignominy of it. He, the chosen king of England, being forced to prostrate himself at the feet of another ruler. To beg for aid in order to take back what was rightfully his. But he would not kneel forever.

No sooner had the ship landed and its mooring been

fixed than he leapt ashore, feeling his legs tremble on solid ground after so long at sea. The brisk air of Alba chilled him, but he had foregone a cloak. These savage northerners could smell the stink of weakness, and Edgar would not offer them the merest whiff.

He turned to help his mother down from the boat, and she gratefully took his hand. Though she had put a brave face on this, her reservations were obvious in the dark shadow of concern that marred her features. They waited as the boatmen helped his sisters ashore, closely followed by Gospatric. The ealdorman had a grim look to his narrow face, but then he had reason to be troubled. He was an earl dispossessed of an earldom. A powerful man with no power. Edgar knew full well he had only presented himself as an ally, and promised to help regain the crown, for his own betterment. Nevertheless, in a land of few friends, Edgar would have to accept help where it was offered. He could only hope the man they had come to meet would make a more trustworthy ally than this Saxon lord.

'Don't look so worried,' Gospatric said, clapping Edgar on the shoulder. 'Trust me, I have known Máel for many years, and he is no friend of the Franks. This is the wisest course.'

Edgar nodded his agreement, but was given no solace by Gospatric's mention of 'trust'. Could he really trust anyone in these savage times?

They struck north from the jetty, along a path that cut through an open glen. Edgar didn't have to go far before they saw men waiting for them atop the hill ahead. There were five of them, each as stout and implacable as the surrounding land, their furs blowing in the breeze, their hair as wild and rampant as Alba itself.

Gospatric stepped forward, sharing brief words with the men in the Gàidhlig tongue. They laughed, eyeing Edgar with little respect before beckoning him to follow. Not for the first time he wondered if this was some kind of trap, if he had led his mother and sisters into needless peril, but what fear could Alba hold that the rest of the country did not? If Edgar was to take his rightful crown he would have to show more conviction.

He turned to make sure his mother and sisters were still close. Though whipped by the wind, the lady Agatha had a firm set to her jaw. Behind her Cristina looked skittish, eyes flitting to left and right as though she expected an ambush to burst from the ground she walked on. In contrast, his sister Margret bore that serene look to her face that always gave Edgar little impression of what she was thinking.

His mother increased her pace, grasping his arm as they followed their guides to the brow of the hill.

'Are you prepared for what we might face?' she asked in the language of the Rus, lest they be overheard. 'Those men look every inch the barbarians we have been warned to expect. At best we might be offered no sanctuary. At worst...' She left that consequence to hang in the cold air.

'Gospatric has reassured me we are safe in the court of Alba.'

'I believe that man less than the Franks.'

'Belief is all we have to rely on right now,' Edgar replied, though he hated to admit it. 'We need allies, and this is our best chance to secure them.'

'And what of your sisters?' Agatha said. Edgar could sense the fear in her usually calm tone.

'I will see no harm come to them. We have been greeted by warriors, mother. Most likely it is a show of strength, nothing more.'

Edgar could only hope that was true. It reminded him of another display of power he had been privy to, when the newly crowned king had offered 'invitations' to the great and good of England. Magnates like Edwin and his brother Morcar, Gospatric himself and his cousin Waltheof, even the Archbishop Stigand, along with Edgar, had been taken to the Dukedom of Normandy. There, William had celebrated his victory, along with displaying his defeated English prisoners, to the roar of the crowd. They had been treated like visiting dignitaries, wined and fed on the finest of fare. Persuaded that it was in their best interest, and the interest of their people, to accept the rule of William and the passing of power to a new regime of ealdormen from foreign shores.

Of course they had agreed, but what other choice was there? Such hospitality was thinly veiled in threat. Accept and be rewarded. Defy and burn along with the country. So of course, the Saxons had accepted with a toasting of wine and cheers for their new king. Edgar had been more surprised than any that King William had believed these treacherous Saxons. If he had known them like Edgar did, he would have realised they would never accept him as their new lord and master. England had been a country riven by division and internecine warfare long before the Normans and the Bretons and the Flemish set foot on its soil. Edgar knew full well that even had he been given the throne, as promised at Berchastede, he would have spent the rest of his reign quelling the ambitions of the very men who had sat him there.

When Edgar saw the huge fort rising from beyond the ridge, all thoughts of past kings suddenly fled, to be replaced by the meeting of a new one. Just beyond the palisade he could see a grim building, half cathedral, half longhall – a monument to the power of the kings of Alba. Outside the gate to the fort more men waited.

As he drew closer, Edgar could see they were bedecked in furs, beards and hair braided. From a distance, he thought that the size of them was perhaps a trick of the light but when he came within ten yards he realised that each one was huge – a bear in human form.

Gospatric stopped some feet in front of them and Edgar came to stand by his side. One of the warriors, his hair red but flecked with grey, took a step forward.

'Greetings to you all,' he said in thick accented English. 'Welcome to the seat of Máel Coluim, son of Donnchada, the Ceann Mor of Alba.'

With that he stood back and the biggest of their number strode forward. Though he wore no crown, around his neck hung a thick chain of iron, bronze bands about his wrists and rings of gold adorning every finger. From the deference shown by his fellows, Edgar knew this could only be the king they had come to beseech.

Before Edgar could thank him for his audience, Gospatric stepped up to the man with a wide smile on his face. 'Great Chieftain,' said the ealdorman. 'It has been too long.'

They grasped one another like long-lost brothers, but it still did little to calm Edgar's nerves. It was all he could do to stop himself shivering and he only hoped that it would appear the cold, and not fear, made him tremble so. When they had done with their greeting, Máel stepped toward Edgar, offering his hand in a more formal greeting. Edgar took it, feeling the strength of that grip. This man was a formidable one and no mistake, his dark hair combed and oiled, his face a monolith of granite, bearing the scars of his victories. He glared down at Edgar impassively, before raising one scarred brow.

'You should have worn a cloak, lad. It's bloody freezing.'

As though to labour the point, the fur of Máel's cloak ruffled in the wind. Was it wolf? It looked like bear, though there had been no such beasts on these shores for hundreds of years. No matter, it still gave him the appearance of a mighty warrior, and one in front of which Edgar was keenly aware of his inferiority.

'You have my gratitude, Great Chieftain. For allowing myself and my family to take refuge, and for meeting with me.'

'Ach, I'm glad of it. The Franks move ever northward in their quest to bring these islands to heel. Their intentions on the kingdoms of Alba are plain to see for anyone with eyes. I would be thankful for English allies at my side.' He clapped a meaty hand to Edgar's back and directed him through the open gate of the fort. 'The Saxons I know. The Franks I know not.'

Of that there was no doubt. For centuries the kingdoms of England and Alba had fought like dogs back and forth across their borders, but they had also traded in times of peace. Edgar knew better than anyone that it was conquest, and not peace, that interested King William the most.

'Were I to sit on the throne of England, there would be only shared respect between our kingdoms,' Edgar said as he walked ahead of their procession and along the road to the great hall. 'Things would be as they were during the most cordial days of our two ancient lands. Better, in fact. You would have to fear no invasion.'

Máel's brow darkened slightly at Edgar's words. 'We do not fear a fight with the Franks, lad.'

'No. I did not mean that—'

A grin crossed Máel's bearded face and he clapped Edgar on the back with a heavy palm. 'I know what you meant. But if we hope to put things back as they were, neither of us should expect it to be bloodless.'

They had reached a patch of open ground, with a hillock that rose to a flat peak. Atop it was a carved red stone laid flat in its centre. Edgar could only think it some kind of pagan idol, left in pride of place.

'I do not fear war either, Máel. My grandfather was a king who fought for his crown. I am in no doubt I will have to do the same. Though I have much respect for your fearsome reputation, I do not ask that you take the crown for me. Merely aid me in this time of need, and I will remember it when I sit on the throne.'

Máel turned to face him with a solemn look. 'You think you have the will to take it and hold it, lad? You think you can defy this Frankish duke and all his noble lords? His knights?'

Edgar glared back with as much grim certitude as he could muster. 'I know I have been a puppet in the plays of other men for too long. Now it is my time. I will claim what is mine or I will fall.'

A warm smile crossed Máel's lips, much to Edgar's relief, and he gestured to the red stone. 'This is sacred to my people. The Clach na Cinneamhain. No king of Alba can proclaim himself as king unless crowned upon it.'

Edgar nodded at the insinuation. 'And no one will accept my claim to the English throne unless I take it for myself.'

'You have a wise head on those young shoulders, Edgar Aetheling. And perhaps you may yet make a good king. So I will help you, in any way I can. Tonight we will feast as friends, and vow that friendship lasts after you are crowned. But first you have an enemy to defeat.' He unbuckled the sword at his belt. It was a beautiful weapon, jewelled at the hilt and wide in the blade. 'So to help you do the deed, and as a gesture of my support, you shall have this.'

Edgar marvelled at the gift, pulling the rune-carved steel from the scabbard and staring in awe at its craftsmanship.

'You have my thanks, Great Chieftain. Someday I will work out how to repay you for such generosity.'

Máel cast a brief glance over one shoulder, to where Edgar's mother and sisters stood. 'Aye. Someday I might well ask for something in return.' He looked back, his face now serious once more. 'But for now I must speak with Gospatric. You know how these English earls need much attention.'

'That I do,' Edgar replied, and with that Máel left him with his sword.

No sooner had he gone than Agatha approached, her face more concerned than ever, despite the obvious display of alliance Edgar now held in his hands.

'Well?' she asked.

No patience, but then Edgar had long since learned to expect none where his mother was concerned.

'We have the support of the Ceann Mor.' Edgar brandished the valuable weapon, before buckling the belt around his waist.

'Do not grow complacent because you have been gifted a bauble, Edgar. You may have struck an alliance with this man, but he might not stay loyal forever.'

Edgar glanced over, seeing that despite his words, Máel was showing Gospatric little attention. In fact he seemed more captivated by Margret as she charmed him with some tale or other. It was as though the Great Chieftain had never conversed with such an engaging woman before.

'Fear not, mother. There might be a way I will have his loyalty for the rest of time. Or until I have the crown. Whichever comes first.'

PART ONE

BETRAYER

I

Dublin, Éire, February 1068

The white sail fluttered in the wind as the tiny ship cruised into the bay. Above shone a bright midday sun, but the sea breeze was biting, the cloak around Styrkar's shoulders doing little to shield him from the chill breath of winter.

He glanced across at his sailing companions. One stood at the tiller, eyes fixed on the city that surrounded the bay. Two more sat facing Styrkar, hands on their oars as they prepared to guide the boat into harbour when the sail had done its work. Not a word had been uttered by any of them as they crossed the sea from England. Styrkar was at peace with that, in no mood for conversation himself.

Though he did not know any of their names it was obvious from their bearing, and the close-set eyes they all shared, that they were brothers. As Styrkar thought on that, it suddenly filled him with sadness.

Soon he would be reunited with three more brothers, who were his kin in all but blood. He would meet them as a long-lost friend before stabbing each of them in the back and betraying the memory of the father they shared. Despite struggling with what he had to do, Styrkar knew he had no choice in it.

The sudden screech of a gull tore him from sullen thoughts. Glancing up he watched the birds wheeling all about the coastline. Would that he had their freedom, that he could fly away and never return, but there were grim deeds to be dealt before that day would come.

Lowering his head, he looked down at the sword across his lap. He had held tight to King Harold's seax for the entire journey and it felt heavy in his grip, reminding him of the weight of this burden. He was not only betraying his brothers, but also the man who had treated him like a son. But Harold was dead and gone. For now, Styrkar had to think about the living. About Gisela. He was her only hope for salvation and he could not let familial loyalty fill him with doubt.

As the ship cruised into harbour, the brothers furled the sail and used their oars to guide it toward the shore. Men at the dock caught the mooring ropes and tied them off, and Styrkar got the impression this was a well-practised routine.

Two of the brothers began to unload what cargo they had brought with them – bales of cloth and wooden barrels – and Styrkar turned to the eldest of the shipmen.

'How long do I have before you return to England?' he asked.

The grim-locking sailor shrugged. 'We're paid to stay and wait as long as it takes,' he replied.

Styrkar had no idea how long that might be, or even if he

would succeed. Still, it was reassuring to know there might at least be one way to escape if his treachery was discovered.

He stepped onto the jetty, pulling the cloak tight around him. The harbour was busy, mostly with fishing vessels, but there were a few foreign ships among them. Styrkar recognised the dragon prows of longboats, and among the crowd were a mix of shaggy locals alongside braid-haired Danes and Norse. They were not here to raid, but to trade, and Styrkar could see their sorry looking cargos. Slaves lined the dockside, each lashed together at wrists and neck. Styrkar was suddenly reminded of his own sorry beginnings in thrall to King Harald so many years ago, but he could not bring himself to feel any sorrow for these wretches. He had his task to think on.

The busy harbour led to a sprawling settlement, thatched houses packed together and stretching into the distance. Styrkar was struck by the stench, as shit and piss from man and animal flowed along the streets to run off into the sea. For a moment he wondered how he might begin to find this King Diarmait, and through him Harold's sons, but as he scanned the rooftops he saw one building towering above the rest. Even from the bay he could tell it was a vast longhouse – where better to enquire after the King of Dublin?

He made his way through the busy streets, passing traders, slavers, warriors and farmers. At various points he had to step aside to let drovers wrangle their animals. A waddling gaggle of geese, an unruly herd of pigs, even a huge bull, bigger than Styrkar had ever laid eyes on, all passed him on the narrow roads.

No one seemed to pay him any mind, and it was clear that

Dublin was a city used to visitors of all kinds. Hopefully that would stand him in good stead, and a single stranger would not be pegged for a Frankish spy.

When finally the great longhouse was in sight, he paused some distance away. Every fibre of him screamed that this was wrong, and he found it hard to walk those final few steps to the entrance, but Styrkar knew he was just delaying the inevitable.

He viewed the huge wooden doors, carved with symbols in a foreign language, the script etched among the tentacles of some great sea beast. Four warriors stood guard, shields and spears held at the ready, watching vigilantly for anyone who might intrude on the longhouse. It was obvious they were king's men – their helms polished, green cloaks embroidered with the same swirling patterns that adorned their shields. They would have intimidated any ordinary man coming here with malicious intent, but Styrkar was no ordinary man.

Raising his head, he strode out from the shadows and walked across the muddy thoroughfare. The warriors saw him coming and raised their shields to bar the red-haired giant's approach.

'Hold there, big man,' said the most senior among them, his greying beard braided into two points. 'You've no business here. This is the house of King Diarmait Mac Mael. High King of Éire.'

'Then this is exactly where my business lies,' Styrkar replied. 'I would speak with the king on a matter of importance.'

'What kind of matter?'

Styrkar regarded the men, sensing their unease. 'I'd say that's between me and him.'

One of the younger warriors stepped forward threateningly, tipping the point of his spear toward Styrkar's throat, but the veteran nudged him with his shield.

'Let's all keep steady now, shall we,' he said, accent thick and voice calm. Styrkar appreciated such a man being in charge; an old hand ready to keep the peace rather than a hot-headed youth. 'What's your name, traveller?'

'My name is Styrkar. Sworn housecarl of Harold Godwinson. Bonded to his service and the service of his kinsmen.'

The veteran nodded. 'I know King Harold's sons. I take it they will vouch for you?'

'Bring them here and you will see for yourself.'

With a nod from the veteran, one of the king's men ran off along the street. 'Very well,' the warrior said. 'You will see the king, but not with that.' He gestured to the seax Styrkar still held in his grip.

For a moment Styrkar considered arguing – it was his master's precious weapon after all – but there was no use in being obstinate. If he was to have these men trust him he had to do as they asked.

Once he had handed the seax over, the veteran pushed open the doors to the longhouse and led the way inside. There was a sound of muffled conversation as Styrkar entered the dark confines. A fire burned in a pit at the centre of the hall and his stomach grumbled as he smelled fresh roasted pig. Thegns lounged about the place, their clothes an array of colours, gold and silver trinkets adorning their necks, wrists and fingers. Some looked up curiously as Styrkar was led through the hall, others standing ready in case of danger.

At the far end, Styrkar could see King Diarmait seated on a wooden throne. The closer he came to it, the more he could discern of the intricate carvings that adorned that seat. Diarmait looked up from a conversation he was having with two men. They leaned in close, one a warrior with thick bands about his arms, the other perhaps a reeve of some kind, a jewelled clasp glittering on his cloak. When he saw Styrkar being led closer, the king dismissed them both with a gesture of his hand.

'And who is this?' King Diarmait asked. His nose was broken, little left of it after it had been smashed so many times. Despite his brutal visage, his eyes were keen and bright blue like a summer sky.

'He says he is—'

Styrkar stepped forward in front of the man, in no mood to let anyone else speak for him.

'I am Styrkar,' he announced. 'Called the Red Wolf. Housecarl to Harold Godwinson, the last true king of England.'

'He brought this, my king,' the veteran said, handing the seax to Diarmait.

As he examined the weapon, Styrkar tried to weigh up the High King. The man was old, but still held himself with dignity. His brow was severe but there was intelligence in those bright eyes. Styrkar had met many such men in his time, some cruel, some clever. Which one this High King was he could not yet tell.

Diarmait slowly looked up from the weapon. 'This is indeed the sword of King Harold. But you are not the Red Wolf. He died at Senlac Hill more than a year ago.'

The three warriors surrounding him tensed, one raising

his shield and bracing his spear, the tip aimed at Styrkar's heart.

'I was at Senlac,' Styrkar replied, ignoring the imminent threat. 'I watched my king perish alongside his brothers. Faced the storm of arrows and heard the thunder of hooves as our numbers were culled by the Frankish onslaught. But as you can see, it was not my time to die.'

Diarmait raised an eyebrow. 'Your time might well come soon if you don't prove the truth of your words.'

As the king spoke, Styrkar's eye was drawn to the row of banners arrayed behind him. Among those he did not recognise was a torn and threadbare pennant, a fighting man displayed on its filth-stained cloth. Harold's war banner, most likely brought here by his sons and gifted to Diarmait as a mark of respect.

Styrkar took a step forward, the men around him bracing their spears to block his path. 'You have the war banner of King Harold in your hall. A banner I have fought beneath more than once. Who other than someone faithful to the king who carried it would recognise such a symbol?'

Diarmait rubbed at his chin, still unsure of the truth in Styrkar's claim. There were other warriors surrounding him now, hanging back in the shadows. Behind him he heard the sharp, slow ring of a sword being stripped from its sheath. Styrkar had no weapon to hand; there was no chance he could survive if they attacked.

'Styrkar!'

The voice called out from the far end of the longhouse. Styrkar turned to see Godwin rushing toward him, Magnus and Edmund not far behind.

As Godwin hugged him, Styrkar saw the warriors surrounding them lower their weapons.

'Brother,' Magnus said joining in Godwin's embrace. The young lad had grown since Styrkar had last seen him and was now as tall and strong as his older brothers.

Edmund hung back, offering a nod rather than giving such a boisterous greeting.

'It seems you speak the truth,' Diarmait said. He stood from his throne and took a step towards them. 'Welcome to Dublin, Styrkar the Red Wolf. It is my honour to host a man of such repute.'

'What are you doing here?' Godwin asked. 'Where have you been?'

'I was wounded after the battle,' Styrkar replied. 'When I recovered I came to join with you as soon as I could. To win back the crown for the Haroldson line.'

'And he brings this,' Diarmait said, handing Harold's seax to Godwin.

'Our father's sword,' said Godwin, pulling the blade free of the sheath, looking in wonder as it winked in the firelight. 'How did you come by it?'

'Your mother...' Styrkar replied. The thought of her stung him like an arrow to the heart, not just because of the painful memory of her death, but because of what he was here to do. She had saved him and shown him nothing but kindness, and here he was ready to betray her sons.

'Where is she?' Magnus asked. 'And Ulf? And our sisters?'

Styrkar swallowed, at first unable to find the words. 'Edith is... Your mother is dead. Your sisters sent to abbeys, your brother taken by William, to where I do not know.

When Edith lost her family it was more than she could bear. She took her own life.'

Magnus took a step back, shaking his head, his eyes already filling with tears as he trembled with rage. With a howl he picked up a stool, smashing it against a pillar. Edmund was quickly by his side, holding him about the shoulders and whispering words of solace.

Godwin took Styrkar by the arm, his expression grave. 'I'm sure you did all you could, brother.'

As Godwin said the word 'brother' Styrkar had to grit his teeth against the pain of it.

'It was not enough,' he replied.

'Fear not,' Godwin continued, a determined look to his eyes. 'We will have our reckoning. William will not sit easy upon his throne for long. With the help of King Diarmait we will return to our home and reap such vengeance as England has never seen. Your arrival is a good omen, Styrkar. With you at our side none will stand against us.'

'And when will that be?' Styrkar asked, eager to know what Godwin's plan was so he could be done with this deception and return to Gisela.

'All in good time,' Godwin said, turning to the king. 'For now, you will find King Diarmait a welcoming and generous host.'

'Aye,' Diarmait said. 'My house is your house, Styrkar. And tonight we will feast in celebration of your arrival. And to mourn Queen Edith.'

'And I am grateful for it,' Styrkar said as a cheer went up from the surrounding thegns.

'Thank you for this,' Godwin said, holding the seax to

his chest. 'Despite the cruel tidings you bring, it is truly a blessing that you have come.'

Styrkar could not answer, but then what would he say? He had come under the guise of friendship to betray his own brothers. He was the worst kind of oath breaker... a deceiver to his kin.

Yet still he would stay and drink and feast, and when the time came he would find out what he had to, and then flee this place like the traitor he was.

2

Cantocheheve, England, February 1068

She clung to the bucket as though her life depended on it. Gisela's head span as she retched, desperately trying to stifle the noise, but there was no way you could throw your guts up and stay quiet at the same time. She could only hope anyone listening thought she was vomiting from fear... not that she was with child.

It had started the morning after Styrkar left. She had hoped beyond hope that she was just stricken with some illness, but deep inside Gisela knew what ailed her. There was a moment of joy at the realisation, and fleetingly she wondered how Styrkar might react when he found out, but that notion had quickly dissipated like smoke on the breeze to be replaced by grim reality. She was a prisoner of the Franks. Of Ronan. This was the last thing she needed.

Gisela heaved into the bucket once more. The tepid gruel she had eaten the night before had already come up. Now all that remained inside her was bile, and it dribbled from her lips into the bucket. She managed to take a breath as the nausea abated slightly, listening for anyone heeding the sound of her sickness. All was silent. Outside she could hear the soldiers going about their business, ignorant of her malady. Or perhaps they didn't care. Either reason was a blessing.

She pulled herself to her feet, breathing deep as she wiped her mouth on her sleeve. Her head still swam with dizziness and fear but she fought against it. Gisela could not give in to the bleakness of her circumstances. She had to cling onto the hope that Styrkar would succeed in his task and return to her swiftly. Whether Ronan would keep his side of the bargain was anyone's guess, but their only chance was to do as he commanded. What might follow was out of both their hands.

When she had gathered her wits she moved to the shuttered window. Opening it she gazed across the small coastal fort. It had once been the home of an English magnate, but now was filled with Frankish knights. There were some signs of the previous occupants and the meagre belongings they had left behind. Their flight must have been in haste, as the small room still had blankets and even spare clothes strewn about the place. Gisela saw a child's doll abandoned in one corner, and she was suddenly gripped with grief at what might become of her own child if Styrkar failed in his task. Would it even be born before she was murdered by Ronan or one of his men?

She walked to the corner, getting a grip on her faculties, feeling somewhat better now the sickness had passed. The doll had been crafted with care, the stitching neat, and when she picked it up she saw its dress had been embroidered with silken thread.

What had become of its previous owner she had no idea, but she could only wish them Godspeed. If they were fortunate, they would be miles away from here.

She knelt in the light that streamed through the window, gripped the doll in her hand, and began to pray. Her lips moved silently as she begged for salvation, begged for Styrkar's safe return and that her child would be born healthy. The Franks might be savage warriors, but they were Christians too. Surely they would not be so brutal as to harm a child. Was that a hope too far? Even as she prayed, Gisela knew it was.

'I would never have pegged you as a God-fearing woman, Gisela of Flanders.'

She opened her eyes, seeing Ronan standing at the doorway. He looked amused as he watched her praying, as though he already knew it was a waste of her time.

Gisela rose to her feet, hiding the doll in the folds of her kirtle. 'Are you so surprised to see me at prayer?'

'I wouldn't think such a pious woman would take a savage heathen dog as her lover.'

She bristled at that, but held her tongue. What did Ronan know of it? He was little more than a beast himself. Styrkar was more gentle and noble than he would ever be.

'I have the right to pray for deliverance,' she said. 'I am held a prisoner despite my innocence.'

'Innocence?' Ronan grinned, entering the room and closing the door. 'You are the consort of a renowned outlaw. You are far from innocent in this.'

She moved to look out across the courtyard. There were no bars on any windows and the gate to the fort lay open, but she knew she may as well have been locked in a cage.

'If you've already decided my guilt, why am I still alive?' Absently, she placed a hand to her belly, before she realised what she was doing and what it might signify. Quickly she returned the hand to her side.

Ronan shrugged. 'I am a man of my word.'

It was all Gisela could do to stop herself laughing, but none of this was funny.

'You and your people are murderers. All you do is spread suffering wherever you go. You kill without thought or sense of remorse, and yet you dare to question my piety? A man of your word? You don't know the first thing about honour.'

He stepped closer to her and she was instantly reminded of that day at Hereford when he had tried to have his way, and to her shame she had fled from him like a frightened girl. She did not flee this time, but stood her ground. Let him do what he wanted, she did not care anymore.

'Be careful how you speak to me,' Ronan breathed. 'I am the only thing keeping you alive. I could hand you to my men for their pleasure, and not give it a second thought.'

'Then do it.' Gisela spat the words, her rising anger beating down her fear. 'Do it if you dare, and see what Styrkar does when he returns. Nothing will stop him—'

Ronan began to laugh. Gisela gritted her teeth, fists bunched as she fought to quell her rage. She had already said too much, and was in enough danger without provoking her captor further.

'You think your lover scares me? You must be more stupid than you look to blindly accept the myth of the Red Wolf like all the rest? He is just one man, and can be killed like any other.'

'No,' she replied. 'Not like any other, and I think you know that. You say I am stupid? If you do not fear the Red Wolf then *you're* the fool.'

The smile wavered on Ronan's lips. 'Maybe you're right. But I have the one thing he values above all else. And while I do, I am safe. You however...'

He left that hanging as he took a step back on his crippled leg. She saw him wince in pain before he stumbled toward a chair and sat down. Leaning forward he rubbed at his ankle.

As she watched him, she suddenly realised how pitiful he looked. Just a crippled man, suffering in the winter cold. But no – he was not just a cripple. He was dangerous and cruel, and if she wasn't careful he would be the death of her, and her unborn child.

'How did it happen?' Gisela asked, as keen to change the subject of her fate as she was curious about his ailment.

'As though you care?' he replied.

'Fine. Keep your secret. I think I would prefer the silence anyway.'

Ronan chuckled. 'Stubborn. I like that. I'm starting to realise what he sees in you. You're not quite the little mouse I first thought.'

She folded her arms, turning back to the window.

'Very well,' Ronan continued. 'It was many years ago. I was little more than an infant. My father wanted nothing to do with me, I was a bastard after all, but as a child of noble blood I was accepted into the house of Count Odo of Penthièvre as a squire. I'm sure I don't need to explain what that means?'

She gave a shrug as she turned to face him once more. 'I

assume it means you learned the horse, the sword and the lance?'

'Yes,' he replied. 'But mostly I polished and washed and carried around a knight's burdensome armour, and groomed his steed. Very dull work, but as the former maid of a highborn lady you'd know all about that.'

'I was happy in my labours,' Gisela lied.

Ronan's wry expression told her he saw through it. 'I'm sure. But I was a spirited child. Impatient. So one day I saddled my master's horse and I rode it. Of course my inexperience was my downfall. I slipped from the saddle, foot caught in the stirrup, but the horse ran on regardless. A mile, perhaps two, before it eventually stopped.'

'It must have been agony,' Gisela said in sympathy, before she caught herself. Ronan did not deserve her compassion and she immediately regretted showing it, but then it wasn't for him; it was for the little boy he had once been.

'I don't remember,' he replied. 'I had passed out almost immediately. But I remember the pain after. The days of suffering as the surgeon did his best to straighten my foot. Of course the Count of Penthièvre had devoted much time and money to my training and upkeep, and would not want to see his investment wasted. I could eventually walk, after a fashion, but I would never fight on foot. Luckily, I could still learn to ride and wield a lance and shield. Eventually, with my ankle strapped, I could fight as well as any mounted knight.'

'It must have been hard for you,' she said, this time feigning her empathy.

All that did was make Ronan laugh again, much louder than before. 'Like you care, Gisela. Like you give a damn what I have suffered. What I have been through to get where I am.'

'Is that why you are consumed by so much hate?' she said, unable to hide her disdain. 'Is there only venom left inside you, after you suffered so much?'

'What, no more sympathy?'

She sighed. 'I just want to know why you are so filled with loathing? Why you detest Styrkar so much that you would put us both through this torture?'

He leaned back in the chair. She expected him to lash out with another cruel barb but instead his eyes adopted a tinge of sadness. 'You know, he killed the only real friend I ever had. Aldus never had much to say, but he was loyal. My companion since childhood. But I don't want Styrkar to suffer because of that. I couldn't give a God damn if he burns in Hell or rises to Valhöll, or whatever imaginary pagan shithole he believes in. The Red Wolf is a means to an end. A tool in my arsenal. And as long as he is useful he will live.' Ronan leaned forward in his chair, sadness replaced by a look of intense focus. 'And so will you.'

'And when he gives you what you want, you will kill us both.' It was not a question.

'That is not for certain,' Ronan replied matter-of-factly. 'As you have already so plainly pointed out; Styrkar is not an easy man to kill. And if he accomplishes the task I have set him, what reason would I have to execute him? Or you? I will have gained exactly what I want.'

'You expect me to trust your word?' she asked.

Ronan grinned. 'I don't give a shit what you expect.'

There was a knock at the door. Ronan struggled to his feet and opened it to see one of his men waiting expectantly.

'My lord, a messenger has come from the east. Earl Brian has sent word that you are needed in Exonia.'

'On what business?' Ronan asked, not even trying to hide his annoyance.

'On the king's business, my lord.'

Ronan let out a resigned sigh. 'Very well. Have the men prepare, we leave within the hour.' With that he turned to Gisela. 'It seems we will have to forego the luxury of these accommodations, my lady.'

'But we have to wait for Styrkar,' she said, feeling panic grip her ripe stomach.

'Don't fear. I'm sure we will return before your lover gets back. I suggest you wrap up warm. It's a cold road to Exonia.'

He left her alone in the room, and Gisela gazed once more out of the window. She could see the open gate to the fort and the road winding away beyond it as Ronan's men began to muster, preparing their horses for the ride. She took out the doll she had hidden in her kirtle, barely able to focus on it through her tears.

Part of her yearned for Styrkar to finish his task and return to her with all speed. Perhaps Ronan would even keep his word and allow them to live.

Another part, a stronger part, wished that Styrkar would run as far away from this danger as he could, and never return.

3

Dublin, Éire, February 1068

Styrkar hunkered behind his shield, making himself as small a target as he could manage – not an easy task at the best of times. Godwin did likewise, but his patience was wearing thin. He suddenly surged forward, slamming his practice sword against Styrkar's shield, unable to wait any longer. Though he was just as impetuous as he'd always been, Styrkar could tell his skill with a sword had improved immeasurably, the blow sending him back a pace so he almost slipped on the frosty ground.

Though the land was still in the grip of winter, both men chose to fight naked to the waist. They had practised since dawn, and now a thin veil of mist was rising from both of them as they sweated in the cold air. Styrkar could see that Godwin was no longer the youth he had known. His chest and shoulders were heavily muscled from repeated swordplay, and if Styrkar hadn't known better he'd have thought the lad at least an inch taller. Perhaps it was just his bearing, but now that Godwin was entering manhood he looked the more fearsome fighter. Either way, the son of King Harold had become every bit the warrior his father was before him.

'Is the Red Wolf losing his bite?' Godwin asked. 'Or is this cold weather infesting your bones?'

Before Styrkar could answer he launched himself forward again, the attack swift and accurate. Styrkar had already got the measure of it though, and he ducked, letting the practice sword sweep past his head. Stepping in, he swiftly brought his own weapon up, nudging Godwin's chin with the blade. He'd meant only to show how Godwin had lowered his guard, but the blow struck squarely, and Styrkar heard Godwin's teeth clash together.

Harold's son took a step back, anger flashing across his eyes. Then it was gone in an instant, as his mouth started to bleed from a cut lip.

'Clearly I spoke too soon,' Godwin said.

'Your attack has improved,' Styrkar replied. 'But at the expense of your defence. Always keep your shield up. Even if you think you have a man dead to rights.'

Godwin smiled. 'I have missed days like these.'

Styrkar had missed them too, and for the briefest moment he also felt like smiling. But he knew there was nothing to smile about. He was not here to reminisce or recapture those lost days. He was here to save Gisela's life, and so far he had made little progress. There was still no firm plan for a counter invasion, or at least none that had been shared with Styrkar. So far he had remained silent, patiently waiting for something to be revealed, but neither Godwin nor King Diarmait seemed keen to disclose their intentions. Now, as he stood alone with Godwin, he felt all too keenly that time was running out. Ronan would not keep Gisela hostage forever, and if the sons of Harold launched their invasion before Styrkar could return with details of when and where, she would surely die.

'This is just the beginning,' Styrkar said. 'Soon we can go home and things will be returned to how they were always meant to be. You will take the crown that is rightfully yours.'

Godwin clapped a hand against Styrkar's muscular arm. 'With your help, brother,' he replied.

Styrkar could hold his tongue on the subject no longer. 'I have been here for some days now, and still there is no plan of attack. Or at least none revealed to me.'

There was a brief flash of emotion across Godwin's eyes. Was it suspicion? Styrkar silently cursed himself for his clumsy tongue. Subterfuge was never a talent he had learned. He was a warrior – direct and to the point. Loyal in all things... until now.

'Fear not,' Godwin replied. 'You will have your chance to avenge our father soon enough. Plans are afoot, do not worry on that score. And when the time is right we will sail at the head of a mighty fleet to wrest the crown of England from the damned usurper.'

Styrkar nodded in acknowledgement, deciding it best to let the matter rest. If he pushed Godwin too hard, surely he would begin to suspect Styrkar's treachery. But if he left it too long his chance to save Gisela would turn to ash. There had to be a way to discover their intentions, and soon.

'My lord,' someone called from the road leading back to Dublin town. Both men turned to see one of the king's thralls making his way up the hill.

Godwin approached the servant, who stopped for a moment, panting for breath.

'My lord... the king... he has asked for you to attend his hall. It is a matter of the utmost importance.'

'What kind of matter?' Godwin asked.

'There is a visitor at court, lord. I know not who, but I am told it is someone who would be of great interest to you and your brothers.'

Godwin turned to Styrkar with his eyebrow raised. 'Great interest? Then we must head to the king's hall with haste.'

The men picked up their tunics and followed the thrall back down the hill. He led a fast pace, and they had to all but run to keep up with him. By the time they reached the town and entered through the western gate, all three of them were huffing for breath.

When they arrived at the longhouse of King Diarmait, Styrkar saw warriors milling outside. It was an uneasy standoff of sorts, with the king's green-clad house-carls standing in grim silence alongside English warriors, their cloaks of red and blue, spears standing proud, shields painted in bright colours.

The door to the hall was opened as they approached, and Styrkar saw Magnus awaiting them on the threshold.

'What is it?' Godwin asked. 'Who has arrived?'

'It's the northern whore,' Edmund said with disdain, appearing from the shadows before his younger brother could answer.

Styrkar and Godwin stepped inside. At the far end of the longhouse, Styrkar could see King Diarmait sitting on his throne. He was listening intently to the entreaty of a woman holding her infant child. Though her back was turned to him, Styrkar recognised her long hair, the colour of jet, as it cascaded down to her waist.

'Alditha,' Godwin breathed, as he approached across the longhouse.

Harold's widow stopped speaking, turning her head to look at the two men approaching. Styrkar did not know what to expect, the sons of King Harold held no love for the woman who had ousted their mother from Harold's family bed. He felt the tension rising, until Godwin bowed graciously.

'My lady,' he said. 'It pleases me to see you are safe and well. And that my new sibling is in good health.'

Styrkar watched from the shadows as Alditha nodded back in equally as gracious a fashion, the infant in her arms wriggling as it gripped a lock of her raven hair.

'I am glad you could be here,' Diarmait said to Godwin. 'The Lady Alditha has requested sanctuary in my court. Sent from England by her brothers Of course, as the widow of my friend and ally I was about to grant her entreaty... unless anyone might object.'

He left that to hang in the air. Styrkar already had the measure of Diarmait. If his mind was already made to grant Alditha sanctuary there was nothing anyone else could say to change it. His offer to Godwin was nothing more than good manners.

'Why would anyone object?' Godwin said. 'We can hardly turn away a mother and her...'

'Son,' Alditha said. 'King Harold's son and heir. And a threat to King William's rule if he stays on the mainland, hence my journey here.'

Styrkar ground his teeth at her words. Alditha proclaiming her own child as Harold's heir certainly would not go down well with his eldest sons. Nevertheless, Godwin chose to ignore the suggestion.

'A fine boy,' Godwin replied. 'But then, he is of kingly stock.'

'Settled then,' said King Diarmait, rising to his feet. 'All the sons of Harold Godwinson are welcome in my house.' He placed his arm around Alditha and began to lead her back across the longhouse. 'Rumour has it your brother Edwin has been betrothed to King William's daughter. Tell me, has the marriage day been arranged?'

As she was led away, Alditha glanced up and her eyes fell on Styrkar as he stood in the shadows. For a moment her visage turned dark, lip curling in the most subtle of sneers, before she carried on her conversation with Diarmait.

'No love lost there,' Godwin said as he stood beside Styrkar and they watched the pair leave.

'No,' Styrkar replied. 'None.'

'What can you possibly have done to upset her so?' Godwin said.

'I was among your father's chosen housecarls when he launched his campaign against the Welsh. And by his side when King Gruffydd's head was given to him as a mark of surrender. Brought with it was Alditha. I was tasked with returning her safely to her brothers.'

'And for that she hates you?' Magnus asked.

'I helped end her first husband's reign. She lost her crown. Her children. I can understand why she would harbour such hate for me.'

Godwin smirked. 'All in the past, brother. Now it seems we are to be one family.'

'That whore!'

The three of them turned to see Edmund still glaring after Diarmait and Alditha. They had left the longhouse now, but Edmund still watched in their wake, as though he might commit murder with his gaze.

'Brother, lower your tone,' Godwin ordered.

In other parts of the longhouse, Diarmait's thegns were watching closely.

'She comes here with her mewling spawn, begging sanctuary. Using our father's name to hide herself from the Frankish king. And what of her brothers? Where are Edwin and Morcar to protect her? Where were they when our father fought at Senlac Hill? Those cowards. That woman does not belong here. She should be thrown in the bay, and her bastard child with her.'

'That is our brother you speak of,' said Magnus.

Edmund fixed him with a disdainful look. 'He is no brother of mine.'

Godwin stood between the two. 'Whether we like it or not, he is our blood. And it's not our choice whether she is given refuge in King Diarmait's house. Squeal all you like, Edmund, the decision has been made.'

'Not by me,' Edmund hissed, and stomped off across the longhouse.

'He'll cool down soon enough,' said Godwin.

'I doubt that,' said Magnus with a grin. 'He's more likely to throw himself in the bay before that happens.'

The brothers laughed at one another as they made their

way after Edmund. Styrkar followed, but he could see no humour in this. Alditha's presence could only be a bad omen. He could smell the stink of trouble ahead, as if he didn't have enough of his own to think on.

4

Dublin, Éire, March 1068

He approached the hut warily. Harold's sons had summoned him, and he did not know what for. Had he finally been discovered? Were they lying in wait to murder him for his treachery?

For days he had tried to discover Godwin's intentions, sometimes listening for any suggestion of when and where the invasion would start. Often succumbing to his frustration and clumsily demanding that he reveal his plans. At every turn he had failed. Now, as he reached their meeting place, he wondered if he had gone too far.

Godwin, Edmund and Magnus were waiting silently inside as Styrkar swung the door open. Each one greeted him with a nod as he entered then closed the door, casting the room in shadow. Godwin looked pensive, but there was a light to his eyes as though he were filled with anticipation. Magnus smiled his easy smile, and it served to put Styrkar at ease momentarily, but then Edmund wore his usual scowl. It would not do to relax just yet.

He walked further into the room. There was no one lurking in the shadows, no men waiting to slaughter or enslave him. That was something at least. Whatever the sons of Harold had summoned him for, it was not murder.

'Please. Sit, brother,' Godwin said, gesturing to the empty chair at the table.

Styrkar did as he was bid. 'What is this?' he asked. 'Do you have news of our invasion?'

'We have made progress, Styrkar,' Godwin replied with a smile. 'A step closer to reclaiming our father's crown. I wanted to let you know that our plans are moving forward and soon we will set foot on English soil once more.'

'And when do we leave?' Styrkar asked, trying not to show his eagerness too much.

'Patience, brother,' Godwin answered. 'It will not be long before your axe tastes Frankish flesh. But first we have to await our army's arrival.'

'What army? Are we not to sail across the sea with King Diarmait and his warriors at our back?'

Magnus leaned in. 'The High King of Éire might offer us sanctuary, but he cannot be seen to pledge his own army for a counter invasion. That would be a provocation the Bastard could not endure. It would cause all-out war, and the Franks would flood this isle faster than they flooded ours. Instead we will have to settle for mercenaries, but fear not – they are fierce.'

'Mercenaries?' asked Styrkar, far from enamoured with the idea. 'How do we know we can trust such warriors?'

Godwin laughed. 'How do you think, brother? The way you buy the trust of all mercenaries – with gold. Thankfully,

King Diarmait will see to the cost in return for the continued friendship of Harold's sons and the nobles of England.'

Edmund slammed his hand down on the table, his face twisted in anger. 'That bitch!' he spat.

Godwin raised his eyes to the roof. 'Must we go over this again?'

'Yes we must,' Edmund snapped. 'You talk of war and conquest across the sea, while you ignore the snake that lies sleeping only feet away. We are in danger.'

'We have talked of this, Edmund, and you have made your feelings clear. The matter is settled—'

'Not to me it's not,' he said, hands balled into fists. Styrkar wondered if the poorly built table they sat at would survive another blow. 'Alditha and her child are a constant danger to us while they live. She flouts her position among the court of King Diarmait as though she were still Queen of England. Proclaims her son the true and only heir to anyone who will listen. That bitch has to be silenced.'

'Peace, brother,' Godwin said, trying to placate Edmund, though Styrkar could see he was losing patience. 'What that woman says matters little in a foreign land. She has no followers here but the few men she has brought with her. King Diarmait was a friend to our father, and is a friend to us, not this pretender queen. Her brothers are in thrall to the Frankish usurper, their power is nothing but a memory. She is no threat.'

'No threat?' Edmund replied. 'So you think Edwin and Morcar will be in thrall forever? That they will sit on their hands and let the usurper take over unopposed? They have already tried to put the Aetheling on the throne so they might be puppet masters to the king of England. Now they have a trueborn nephew with a legitimate claim. You think they will just forget that? You think they won't do everything in their power to see the Bastard dethroned and their own kin put in his place? That would make them the most powerful men in England. And then where will we be?'

Godwin shook his head. 'You worry needlessly. They had their chance to back Edgar the Aetheling, but when faced with William's might they knelt like the rest. They have no power anymore. They lacked the nerve to defeat Harald Sigurdsson and our uncle when they came to ravage the north. They failed to support our father when called on to fight in the south. They are cowards, Edmund. Their sister and her offspring are no threat to us.'

'You're a blind fool. She and the child must be disposed of.'

'Enough,' Godwin barked, rising to his feet. Styrkar resisted the urge to get in between them as he had done in the past. These brothers were men now, and had to resolve their differences in their own way. 'I have made my judgement on the matter. Do not defy me on this.'

Edmund tried to hold his elder brother's gaze but could not, turning his attention back to the table. Styrkar could see his fists were still clenched, but the fire inside him was waning.

'Styrkar,' Godwin said after taking a breath to calm himself. 'Diarmait has sent heralds to seek aid from Norse mercenaries. Knowing your past, how you were enslaved by the Norse, held in their thrall, I wanted you here to ask one thing of you. Will you still stand as our brother when we return to our homeland? Are you still willing to fight beside us and the Norsemen?'

Though the prospect was not one he relished, Styrkar grasped Godwin's arm. 'Always,' he replied.

Even as he said the word he felt a stab of regret. He was betraying the only men left alive he could truly trust, and who trusted him in return. Nevertheless, Godwin grinned his pleasure.

'Then there is nothing that can stop us, the sons of Harold, taking our vengeance on the usurper and the rest of his Frankish bastards.'

Magnus stood and embraced him, his smile wide as they laughed about the victories they would have over the Franks. Even Edmund raised himself from his ire to clap Styrkar on the shoulder.

Finally they bid one another farewell, after much talk of conquest and the justice they would reap, but as Styrkar stepped out into the open air he could only grit his teeth against the pain in his heart. He had a duty to those brothers, a bond stronger than any other, but there were other oaths he had made that had to be honoured. It had been weeks since he had seen Gisela, and he had no idea how she fared in bondage to that bastard Ronan. Yet that was not all he had to think on.

Hearing Edmund's words, Styrkar realised there was an oath to his former master he would also have to keep. Despite Godwin's command that Alditha and her son should be spared, Styrkar knew it was doubtful Edmund would obey. Despite appearances, he was as wilful a son of Harold as either Godwin or Magnus. Edmund would soon have his reckoning, of that Styrkar was sure.

He made his way across the town, thinking of his burden more than ever. Styrkar was here to betray Harold's eldest sons, but perhaps he could redeem himself by doing something for the youngest.

Alditha's lodgings were not too far away, and as he drew nearer Styrkar could see there was but a single guard at her door. He approached, all too aware that the only weapon he was carrying was an axe at his belt. As he did so, it was obvious the guard recognised him, for he drew himself up, bracing his shield and placing a hand to the hilt of his sword.

'That's close enough, Red Wolf,' the guard said.

His hair was shorn close to the temples, a single braid running down his back. His beard was greying at the edges and the scars on his face and arms, along with the cold set to his eyes, spoke that this man was a seasoned fighter.

Styrkar stopped a few feet away. 'It is important I speak with your mistress.'

'It's important you come no closer,' the guard replied. 'Unless you've come for trouble.'

'I want no trouble. But I would speak with Alditha, and I will not be turned away.'

The guard offered a sidelong glance. 'Don't know who I am, do you?'

Styrkar did his best to quell his growing impatience. 'Why would I?'

'I am Tonbert Uffasson. Loyal housecarl to Earl Aelfgar, and his son Edwin after him.'

Styrkar could not remember the name, but it was clear this man thought it of some importance.

'I have met Earl Edwin,' he replied. 'You I don't remember.'

'No? So do you remember how Harold and Aelfgar

fought? How they hated one another to the core? Some of us have not forgotten.'

Styrkar knew well how deep the feuds of the Saxons could run. How they would pass on their grudges from generation to generation until all that remained were corpses. Clearly this Tonbert still harboured Aelfgar's old hatreds, and Styrkar might gladly have accommodated his need for redress had he not a more pressing matter to attend.

'Perhaps you should. Our masters are dead. Their blood-feud has followed them to the grave.'

'So easily you forget your oaths, Red Wolf. But then what can one expect from a Dane?'

'I remember my oaths,' Styrkar replied, hand straying to his axe. 'And my enemies. But I have no quarrel with you. Unless you want to start one.'

Before Tonbert could reach for the sword at his side, the door to the house opened. Alditha stood in the doorway, regarding both men with a look of annoyance.

'You'll wake the child,' she said quietly, but there was steel to her tone.

Tonbert bowed. 'Apologies, my lady. But this—'

'I know who this is,' she said, regarding Styrkar curiously. He remembered the disdain with which she had looked at him when first arriving in Dublin, but now her animosity seemed to be forgotten. 'I would not have expected the fearsome Red Wolf to call at my refuge. Have you come seeking vengeance after all this time? Come to redress the slight against your mistress Edith?'

'No,' he replied. 'But I would speak with you on a matter of grave importance.'

A smile crept up the side of her face. 'Would you, indeed? Then you had best come in.'

As Styrkar stepped across the threshold, Tonbert made to protest but he was silenced by a raised hand from Alditha.

Inside her hut the air was warm and fragrant. It reminded Styrkar of fresh wildflowers, but he could see none about the place. In one corner he heard young Harold mewling in his crib, gurgling as babies do.

'So why have you come here, Styrkar?' Alditha asked as she laid a hand on her son's crib, gazing down at the infant. 'Somehow I doubt it is to talk of old times.'

There was no other way to say it. 'You are in danger, my lady. I have come to tell you that it would be best if you left this place. Flee from here, anywhere you please as long as it is far away.'

When she turned back to him there was a smile on Alditha's face. 'And what is the nature of this danger you speak of?'

'I cannot say. But you must heed my words. You are not safe here.'

'I am under the protection of King Diarmait,' she replied, fixing him with a determined expression. 'The sons of Harold would not dare do me harm as long as I am his guest.'

So she already knew the source of the danger. Then again, she had always been a shrewd judge, but still she had to be persuaded to leave. 'You do not understand. The brothers are—'

Alditha laughed. 'Oh, but I do understand. It is only natural they would be threatened by the true king of England.' Alditha smiled down at her child. 'But I am curious, Styrkar –

why would you come to tell me? Why would the man who slaughtered so many of my first husband's kinsmen come and warn me of such a threat? Especially when I was the one who stole away your master from his beloved wife.'

Styrkar shook his head. 'I held no grudge against King Gruffydd, I merely did as I was bidden. And I hold no resentment for you. King Harold made his own choice.'

Alditha laughed again, her voice like the tinkling of a forest stream. 'Whatever the truth, it is of no consequence. I know you were loyal to Harold to the end. And I know the oaths of loyalty you have spoken to his sons.'

'They are as brothers to me.' Styrkar could not hold her gaze. If only she knew the truth of his betrayal, for the real reason he was here, she might not think him so loyal.

'So are you true to all your master's sons?' she asked.

Styrkar looked up at her, feeling the need to unburden himself but managing to hold his tongue on the matter.

'I am,' he replied. 'Until my dying breath.'

Alditha reached into the crib and picked up her child. She took a step forward, showing Harold's infant son.

'Is he not handsome?' she asked. 'Do you not think he has the look of his father?'

Styrkar gazed at the child. Truth be told, the boy looked like every other squalling babe he had ever seen.

'Yes, my lady,' he replied. 'And if you would see him safe, you will leave Dublin today.'

Alditha shook her head. 'I have no intention of running from this place. I am protected by the High King of all Éire. And if you are still as loyal as you say, Styrkar, then you will give your oath to my son.'

He felt a sudden dread grip him – more oaths to counter

those already sworn… and broken. 'Are you asking me to protect your child?'

'Of course,' Alditha replied. 'Young Harold deserves your fealty. He is the rightful heir to the throne of England. His claim is more legitimate than any of his brothers. They are the sons of Edith, Harold's wife in the eyes of pagan laws. I was his wife before God. Our son is the rightful king.'

'I know you believe the truth of your words, and you may be right. But you should be careful to whom you speak them.'

'If you truly believe the life of my child is in peril, then perhaps you will soon have the chance to test your loyalty.'

'I have brought you fair warning, my lady,' he said. 'I can do nothing else to protect you.'

With that he bowed to her. When he looked up, she had already turned her back to him.

As he stepped out into the daylight, Tonbert gave him a stern look, but no more words were spoken. Styrkar left the house behind him, wondering if he had done the right thing after all. Should he have obeyed her and offered his fealty, placing young Harold under his guardianship?

No. Styrkar already had too many oaths to satisfy. Oaths he was about to betray. Why make more, when he was bound to break those too?

5

Dublin, Éire, March 1068

Two dozen warriors squinted in the sun as gulls wheeled noisily above them. King Diarmait's men stood in their finest regalia, green cloaks resplendent, helmets glinting in the bright summer sunlight. Styrkar could only feel some amusement when a gull shat on one of those helmets, making a tinny sound as it spattered against the steel.

This was all for show, and it bored Styrkar to his core. The mercenaries were coming, and by every account they were a savage and brutal bunch. This all seemed an overblown gesture, but it was what King Diarmait had ordered, and so they stood and they waited.

Godwin shuffled uncomfortably at Styrkar's shoulder. He was putting a determined face on this, but Styrkar could sense his trepidation. The men rowing toward the harbour would be instrumental in helping Godwin take the crown, and he had already expressed his doubts as to whether they would follow an untested youth into battle. Styrkar held no such qualms – they were mercenaries, and they would fight for whoever paid them.

To the east the longboats were almost at the harbour, and memories of Norsemen and their ships came flooding back to Styrkar in a storm-swept wave. The men on board looked familiar – their long hair and beards braided and combed, scars and swirling marks upon their flesh. Styrkar knew well what great fighters these men were, but also how savage and untrustworthy. Godwin would do well to remain wary of these warriors until he had earned their trust. Until then, Styrkar could only hope the Norsemen held enough respect for King Diarmait to serve his friend Godwin faithfully.

The ships reached the sturdy wooden quay, and several of the Norsemen debarked before they had even come to a standstill. Ropes were thrown ashore and secured while the rowers stashed their oars.

When a burly, bearded warrior stepped from the lead longship, King Diarmait moved forward to greet him. They embraced, laughing like old friends before the king guided the warrior toward his waiting guests. Godwin stepped forward and bowed to the man, who glared back with barely masked amusement. His shoulders were broad, waist thin and his dark brow creased, despite the smile on his face. An old scar lanced down across his right eye and his oily black hair cascaded across his shoulders.

'Godwin,' said Diarmait. 'This is Oskell Blackhand. Leader of this rough band of devils. You will not meet a more fierce warrior on all these islands.'

Styrkar glanced along the quay at the dozen or so ships that were landing. If Diarmait had spoken true it was but a fraction of Oskell's fleet. This warrior must have been powerful indeed to command such a large force of raiders.

Godwin grasped Oskell's arm. They almost wrestled as the Norseman tested the young man's strength, but Styrkar felt a swell of pride when Godwin held his own. As Godwin spoke his greeting, Styrkar saw that Oskell had fingers missing from his left hand. Perhaps they had been cut off in his many battles, though more likely they had frozen off during a voyage on the frigid northern seas, and resulted in the warrior gaining his distinctive name.

More men came across the quay to join their leader, and Diarmait greeted them with equally boisterous affection. The first he introduced as Kjarval the Beard, which Styrkar could see the mirth in since the man had no beard to speak of. The second Diarmait introduced as Hingar Eriksson. He greeted Godwin with a curt nod, and Styrkar regarded him warily. The man was heading into his old age but still looked stout enough to level any enemy he chose. His wrinkled head was bald and discoloured with liver spots, and a dozen rings adorned each ear. The man was sallow but keen-eyed, and Styrkar thought that of all the men debarking their ships this should be the one they were most wary of. There was nothing more treacherous than an old veteran – if he'd survived for so long among such violent company he was a man to regard with caution.

'I am glad to have united you,' Diarmait said when the introductions were done. 'Oskell leads his fearsome band with an iron fist, and young Godwin's cause is a righteous one. Together you are sure to win victory over the Frankish usurper. But first, we feast and drink, and become as brothers.'

That provoked a cheer from the Norsemen, as Diarmait led them toward his longhouse. Godwin was ushered away by both Diarmait and Oskell, and the two older warriors seemed only too keen to regale him with stories of their past victories.

Styrkar hung back as he and Magnus watched the Norsemen head off, eager to glut themselves on King Diarmait's meat and mead.

'This is a good day,' Magnus said, unable to hide the grin on his face. 'These men look more seasoned an army than any I have seen. I've heard many tales of the Norse, their reputation for war precedes them.'

When Styrkar did not answer, Magnus clapped a hand to his shoulder.

'Are you not pleased, my friend? This is the first step to reclaiming our homeland.'

'Yes, I am pleased,' Styrkar replied, forcing a smile. 'Soon this will all be over.'

Magnus nodded his assent, and they both made their way toward the feasting hall. Styrkar had spoken the truth at least – he was pleased this was almost over. Soon he would learn enough to return to England, to Gisela. That was all that mattered now.

Trying his best not to think on that, he followed Magnus inside the longhouse. Chairs and benches had been set along each side of the huge table and Diarmait's thralls were already pouring mead for the Norse. Godwin sat at the head of the table between Oskell and the king, and the closest Styrkar could get was a few feet away. Magnus seemed in his element, and soon he was laughing along with them at nothing in particular. For Styrkar it took him back to the court of Harald Sigurdsson – to the days he had been a slave, pouring mead and ale for violent, unpredictable men. He would have warned Magnus not to get too comfortable in their company, but that would have done neither of them any good. They could not show weakness here, not for a moment, not even if it seemed they were among friends. Styrkar knew full well how such rowdy company could turn vicious at the most inoffensive slight.

They drank and ate of Diarmait's spitted pig as the day turned dark, and torches were lit along the walls. As Styrkar ate he began to miss the more sedate feasting held in King Harold's halls, and he could only watch as the Norsemen howled with laughter and bragged of the violence they had done, and would do again. At the head of the table, Godwin looked out of his depth between Oskell and Diarmait – those two old warhorses bragging to one another and reminiscing over times past. But then he was not a tested warrior like these men. He had accomplished nothing on the battlefield. To Styrkar's knowledge he had not even bloodied his sword. Of what would he boast to these hardened veterans?

Oskell's deep laugh cut through the air, and he suddenly slapped Godwin on the back. For his part, Godwin took the gesture with good grace.

'I will place the crown of England on your head myself, boy,' Oskell bellowed to the delight of his men. 'They will call me the kingmaker.' He laughed and his men along with him. Someone half-heartedly tried to begin a chant of 'kingmaker' but it died as soon as it began.

Styrkar could see Godwin's discomfort. The suggestion that Godwin could not fight his own battle hung heavy over them. Styrkar would have offered him a gesture to take the perceived insult in silence, but Godwin was not to be cowed.

'I will prove I am worthy,' he said above the noise. 'I can place the crown on my own head, Blackhand.'

Some of the Norse cheered at that, impressed with Godwin's bravado, but others fell silent. Godwin was standing up to the Norse leader, and some of his men would see such a thing as a challenge to Oskell.

Kjarval leaned across the table, a smile on his clean-shaven face. 'The boy is testing you, Oskell,' he slurred.

The dark-haired Norseman shrugged. 'What do I care about the English crown anyway? I will do my part and take my gold. Godwin is welcome to his kingdom.'

'Yes,' shouted Kjarval. 'What's left of it after we've had our fill. I for one am looking forward to the taste of an Englishwoman. Or a Frankish knight, maybe. I'm none too fussed either way.'

The Norsemen laughed at that, but Styrkar could see Godwin was not amused.

'Our goal is not pillage,' Godwin said, slamming his cup on the table. 'We sail to reclaim my father's kingdom, not rape it. Once we land, its people will flock to our cause. Burning villages to the ground and enslaving their women will do nothing to win support.'

The Norse fell silent. Kjarval once again leaned forward, and Styrkar's hand instinctively reached for the axe at his side.

'We will do as we please,' said the Norseman. 'And no upstart prince will stand in our way.'

Before Godwin could reply, Styrkar growled across the

table, 'You'll struggle to pillage anything with my axe in your fucking neck.'

More silence as Kjarval lurched to his feet. This was an insult no man could ignore, let alone one of the fearsome Norse.

'You bait me, boy,' said Kjarval. 'So why do you still sit?'

'If I stand,' Styrkar replied, 'blood will be spilled. This is a feast, and I would not offer insult to our host.'

'Then step outside you—'

'Sharp tongues,' said Diarmait, rising to his feet. 'I would expect nothing less from two such esteemed warriors. But that's enough. Save your ire for the Franks.'

Kjarval glanced toward Oskell, who raised his fingerless hand slightly, signalling for his warrior to be calm. Obediently, Kjarval returned to his seat.

'King Diarmait is right,' Oskell said. 'We are all friends here. There will be more than enough blood to spill once we reach the English coast.' He turned to Godwin. 'My apologies to you, Prince Godwin. Of course, pillaging the land you hope to rule would be foolish. You are clearly as wise as your father before you.'

Styrkar allowed himself to relax, hand moving away from his axe. Oskell's words seemed sincere enough, though he had not proved himself trustworthy yet.

Godwin rose to his feet. To Styrkar's relief, the Norsemen kept their silence. Perhaps he might yet gain their respect.

'My thanks,' he said, raising his cup. 'Together, we will have victory. Of that I am certain. In reward for your support, Oskell Blackhand, you will always be welcomed on English shores.' That was enough to provoke a cheer from the Norsemen. Oskell loudest among them. 'Now I would bid you good evening. My brothers and I still have much to plan for.'

He nodded his thanks to the king, before making for the door. Styrkar and Magnus followed him out, and as he did so, Styrkar thought it wise to ignore the baleful glances he was getting from the Norsemen, not least of all from Kjarval.

Once they were outside, Godwin turned on Styrkar.

'Never presume to speak for me again, brother,' he said. His voice was measured, but Styrkar could sense an undertone of anger. 'You made me look weak.'

'Godwin, this is folly,' Styrkar replied. 'These men only want gold and slaves. You can never win their loyalty; you cannot trust any of them.'

'And what choice do I have?' Godwin snapped. 'I know these are nothing more than mercenaries. That is why I have to keep as many loyal men as close to me as I can. That is why I need *you* by my side, not undermining me at every turn.'

'I am always by your side,' Styrkar said.

Godwin nodded, seeming to calm himself. 'I will remember those words, brother. And I will hold you to them.' With that, he turned and left Styrkar outside the longhouse.

Magnus sighed, stepping up beside Styrkar.

'You're right,' he said. 'We do need to be wary. But then Godwin is right too – we have no choice in the army that fights for us. We can only hope that Diarmait's gold keeps the Norse loyal for as long as we need them.'

He clapped Styrkar on the arm, and left him alone.

Night was drawing in, and there was another raucous laugh from within the feasting hall. Despite the mirth of the Norsemen, Styrkar knew what a dangerous game Godwin was playing.

But then, weren't they all.

6

Exonia, England, April 1068

Ronan's horse was unsettled as darkness descended, snorting and stamping its front hoof in frustration. He sat among a row of other knights, just out of arrowshot of the town. They had waited most of the day as the enemy jeered from beyond the high palisade, but the English had gone quiet now. They all knew the end was near, one way or another.

A raindrop tamped against the metal of his helm, then another, before the heavens opened and began drumming a galloping beat on the waiting horsemen. Ronan sighed. As if this couldn't have got any worse, now it was pissing down. Damn these English and their bloody defiance. Why could they not submit? Why could they not just kneel before their betters?

The siege had been going on for days now, eighteen if Ronan had counted right, and all the while the Englishmen of Exonia had remained stubbornly rebellious. Earthworks had been dug, tunnels burrowed beneath the ground to loosen the foundations of the walls, but so far they had achieved nothing but to collapse in on the diggers and crush them where they worked. Barriers had been erected a few yards from the palisade so the besiegers could avoid being picked off by any keen-eyed archers. Ronan suddenly thought what an ignominious end that would be. To die pierced by an arrow in the piss wet, bleeding his last in front of one more cesspit town in this dung heap country.

To add insult to injury, the English had not seemed the least bit intimidated by the gathered might of King William's army. They had screamed their abuse and hate every day, flinging their shit from the town walls at the waiting Franks. Lady Gytha herself had come to refuse William's offer for them to surrender, her foul mouth cutting the air like a blade. The gathered knights had found her tirade amusing, but not so Ronan. Most of his peers spoke not a word of English, but he had heard every curse and barb shot at the king. He knew William would not take such insults with a calm head.

Ronan would have been surprised that the mother of a king might choose to hurl such tawdry language at her enemy, but what else could he expect? These were savages of the worst kind, and King Harold's mother seemed the most base and shrewish of the lot. Even today one of those peasants had stuck his bare arse over the edge of the palisade and farted his defiance. William of all people had not seen the funny side. His patience had run dry days ago. Ronan had already witnessed one English prisoner have his eyes put out. When they finally breached these walls, he guessed that an equally grisly fate would await everyone inside.

He glanced along the row of knights to his left. Mainard

was beside him and Ronan could see the eagerness in his visage. He was as keen to have this over with as the rest of them, but there was also a sense of trepidation in those eyes. For his part, Ronan felt no fear. He had been here before – waiting for battle while you slowly froze in the cold or drowned in the rain. It was more frustrating than anything; this siege was a pointless diversion. There were much more important things that required his attention, but for now he had to settle for serving as the faithful soldier.

Ronan was just another knight in William's army. Just a member of the rank and file, come to this foreign land on the promise of riches. No one could know the importance of his plans, the mission he had set himself, the ambition to be satisfied. All this was but an obstacle, a barrier to his rise to fortune. There was nothing he could accomplish here that would aid that rise as much as meeting Styrkar and hearing news of King Harold's sons. It would certainly not be helped by putting down yet another rebellion. Ronan knew he would get no thanks for this, and he was risking his bloody life here when there was choicer game to hunt.

He was dragged from his dark thoughts by a sudden rumble. Through the rain he could see the wall to the east begin to waver. Shouts of panic echoed out into the night as the wall's foundations gave way. There was a crack of timbers; someone screamed as William's entire army witnessed the wall begin to collapse. It seemed the diggers had managed to do their job after all.

'Prepare to advance,' someone cried from along the row of horsemen. Ronan couldn't identify the voice, but it spoke with authority. Lances were hefted, reins gripped in mailed fists as they girded themselves for the attack.

'Charge!' screamed the voice above the sound of the rain.

Ronan didn't even need to set heels to flanks as his horse bucked, lurching forward on the soft earth as the rest of the conrois began the gallop toward the fallen wall. His steed raced ahead on instinct, well drilled and disciplined like the rest.

With his heart beating faster they headed toward the breach. The panicked cries of the English were drowned out by the drumming of hooves and the enthusiastic whooping of his fellow knights. Ronan did not share their zeal, and he hung on tight, gritting his teeth, brow furrowed against the rain spattering his face.

An arrow zipped past his head. Then another, forcing him to duck. A volley flew, ricocheting off helmets and thudding into shields. He heard a horse squeal, the battle cry of a man just behind him cut short as he was struck by a flung lance. Still they rode on, unstoppable, implacable in the face of the English defenders.

The first of their horses had leapt through the gap in the wall. As Ronan's steed followed he saw dead English littering the ground. He held a breath as he galloped across broken timbers and piled earth. Then he was through, coming out into the town, seeing angry faces in the torchlight. Up ahead, the lead knights had already engaged, their lances striking out to spear the hapless peasants where they stood. The English were quick to counter, rushing in a horde at the Frankish riders.

A spearhead prodded at him as he struggled with the rein, and Ronan managed to turn it on his shield at the last moment. He countered without thinking, his lance thrusting down at an English face. Ronan felt that familiar horror as flesh was parted from skull, the man's cheek turning crimson before the lance was pulled from Ronan's grasp.

His steed bolted forward and he rode on amid the column of knights, wrenching the sword from the sheath at his side. Ronan gripped the blade tight lest it slip from a mailed grip slick with rain. Deeper they rode through the town, hearing the jeers and cries from the surrounding folk of Exonia, until they reached a central market square.

Ronan felt the fury rising within him now. He was ready for the fight. Gone were all thoughts of the Dane and the plot of Harold's sons. Now he was among his fellow knights and hungry for the slaughter.

Ahead was a wall of bodies, the townsfolk crowded together. Ronan readied himself to charge into their midst, but through the rain he could see the fight had already gone out of them. Many were already on their knees, begging for surrender. One held up his arms, crying in English for the knights to cease their onslaught. Ronan could not stop himself.

He pulled back on his reins, horse rearing on the muddy ground as he swept his sword down in a devastating arc. He heard the crack of a man's skull above the din, before he fell like a wet sack of shit to the sodden earth.

As the impact of the blow jarred up his arm, all the bloodlust, all the killing spirit fled from Ronan in an instant. He was left sitting atop his horse, glaring down at the corpse he had made. A man ready to yield, now lying dead.

Glancing about the marketplace he saw the English were surrendering en masse, throwing down their arms, hands held up, pleading to the formidable force that had come to meet them. Some of his fellow knights were not so quick to accept surrender, and Ronan witnessed more of the unarmed English cut down before it became obvious the fight was done.

It appeared their attack was over as quickly as it began.

Ronan had expected so much more – a fight at least, but it seemed that after eighteen days the remaining townsfolk were as eager for this to be finished as the besiegers.

He sat and watched as knights flooded the place, corralling the English into an agitated crowd at the centre of the town. Perhaps he should have done his part and helped wrangle these rebellious natives into the square, but despite the brevity of the battle he suddenly felt exhausted. More peasants were led from elsewhere among the settlement, row upon row of prisoners forced to face the mercy of the Franks. Ronan didn't rate their chances.

As they stood there, pitiful and shivering in the rain, he saw that most were half-starved wretches. No wonder they had given up so willingly. Their previous defiance had been nothing but an affectation. These people were beaten even before the wall collapsed.

The rain began to relent, leaving a mass of sodden figures standing in the torchlight. Before long, two riders entered the marketplace; King William was first, looking resplendent, the crown of England atop his head. The statement was obvious. Beside him rode his brother, Bishop Odo, looking almost as imperious as the king. As the two men brought their horses to a stand, Ronan braced himself for further violence.

Odo raised himself in his saddle, peering down at the mass of townsfolk.

'Who will come forward and speak for the town of Exonia?' he proclaimed in the English tongue.

At first nothing, but then Ronan would have expected no different. Who would willingly throw themselves among this pit of leopards?

Then, as the townsfolk were wondering who they might push forward to speak for them, an old man stepped out of the crowd. He did not look like any magnate Ronan had ever seen, he was as wan and bedraggled as the rest, but he held himself with as proud a bearing as he could muster.

'I will speak,' said the elder, his voice surprisingly strong despite his obvious trepidation.

'All we want is the Lady Gytha and her conspirators,' Odo said. 'Tell us where they can be found and the rest of you will be spared.'

Ronan doubted that. He could see from the elder's raised eyebrow that he doubted it too. 'They are gone, my lord,' he replied. 'Gytha and the rest of the town's stewards fled before the wall fell. We are all that remain.'

Odo turned to the king, relaying the news in their language. William seemed unmoved by the escape of his enemy, merely shrugging at his brother in reply.

Silence filled the square. Ronan could feel the tension, sensing the hot blood of his fellow knights. These English had been subdued with little effort, and the lust for further bloodshed hung heavy in the air. It was as likely they would burn this place to the ground and every peasant along with it, than let them live.

'Very well,' Odo replied. 'The king understands and he is willing to be merciful. As long as you show your fealty now, and vow never to defy his rule again.'

There was a discomforted murmur from the crowd, but the elder was undeterred. He stepped forward, then gingerly crouched on one knee.

'We swear it, my lord,' he said, before bowing his head in supplication.

At first Ronan thought some in the crowd might be less willing to show their loyalty, but as he watched they too dropped to their knees. One by one, the crowd bowed their heads until the whole town had submitted to their new king.

Ronan could only think that if they'd not followed that harpy Gytha, and done this eighteen days ago, they could all have saved themselves a lot of pain.

As the rest of the knights began to usher the English back to their homes, consolidating their hold on the town, Ronan turned his horse and rode away. He would not be missed, and he had suffered enough in the wet night.

When he finally rode back to the Frankish camp it was all but deserted. A single squire came forth to take his horse as he dismounted, and he painfully limped his way back to his tent. The cold and damp had infested his lower leg, and he gritted his teeth against the pain. All he could do was console himself that this was finally over, and now he could get back to the job at hand.

As he stepped into his tent, Gisela was waiting for him. She stood to one side, and for a moment Ronan wondered if she had been standing there all night.

Neither of them spoke as he unbuckled his helm, laying it down in one corner, and began to unstrap his byrnie. He was thirsty, but there was no wine to be had. After eighteen days of the siege supplies were scarce, and he could not wait to leave this place behind.

'Was there much slaughter?' Gisela asked, breaking the silence.

Ronan continued to disrobe. 'Not as much as I expected,' he replied, pulling his mail over his head. 'In fact it was an altogether peaceful end to a mostly uneventful battle.'

'Then why are your hands still shaking?' she said.

Ronan realised she was right. Both his hands trembled as he fumbled at the straps of his jerkin and he hadn't even noticed. He clenched his fists, stopping the shaking immediately. Was he losing his nerve? No, that was impossible. Not after everything he had suffered, everything he had been through to get here. What happened tonight could hardly be called a skirmish, and he was a veteran of more battles than he could count.

'It's nothing,' he replied, turning his attention back to the straps of his jerkin.

As he did so, he felt something within a pocket of the lining. Reaching inside, he pulled out the small wooden carving of the wolf he had taken from Styrkar's home. He had kept it to remind himself of the urgency of his true mission. So he might not forget what really mattered. He didn't remember taking it with him into battle though. Now, as he stared at it, the carving only served to remind him of all he had left to achieve.

'Are you sure you're all right?' Gisela asked.

'Christ, woman,' he snapped, turning on her. 'I am fine. Don't you know when to be silent?'

Slowly, Gisela backed away and took a seat on the palette bed he had provided for her. For an instant Ronan regretted his harshness. Perhaps her show of concern had been genuine? No, more likely she was trying to play him for the fool. To worm her way into his affections until she could escape him. Ronan would not fall for such a charade and open himself wide for betrayal.

As he placed the carving back in his pocket, he realised this was no time for weakness, not when he was so close. It would not be long now. When Styrkar returned with his information, Ronan would be waiting. Then he could make his name, and leave all this campaigning to lesser men.

He could only hope the savage Dane was cleverer than he looked, and had not already given himself away.

7

Dublin, Éire, April 1068

Gulls screeched outside his window, but Styrkar had been awake since long before dawn. Always those gulls, they were his constant companions and he would often lay until sunrise listening to them, wondering how much longer he would have to endure their piercing calls.

The sun shone bright, the wind shaking his poorly constructed hut. As he swung his legs over the side of the bed his thoughts went to Gisela. Styrkar knew he had tarried here for too long. He had failed to learn of the coming invasion, and after weeks of trying he was no closer to his goal. His lover had waited long enough for his return – she would wait no more.

He stood and walked to the bucket that waited in one corner, cupping a handful of water and wetting his face. The cold of it brought him out of his reverie and he quickly donned a tunic. Since the Norse had arrived Styrkar had seen it as his duty to remain at Godwin's side as much as possible. The mercenaries were growing evermore restless and eager for battle, but had to satisfy themselves with practising their swordplay, then drinking themselves into a stupor. Fights had broken out among their ranks and two of them were already dead. Styrkar could not allow Godwin to embroil himself in such deadly brawls, and he had become the king-in-waiting's constant companion. Despite that, Godwin had been reluctant to reveal any of his plans.

Did his brother suspect Styrkar of betrayal? Keeping him at arm's length because he had discovered what was going on? Whether that was true or not, he knew he had waited for too long. He had to leave – return to England and find Gisela. Perhaps if he told Ronan what he had learned so far it would be enough to see her set free. If it wasn't, he would kill Ronan and take her from him. More likely he would die in the attempt, but anything was better than waiting here for a day that might never come.

The air was chill despite a bright sun, as Styrkar made his way to the dockside. Longships lined the harbour as they had done for days now. When they would set sail once more was anyone's guess. All the more reason for him to leave now.

As he reached a mooring on the far eastern side of the dock, he saw the boat he had rowed here from England. Nearby were the three brothers who had brought him, sitting silently in the shade of a rickety shack, watching the bustle along the bay as ships were loaded with goods, some already sailing along the estuary toward the sea.

The eldest brother nodded in greeting as he approached, the other two not even acknowledging him.

'We are done here,' Styrkar said. 'See the boat is ready to sail by the morrow.'

The eldest of them rubbed at his teeth with the worn end of a stick, though from the state of them he should have done it much more regularly. 'Get what you came for?'

Styrkar clenched his jaw in frustration. He had failed in his task, but these men didn't have to know that.

'We leave at first light. Make sure you're ready.'

The man nodded as though he couldn't have cared one way or another. Styrkar would have grabbed him, shook him, made him care, but he needed these men on side, at least until they returned him to English shores.

When he turned back toward the town, he saw Edmund watching him from the dockside. Styrkar felt a prickle of dread at being discovered, but he managed to feign a smile of welcome as he approached Edmund.

'You have risen early, brother,' Styrkar said.

'As have you,' Edmund replied, nodding toward the trio of boatmen. 'Who are your friends?'

'No one. Just fishermen I was passing the time with.'

Edmund raised an eyebrow. 'Is the Red Wolf planning a new path in life? Catching fish out on the sea?'

Styrkar shook his head. 'My path is the same as it always has been, brother. I will fight at Godwin's side and reclaim the crown for him.'

The lie burned on his tongue, but to Styrkar's relief it seemed to satisfy Edmund.

'Good. Then you should meet us later at King Diarmait's longhouse.'

'Why? Is he to lay out his plans for invasion?'

Edmund grinned, gently placing a hand on Styrkar's shoulder. 'Patience, brother. Always with the questions. I can tell you this – King Diarmait has a visitor he would honour tonight. It will be an auspicious event. One you will not want to miss.'

Before Styrkar could ask anymore, Edmund offered him a nod, before leaving the dockside. Watching him go, Styrkar could only wonder if he should forget the invitation and leave anyway, perhaps even right now, but the lure was too tempting to ignore. Perhaps this was another ally in the fight against the Franks, and that might mean their planned attack was imminent. If so, Styrkar would have to stay and learn what he could.

He returned to his shack and waited. The day passed slowly, so that by the time night drew in he had grown wary of what was to come. So wary he concealed a knife beneath his jerkin before he left the hut and made his way toward the feast hall.

Despite his fears, Styrkar was greeted with a familiar nod from the guards at the open doors. From within he could hear the sound of revelry drifting out into the night. Inside awaited a host of unfamiliar faces among those he knew. At the head of the feast table sat Diarmait flanked by two men. One was as old as he, though less grizzled and retaining the jet black of his hair for the most part. The other was younger, and by his look was a close relation of the king.

'Styrkar!'

He turned to see Magnus gesturing to him from the other side of the hall. Godwin and Edmund were nearby, but on seeing Styrkar they offered no word of greeting. He made his way through the bustle of the hall to stand with Magnus, who stank of ale.

'I thought you weren't coming.'

Styrkar gazed across the hall at the revellers, seeing Oskell, the shark-eyed Hingar, and some of the other bastard Norse among their number. 'I was told this was not a gathering that I should miss.'

'Indeed.' Magnus gestured toward the king and his guests. 'Diarmait's son, Murchad, has come to join his father, and he has brought an old ally. Turlough ua Briain is the King of Munster. They are friends bonded in blood, and together they have quelled all opposition in the kingdoms of Éire. Diarmait's fierceness and Turlough's cunning have seen them rise, where so many others might have fallen.'

'It is obvious you admire them, Magnus. So has this King Turlough come to offer us help against the Franks?'

Magnus shook his head. 'Doubtful. More likely he has just come to drink and feast in honour of their alliance. To ensure the bonds of friendship endure. You know how kings are.'

His brother smiled, but Styrkar did not see the humour in it. He knew full well the nature of kings, and how likely they were to stab one another in the back as raise a cup in toast. And if Turlough was not here to help them, Styrkar was wasting his time. He could not tarry, feasting and drinking, while Gisela was still held in bondage.

'So we have still not decided on when we will set sail for England? There must be a plan by now.'

Magnus shook his head. 'If there is one, only Godwin and Diarmait know of it. I am as in the dark as you are, brother.'

Styrkar turned to look at Godwin, but again he did not meet his gaze. Was there something wrong? Had Edmund raised some suspicion? But surely if Styrkar's betrayal had been discovered Godwin would have been in a fury.

There was a loud knock as one of Diarmait's men hammered on the floor with the butt of his spear. A hush descended on the feast hall as the king rose to his feet. All eyes turned toward him as he laid a hand on the shoulder of King Turlough.

'It warms my heart to see so many friends gathered here in my hall,' said Diarmait. 'Both the old and the new.' He nodded toward Godwin, who returned it in kind. 'Loyal allies are hard to find, even for a man of my years. Turlough, you have been one such ally, and I am honoured to have you at my table. Our brotherhood is as strong as any bond of blood, and I would show you my appreciation for the years we have stood at one another's side.'

Turlough rose to his feet. At first Styrkar thought he might show humility and thank Diarmait for his words, but instead he stood imperiously, waiting for the King of Dublin to demonstrate his gratitude.

Diarmait held out a sinewy arm, and one of his men came forward, presenting him with a sheathed blade. It looked old and unadorned. A simple weapon, rather than a lavish gift suitable for kings.

'I have kept the sword of Briain Bóruma for many years, and acted as its steward. Now it is time for you, his rightful heir, to take it into your safekeeping.'

Turlough held out his hands for the weapon, gazing at it as though he had been gifted his own weight in silver. A cheer went up from the gathering, as Turlough gripped the weapon tight, but there was no nod of appreciation. Instead he regarded Diarmait with a wry look. The crowd, sensing something was amiss, fell silent again.

'I have waited a long time for this,' Turlough said, voice

hushed almost to a whisper. 'Have travelled far to receive it. But can it be called a gift? The sword of my grandfather that is mine by right?'

The room had fallen so silent they might have heard a mouse scurrying along the floor. Diarmait's eyes narrowed, and Styrkar thought it a dangerous game for Turlough to play, suggesting his host was a miser in his own longhouse. Nevertheless, Diarmait raised his chin and smiled.

'Which is why I have more to offer you, my friend.' He gestured to one of the men behind his throne. From the shadows, a housecarl stepped forward carrying a standard, torn and threadbare, with the fighting man emblazoned on the front. Harold's war banner. 'Take this as a symbol of my friendship. It is—'

'No!' Styrkar snarled, unable to quell his sudden fury. 'That is not a mere trinket to be bartered for favour.'

Every eye turned toward him. Diarmait's son, Murchad, rose from his seat and glared across the feast hall.

Turlough narrowed his eyes as he regarded Styrkar, who glared back defiantly. 'Who is this to judge what might be offered between kings?'

Godwin took a step forward, bowing his head. 'My apologies, King Turlough. This is Styrkar, the Red Wolf. He was a loyal servant of my father. And that banner—'

'That banner is sacred,' Styrkar growled. 'As sacred as any relic of your White Christ.'

'To who?' asked Turlough.

'To me!' Styrkar bellowed.

He was conscious that some of the warriors watching were getting twitchy. Glancing about nervously, sensing violence to come. Styrkar didn't care. He had endured much since he arrived on these shores, suffered in silence, dwelt in frustration, but now he could hold his ignominy at bay no longer.

'Peace, brother,' Godwin said, laying a hand on Styrkar's shoulder. 'I am sure King Turlough appreciates the value of the gift he has been given.'

'Does he? Does he know how many of us have bled in the sight of that banner? How many of us followed it faithfully? How we lamented when we believed it was lost?'

Turlough took the banner in his hand, gazing up at the torn pennant. 'I do appreciate it, Red Wolf. And it shall take pride of place within my fortress.'

'I am sure,' said Godwin. 'And so that we can be certain it reaches your homeland safely, Styrkar will accompany you on your journey home.'

'No,' Styrkar said, unsure if he had heard right. 'My place is here, at your side. I cannot leave when we are so close to returning to England.'

'Do not fear. It will set your mind at ease to see our father's banner sent to Turlough's kingdom securely. I understand more than anyone how much it means to you. It is what King Harold would have wanted. Then, when you return, we will be ready to set sail and reclaim his crown.'

'But I—'

'Just a few days, brother.'

Godwin held his gaze more forcefully than Styrkar had ever seen before, and spoke his words in a voice that would brook no argument. It seemed Styrkar had no choice in this. Despite his need to leave, to find Gisela, he would have to do as he was bid. At least when he returned he would know with certainty where they would land in England, and that was more valuable to him than anything else.

'Very well. It would be my honour to accompany King Turlough on his journey.'

Diarmait grinned. 'That settles it then. My friend will have the protection of King Harold's fiercest housecarl when he makes his journey west.' He picked up his tankard from the table and raised it. 'To King Turlough.'

The rest of the room raised their cups in honour of the visiting king. Once they had drunk to his health, the revelry began again. Styrkar could not stay and watch, instead choosing to retreat from the hall and return to his bed. There might be a long journey ahead of him.

8

The day had started brightly enough, but now no matter which direction they turned their horses it seemed to be straight into the cursed rain. Styrkar might have thought this country held a majestic beauty if he could have raised his head long enough to see it.

He rode at the rear of the column. At its head was King Turlough flanked by his cloaked housecarls. Behind him was Murchad, his own men sticking close, occasionally talking to one another conspiratorially when the rain relented enough for them to do so. On the back of Murchad's horse was strapped Harold's banner, folded in sheep's hide. It should have been proudly displayed in the hall of an English king, but instead it had been given away like a roll of cheap cloth.

Styrkar yearned to claim it for himself, to hold it aloft as he rallied the Saxons against their invaders, but instead here he was, soaked to the skin and forced to follow on this relentless journey. Ironic then, that in a previous life he had followed that banner willingly. Fought in its shadow alongside King Harold. But those days of glory were over. All he had to think on now was returning to Gisela's side, and the only way to accomplish it was to suffer this trek through the wilds, then return to Dublin with all haste.

His horse stumbled on the rock-strewn path. Not for the first time he thought that perhaps he'd been given this old nag on purpose, to demonstrate his lowly position among this esteemed company. Best not to entertain that notion lest his rage get the better of him and he show these men who the Red Wolf really was. Instead he swallowed down his pride, enduring the ignominy through gritted teeth.

Just as he thought the journey might be more than he could bear, the rain stopped. Styrkar pulled back his hood, letting the sun bathe his face. Yes, he had been right – this truly was a majestic country, but just as he started to enjoy it, Murchad slowed his horse and fell back to ride beside him.

'This banner must mean a lot to you, Styrkar, that you'd join us on such a miserable journey to see it protected.' Murchad patted the hide roll strapped to the back of his saddle.

Styrkar glanced down at it, again counting the reasons why he shouldn't just seize the thing for himself, no matter how many corpses he had to leave in the taking of it.

'Yes,' he replied.

Murchad nodded at the answer. 'I met him once, you know. Harold. Before he was king of course, but it was obvious he was destined for greatness. Truly you are loyal in showing such devotion to a man long dead.'

That much should have been obvious. 'Yes.'

Again, Murchad nodded at the curt response. 'And are

you just as loyal to his sons? I hear Godwin for one has grown to rely on you.'

Styrkar turned to face him, looking deep into those grey eyes, searching for something, anything that might tell him Murchad was somehow trying to bait him. He found nothing.

'Of course.'

Murchad let out a long frustrated sigh. 'Anyway, it's been good talking to you, Styrkar the Dane. You have certainly helped liven an otherwise dull journey.'

With that he kicked his horse on, leaving Styrkar at the rear of the column once more.

Perhaps he had simply been seeking genuine conversation, to learn a little more about the Red Wolf, but Styrkar was in no mood to parley. He just wanted this done with, so he could get back to Dublin and learn what he needed to before returning to England.

For the rest of the day they trekked west, and Styrkar was left in peace until they eventually neared a settlement on a river. It wasn't much more than a few fishermen's huts and a stone-built redoubt, but as the dark sky rumbled ominously it made for a more welcome resting stop than the wilderness of Éire. More than anything, Styrkar was grateful his struggling horse would have a chance to rest before continuing its journey along the poorly-laid road.

They were met by a steward, King Turlough greeted with all the respect due his station, and led inside the fort. Styrkar took some time to see his horse stabled and cared for, before he joined the others inside.

A boy was already playing a wooden flute in one corner as another, perhaps his brother, kept time on a small drum placed between his knees. Murchad and his men sat close to the door, still talking to one another in hushed tones, as Turlough hunkered by the fireside examining his grandfather's sword. From his stature alone, Styrkar was convinced the king was no warrior, but then Murchad looked little better suited to war. Their men however, were stout of shoulder and watchful of eye, and Styrkar was careful to sit himself with his back to the wall as he warmed himself near the hearth.

'Will you drink with us, Dane?' said one of Turlough's men, holding up a mug.

Styrkar shook his head in reply, turning his attention back to the fire and ignoring the resulting grumble at his refusal. He had no desire to fall to drunkenness at the best of times, least of all now when surrounded by strangers.

Instead he watched Turlough as he caressed the sheathed blade on his lap. Eventually the king looked up and smiled, pride beaming through his white teeth.

'I know it may not look like much,' he said. 'But this weapon is legendary. Briain Bóruma, my grandfather, was a great king, as I'm sure you've heard.'

Styrkar shook his head. 'I do not know of him.'

Turlough raised his dark brows. 'It surprises me that a man with a reputation like yours would not know of such a respected warrior.'

'I have known a great many respected warriors. And I have seen most of them buried. No one will ever hear their names.'

He thought Turlough might see the comment as disrespectful, but instead the king nodded his agreement. 'Aye, the dirt waits for us all. It's what we do while we're above it that counts.'

Styrkar looked back into the fire, remembering the task he had to do. Yet here he was, wasting his time with these strangers, allowing himself to be distracted by the war banner of his dead master. A master whose memory he had to betray. This had been folly – he had allowed himself to become waylaid by memories of a better time, by symbols from the past that held no bearing on his future. What did it matter if Harold's banner was handed to an undeserving king? Styrkar had to think on the living.

As those boys continued to play their doleful tune, he rose and made his way to the door. Murchad called out, asking where he was going, but Styrkar ignored him. Outside, the night air was cold but so far the storm had held off. If he was to ride through the night he might reach Dublin before sunset the next day.

The stable was dark as he entered, his eyes taking some time to adjust as he listened to the snort of horses. Among the twenty-or-so steeds he managed to find the one he had ridden on, wondering if it might be best to take another for the long ride back to Dublin. Before he could make his decision, the stable door opened behind him with a creak.

Styrkar caught sight of two figures entering, a glint of steel in one of their hands, and he slipped further into the nearest stall. The horse within whickered nervously, and he held his breath as one of those hooded men drew closer.

Slowly he drew the knife he kept at his side, crouching low, waiting for the first one to get close. There could be no misunderstanding here – these men had come for murder. And murder he would give them.

As the knife came into view, Styrkar snatched the wrist that held it, plunging his own blade into the man's neck.

He fell before he had a chance to cry out, slipping on the sodden floor and taking Styrkar's knife with him.

The second killer came at him, hacking desperately with an axe. Styrkar dodged away, feeling the keen edge of the weapon open up the flesh of his shoulder before grabbing hold of the man's cloak. He grunted as Styrkar slammed him into the side of the stall and clutched his wrist. The assassin grasped the axe with both hands, pushing with all his strength, the keen edge teasing the flesh of Styrkar's chest. A bridle hung from a hook nearby, and Styrkar snatched it, throwing it over the man's head. The leather strap tightened about his neck and he clawed at the bridle as Styrkar twisted it in his fist.

In the moonlight he could see the man's eyes widen, desperate, as Styrkar tightened his grip, shortening the length of leather, cutting off his airway. The axe fell from his hand as he desperately pulled at the bridle, but Styrkar had it in both hands, twisted, throttling, until the man went still.

He let him drop to the ground before scrabbling in the straw for the fallen axe and glaring at the door, waiting for more killers to come in from the night. In the scant moonlight, he was sure he could see someone waiting outside, their shadow falling on the wet earth beyond the door.

Styrkar crept closer, just as the door opened. Another hooded figure stood framed in the doorway, and he darted forward, grabbing the man by the throat and dragging him into the stable. As he slammed him against the wall, he recognised the face of Murchad, eyes wide in fright.

'Why?' Styrkar snarled.

Murchad raised his hands to show they were empty. 'Peace, Red Wolf. None of this was my idea.'

'Then whose?' Styrkar pressed the axeblade closer to Murchad's neck.

'Godwin. It was Godwin and his brother Edmund who ordered this.'

'I don't believe you.'

'Why would I lie? He says you betrayed him. Wanted you out of the way, but for the sake of the father you shared he couldn't do the deed himself. Paid handsomely in gold for me to do it too, and what kind of man would I be to refuse the future king of England?'

As much as Styrkar didn't want to believe it, he knew it must have been the truth.

'How did he know I would betray him?'

Murchad offered as much of a shrug as he could manage in Styrkar's grip. 'I don't know, but he was pretty convinced. That's not all you should know though.'

'Speak it,' growled Styrkar.

'Ah, well, first you must agree to let me live.'

The notion did not sit well with him, but Styrkar nodded anyway. 'Very well. If what you tell me is worth your life, I will spare it.'

Murchad quickly weighed his options, realising he'd have to take Styrkar at his word. 'The woman, Alditha, and her child. He intends to kill them both.'

Styrkar tightened his grip on Murchad's throat. 'You lie. She is his father's bride, her child his brother. Godwin would never agree—'

'And yet he has. The other one, Edmund, he persuaded him.'

'But your father offered her sanctuary.'

'My father knows nothing of this. And to hide his part in it, Godwin has tasked his mercenaries to see the deed done. If you leave now, there might be time to stop them.'

Styrkar released Murchad and took a step back, wondering whether to silence him forever. Before he could decide if he should use the axe, he heard voices from outside.

'In here!' Murchad shouted, dashing away from Styrkar and deeper into the stable.

Men had come from the fort, half a dozen of them with swords drawn. Styrkar had no time to exact his vengeance, no time to even saddle a horse. Instead he dashed out into the night, turning to the road they had travelled along, and running back toward Dublin. With luck, he would get there before Alditha fell victim to Godwin's wroth.

9

Wiltescire, England, April 1068

Gisela had never walked so far in her life. The road east
to the capital was a long one, mercifully straight, but
hatefully monotonous. All she had for company was the
incessant squeak of a cartwheel as it turned and turned,
playing out the rhythm of their journey. At first it had all but
driven her mad, but she'd soon learned the sound of it was
far preferable to the endless blether of the camp followers.

A gaggle of them dogged the Frankish column as it
made its way east. Serfs and whores walked together in a
throng, along with other waifs whose purpose Gisela had
not managed to discern, but she guessed they must have
brought some value to the Franks or they would never
have been allowed to tag along. A group of women babbled
incessantly, gossiping like washerwomen, their banal
conversation making Gisela feel even more sick.

Perhaps joining in their conversation might have helped
break up the monotony of the journey, but Gisela would
be damned if she'd resort to that. Instead, she suffered the

soreness of her feet and the aching in her legs as they trudged ever eastwards. All she wanted was to stop and rest, if not for her but for the life growing in her belly, but she knew that was not about to happen. For now, if she wanted to live she had to walk. One foot in front of the other, until the mounted riders at the head of the column showed enough mercy to allow them some respite.

She glanced along the ragtag column of travellers, to the mounted knights up ahead. From her position at the rear she could make out few details, but she knew Ronan would be among their number. After they had subdued the town of Exonia, the victorious knights had been summoned to the capital by the king. William himself was leading his forces east, most likely beneath his leopard standard, regaling himself in his glory. Satisfied that the country was now firmly within his grip of iron.

Gisela found herself momentarily grateful that she was at the back of the column, away from these men of Normandy and Bretagne, and the arrogance they had brought across the sea with them. The more distance she could put between herself and Ronan the better.

The crippled knight had been furious when he received his orders to ride to the capital. He ranted about his plans, about securing his position, raging like a madman, but in the end he had no choice. And consequently, neither had Gisela. Though it had pained her to leave, to think that Styrkar might return to the English coast and she would not be there waiting for him, there was little else she could do.

She dragged her gaze away from the backsides of the horses in front of her, glancing furtively at her travelling companions. No one gave her so much as a nod of acknowledgement. Another reminder she had no friends here.

Absently she placed a hand to her belly, feeling the ripe bump that was growing by the day. It would be obvious to some that she was with child, but so far no one had deigned to make comment on it. No one gave a damn but her.

At least back in Hereford even strangers would perhaps have crossed themselves and offered a blessing for her child. Here there was nothing. She was in the company of beggars, cooks and cobblers. Smiths and coopers and sinners, dragged together by their need to please the men who had come to burn their land and overthrow their king. How low had she fallen? Certainly far enough to be surrounded by people who didn't care if she lived or died. In Hereford she had been Lady Agnes' maid. She had mattered, at least to her mistress. Now she had nothing and no one. Her lover was across the sea, and she didn't know if he was alive or dead. Even if he did return he would never find her now. She was more alone than she had ever been.

A shout from up ahead halted the column. The horses and the squeaking cart in front of her came to a standstill. One of the knights turned in his saddle and called for them to rest awhile.

Gisela gave a sigh of relief – all she wanted to do was rest. To take food and water and prepare herself for the remainder of the journey. But as she watched the rest of the camp followers sit themselves by the road, massaging their aching feet and carrying on their nattering, she knew she had to take her chance.

No one was watching her. The knights up ahead paid her no mind, and the rest of the vagabonds she had fallen in with didn't even know her name. Surely she would not be missed were she to slip away into the surrounding forest.

As someone broke out a bottle of mead to share among their group, Gisela backed away, shuffling toward the edge of the road. The treeline was but a few feet distant. She could take a single step and be gone before anyone would see her. And yet she paused.

What would she do in the wilderness, alone and with child? Where would she run to? Who would take care of her?

No one. But was that not a better fate than the one awaiting her at the capital? Was death by exposure to the wilds not a more fitting end than the one Ronan would inevitably grant her?

Without another word she stepped from the road, turning her back to the column and walking casually into the forest. She resisted the urge to run, that would surely give her away, and so she walked as though she were just finding a private place to relieve herself, away from prying eyes. Any moment she expected someone to call after her, but there was only the sound of aimless chatter and the tweet of birds in the trees above.

Gisela walked until the sound of horses grew distant, those voices fading on the gentle breeze. Then she ran.

All she could see was the dense woodland surrounding her on all sides as she rushed through the brush. A smile broke across her lips at the sudden excitement, the feeling of freedom she had missed for so long. It was a fleeting release, as above the sound of her footfalls there came a shout from behind.

Desperation gripped her as she fled. Perhaps she had not

been so anonymous after all, but it was too late to regret it now. There was no question of surrender, and so she did not stop. *Could* not stop.

She dodged through the trees, feeling her feet ache all the more, but ignoring the pain. The leather of her shoes had all but worn away after miles of walking the road and they did little to cushion her tread. Gisela could not let it slow her. If she gave in to the agony there would be more suffering to come, of that she was certain.

Her foot snagged on a tree root and she stumbled, the shoe coming off altogether. One hand instinctively went to her stomach to shield her unborn child, but Gisela managed to stay on her feet. Feverishly she tore off her remaining shoe and carried on her flight barefoot.

The woodland began to slope upwards. Behind her came more calls of alarm, this time closer than before. They were gaining, and in her exhausted state she would only get slower. She could not give in – not to the fatigue, not to despair nor any notion that she might be captured once more.

With another surge of effort, she came out of the woodland into the bottom of a long valley. Up the slope she saw an old ruin, and with nowhere else to hide she rushed toward it. Breath came in fevered gasps as she reached the ramshackle stones. It must have been some ancient monastery, abandoned and left to the vagaries of the wild, but to Gisela it might as well have been the highest bastion.

She rushed inside; all that lived here now was a mass of vines, twisting their way through the old stones. A worn staircase led upwards to the crumbling parapet, and she all but crawled to the summit.

As she rested her back against the worn bulwark she panted for air. From the top of the structure she could see for miles, the wind blowing in strong gusts through open fields as she listened for the approach of her pursuers. Strangely she considered what a beautiful sight it was. Green and verdant land. A place she could get lost in. A place she could finally find freedom.

There came the sound of feet on the stone stair. Gisela gritted her teeth as they came closer, but there was nowhere else for her to hide. As the Frankish knight turned the corner and saw her, she gritted her teeth, a growl of anguish and hate issuing from her throat.

She recognised this young knight immediately – the one who acted as Ronan's right hand, and in turn he smiled back at her, then shook his head.

'Did you think you wouldn't be missed?' he asked, almost out of breath. 'Trying to escape was foolish. Ronan will not give up his prize so easily.'

'Please,' Gisela begged. 'You have to let me go.'

She fought back the tears, realising her hand had gone to her belly yet again. She could have wept, but instead she gritted her teeth, awaiting the knight's mercy.

'I cannot,' he replied. 'And why would I?'

'I… I am…' Could she tell him about her condition? Would it soften his heart? She doubted it, but then what choice did she have. 'I am with child. Please, I beg you. I don't ask for mercy for myself, but for the unborn soul inside me.'

A shadow of doubt fell across the knight's face, as he glanced down at her stomach. Before he could answer, there were more footfalls on the stair, and two more knights appeared.

'You've found her,' one of them said with a grin. 'Bitch led us a merry dance.'

He strode forward and grasped Gisela about the neck, dragging her from the wall. Before he could bundle her down the stairs she glanced to the young knight. She could still see the look of doubt on his face, but there was little he could do now.

Her flight through the dense woodland had gone by in a flash – the walk back seemed to take an age. All the while the sense of foreboding grew inside her, and by the time she reached the column of horses on the road she was shaking.

Ronan sat in a clearing nearby, surrounded by more men, carving a slice from the apple he was eating. When the knights appeared, grasping Gisela between them, he looked up and raised a dark eyebrow.

She prepared herself for his fury, no longer caring what he did to her, but she would do her utmost to protect her child. Before she could begin to wonder what he might do, a smile crept up one side of Ronan's mouth.

'Back so soon?' he said.

Before she could spit in his face, the young knight who had found her at the ruin stepped forward. 'My lord, I have something to tell you.'

Gisela felt herself gripped by panic. She had told this knight of her state in the hope he would show mercy. She doubted she would get any from Ronan. Worse still, he would only use her unborn child against her.

'If it's that she is expecting, then don't bother,' said Ronan. He gestured to her burgeoning belly with the knife in his hand. 'It's as plain as the nose on that filthy face of hers.'

He had known, but for how long she could not say. Perhaps there was a spark of hope after all.

'Then you will spare me?' she said. 'And my child?'

'Spare you?' Ronan replied. 'From what? Gisela, what fate did you think awaited you in Ludenburgh?'

'You have imprisoned me. Threatened my life. There's no evil I wouldn't expect from you.'

That seemed to amuse Ronan even more. 'I can see why you'd think me a monster. So what makes you think I will spare you because you're carrying the get of some pagan whoreson? It only makes you more valuable to me. Your barbarian lover will be much more compliant now I hold his child as well as his woman.'

'Bastard,' Gisela snarled, all thoughts of safety now fled.

She struggled from the grip of the knight holding her, lurching forward with no other thought than to claw the eyes from Ronan's head. Before she could reach him, two more knights blocked her path, grabbing her and pulling her away.

'You are an ungodly creature, Ronan of Dol-Combourg. And you will rot in Hell for what you've done to me.'

Before she was dragged from the clearing, she had enough time to see Ronan shrug.

'I'll rot for more than that,' was all he said, before she was bundled away.

IO

Dublin, Éire, May 1068

For a night and a day he raced along the road back toward the great port of Dublin. The wounds he had suffered to chest and shoulder had stopped bleeding, but the niggling pain served to urge him relentlessly onward. Now night was falling once more and his legs burned from the effort, his breath coming in strained gasps, but still he had to run. If Godwin had truly been swayed by his brother Edmund, and meant Alditha and her child harm, he had to do all he could to save them, if only to honour Harold's memory.

The weather had grown inclement, the rain and wind harrying him on his journey, but as the city came into view, Styrkar was grateful for Thor's humours. The dark of night, and the driving rain would hide him as he entered.

No one saw him as he climbed the palisade. No alarm bell rang as he dropped down from the battlement to slip into the narrow streets. Gripping his axe tight he made his way along the mud-bound alleys, silently cursing the day he had ever come here. His betrayal had been discovered and he was no closer to learning when the invasion might take place. The only thing left was to salvage what little he could from this place, and that meant rescuing Harold's widow, even if it cost his life.

As he stole towards Alditha's hut he crossed the abandoned marketplace, and looking up he saw how he had been discovered – the reason Godwin had tasked Murchad with his murder. Three heads were mounted atop a gallows. Despite the darkness and the storm rain, Styrkar recognised them as the three boatmen who had brought him to Dublin. Edmund's suspicions must have been raised when he saw Styrkar talking to them at the dock. He could only imagine the torture they had undergone before revealing what they knew of Styrkar's mission for the Franks.

Now was not the time to think on that, as he moved along the quiet pathways of Dublin. Finally he made his way to the dwelling King Diarmait had offered Alditha and at the door he paused, glancing up and down the path to ensure he was not seen. All was silent but for the wind.

A sharp knock, and the door opened a crack. Styrkar recognised the man who glared at him, wondering who had come to visit in the dead of night. Tonbert opened the door wider, showing Styrkar the blade he held in his hand.

'What does the Red Wolf want with Lady Alditha at this hour?' Tonbert demanded.

'I must speak with her,' he replied. 'It is a most urgent matter.'

'Fuck off, Dane. Urgent or not, she won't want to speak with you. Come back in the morning and—'

'This cannot wait,' Styrkar snarled.

Tonbert didn't move, and behind him Styrkar saw more

of Alditha's loyal men advance to see who was visiting in the dead of night.

'Who is it?' A 1ditha's voice from inside.

Tonbert kept his eyes fixed on Styrkar. 'The Red Wolf, my lady. Says he has to speak to you on an urgent matter. Looks half drowned too.'

Before Styrkar could call out to her she appeared at the door. 'It must be urgent indeed for you to visit me in this weather.'

'May I come in?' Styrkar asked.

Tonbert opened his mouth to protest, but A1ditha opened the door, raising a hand to silence her faithful bodyguard. Styrkar entered and she closed the door against the squall.

Inside there was a fire burning in the hearth. Young Harold lay sleeping in his crib at the far side of the room. Three more of A1ditha's guards waited there, weapons drawn.

'My lady,' Styrkar said as he shook the rain from his cloak. 'Time has run out, and we must leave Dublin tonight. Your life is in danger here. And that of your son.'

'We have already discussed this, Red Wolf. I am under the protection of King Diarmait. It would be foolish indeed for someone to try and harm us.'

'Foolish or not, Edmund seeks to right the wrongs against his mother Edith, and he has now persuaded Godwin. They intend to carry out their revenge with the help of Norse mercenaries.'

A1ditha glanced toward Tonbert. They did not speak, but Styrkar could tell by their expression that this news was not entirely unexpected.

'No, I will not leave,' she said. 'We will inform King Diarmait of this plot. Let him decide what to do about it.'

If Diarmait learned Godwin had betrayed his trust, the consequences could be dire. Even though Godwin had ordered him killed, Styrkar could not see one of Harold's sons face such a grim fate.

'It is better if we leave,' he said. 'We could steal a boat at the dock. Be back in England by tomorrow. I will see you safely taken to your brothers in the north.'

Alditha shook her head. 'My son would face more danger in England than he does here. No, I will speak to the king at first light. Then we shall see what Godwin has to say in his defence.'

'You heard, Red Wolf,' Tonbert said, standing in front of Alditha, that blade still in his hand. 'You've delivered your warning. Now piss off.'

Styrkar didn't move. His hand twitched as he fought the urge to draw his axe and bury it in Tonbert's head. At the edge of the room he was aware of Alditha's other housecarls shuffling uncomfortably. He should have spoken further, made her understand, but words had never been Styrkar's strength. Only violence. As he turned back to the door he forced himself to believe that right now violence would only serve him ill.

As the door was suddenly kicked inward, all that changed.

In stalked a man he recognised – squat, muscular, ears covered in iron rings. Hingar Eriksson held murder in those dead shark's eyes of his. It was obvious why he was here – to do the deed Godwin had agreed on.

Styrkar stripped the axe from his belt as more Norsemen rushed into the dwelling, along with the howling wind.

Alditha was already rushing to Harold's crib. One of her housecarls let out a bellow of rage, throwing himself at the Norse. Tonbert was quick to follow as blades clashed in the tiny house. Styrkar kept his eyes on Hingar, who slipped past the violence like a snake, slinking toward Alditha, blade held tight in one meaty fist.

Before he could reach her, Styrkar barred his path. There was a twitch of the Norseman's mouth perhaps half a smile, perhaps anger at being kept from carrying out Godwin's bidding. Then he rushed to attack.

Styrkar brought his axe down, intending to cleave that big bald head in two, but Hingar dodged aside, lashing out with his sword. It cut a strip in Styrkar's cloak as he lurched backwards. The howling wind rattled the shack as the other men fought in desperation, and Styrkar stared at Hingar. There were no words to say, each knew what the other was about. In that moment both knew that one of them was about to die.

Hingar dashed forward, and Styrkar was ready, bringing his axe down. Hingar caught the handle in his fist, stabbing forward with his blade. Styrkar managed to twist his body aside, but the blade scored a slash in his tunic before he grasped Hingar's wrist. There they stood, testing one another's strength for a moment, before Styrkar butted Hingar in the face.

There was enough time to see the blood spill from the Norseman's nose before he butted Styrkar right back.

Then they were at it, Styrkar driving him into the wall, Hingar driving right back and toppling a table and chairs. Their weapons were gone from their hands and they grabbed one another by the throat, losing balance, falling to the floor as the other warriors still fought, metal clashing, blood spilling.

Hingar clawed at Styrkar's face, and it took all the strength in Styrkar's arms to stop him gouging out an eye. The man was a thick ball of muscle, those years at the oar and the axe making him strong as oak. But in turn, the Red Wolf had been forged from iron, and he wrestled an arm around the man's bull neck and squeezed. Hingar managed to grasp his wrist, slowly pulling it free of his throat.

In desperation Styrkar bit down, teeth clamping onto Hingar's ear. He could taste the tang of those iron rings and blood spilled over his lips as he clenched his jaw tight. With a snarl of rage he wrenched his head back, tearing the ear off and those rings with it, but still Hingar made no sound. Instead he smashed his elbow into Styrkar's jaw, sending him reeling back before spitting rings and flesh onto the floorboards.

Hingar scrabbled across the floor toward his fallen sword. Styrkar's eyes darted around for a weapon but he saw his axe was feet away across the room at Alditha's feet. His eyes locked on hers for an instant before she glanced down, seeing the axe in front of her. With a swift kick she sent the weapon skittering across the floor toward him.

Just as Hingar grasped his sword, Styrkar took up the axe and leapt toward his foe. The Norseman turned in time to be greeted by an axeblade to the centre of his skull. The crack rang out through the tiny shack, and Styrkar watched as a drop of blood ran from the Norseman's dead eye before he slumped to the ground.

But for the wind, all had gone silent.

Styrkar rose to his feet. The Norsemen were dead but so were all but one of Alditha's housecarls. Tonbert Uffasson lay on the ground moaning quietly, hand clamped to a wound in his thigh.

'We have to leave,' Styrkar said, turning to Alditha and holding out his hand.

Ignoring it, Alditha made her way to the door, but stopped beside Tonbert. 'You have to help him.'

Tonbert glared at Styrkar, teeth clamped together as he fought back the pain. It was clear he would ask for no help for his own sake. For a moment, Styrkar considered leaving the man but, despite their differences, right now they both wanted the same thing – for Alditha to reach safety.

Without a word he hauled Tonbert to his feet and dragged the groaning housecarl out of the shack and into the rain. Alditha clutched her child tight to her chest as she helped the limping Tonbert on toward the docks.

Boats lined the harbour, and Styrkar guided them toward the one that looked most able to get them across the sea to England. He secured the oars in the rowlocks, feeling excitement build at the thought of making his way back home, back to the woman he loved. All hope was dashed when he heard a shout from behind them.

Two figures were approaching, weapons in their hands. Through the rainfall, Styrkar recognised Edmund's rangy gait as he hurried toward them.

'What are you doing?' said Edmund as he drew closer. 'You would take sides with that bitch? You would spit on the memory of our mother?'

Styrkar shook his head. 'This is not what your father would have wanted, Edmund.'

'How the hell do you know what my father would have wanted?' Edmund spat. 'You were just a bloody slave.'

Styrkar could see the Norseman at his side was growing agitated, itching to attack.

'Just let Alditha and the child go.'

Edmund's face twisted into a scowl. 'You have betrayed us, and damned yourself, Red Wolf. I curse your name.'

With that, the Norseman darted forward.

Styrkar was ready for the attack, bringing his axe up in an arc that took the Norseman's sword hand off at the wrist. He screamed, clutching the stump, before Styrkar hacked him down with a swift blow, opening his neck.

Edmund was already racing forward, but he had never been the most accomplished fighter. With a swipe of his axe, Styrkar sent Edmund's sword spinning from his grip.

The two faced one another, rain drenching them as they stared – Edmund's eyes filled with hate, Styrkar's with sorrow.

'I had no choice,' Styrkar whispered, before turning and making his way back toward the waiting boat.

After climbing aboard he pushed it from the dockside with an oar, and began rowing toward the open sea. When they were far enough out he unfurled the sail, and secured it from the whipping wind, before glancing back at the harbour. He could see Edmund standing at the dock, still glaring his hate. Styrkar could only hope he would never have to see his brother again, lest he be forced to do more than just betray him.

II

Ludenburgh, England, May 1068

Though it pained Ronan to admit, Saint Peter's Abbey was an impressive construction. Comparatively speaking, at least. When placed beside most other structures he had seen in these lands it was virtually magnificent. Built by their confessor king a few years before his death, it stood as a glorious testament to the skill of English builders, and a towering monument to the glory of God. If only King Edward had spent more time fortifying his castles rather than creating glorious churches, the English might still have their lands intact. As it stood, this was William's church now, as was the rest of the country.

Ronan was well aware of the significance of this place to the English. It was why King William had chosen it as the site of his wife's coronation, and on Pentecost of all days. The holiest place in the country on one of its holiest occasions, to crown Mathilde as queen. It was a shrewd move. Not that many of the English would appreciate it.

Even now those peasants stood watching from a distance

as Ronan and his fellow knights waited outside the abbey. Most of the crowd looked on with glum expressions. Faces of defeat. There were a few enthusiastic bystanders, children and youngsters who thrilled at the spectacle, but they were most definitely in the minority. Ronan wouldn't have been surprised if William had paid them for their support. Anything to put on a show for his beloved wife.

Despite the lack of a clear threat, every knight was armoured in mail and bore a sword at his side. There was no point in taking chances. The last time they had been here to crown William as king, his men had set fire to half the city. Ronan could only hope there wouldn't be a repeat of that.

Muted cheers came from up the road and every head turned to see the procession approaching the abbey. Knights rode at the head of the column, pennants flapping in the breeze bearing the papal cross and the leopards of Normandy. Behind them was King William on his black warhorse, Mathilde at his side on a dappled white mare.

The knights made way as the procession came to a stop outside the abbey, and the king dismounted. He raised a hand to help his wife down from her mare, though by the looks of her she needed no aid from William. Ronan had heard she was a tiny woman, barely taller than a dwarf, but it seemed those rumours were unfounded. If anything she was as robust a queen as there had ever been in these lands, and she ignored her husband's gesture as she climbed down from her mount.

As the king and his bride made their way up the stairs to the abbey, the knights and nobles of Frankia gathered together to join them. Ronan found himself walking beside

Brian as they both filtered into the vast abbey. The Earl of Cornualge, as he was now known, struck a regal figure, and Ronan almost felt inadequate as he limped along beside his old friend. His first thought was to complain to Brian about his recent obligations, and how they had scuppered his plans to learn of the coming invasion. When they entered through the vast arch, the scent of incense, along with the low buzz of the choir struck them full in the face, and now seemed far from the right time.

Brian took his place close to the front, and Ronan made sure he was at the earl's side as he did so. There were prominent magnates and nobles in attendance, and it would do his reputation little harm to be seen with one of the most powerful men in England.

Before them, Bishop Ealdred stood at the altar, patiently waiting to preside over the coronation. He could not have looked happier to receive his new queen.

'That wrinkled old bastard's come to heel quickly,' Ronan whispered, as the rest of the congregation took its place.

'If only the rest of the country was so eager to demonstrate its fealty,' Brian replied, keeping his eyes locked forward.

'What makes you say that? The rebellion at Exonia has been quelled. Harold's bitch mother has fled the country. Surely there's little left to fear from the English on these shores.'

'As soon as one weed is pulled another grows. There is still much for us to do before the country is secured.'

'For *us* to do?' Ronan said, feeling the dread pull of tension in his stomach.

'Of course,' Brian replied. 'We all have our part to play.'

Ronan felt a swell of anger and he clenched his fists

to subdue it. He had already been waylaid in his task to discover the Haroldsons' invasion strategy. Now it seemed he might have to abandon it altogether.

'But there are things I already have to do. I have plans afoot—'

Brian raised a hand for him to be quiet as Ealdred started his sermon. Heads bowed in prayer as they began to invest their new queen, and Ronan clasped his hands together till his knuckles were white.

He had already been away from the west for too long. If he was to find out what the sons of Godwinson were plotting he had to return with all speed. Other rebellions were not his concern, and any further distractions might ruin his ambitions. But now was not the time to enquire. First he would have to wait for his new queen to be crowned.

The feast was a raucous affair. King William and Queen Mathilde had shown their faces and accepted a host of sycophantic platitudes with grace, but not partaken of the revelry that followed. That much was unusual for the king. By all accounts he had become very partial to wine and game since his victory at Senlac Hill. Ronan could only guess that with his wife present he was in no mood to demonstrate his new-found love of gluttony.

For his part, Ronan had nursed a single cup of tepid ale for most of the evening. Earl Brian had been preoccupied with other men of wealth and property, and Ronan had to pick his moment carefully. When the opportunity to approach his old friend arrived, Brian was already well into his cups.

'Can we speak?' he asked, as the rest of the gathering were laughing at a juggler who kept dropping his balls.

Brian turned with a smile, throwing his arm around Ronan's shoulder. 'Of course, my friend. What ails you?'

Apart from his crippled leg and the constant need to gain wealth and fame, Ronan had little to complain of. Other than...

'You mentioned rebellion,' he said. 'Are we still speaking of the threat from Godwinson's offspring? Because I have that in—'

'No,' Brian replied, his expression turning grave. 'There are other problems.'

His arm still around Ronan's shoulders, Brian guided them away from the shouting knights, who had now taken to throwing random objects for the beleaguered juggler to catch.

'There is trouble brewing in the north,' Brian said. 'To keep the English lords compliant, William had offered the hand of his daughter Adela to Earl Edwin. That offer has now been rescinded, most likely on the word of Queen Mathilde.'

'And the fact that she is barely a year old,' Ronan replied.

'Indeed. It was stupid of Edwin to even consider the match. Despite that, he is said to be furious that the chance to gain power, and the favour of the king, has been snatched from his hands. Rebellion is stirring in the north once again.'

Ronan's sense of foreboding was growing, but he knew he had to ask the question. 'What does this have to do with me?'

Brian sighed. 'The king is sending men north to quash any notion of an uprising before it can begin.'

'And you are the man he's sending?'

Brian shook his head. 'No, I will not be going. I am to secure Cornualge in case of any uprising there. But the king has asked every one of his earls to pledge men to the northern cause. I need you to go and represent me.'

'But I have to return to the west. The sons of King Harold are spoiling for a raid, and I am on the cusp of discovering where and when they will land.'

'There has been no word from them for months. The king would rather concentrate on enemies he can see, rather than rumours from Éire of an invasion that might never come. You are to travel north under the command of Robert of Comines and quash this new uprising before it can begin.'

Ronan shrugged Brian's arm from around his shoulder, staring his old friend in the face.

'Robert of Comines? The man is little more than a mercenary. A beast, if the rumours are only half true. You expect me to obey his orders? I have important work to do back in the west. Work that will see me gain the favour of the king.'

He could feel all his plans slipping through his fingers. Every carefully placed chess piece was being swept from the board right in front of his eyes.

'This is important work, Ronan. If Edwin and Morcar are not stopped it could spark more rebellion elsewhere in the country.'

'And the king thinks it wise to send Robert? He is unhinged.'

'Send a rabid dog to quell a rabid dog. That is his reasoning. And Robert must be supported in his endeavour.'

'But why me?'

Brian clapped Ronan on the shoulder. 'Because I trust you. More than I trust anyone else.'

Despite the compliment, Ronan shook his head. 'No. I cannot do this. You'll have to find someone else.'

Brian's expression grew grave, and his gentle hand suddenly grasped Ronan tight by the shoulder.

'My dear friend, I'm not asking.'

They stared at one another for some moments before Ronan could hold Brian's gaze no longer. He averted his eyes and nodded.

'Very well. If that is what you command, then I will obey.'

The smile returned to Brian's face and he clapped Ronan on the arm. 'Then it's settled. Trust me, this will be good for you. A chance to improve your already stalwart reputation. Go with God, Ronan. Not that you'll need his help.'

With that Brian turned back to the boisterous revels of the knights, and left Ronan standing alone.

He could only watch as the knights laughed like madmen. One of them was kicking the juggler as he floundered on the ground, their patience with his incompetent skills now frayed to nothing as they made their own entertainment.

Ronan could only look on as the man squealed in protest and the knights continued to kick him bloody. He could feel little pity. After all, he had just been kicked much worse.

12

Dunster, England, May 1068

By the time they sighted the coast, the rains had passed and dawn was breaking on a sunny day. Styrkar was unsure how he felt about being back on English shores. He had failed in his task for Ronan, but at least he had an idea of the numbers Godwin might be bringing with him, and that their invasion was imminent.

As he rowed towards the distant port, young Harold began to mewl. Alditha bared her breast to feed the infant, sitting silently at the prow. She had said nothing to him since they fled Dublin, not that Styrkar had expected any thanks.

At the bow, Tonbert stirred. The housecarl sat up gingerly, wincing in pain. Styrkar had done his best to strap up the man's leg and halt the bleeding, but he would need the attention of more adept hands before long. For his part, Tonbert offered a brief nod, though he fell short of speaking his thanks.

Styrkar was about to row harder for the shore, when Alditha turned to him.

'What will the Red Wolf do now he has lost the favour of his brothers?'

The cold reality of that struck Styrkar like a blade to the gut. 'I will find another way to fight back against the Franks, without them by my side.'

But was that even true? Did he care any longer about his vengeance? All that mattered now was finding Ronan and seeing Gisela safe.

'Revenge?' she replied. 'That is all you can think of? To punish those who overthrew your dead king? Perhaps that is admirable. It shows the depth of your loyalty. And for all your fierce reputation, Styrkar, I have never doubted you loved my husband.'

He watched Alditha as she finished feeding young Harold. The boy was the true heir to the crown of England, according to the laws of the land. Alditha had been Harold's rightful queen under the English God, his firstborn sons disinherited of their claim due to their mother's handfast marriage. Styrkar began to wonder what Alditha had planned for the child, but there was a more pressing question that came to his mind.

'Did *you* ever love Harold?' Styrkar asked.

Alditha's mouth twisted into a bitter smile. 'How do I answer that? I was gifted to a Welsh king by my father. Gifted to Harold by my brothers. No, I never loved your precious king. But I love his son.' She glanced down at the boy, who was settling into sleep after his feed. 'And he is all I have left.'

As he watched mother and babe, Styrkar could only think how much he was reminded of Edith and Ulf. That bond between mother and child appeared unbreakable as iron, but it could so easily be struck asunder. He only hoped Alditha would have the chance to cherish her son for much longer than Edith had.

They were fast approaching land, and could now see fishermen labouring at the shoreline. Nets were being loaded on their small fishing vessels and a trail of men were making their way down to the tiny harbour.

Styrkar scanned the town above for any sign of Frankish occupation, but he could see no armoured knights patrolling. It could have been any other day in any other English port during Harold's reign. How little things had changed in some places since their king's death, but he could not blame these people for carrying on with their lives. Styrkar had learned some time ago that ordinary folk had little invested in who ruled their lands as long as they were left in peace.

Once he had rowed to the nearest jetty, Styrkar stepped ashore and helped Alditha and her child from the boat. Tonbert did his best to limp aground, but he too needed a strong arm to pull him up, wincing all the while at his injury.

'What do they call this place?' Styrkar called out to a passing fisherman.

The man regarded him with a frown, baffled by the curious question. 'This is Dunster. At the north of Sumersete.'

Not too far from where he had set sail for Dublin. Perhaps this was a good omen and his fortunes were finally changing for the better.

Styrkar thanked the man with a nod as he, Tonbert and Alditha made their way from the jetty and up the steep incline toward the village that was perched on the headland. They drew little attention when they entered the tiny port, and as Styrkar began to wonder what her next move might be, Alditha regarded him curiously. Was there a hint of gratitude in her cold eyes? She certainly bore no disdain, which was a surprise in itself.

'It seems we are safe for now, Red Wolf, and perhaps I should be grateful for you saving us.'

Styrkar shrugged in response to her begrudging thanks. 'It was my duty. As you have already pointed out, I had little choice in it. But I am glad you are safe.'

'How long I remain so, only time will tell. If the Franks find me they will surely take me and my son away. We will be King William's hostages.'

'When you return to your brothers they will find sanctuary for you once more.'

'And will you be accompanying me on the journey, as you did when my first husband was defeated?'

Styrkar shook his head. 'I have other matters of urgency to attend. But I am sure Tonbert here will keep you safe on your travels north.'

Alditha looked her housecarl up and down. He hardly looked fit to protect himself, let alone a woman and her child.

'If you don't find someone to treat his wound, he'll be dead before we've covered ten miles.'

Tonbert did not protest and Styrkar could not argue with her assessment. 'Perhaps you should secure horses for your journey. I will see to Tonbert.'

Alditha looked about the port. 'I'm sure horses won't be hard to find, and I have penigs enough to pay for them. I would ask you make sure my housecarl does not die before I do.'

With that she carried young Harold toward the smithy in the distance.

It took little enquiry before Styrkar discovered someone who might see to Tonbert's wound. The local midwife had skills enough to treat the man's leg, and Styrkar stood by as the old woman sewed Tonbert's wound shut. As she did so, Tonbert regarded Styrkar with something akin to respect.

'I suppose I should thank you as well,' said the old housecarl. He sounded bitter at having to admit it.

'Save it,' Styrkar replied. 'Had it been up to me I would have left you to die in Dublin.'

'Still,' Tonbert said, wincing at the none-too-gentle ministrations of the midwife. 'I am in your debt. And no doubt you will have earned the favour of Edwin and Morcar for delivering their sister from certain death.'

'What would I care for the favour of those two? I have no desire to make allies of Edwin and Morcar. Had those cowards fought at Senlac Hill for their king, then perhaps none of us would be here now. Alditha would still be queen and the Franks would have been pushed back into the sea.'

'What you say may be true,' Tonbert replied, as the midwife tied off the stitches in his leg and began to bandage the wound. 'But they are still powerful men. While they hold lands on these shores it might serve you well to have them in your debt.'

'I want nothing from either of them,' said Styrkar. 'They can rot for all I care.'

Tonbert shrugged, and let the midwife finish her work. When she was done, he managed to limp out of her tiny shack and the two of them made their way back toward the centre of the settlement. When they reached it, Alditha was already waiting atop a small wagon, drawn by a single pony. A second was hitched to the back of it.

'This is where we part company, Red Wolf,' she said, as Tonbert struggled to climb up beside her. 'I have bought you a parting gift.' She gestured to the pony lashed to the wagon.

'My thanks,' Styrkar said, as he untied its reins. Before he mounted up, he was struck by one last thought – Alditha was not yet safe, and would not be until they managed to find Edwin and Morcar. The English roads were more dangerous than ever, and he could no longer protect her from what might be waiting on her path north.

Styrkar took the axe from his belt, his only weapon, and handed it to Tonbert. 'You'll need this if you're to protect yourselves on the road. Safe journey, my lady.'

With a last nod, Alditha pulled the hood of her cloak over her head as Tonbert offered a brief wave of his hand. Styrkar wasted no time as their wagon trundled from the village, and climbed atop the pony. Steering the beast southeast he proceeded as fast as it would carry him. If he was to find Ronan he would need to parley with the Franks. The best way was to find a fort, and see if they knew of a crippled knight. It was a slim chance, but the only one he had.

As he made his way along the quiet road, Styrkar could only wonder what he would tell Ronan when he found him. There was no lie that would see Gisela freed, but would Ronan accept the truth? That he had failed to learn where and when Godwin intended to land? No matter, first he had to find the Frankish bastard and right now he might be miles away.

Not much further, and he saw a fort in the distance. Its wooden palisade looked roughly made, as though built in haste. Nevertheless he gripped the rein tight as he prepared to treat with his enemy.

Styrkar slowed the pony to a walk as he approached, but before he even reached the open gates he could tell the place was abandoned. As he rode into the courtyard, he saw signs that the fort was being prepared for occupation. Two men were rebuilding a collapsed wall with stone and mortar, and inside one of the buildings a woman swept the stone floor.

'Where are the Franks?' Styrkar asked, as one of the workers turned to see him sitting expectantly atop the pony.

The man shrugged, picking at a scab beneath his eye. 'Not been here for weeks,' he replied. 'This place and its surrounding lands have been bequeathed to the local lord for his loyalty.'

Styrkar gripped his reins tighter. Another Saxon lord had forgotten his vows to King Harold in exchange for kneeling to the invaders.

'What is the name of this lord?' he demanded.

'Eadnoth the Staller is constable of this stronghold,' the man said. 'You'll find him—'

Styrkar held up a hand. He recognised the name and knew where he dwelled. Eadnoth had been a loyal servant of Harold in years past, and Styrkar had met the man once before.

'Which way is Tantone?' he asked.

The man waved a hand along the southeastern road, before turning his attention back to the wall.

Styrkar kicked his pony, and made his way from the fort. The estate of Eadnoth the Staller was not too far away. If anyone might know where Ronan was, it would be him.

13

They were only a day north of the capital and already Gisela's backside was sore from the saddle. At least this time she had been given a horse and not forced to walk the road for miles with the rest of the camp followers.

Their contingent was small, no more than a handful of knights in the conrois. Ronan rode at their head, silent and dour. It was as though he bore the weight of the world on his shoulders, though Gisela thought it only a morsel of what he deserved. At least he was suffering as much as she was, but it gave her little solace.

She only recognised one other among their ranks – the young knight Mainard, the one who had chased her through the woods and snatched freedom from her grasp. He rode close by, with orders to keep those beady eyes on her at all times lest she make another attempt to escape. But escape was the furthest thing from her mind.

Her stomach was swollen for all to see. Gisela could not have hidden it even if she'd tried. It was clear she had fallen pregnant outside wedlock – no better than the whores who would swarm to the scent of warring men. Not that these Frankish knights seemed to care. They paid her little attention, which gave her some comfort in itself.

As they travelled northward Gisela could only wonder what fate awaited her and her unborn. With every passing mile she felt more alone, more scared for herself and her child until she could barely endure it. She could only imagine where Styrkar might be, what he might be suffering even now, but she could not linger on that – the thought of him in danger might push her over the edge of grief. For now she had to remain strong and face whatever obstacles were to be thrown in her path.

Putting heels to her horse she rode up beside Ronan. He acknowledged her with a brief glance before focusing back on the path in front of them. She could tell he was unnerved, his eyes furtively scanning the trees at the side of the road for any sign of attack. Deep down, Gisela yearned for Saxon rebels to come howling at them from the dense woods. To fall on these Franks and take their vengeance. At least then she would have had an idea of her fate.

'Where are we going?' she asked.

Ronan sighed. 'It would seem we are travelling ever northward.'

'Why? What's the purpose of this? And what has it to do with the task you set Styrkar?'

This time Ronan raised his eyes to the heavens before offering another sigh. 'So many questions, Gisela. And all of them of little consequence. It would seem the task I set your lover so many months ago has been rendered utterly pointless, and now I forge on to a new horizon.'

Gisela was unsure what Ronan was wittering on about, but it was obvious his plans for Styrkar had changed.

'Perhaps you should let me go then,' she said. 'If the task you set Styrkar no longer matters I am of no further use to you. Why do you even need me?'

Ronan glanced across at her, then down to her belly. He raised an eyebrow. 'I was starting to wonder that myself.'

'So instead of letting me go free you are riding me into danger. Along with my unborn child.'

He sighed, as though already thoroughly bored with the conversation. 'We are riding north to quell yet another English rebellion. Rumblings of dissent have been heard and the king has decided I am to join his valiant forces and quell the Saxons before they can make a nuisance of themselves. Don't fret, my dear, you will be quite safe. I'm hardly going to don you in mail and make you ride at the head of the conrois.'

'Who do we face?' she asked, realising there was no 'we' at all. She would gladly have seen the English destroy these Franks before they could claim another inch of English soil.

'Earl Edwin was promised the hand of the king's daughter. That promise has now been broken and Edwin is none too happy about it. It would appear these Saxon magnates want their thirty pieces of silver and will not stand down till they have it. Even if that means yet another rebellion. I would have thought they'd learned their lesson by now, but it would seem they don't know when they're beaten.'

'So there will be war?' she said, a sinking feeling gripping her. Gisela had seen more than her share of violence and hated the prospect of yet more wasteful slaughter.

Ronan shrugged. 'I'm hoping it won't come to that. But

if it does we'll show the English the folly of their defiance. Hopefully for the last time.'

Along the road ahead a camp came into view, and Ronan touched his heels to the flanks of his horse to urge it on. Together the group rode faster until they reached the edge of a clearing. Gisela could see tents had been erected, covering a wide expanse of open ground. There must have been almost a thousand of them.

A sense of foreboding rose within her as they rode their horses into the midst of the camp. Most of the knights looked up with little interest, though she did find herself being eyed curiously by several men seated around campfires. It was obvious they were preparing for battle and Ronan's notion that they might avoid a fight was clearly not shared by this contingent. Swords and spears were being sharpened on whetstones, two men fought a friendly duel at one side of the camp, while others saw to their mail and polished their helms. There was an eager atmosphere about the place, as though they relished the prospect of the battle to come. And here she was, stuck right in the middle of it.

When they reached the centre of the camp, Ronan dismounted. His men did likewise, not one of them offering a hand to help Gisela as she struggled down from her own saddle.

'Find somewhere to pitch your tents,' Ronan ordered. 'Get yourselves some food and see to the horses. It's time I introduced myself to the leader of this merry band.'

Mainard took his reins from him and Ronan turned to leave.

'What about me?' Gisela asked.

Ronan gave her a look that suggested he'd forgotten she

was even there, before glancing around at the camp full of knights.

'I suppose you had better stay close to me. It might not be safe for you to be left roaming amidst a camp full of soldiers. Especially in your... condition.'

She walked close to his shoulder as he made his way through the boisterous gathering of men. After asking someone where he could find Robert of Comines, Ronan was directed to an area at the northern end of the camp. A flag flew beside one of the tents depicting three sheaves of corn on a field of blue, and as they made their way toward it Gisela could sense Ronan's unease. His fists were bunched as he limped closer, his eyes looking woefully at that flag, and she could barely quell her own apprehension as they reached the tent.

Ronan paused some yards away before turning to her. 'It's probably best you keep your mouth shut. Robert has something of a... volatile temperament. Or so I'm led to believe.'

Gisela nodded, despite how ridiculous that sounded. To suggest one of these barbarians might be more fierce than any other seemed ridiculous to her. Nevertheless, if this Robert had a reputation among them as a fiery individual it was advisable she do as Ronan suggested.

The flap of the tent lay open as they approached. Inside, Gisela could see the man she guessed was Robert of Comines. He sat slouching in a wooden chair, one hand resting on the arm as he swilled the dregs of a brass goblet in the other. His head was shaved to stubble and he lazily glared from the tent, his face a beaten testament to the violence he had seen – nose broken, scar running down his left cheek. Even in repose, Gisela could tell he was a brute.

Robert regarded Ronan with something resembling contempt as they stood on the threshold of the tent.

'My lord,' Ronan said. 'I have been sent by Earl Brian of Cornualge to join you on your expedition north. My name is—'

'Ronan of Dol-Combourg,' Robert slurred, a leer spreading across his lips. 'The cripple. I know you.' He lazily wiped wine from the corner of his mouth, taking the leer with it. 'Tell me, how is my old friend Earl Brian? Pious as ever?'

'Most certainly, my lord,' Ronan replied. 'As faithful to God as he is the king.'

'And how does he enjoy his new estate in Cornualge?'

'I believe he enjoys it very well.'

Robert sniffed his disdain at the fact. 'What he must have done to gain such favour with the king.'

Ronan shrugged. 'We all benefit from the favour of the king. In one way or another. I am sure we shall get the rewards we are owed, with time.'

That brought a smile to Robert's face. 'Yes of course. And when we have crushed this upstart Saxon we will receive gifts aplenty I am sure. So, Ronan of Dol-Combourg. What have you done to deserve being sent north to join me on my quest to bring these English dogs to heel?'

Ronan shuffled uncomfortably on his crippled leg. 'I am just lucky, I suppose.'

Robert snorted at that before his gaze moved from Ronan and fell on Gisela. It was as though he had only just noticed her, his eyebrow raising in interest.

'Lucky indeed,' he said. 'You have been blessed with a most beautiful wife.'

Ronan shuffled uncomfortably again. 'This is not my wife. She is...'

He seemed unable to find the right word. Gisela would have spoken for herself, but the warning from Ronan still echoed in her head.

For his part, Robert only shrugged. 'Wife. Whore. What does it matter? You're lucky such an ugly cripple holds the attention of a woman like this. And her belly is ripe. How good of you to keep your future bastard so close.'

Gisela should have held her tongue, but her rage burst to the surface as she laid a protective hand to her belly. 'I am no whore,' she spat.

She regretted it as soon as she said the words, cursing herself for not heeding Ronan's warning, but Robert seemed more amused than angry.

'A whore who thinks herself a lady then? I've had plenty of women like that in my time.'

'You have never had a woman like me,' Gisela replied, unable to keep her peace now. Not caring what the consequences were. 'I'd wager you've never had a woman you haven't forced or paid.'

There was silence, and Gisela began to regret the taste of her own words, before Robert suddenly barked a laugh, slapping the armrest of his chair. 'You have yourself a sharp- tongued harpy there, Ronan. Your work's cut out for you, that's for sure. But I suggest you soon bring the bitch to heel.' The humour drained from him in an instant. 'Lest someone else has to do it for you.'

'My apologies,' Ronan said. 'I'll be sure to keep her muzzled in future. And I look forward to joining you in crushing this rebellion. For the glory of the king.'

Robert lazily waved his hand in response as Ronan grabbed Gisela's hand and dragged her away from the tent. He said nothing as he limped through the camp and back to where his men were readying themselves for a night in the open. Gisela was pulled past them toward the edge of the camp where there was a stand of trees. She expected Ronan to rage at her, but as soon as they were out of earshot of the rest of the knights he released her hand, leaning wearily against one of the trees.

'Are you going to make any more trouble for me?' he asked in a strangely calm voice. 'It would be best for you and the child if you watch that mouth of yours in future.'

All Gisela could do was nod. Her tongue had already got her in enough trouble, and it was best she curb it for now.

'I know what you think of me,' he continued. 'Of us all. But these are dangerous men, and we are riding into dangerous territory. It would be best if you did not make the job of protecting you any harder than it already is.'

With that, Ronan let out an exhausted sigh before limping back toward his men.

Gisela knew how much danger she was in, but oddly it seemed that danger was not from Ronan. Did he somehow now see his job as protecting her? No, that could not possibly be. He was her captor. Her enemy.

But it seemed in this place, among this army, Ronan might well be the only protector she had.

I4

Tantone, England, June 1068

His pony went lame not long into the journey toward
Tantone. It was in a sorry state, and Styrkar felt some
guilt at riding the beast so hard when it was clearly unused
to such exertion. He should have slaughtered it then and
there and eaten of its meat, but without a weapon he had no
means to do the deed. Besides, it was a doleful animal, and
had obviously been treated little better than a village cur.
Styrkar thought it best to just unsaddle the thing and let it
live out the rest of its short life in peace.

The walk was beginning to grate on him as he neared
Eadnoth's estate. His stomach rumbled and his legs ached,
but still Styrkar strode on, resisting the temptation to curse
his ill luck and remaining focused on his destination. He
had to reach the place before it was too late. Had to find
Ronan, at least before Godwin launched his ships. As he
drew close to his goal, Styrkar began to realise he might
already be too late.

Cresting a hill, he saw the estate of Eadnoth in the distance –

a fort surrounded by its palisade. The main gates were open and groups of warriors were entering in their ones and twos. Men laden for war, spears and shields slung over their shoulders. Eadnoth was mustering his fyrd for battle, but Styrkar had already learned the Staller was loyal to the new king, and if he was not rousing his men for rebellion...

It could only mean one thing – in the time he had crossed the sea from Éire and made his way here, Godwin and his Norse fleet must have followed. And now this Saxon was making ready to resist their invasion. Styrkar was too late to warn Ronan, too late to save Gisela.

But perhaps not. Maybe there was a chance he could still stop this.

He made his way down the hill toward the open gate. As he did so he joined the road behind two warriors, making their way toward the estate. One was old, seasoned and going to fat about the middle. The second was younger, his eagerness writ large on his wide-eyed face. They stopped their good-natured conversation as Styrkar drew closer and the elder of them turned to regard him curiously.

'You are here to answer the constable's call, brother?' he said.

At first he thought about ignoring their friendly greeting, but perhaps the only way he might gain entry to the estate was to pretend he was one of these warriors.

'I am,' he replied.

'Were you robbed on the road?' the younger warrior asked. 'Where is your spear and shield? Your helm?'

'This is all I have,' Styrkar replied, unable to come up with a convincing excuse for his lack of arms and armour.

'Well, you're a big one, and no mistake,' laughed the

older man. 'Fearsome enough without a coat of mail. Glad you're on our side.'

Styrkar had nothing to add, joining the pair as they made their way to the gate. The housecarls guarding the palisade nodded their greeting as the three of them approached, and made no move to stop them entering the estate. One of them looked Styrkar up and down curiously but said nothing as he made his way inside to see yet more fyrd gathered within the perimeter of the settlement.

Atop a mound at the centre of the fort stood a longhouse of stone and straw. Styrkar knew this must be the dwelling place of the man he sought, and he wasted no time making his way toward it.

Surrounding him was a familiar sight, men drawn from all across the land making their way inside to pay fealty to the constable of Tantone. Styrkar joined them as they filed into the longhouse, hoping he looked enough the part to not be questioned. At the far end of the building he could see the man they had come to meet, Eadnoth the Staller, seated in his wooden chair – a crude approximation of a throne. He was a thin man with a gaunt face and sharp cheekbones. His hair was receding and his limbs were wiry, with long-fingered hands gripping the arms of that chair. Eadnoth watched through small piercing eyes as each man came to kneel before him, bowing his head and vowing to fight for their constable.

Styrkar waited in the shadows of the longhouse as the line in front of him dwindled, then finally it was his turn. As he walked forward into the torchlight, Eadnoth raised his bushy brows in surprise. It was the first emotion Styrkar had seen on the old man's face, and as he stood in front of the Staller, a sly smile crossed his lips.

'I know you,' Eadnoth said. 'Thought you were dead, along with the rest who harkened to Harold's call. But it seems your reputation for survival is well deserved.'

Styrkar could see the men surrounding Eadnoth growing nervous. 'Had you fought with us at Senlac you would have seen for yourself.'

'And I'd be dead along with the rest, Styrkar the Dane.'

At the mention of his name a discomfited murmur rippled through the longhouse. From the dark surrounding Eadnoth's throne, a young warrior stepped forward. He was tall and fit, bearing a striking resemblance to the constable of Tantone.

'The Red Wolf?' the man said. 'This is an outlaw in our house. We should seize him. Hand him over to the Franks.'

Eadnoth shook his head. 'No, I will hear what he has to say. We owe him that much at least.'

'We are allowed to keep our estate by the grace of the king,' the young man said, not taking his eyes off Styrkar. 'Even allowing this man to speak is a betrayal.'

'Step aside, Harding,' Eadnoth said, his humour gone. The young man reluctantly moved back to the shadows as Eadnoth regarded Styrkar. 'Speak quickly, Dane. My son has a mind to clap you in irons, and I'm not yet sure if it's the wrong idea.'

Styrkar stepped forward into the light so everyone could see him. 'You know me. My reputation is as a man of war, but I have come to stop it. I ask that you give me a chance to treat with the sons of King Harold so that we might find a way to end this without violence.'

Eadnoth shrugged. 'You're too late. Godwin and his raiders have already harried the coast. It would seem your hopes for this to end without bloodshed have been dashed, Red Wolf.'

'And that is why you have raised the fyrd? To battle the sons of your rightful king?'

'It is,' Eadnoth replied. 'I am faithful to the new king, and in return he has allowed me to keep my lands. Do you think that treacherous of me?'

Styrkar did, but he knew it would be foolish to say so. If he had any hope of ending this peacefully he had to make Eadnoth trust him.

'You have done what's best for you and yours. It has become a common trait among the magnates of England.'

As much as he tried to hide his contempt, Styrkar was sure he had failed. Before Eadnoth could answer, his son Harding stepped forward again.

'We don't need approval from a common outlaw,' he said.

Eadnoth raised a hand to silence his son. 'Oh, this is no common outlaw. There is nothing common about the Red Wolf. Loyal as a hunting hound to King Harold. Fearsome. Deadly with both axe and blade. He might not look it, but this is a man to be admired. And for that reason, Red Wolf, you may leave here unmolested. No one will try and stop you, outlaw or not.'

Styrkar considered the offer, but where would he go? What would he do now he had failed in his mission for the Franks? Even if he could get word to Ronan it would be too late for him to meet Godwin on the field. Styrkar had to stop this battle himself. If he could persuade Godwin to leave and avert this invasion it might be enough to persuade Ronan to release Gisela. Even though Godwin had marked him for death, he had to at least try, for his lover's sake.

'I would stay,' Styrkar said. 'I would join your fyrd and face Godwin and his brothers.'

'You would fight against the sons of your dead master?'

He might well have to, if he was to save Gisela. But would Eadnoth accept that? Would he understand that Styrkar was doing this because the Franks had taken her as a hostage?

'There has been enough death on these shores. Enough fighting between Saxon and Frank. The only way for it to end is to accept the Bastard as our king. Godwin will never be crowned, he is not strong enough to take the throne from the Franks, but perhaps this can still be ended peacefully. He is my brother. He will listen to me. I can make him see that there is no one on these shores willing to risk their lands and titles to support his claim to the crown. We can stop this war before it starts.'

Eadnoth rubbed his stubbly chin, considering Styrkar's words. 'Very well. If you think Godwin will listen, then you may join us. But if you fail and we have to fight, Red Wolf, you had best remember whose side you're on.'

Before he could answer, someone rushed into the longhouse. Styrkar turned to see a young man, out of breath and filthy from the road.

'Constable,' he said, approaching Eadnoth's wooden throne and kneeling before his lord. 'I have word from Brygstow.'

'Speak it,' Eadnoth commanded.

'Godwin Haroldson and his brothers have landed at the port. Their mercenaries have razed the town and they are already moving along the coast, ravaging the land as they go.'

Eadnoth lifted himself from his chair, eyes darkening as he clenched his jaw.

'Then the time is upon us,' he said. 'Gather the fyrd. We'll go and face this invader.' He fixed Styrkar with a stern expression. 'You'd better hope you're right about your brothers, Red Wolf. I may have been faithful to Harold, but I have a new king now. If Godwin thinks he can piss all over my lands I'll see him buried beneath them.'

Styrkar watched Eadnoth leave. He was an old man, but determined, and Styrkar could only admire his grit. The longhouse cleared until there was only one man remaining. Harding, Eadnoth's son, came to stand beside Styrkar.

'You'd better decide where your loyalties lie, Red Wolf,' he said. 'My father risks much by allowing you your freedom.'

'He has my loyalty,' Styrkar replied, though he realised how little those words meant nowadays.

'So you'll fight for him if needed?'

Styrkar turned to regard Harding. He was a head smaller, but still looked as tough as his father. 'Give me an axe and I'll prove it.'

A slow smile crossed Harding's lips. 'You'd better, Red Wolf. You'd better.'

15

Flames licked the sky everywhere he looked. This had been far from the biggest settlement Ronan had ever ridden into, but it certainly burned like Hell itself. The sounds of screaming villagers echoed like the damned as they were consumed by the flames or pierced by the lance. And all the while he sat and watched.

Ronan was the only calm amidst the chaos. His horse remained stalwart as he sat atop its back, witnessing the knights of Robert of Comines run rampant throughout the small town. Some charged their horses, spearing the hapless peasants as they fled. Others had chosen to dismount, grinning in delight as they drew their swords and axes and got in close. Whatever method they chose, they executed it without mercy.

A sharp cry made Ronan turn and he saw a woman dragged from a house by two armoured men as the building was consumed in flame. He quickly turned away before he could see what was about to happen, in no mood to view the grim proceedings. His stomach was already tied up in a knot, lance held loosely in his hand, impotent and unused. The sword still in the sheath at his waist, his grip on the rein tight in case he let go and see that his hand was shaking.

Ronan closed his eyes, vainly hoping it might block out some of this madness. In an instant he regretted it, as visions of a torched hut danced before his eyes. A hut by a river. A hut he had ordered burned along with those trapped inside, so many months ago.

His eyes flicked open, but the screaming and the flames and the death were still there. He could not escape them no matter what he did. Anarchy reigned whether he closed his eyes to it or not.

What was wrong with him? Was he losing his stomach for this? Or was he afflicted by a worse malady? A fault of the mind much worse than the one in his leg? Was this simple cowardice or was Ronan of Dol-Combourg finally losing his wits?

A horse cantered up beside his own, snorting in protest as its rider pulled hard on the reins. Ronan recognised the rider despite the blood spattering his face and armour. Mainard looked to be relishing his part in the carnage.

'Are you all right, my lord?' said the young knight. 'Are you wounded?'

Ronan took a second to glance at the sorry display before him. If there had been any among this pathetic settlement capable of wounding a mounted knight, they had not shown themselves.

'Of course not,' he replied, trying his best to quell any doubt in his voice.

Mainard frowned in confusion. 'Then what ails you?

Why have you not joined in the fight? There could be much treasure to be had.'

Again, Ronan considered his surroundings. Calling this a fight was overstating it by several degrees. 'What treasures could I possibly hope to find in this shithole? A rusty shovel and a half-eaten cabbage might seem like riches to you, Mainard, but I have much higher standards where that's concerned.'

Mainard opened his mouth to answer but thought better of it. With a browbeaten look, he put his heels to his horse and rode off to send more helpless villagers to their doom. Ronan watched him go before cursing his harsh tongue. Mainard was one of the only friends he had in this misbegotten place. It wouldn't do to make him resentful. And neither would it do to just sit here and watch another town burn.

Pulling on the rein he turned his horse and rode as fast as he could from the massacre. It took some time before the image of flames left his mind.

They built their camp some way from the burned village. Ronan found he couldn't quite manage to snort the stink of it from his nose – charred wood and burning flesh still lingering in his nostrils, haunting him as he stood in the dark. At least the noise had abated. That was one mercy at least.

Though Robert's men had camped down and were now making merry, Ronan was in no mood to join them. He stood apart in the shadows at the edge of the encampment, trying to expel the spectres that plagued him. He'd drunk plenty of wine, but even that did little to exorcise those ghosts.

Still, it was a quiet night. Ronan might as well take advantage of some respite before the slaughter began all over again. The rest of the men sat in their repose as though it had never happened. Someone was even singing a cheerful song as they laughed and talked. That someone had most likely been raping and murdering until the sun set.

Had Ronan once been able to flit so easily from brute to minstrel? To forget the violence he had inflicted and act as though this were any other day? Before he could even try and recall, he saw the outline of someone approaching from the camp. They were framed in the glowing light of the campfires, and it took him a moment to recognise the silhouette. When he realised it was Robert, he tried his best to drag himself from his malaise.

'Not in the mood for celebration?' Robert said as he came to stand at Ronan's side. He held a cup in his hand, swilling the dregs of whatever he had been drinking before taking another sip.

'No,' Ronan replied. 'I thought it best to ensure the perimeter was secure.'

Robert flashed him a cynical look. 'Our perimeter is quite secure, cripple. I think you just don't like mixing with the rest of my men. That makes me suspicious. I've always been wary of men who see themselves apart from their fellows.' He peered closer, the smell of booze on his breath drifting toward Ronan despite the breeze. 'Do you think you're above the rest of my men, Ronan of Dol-Combourg?'

Of course he did. He was the son of a nobleman. Friend

to earls and lords, and servant to a king. 'No. I am just a soldier. Doing his duty.'

'Just a soldier,' Robert replied with a nod. 'I like that.'

Ronan was relieved the answer seemed to satisfy him. Perhaps he should have cherished the fact and accepted the silence that followed, but he could not help himself.

'I would ask, is this harrying necessary? We have not even reached Waruic and yet you seem determined to salt every inch of ground on the way.'

Robert drained his cup. When he finished Ronan could see he was smiling in the dark. 'Of course it's necessary. I have been sent to curb a rebellion before it takes hold. These villages and burhs are insignificant, but their destruction sends a message.'

'But these people have demonstrated no loyalty to Edwin. It's just as likely they are loyal to the king. They probably don't even know what Edwin's plans are; they are not rebels.'

'Not yet. And neither will they be when Edwin puts out the call. Towns we destroy now won't have to be put down in the future. I am surprised at you, Ronan. I had heard you were reliable, ruthless, not scared of making hard choices. Not one to balk at the death of worthless peasants.'

'Don't think to question my determination,' Ronan replied, eager to make it clear he was no coward, no matter how much he suspected it himself. 'When the time comes I will do what's needed.'

Robert took a step closer, staring into Ronan's eyes. He was not a big man but Ronan still thought him imposing.

'You had better,' Robert said. 'Because I've seen little evidence of your resolve so far.'

'When we find an enemy worthy enough, you will witness my value.' He could smell Robert's breath much more keenly now, a hint of raw meat behind the wine. It took all his strength to stare down those mean eyes of his. 'When we face Edwin on the field you will see how I fight. Just as I did against King Harold at the Hill.'

Robert held his gaze for a long lingering moment, before nodding.

'I hope so, Ronan. For your sake.' With that he took a step back, and it was all Ronan could do not to let out a sigh of relief. 'My goblet is empty. Time I filled it. I suggest you do the same.'

He left Ronan standing in the dark and made his way back toward the camp. It would have been wise to heed his suggestion, but Ronan just stood there, watching him go. All he could do was try and quell his disdain for the man he had been forced to serve. It was no easy task, but Ronan had spent a lifetime eating shit from men of little worth in order to rise through the ranks. He struggled to understand why this time it was so difficult.

As he tried to work out the answer, his crippled leg began to ache, his knee trembling so much he had to walk off the pain. As he circled the camp, passing a couple of sentries, he began to entertain the notion that Robert was right. Perhaps he should join the rest of the men. Try to fit in. Was he as arrogant as Robert suggested? Should he really think himself above the rest of these knights? They would have to fight alongside one another in the days to come. After the burning of helpless villages was done, there might be a hard battle ahead at Waruic. It would not do for him to be regarded as a pariah when he might need these men to watch his back.

The sudden thought of another battle made his stomach churn unexpectedly. The wine he had drunk roiled in his gut and he staggered toward a nearby tree. Ronan barely reached it before he threw up hot vomit onto the grass. His stomach heaved again, this time there was barely anything to evacuate but still he retched. Perhaps he should have been wary that someone had heard him, that he might gain a reputation for a lack of tolerance to wine, but he had stopped caring. His head was spinning, legs shaking as he fought the urge to puke once more.

'Are you all right?' someone asked.

Ronan forced himself to stand up straight, recognising the voice, though he could barely see her through the dark and the tears that filled his eyes.

'I am fine,' he snapped.

He hadn't meant to react so aggressively, but the shame of showing such weakness filled him with anger. Gisela moved closer. He could see she had one hand placed protectively on her swollen belly, but her eyes were filled with genuine concern.

'Shall I fetch you some water?' she asked.

'I doubt that will do much good,' he replied, the thought of filling his gut with anything almost causing him to retch once more.

'Are you sick?' Gisela asked.

How to answer? Ronan had no idea what was ailing him, but it was no pox, and it certainly wasn't the meagre amount of wine he had drunk.

'No. I am well. Just…'

Just what? He had no idea how to answer. Instead he stood there leaning against a tree. The two of them regarded one another as gradually the bilious sensation inside him began to relent.

As they stood in silence he found he could not take his eyes from her stomach. He had never been so close to a woman with child. It was a novelty that provoked an unfamiliar feeling within him. Curiosity perhaps?

'Does it kick?' Ronan asked. It seemed the right thing to say, and anything to break this uncomfortable quiet.

Gisela took another step forward. 'Would you like to feel?'

'I would not,' he replied. But did he? What was he scared of?

She took another step forward, reaching out with her hand. 'It's all right. You can touch if you wish.'

Ronan let her take his hand and press it to her belly. It was warm to the touch. Smooth and firm and burgeoning with life. No sooner had he laid his hand to her than he snatched it away. Again, dizziness overcame him. Nausea threatening to rise up and make him puke once more.

'It's all right,' she said.

'Damn you woman, leave me in peace,' he snarled, pushing himself away from the tree. 'And have a care. You should be more wary of who you allow to touch your unborn bastard.'

He staggered away from her and into the dark, leaving Gisela and the camp behind. In the distance he could hear the knights becoming more raucous, the sound of them haunting him more than the screams of dying peasants.

Ronan had to clear his head of distractions. Had to think on the task at hand. This was no time for celebration, no time for weakness. Soon he would be called upon to prove his worth, and he had to curb this malaise. If he couldn't, it may well be the death of him.

16

Wain's Hill, England, June 1068

L ight bathed the green fields as Styrkar sat at the edge of Eadnoth's camp watching the sunrise. He had barely slept. All he could think on was what would be coming. If there was battle on its way he would have to fight his brothers – the sons of his master. It would be Styrkar's final betrayal, and he may as well have driven a spear through Harold's grave and spat on the mound that marked it. Not that there was such a thing. King Harold had no grave, and now Styrkar might be forced to send his sons to join their father in the afterlife.

Godwin had learned of his treachery and it had moved him to such a fury he had ordered Styrkar's murder. Whatever kinship they held was gone now, but still he had to face him. If he could halt this raid before it started it might be enough to bargain for Gisela's freedom. He had to speak with his brother again, no matter the danger.

As the fyrd began to rise, rubbing warmth into their limbs and starting fires to break their fast, a rider approached from the north. Eadnoth and Harding greeted the man as he dismounted, and Styrkar walked closer, eager to hear what the messenger had to say, hoping against hope that he would deliver news of Godwin's retreat back across the sea.

'My lord,' the rider said, bowing before his constable. 'The raiders are camped five miles beyond the hill. They have a large force. Norsemen if my eye is right.'

Eadnoth nodded at the news, thanking his messenger before turning to his son.

'Prepare the fyrd,' he said. 'Today is the day.'

Harding nodded, looking much more eager for the fight than his father. 'We'll push those bastards back into the sea. This will be a day for the histories.'

Eadnoth the Staller looked much less keen to write his name in the annals. 'Just prepare the men,' he replied. 'The best we can hope is to offer enough resistance to force a retreat and prove the king was right to let us keep our estates. The histories be damned.'

Before Harding could muster their army for battle, Styrkar moved closer.

'Staller,' he said. 'I would ask a favour. One that might benefit us both.'

'Speak it,' Eadnoth replied.

'I told you I wanted this to end without bloodshed. Let me ride to their camp. Let me try and persuade Godwin of his folly. His mercenaries might have come for slaves and plunder, but Godwin only wants his rightful crown. If he sees he has no chance to regain it, maybe he will leave. It might not mean the raiders will retreat, but at least you will not have to face the sons of your former king in battle.'

Eadnoth considered his words, but Harding was quick to step forward.

'The sons of Harold have made their intentions clear. They are traitors to the king of England. And you've not yet proven yourself loyal, Red Wolf. Best you be silent lest—'

Eadnoth laid a firm hand on his son's arm. 'But he speaks sense. We may have a new king but we were once loyal to Harold, and he did right by us. Least we can do is offer clemency to his sons. Who knows, maybe this can all be ended without a drop of blood spilled. Take a horse, Red Wolf, and go see Godwin. But I warn you – betray me and I'll have your head sent to the king.'

Styrkar nodded his thanks before one of Eadnoth's men brought him a pony. As he rode up the hill toward Godwin's camp, he could not suppress the rising sense of dread within him. How would he ever persuade the ambitious young warrior to abandon his invasion? This country was his birthright after all. And even if Styrkar could make Godwin reconsider his rightful legacy, would he take the mercenaries with him? More pressing still – would he even listen to Styrkar, or would he simply have him killed?

That thought was one he had to ignore. If he could stop this battle and save his brothers, then perhaps he could save Gisela too. The chance was slim, but it was one he could not spurn.

He mounted the hilltop and rode north until he could just see the Norse camp in the distance. The sense of foreboding never left him as he made his way across the fields. Styrkar was acting as herald and peacemaker. He had no weapon but still rode right into the heart of the enemy. Even in his darkest days in the wilds, as he fought the Franks with little more than an axe and his grit, he had never felt so vulnerable.

The horse swiftly carried him toward his goal, and the closer he got the more imposing the mercenary camp looked. Hundreds of warriors were entrenched atop a great hill and the noise they made only served to unnerve Styrkar the closer he got.

No sooner had he reached the edge of the camp than he reined his horse to a walk. Several of the mercenaries saw him coming, and at first they seemed unconcerned. What threat would one unarmed rider be to an entire army? But the deeper into their encampment he delved, the more the murmurs of disquiet spread. Some of them recognised him, and he heard his name repeated in hissing tones. Styrkar clenched his fists about the rein as he saw men drawing their weapons, some approaching with spears, but no one moved to attack until a warrior he recognised pushed his way through the gathering crowd.

Kjarval the Beard eyed him with barely masked hatred. 'You've got some stones coming here unarmoured and empty-handed, Red Wolf. Or maybe you're just as mad as they say you are.'

'I would speak with Prince Godwin,' Styrkar replied.

'Would you?' said Kjarval. 'And I would sit on a throne of gold with slave girls rubbing oil into my toes. But we can't all get what we want.'

Styrkar had no time to react as the first mercenary darted forward. He was grabbed, dragged from the saddle, and barely raised his arms above his head as the first blow landed.

A foot hit his ribs, all the air suddenly kicked out of him.

Fists pummelled his head and he struggled to suck enough air into his lungs and shout for Godwin as loudly as he could. Still the mercenaries did not relent as he tried to crawl, tried to stand, tried to fight, but the Norse were at him with a fury.

A club struck the back of his head, stunning him, but he managed to keep his wits. He tried to curl into a ball and make of himself a smaller target, but there were too many to avoid. Just as he anticipated the thrust of a spear in his side, he heard someone shout before the violence relented.

Looking up he saw Magnus staring down at him. Styrkar could only breathe a sigh of relief as his brother held out his hand. He took it gratefully, allowing himself to be hauled to his feet.

'Step back,' Magnus snarled, guiding him through the hostile crowd. 'By God Almighty, Styrkar, what are you doing here?'

'I must speak to Godwin,' he replied. 'We have to stop this.'

As they moved through the camp, closely followed by the crowd of angry mercenaries, Magnus shook his head. 'Godwin will not listen to you, brother. You should never have come here. There's a horde of Norse ready to cut your head off and stick it on a pole, unless you hadn't noticed. And Godwin... he is convinced you betrayed us.'

He stopped, looking deep into Magnus' eyes. 'You have to believe me, brother, I had my reasons. But all that matters now is that we stop this madness before we are all killed.'

Magnus could only shake his head in frustration as he guided Styrkar through the camp. Up ahead, Styrkar saw Godwin approaching, alerted by the commotion. The hope he felt at seeing his brother melted away as he also saw Edmund close behind, accompanied by Oskell Blackhand.

'Red Wolf,' Godwin said. 'Why have you come here?' His expression was stern, but his voice was steady at least. No sign of rage. Not yet anyway.

'I have come to ask that you see sense, Godwin. This raid is destined to fail. Eadnoth the Staller has gathered his fyrd and awaits you over yonder. Even if you can defeat him on the field, the Franks will soon follow. This raid of yours is doomed. Take your men and leave. Go back to the court of King Diarmait before it's too late.'

Godwin's jaw worked frenetically as he tried to stay in control. 'You betrayed us, Styrkar. You would have told the Franks of our plans, had them wait for us, trap us, annihilate us. I never thought—'

'Neither did I,' Styrkar replied. 'And I have suffered for it, as the gods are my witness. But we have both done things we should not be proud of. I would never have thought you would set another man to slay me. Or that you would order the murder of a mother and her child.'

He could see from Godwin's sorrowful look that he regretted both those choices, but it was only fleeting, before he glared at Styrkar with malice in his eyes.

'It doesn't matter now. All that matters is our victory. All that matters is that I regain my father's crown from the usurper, and restore our family's legacy.'

'Then why are you here on this coast, Godwin?' Styrkar asked. 'Why are you not marching your army to the capital instead of pillaging helpless towns? And in the very lands you seek to rule? Can't you see you're only making more enemies when you should be gathering allies?'

'We… we need gold. We need resources to build an army strong enough to face the Franks. When the ealdormen and magnates of this country see how mighty I have become they will flock to my banner.'

'You would seek to buy their loyalty, Godwin? The ealdormen have already turned their backs on you. You cannot earn their fealty through pillaging these lands. The only ones to gain will be the mercenaries you have brought with you.'

'No,' Godwin growled. 'I will show them their folly. I will make them pay for kneeling to a foreign king. And Eadnoth will be the first of them to taste his regret.'

'This is a battle you cannot win, brother. Even if Eadnoth's army falls there will be more to follow in his wake. You have to turn back.'

Godwin's mouth twisted into a sneer. 'The words of a coward. I would not have expected them to come from the mouth of the Red Wolf. Do you think my father would have faced his enemies at Senlac Hill had he brooked the notion of defeat?'

'Your father died at Senlac Hill,' Styrkar bellowed, unable to hide his desperation. 'And if you do not turn back you will die on this one.'

Godwin fell silent, but Oskell Blackhand had heard enough. He stepped in front of Godwin, his eyes filled with fury. 'Enough of this shit. I demand the head of the bastard who murdered Hingar Eriksson.'

'No,' said Godwin. 'Styrkar has come as the herald of our foe. He will be treated as such. No harm will come to him.'

'But brother,' Edmund said. 'He has betrayed us. And the memory of our father. He deserves the axe.'

Godwin said nothing, but stared down Edmund, who eventually lowered his gaze. Then he looked back to Styrkar with sadness in his eyes.

'You should leave while you still can. I have heard your words, but they do not move me. Tell Eadnoth we will face him, and he will pay for his lack of loyalty to my father with his blood.'

There was nothing more to say. Magnus had already brought Styrkar's pony, and held out the reins for him. When he was mounted, Godwin walked forward and took the steed's bridle.

'Know this, Red Wolf. My brother you may have been, but you are kin no more. If I see you on the battlefield I will kill you myself.'

Styrkar could only nod his acknowledgement of the challenge before he spun the pony and rode from the mercenary camp.

As he made his way back towards Eadnoth's army, he knew there was no way he could avoid the fight now. He could not simply run, not when his brothers faced such danger, no matter how much they hated him. He owed Harold that much.

A battle was coming that he was destined to fight, but the Red Wolf had yet to decide just which side he was on.

17

Banesberie, England, June 1068

Her back ached and the empty bucket in her hand felt so heavy it might have been filled to the brim with rocks. Gisela had not anticipated how difficult it would become to perform the most menial of tasks in her condition, but perform them she would. She was desperate to prove her continuing usefulness. Once she was no longer of any benefit to Ronan, God only knew what fate would befall her.

She made her way down to the riverbank, struggling not to slip on the muddy surface. If she fell over she might never be able to rise again – stuck like a beetle on its back until someone came to turn her over. Gisela had abandoned her shoes days ago, her feet having swollen too much to fit them, and she felt the cold mud slide between her toes.

At the river's edge she dipped one foot in the water, gingerly lowering the bucket. As she did so, her eyes were drawn across the river to the opposite bank. Green fields ran toward woodland in the distance. Beyond that was the town of Waruic, stronghold of the Saxon rebels. It was there Robert of Comines' army would eventually face the earls Edwin and Morcar. Behind her was a huge camp of Frankish knights only too eager to cross the river and bring those nobles to heel. More killing was inevitable.

Would these wars never end? Would King William's reign be plagued by perpetual uprisings until the end of his days? Gisela could only hope not, and a small part of her yearned for the Saxons to be defeated utterly so that peace might prevail. At least then the needless slaughter would end, the murder and rape as the Franks stamped their authority on the defiant English.

It made her ashamed to think it, especially since the father of her unborn child had fought so long and so hard against the invaders. But if her baby was to be born into a peaceable land then perhaps it was better the rebels be curbed and the king allowed to sit on his throne unchallenged.

The bucket was full now, and Gisela struggled to pull it from the water. She hitched up her skirt as she walked barefoot back onto the bank and all but waddled toward the camp. She had not taken more than three stumbling strides before she saw Stanhilde and Wealdberg approaching along her path. The two women carried buckets of their own and were locked in conversation as always – a perpetual wall of noise Gisela always did her best to avoid.

On seeing her, the women ceased their prattle, Stanhilde adopting a grave expression.

'You shouldn't be carrying that heavy a load in your condition,' she crowed, dropping her own bucket and moving forward to take Gisela's burden from her.

'Nonsense,' Wealdberg said. 'I used to carry two buckets

that size when I was much further along with my bairns. She's with child, not bloody crippled.'

Despite Wealdberg's chastisement, Gisela was happy for Stanhilde to take her burden from her. The young woman might have a jaw you could break rocks with, but she was considerate at least. But then so was Wealdberg, despite her sharp tongue. She might also have been a handsome woman in her youth, but hard years had taken their toll on her. Both women had become friends of a sort in the days Gisela had spent in the camp, though they still treated her with some mistrust. Not that Gisela would expect anything else – these were English women born and bred, and she still bore a hint of the accent that marked her as a native of Flanders. To them, she was just another foreign invader.

When the women had filled their own buckets, the three of them made their way back along the path to the camp. Stanhilde carried Gisela's burden as well as her own, but she was happy to have someone else aid her, at least for now.

'Thank you for the help,' Gisela said as they walked the road.

'It's no bother,' Stanhilde replied, and it looked as though she was right. She carried both buckets as though they weighed nothing, but then her shoulders were broad for such a young girl.

'You look like you've done more than your share of labour. What brought you to a camp full of Frankish knights?'

That brought a smile to Stanhilde's face. 'Where else would I be in times like this? Scrabbling in the dirt on some farm? Here I have my pick of fine young knights. With luck I'll win the favour of one of them before long.'

Wealdberg seemed unmoved by the comment, but Gisela was shocked by her answer. 'Why would you want to win the favour of men such as this?'

'Why not?' Stanhilde replied. 'Perhaps one of these brave warriors will take me back home with him to Frankia. I've heard stories about that place. How they treat their women like proper ladies. There's food aplenty for everyone, and even the poor get their share of fine, sweet wine.'

Gisela was about to shatter her illusions with the truth of it, when Wealdberg barked a shrill laugh.

'You're as dumb and naïve as you look if you think that's the truth,' the older woman said. 'Best you keep your legs closed more often than you do, or the only thing you'll be getting a share of is the clap.'

Stanhilde's face twisted into a grimace. 'Piss off you old hag. You're just jealous cos no one pays you no attention.'

With that she slammed Gisela's bucket to the ground and stormed off toward the camp. Gisela struggled to stoop and pick up her load, feeling a little sorry for the girl, but it was best she was given a true picture of things lest the reality of it bite her in the throat later.

As she and Wealdberg continued on their way, Gisela found herself growing curious about this older woman. She could understand why Stanhilde was here, with her misguided dreams of foreign lands and gallant lovers, but Wealdberg looked as though she had learned good sense the hard way.

'And what about you?' Gisela asked. 'Why are you here among the enemies of your kinfolk?'

The older woman cast a wistful glance across the fields before turning back to Gisela with a stern look. 'My sons fought for Harold and never returned. My town was burned to ash. Everyone I knew was murdered or scattered. I have no place left to go.'

'So you serve the very people who brought you to ruin?' Gisela could hardly believe it. Surely Wealdberg should be doing all she could to fight the men who had brought her low.

'I do what I must. There's not much use for pride or conscience if it leads to starvation.' Wealdberg cast a glance down to Gisela's ripe belly. 'So why are you here?'

'I... I have no choice either,' she replied, reluctant to reveal her tale to a stranger. What good would it do to tell this woman of her lover's blackmail? That she was a prisoner so he might do as Ronan had ordered? That it had all been for nought?

Wealdberg nodded her agreement. 'So we are both here for the same reasons.'

Gisela felt a momentary pang of guilt for judging the woman so harshly. It was obvious she was just doing what she had to in order to survive. 'I am sorry,' she said.

'We are all sorry. But we do what we must. And you should do what you can to see that child safe. No matter what it takes.'

They had reached the edge of the camp now. Gisela offered Wealdberg a nod of thanks and the two women parted.

Wealdberg's words resonated with Gisela as she made her way back to Ronan's tent. She thought she had already done all she could to keep herself safe. Her attempt to escape had been in vain, along with her efforts to gain Ronan's favour, but she had to keep trying for the sake of her child.

When she entered Ronan's tent he didn't even acknowledge her or move from the chair to help. She placed down the bucket, seeing the troubled look on his face as he stared at empty air. There had been a change in him over the past few days, and the cocksure warrior she had first met at Hereford was gone, replaced by a man who seemed lost and vulnerable.

'I have brought the water from the river,' she announced.

Still Ronan failed to even notice her. She might as well have been a ghost.

'It looks clean enough to drink. I don't think there's a settlement upriver, so should be safe of any swill.'

Of course there were no settlements upriver. And if there were, these Franks had most likely burned them all to the ground, as was their way.

Ronan's eyes shifted to regard her with annoyance. 'Don't you ever shut up?'

Gisela felt dread rising within her. She had only wanted to endear herself to him, to find some way of consoling him, but it seemed all she did was annoy.

'I am sorry,' she replied, bowing her head before she could get as far from him as possible.

'Wait,' Ronan said as she turned to leave. 'I should be the one who's sorry. And I thank you for the water.'

His response made her stop in her tracks, and she turned to face him, seeing genuine regret in his eyes.

'It's all right. I understand, this must be difficult for you. For all of you. Any day now you could be riding into danger. That cannot be an easy thing for any man. Even a warrior such as you.'

'Best not to dwell on it too much,' Ronan replied,

gesturing to the other chair in his tent. 'Please, sit. You must be tired.'

'I'm not so bad,' she lied, only too grateful to accept his offer. Once she had sat she regarded him awkwardly, the silence only worsening her discomfort.

'Do you think you will have a son?' Ronan asked suddenly.

Gisela laid a hand to her stomach, feeling the baby kick at her touch. It brought a smile to her face, but also a sudden feeling of unease. She could only hope it would not be a son. To bring a boy into such a violent world as this, where he would be brought up to fight and die like so many others, was too painful a notion to bear.

'It is a girl. Or at least I hope. Then she will not have to be raised as a warrior in these times of strife. She will be born to give life, not take it.'

Ronan nodded as though he agreed. It was the last thing she would have expected. His face seemed to move through a range of emotions – sorrow, regret, even anger, and she wondered if he was about to fly into a rage. Eventually he sighed.

'Yes, you're right. It might be best if you had a girl.'

His eyes were drawn to the ground, and Gisela thought he might be about to weep. She struggled from her chair, moving to his side and placed a hand on his shoulder.

'Are you sure you're all right?' she asked.

Ronan slowly shook his head, and when he spoke she could hear his voice close to breaking. 'I don't think I am. I have not been myself for many days. There is a battle coming and I know… I know I will likely die. I am not sure how, but I feel it, more than I ever have before.'

'You cannot know that. It is impossible for you to foresee such things. Only God knows our fate, Ronan. Perhaps you should offer a prayer for your salvation. We can both pray together.'

He laughed at that, regarding her with a wry expression. 'That would be a pointless gesture. God abandoned me many years ago, and I Him. And you would pray with me? Did you not abandon God yourself when you lay with a heathen out of wedlock, and let him plant his seed in you?'

There was the spiteful Ronan she knew. Gisela backed away and returned to the chair, easing herself down gently.

In the following silence she saw his expression change again. He was torn, the emotions fighting within him roiled like a storm. Eventually he stood, moving to a leather saddlebag in the corner of the tent. He fished within it for a moment before finding what he was looking for and brought it to her, holding it in his fist.

'You should have this.'

He opened his hand to reveal a carved wooden wolf. Gisela recognised it as one Styrkar had crafted months before. It had stood with others on their mantle, and the sight of it almost brought her to tears.

'Thank you,' was all she could say as she took it from him.

Ronan sat in his seat once more before turning to her. 'You won't believe me, but we're not so different, you and I. Both brought up in service to powerful masters. Both far from our homelands, doing what we can to survive. Had things been a little different we might have grown up together in the same household, Flanders is not that far from Bretagne. We could have lived like siblings.'

Gisela heard every word but could not take her eyes off the tiny carved wolf. What he said was ridiculous. They could never have lived like brother and sister. He would still have been the same spiteful boy he was, and she would have done all she could to escape him.

'Anyway, you should get some rest,' he said. 'You will need all your strength in the coming days, and I might not be around to protect you forever.'

She stood, still not finding it within her to look him in the eye. With another nod of thanks she left his tent and headed back to her own meagre shelter.

Ronan might not be there to protect her forever, but as she gripped the wolf in her fist, she could only hope that soon there would be another man who would.

18

Bledone, England, June 1068

Styrkar stood in the centre of the line, those familiar old feelings battling for supremacy. Dread and apprehension, tempered by furore – an eagerness that gnawed at the flesh, burned in the blood – the tension gradually twisting into anger. His calm, even breath became more feverish in anticipation of the kill. It would begin soon, and the Red Wolf would come. Then savagery would consume him whole.

This time was different though. The men who stood at his shoulder were not experienced housecarls, they were ordinary folk – the fyrd. Farmers or landowners with enough wealth to provide their own arms and armour, gathered from surrounding estates. They would have little experience of real battle, but it was the only army Eadnoth could muster to face the mercenaries that would soon bear down on them.

Styrkar wore a shirt of poorly fitting mail, tight about the shoulders and falling apart at the seams. Some of the rings hung loose where its previous owner had been wounded. He could only hope it was not a bad omen. The axe in his hand looked keen enough and his shield was reassuringly sturdy, but there was no way to know just how useful they'd be until he put them to work.

Glancing along the line he saw faces both young and old. Some bore grim expressions, the determined features of men ready to do their duty. Others, mostly the young and inexperienced, looked fearful, like they were struggling to keep the shit in their bowels. He'd seen men scared like this before, and there was no way to tell if they'd turn tail and flee at the first sign of the enemy. But Styrkar also knew not to underestimate any man on the battlefield, even if he looked ready to weep. Oftentimes the most scared-looking youth would find his strength in battle; summoning a rage they never even knew they had, and they'd fight till the end like wolves on a bear. He could only hope this would be one of those times.

The sun had almost reached its zenith, the buzzing of flies the only noise to break the silence as he looked up the hill and saw their enemy crest the brow. Murmurs of disquiet began to spread along the line as Eadnoth's army realised what was coming. If any of them had hoped the Norse might reconsider their ambitions for conquest, it was dashed as those armoured warriors spread themselves along the entire span of the hilltop.

Styrkar squinted in the midday sun, scanning the line of helms to see if he could spy Godwin among their number. From such a distance he could barely make out any details, but still he looked, hoping against hope he could spot the prince. Perhaps there was still a way Styrkar could make him see sense. One last chance to change Godwin's mind and end this bloodshed before it began.

'Here they come,' cried Eadnoth, tramping the ground in front of his men, eyeing the army of mercenaries on top of the hill.

He struck a much more imposing figure than when Styrkar had first seen him. In his mail and gold-burnished helm he looked every inch the noble leader – no longer the frail old man Styrkar had met at his estate. His arms and armour looked worth a king's ransom, and it was easy to see why he had so readily struck a deal with the new king. Eadnoth the Staller would not have wanted to forego such riches to remain loyal to a dead master.

There were no rousing speeches, as the shout of challenge echoed from high up on the hill. Instead, Eadnoth barked for his archers to step to the fore.

For a moment, Styrkar was reminded of that day on Senlac Hill, when Harold and his army had stood resolute against the arrows of the invading Franks. They had sent volley after volley against English shields, but the Saxon army had stood firm. He could only wonder if the Norse would likewise hold their advantageous position, but they were already bellowing in fury, hammering their weapons against shields. Their eagerness for battle was about to overcome their sense of tactical advantage.

'Wait,' Eadnoth said, holding his arm aloft.

Styrkar watched the rows of archers, arrows nocked, bows braced in position. Many of those bow arms shook in fear as the cries of the Norse grew louder. Then, with a single bellow, the enemy raced down the hill to attack.

A few men surrounding Styrkar took a step back, ready

to bolt for the distant fields, and someone among their ranks ordered the fyrd to stand firm. Among the advancing Norse, Styrkar spied the shining helm of Oskell Blackhand, leading his men in the charge. A well of hate rose up within, and it was all Styrkar could do to hold himself back and not race forward to face the mercenaries alone.

The Norse covered the open ground with frightening speed, reaching the bottom of the hill at a run. No sooner had they set foot on the flat than Eadnoth bellowed, 'Loose!'

A hail of arrows turned the bright sky dark, scores of bowstrings thrumming their tune like a swarm of bees. As the arrows were put to flight, the cry went up from Oskell.

'Shields,' he bellowed.

Before the word had even left his mouth, the charging Norse halted their advance, raising shields as one, and forming a solid wooden wall. Styrkar had never seen such discipline, nor a shield wall look so impenetrable, as the arrows struck. The shields were linked three high, and he could not count how many abreast. Immediately they were peppered by arrows, quivering shafts hitting the wooden wall with little effect. Only a couple of mercenaries were not fast enough to react to Oskell's order and were pierced by half a dozen shafts before they could join their fellows. The rest hunkered behind the shield wall as Eadnoth shouted at his archers.

'Again,' he screamed, voice almost breaking in his fury.

The archers fired desperately at the immovable wall that sat only a score of yards away. More arrows struck their targets, shafts quivering uselessly in the sea of shields.

Styrkar watched as volley after volley was set to flight. Each one struck the shield wall and the surrounding earth, but not one more of Oskell's mercenaries was hit by the hail. The men around Styrkar grew more unnerved with every passing flight as Eadnoth paced along their line, his face twisted in frustration.

'We're wasting our bloody time,' the constable growled, wrenching his sword from its sheath. He turned to his men, raising his voice for all to hear. 'Let's give these bastards a taste of Sumersete steel!'

More swords rang from scabbards, and axes were gripped tighter in white-knuckled fists. Along the front of the line, men braced their spears in front of them, readying for the charge. Eadnoth turned toward the Norse shield wall, his sword thrust high in the air before he issued a feral cry from his old lungs and charged.

Styrkar heard Harding shouting his encouragement for slaughter as they advanced on the Norse. They began at a walk, covering the distance relentlessly as the mercenaries held their disciplined wall. Then Eadnoth led them in a trot as he lengthened his rangy stride. After ten yards they were running, cries of encouragement rising from among their ranks.

As he began to charge toward the enemy, Styrkar forgot about the men at his side. Only he and the Norsemen remained – all that existed was his hunger for blood and he would have it sated, or die here on this field. The Red Wolf was coming.

His teeth clenched tight as Eadnoth's men smashed into the shield wall. Shouts of fury turned to fevered grunts as they assaulted the wooden barricade. Styrkar's axe smashed into the first shield, sending splinters flying. To his right, one of the fyrd thrust his spear through a gap and a scream issued from behind the barrier, but still it stood fast. In return, the Norse thrust spears of their own, and Styrkar was almost deafened by a shriek to his left as a man went down clutching the bloody ruin of his face.

Styrkar hacked again, battering the wall of shields as though he were chopping down a tree. Each time he heard wood crack, until eventually one of the shields was split down the middle. It revealed a grim Norse face behind, that twisted in surprise as Styrkar swung again, catching the side of the mercenary's head. He fell back silently before the breach was closed.

Before he could go at it again, a spear was thrust at his face. Styrkar barely had time to raise his shield and turn the shaft aside, lest it pierce his eye. It only served to stir him to greater effort and he attacked with renewed vigour, but no matter how hard the fyrd battered the shield wall there was little they could do to bring it down.

The furious cries of Eadnoth's men began to wane as the impetus of their charge died. More and more of them were brought down by Norse spears thrust through the defensive wall, and Styrkar began to wonder how long he could avoid the weapon that would soon impale his own rotten mail.

Just as he thought the fyrd might give up their attack and begin to rout, a roar erupted to the east. From a copse of trees, Styrkar saw more fyrd rushing to attack the Norse flank. Eadnoth had hidden reinforcements, waiting for the right time to strike, and a wave of relief rushed over his men as they saw their allies racing to join the fray.

Oskell's gruff voice bellowed from behind the shields as the mercenaries saw what was coming. Desperately they tried to adjust their defensive line before the reinforcements smashed into their flank, but they would never be quick enough.

The dull clash of steel striking shields echoed down the line of fighting men as the mercenaries were caught adjusting their formation. In front of Styrkar the shields buckled, as the mercenaries were caught unawares, unsure of whether to defend their frontline or face this new threat.

In the confusion, Styrkar fought with renewed fury, driving his shield forward and pushing the mercenaries back. The fyrd to either side of him, emboldened by his effort, followed suit, and Styrkar managed to smash his way through the breach.

A Norseman staggered backward to his left, and Styrkar brought his axe down, smashing it into the warrior's face. As he fell screaming, Styrkar bellowed in discordant harmony, hacking at anything that moved, taking another mercenary in the shoulder and driving him to his knees.

There was a momentary lull in the violence as Styrkar scanned the Norse line for his next enemy. The mercenaries had crumbled under the surprise attack, some of them already backing away, ready to flee. In their midst, shouting at his men to hold fast, stood the imposing figure of Oskell Blackhand.

Styrkar raced forward, eager to face the bastard who had come to pillage the lands of Harold Godwinson. Before he could reach him, their eyes locked and Styrkar saw the mercenary's face twist in fury.

'Come to me, Red Wolf,' Oskell snarled. 'I'll show you what fate awaits traitors.'

Styrkar stalked closer, tightening his grip on the axe.

'Fight or run, Blackhand. But spare me any more of your piss-stinking words.'

Oskell screamed from the bottom of his lungs, raising his sword high and racing forward to reap his vengeance. Styrkar braced his shield the instant before Oskell's sword fell, feeling the resounding blow hammer against the wood. In return his axe struck out, smashing against Oskell's shield, and the two traded more blows as anarchy reigned all about them.

The mercenary struck again, Styrkar batting the sword away with his axe before countering, and kicking Oskell's shield aside. The mercenary was left exposed as Styrkar hacked down, axe striking the Norseman's shield arm, cracking it just above the wrist.

Oskell staggered back as his arm hung limp, the bone of his forearm snapped in two. He let out a feral cry of pain and anger, opening his mouth to spew more vile curses. Styrkar had heard enough. Another swing of his axe and Oskell was sliced across the jaw. All he spewed was blood as he fell back to the dirt.

Shouts of panic issued from the ranks of the Norsemen as they saw their leader slain. Many began to retreat in orderly groups, others turned tail and fled for their lives back up the steep hill. Eadnoth's men cried their victory but they were not done yet, harrying the mercenaries every step of the way. With a last glance at the corpse of Oskell Blackhand, Styrkar set off in pursuit.

His heavy stride churned the earth as he made his way up the hill. Blood pumped in his ears, the lust for slaughter only growing as he searched for the nearest Norseman to whet his axe on. When he reached the top of the hill, all thought of killing fled in an instant.

There, alone among a group of Eadnoth's fyrd, stood young Magnus. He fought with a fury, holding Eadnoth's wolves at bay, but Styrkar could see he was already wounded, his helm lost, his shield little more than kindling in his fist.

Without thinking, Styrkar rushed forward. One of Eadnoth's men jabbed with a spear, catching Magnus in the side and he cried out, spitting his hate as he hacked the shaft in two with his sword. Another raised his blade, ready to hack down this stubborn warrior.

Styrkar was upon them before they could deal the killing blow. His axe moved of its own accord, powered by desperation as he smashed the spear-wielding fyrd in the back of the head. His next swipe caught the swordsman about the shoulder and he fell back with a wail. Seeing the fearsome Red Wolf come at them, the other men backed away, too afraid to fight on.

As Magnus dropped to one knee, Styrkar rushed to his side, grasping him before he could fall.

'Brother,' Magnus gasped, the sword falling from his fingers. 'I never thought to see you here.'

Styrkar lowered Magnus to the ground as his lifeblood ebbed from the wound in his side. 'You think I would have missed this?' he replied, trying to smile through his sudden grief.

Magnus smiled back. 'You should not have come. But it... it pleases me that you are here.'

'It pleases me too, brother,' Styrkar said, but Magnus

could not hear him. The son of Harold Godwinson stared blindly at the bright midday sky. He would see nothing more.

Styrkar closed his brother's eyes, realising the battlefield had all but gone silent. When he looked up, he saw he was surrounded by fyrd, men he had fought beside, men he had now betrayed. On the ground nearby lay the two men he had slain to defend Magnus.

'I knew we should never have trusted you, Dane,' a voice said. Harding pushed his way through the crowd of fyrd, a look of murderous intent on his face. 'Take him.'

Some of the warriors glanced at one another with uncertainty, fearing the wrath of the Red Wolf, but with the death of Magnus all his fury had fled. Styrkar rose to his feet, dropping shield and axe to the ground. His battle was over. He had done all he could to halt this bloodshed, and failed. Now his brother was gone. What use in fighting on.

As the fyrd surrounded him, and took him by his arms, Styrkar did nothing to stop them.

19

Ronan's horse snorted and whickered, almost as unnerved as he was. Damn it was hot. He was drenched within his layers, jerkin sticking to him like tar, mail byrnie heavy and cloying. Flies buzzed around them in clouds, noisily pestering man and beast as Robert's army sat impatiently outside the town.

'What are they bloody doing in there?' Mainard hissed.

Ronan didn't answer, but frankly he had no idea. The last thing they seemed to be doing was preparing for a siege. There were no archers mounted on the palisade, no arses farting their defiance as there had been at Exonia. The town of Waruic appeared all but abandoned.

The rest of the men looked ready for the assault. Eager to the point of zealotry, doing all they could to restrain their mounts as they waited for Robert to give the order to advance. Ronan glanced along the line, seeing their leader sitting atop his dark steed, no helmet, bald head shining in the bright sunlight. He stared at the walls of Waruic as though he might surmount those walls with the power of his hate. As it was, they had ladders for that. Ranks of men-at-arms waited patiently with shields, ready to mount the palisade and open the gates. Once inside they would raze the town and end this rebellion before it had begun.

'I think they've had long enough to surrender,' Robert cried from down the line. 'What say we deliver a message from our king?'

Shouts of approval went up from the gathered knights, but Ronan wasn't inclined to join in. The dread he had felt for days had all but consumed him, and it was impossible to quell his sense of panic. His horse felt it too, and struggled against the rein, but Ronan held on fast. He could not show his doubt or cowardice, not in front of these men.

Perhaps he should have fled days ago. Abandoned this folly and gone back to Cornualge. What was the worst that could happen? Brian would castigate him for his defiance and exile him back to Bretagne? Would that have been a worse fate than this?

Too late now.

Robert's arm was raised. The shield bearers braced themselves for the attack, but still there were no archers at the town's palisade to repel them. Men lifted their ladders, ready to cross the killing field. Horses grew skittish in anticipation of battle, and Ronan took in a deep breath as he prepared himself for the coming violence.

'Ready,' Robert shouted, his voice peeling out across the open ground, his arm still held high.

The gate to Waruic opened with a squeak of hinges and creak of old timbers.

In the distance, Ronan could see a single figure make

his way through the opening and approach along the road. Both his arms were held in the air, and in one hand he carried some kind of pennant.

'Who is that?' Mainard asked.

'I have no idea,' Ronan replied. 'But he hasn't come to fight.'

The man had no arms or armour and wore no helm. As he drew closer, Ronan could see his beard was unkempt and his hair thinning and grey.

'Is that a bed sheet he's carrying?' Mainard said.

Despite its tattered appearance, Ronan saw the man carried a flag. A yellow cross on a blue field. The symbol of ancient Mercian kings. Edwin's flag. For a moment, Ronan allowed himself to hope this whole thing might be over before it began.

When the man was within twenty yards, Robert urged his horse forward to greet him. Ronan could see a fearful look about those old features, but the herald managed to stand tall before the mounted knight.

'My lord,' he said, bowing his head and offering up the flag. 'I am the town steward, and I have been sent to announce that Waruic offers its surrender.'

Robert looked disappointed at the news, and there was a disgruntled murmur among some of the mounted men. Ronan felt his heart soar, but he did his best to quell his joy. He had not been reprieved yet.

'What about the brothers, Edwin and Morcar,' Robert asked. 'Do those English bastards surrender too? Or do I have to root them out?'

'Yes, my lord, they are the ones who sent me. They have opened the gates of Waruic in return for clemency. Edwin himself sent me to offer you the saltire of Mercia as a gesture of good faith.'

The old man held out the tattered flag once more, but Robert ignored it, swinging his horse about to face his men. As his brow furrowed in thought, one of his knights nudged his horse from the line.

'My lord Robert, this could be a ruse. This man could be luring us into a trap. Lowering our guard for an ambush once we enter the city.'

Ronan hadn't even considered the notion, and neither had Robert by the looks of him.

'You're right,' he replied, glaring down at the steward, still gripping his flag protectively. 'We can't take any chances.'

Just as Ronan thought he might cut the old man down where he stood, Robert looked up and smiled.

'Ronan of Dol-Combourg. You told me not three days ago that I would soon see your worth. Well, I would see it now. Ride into the town. Ensure the populace is suitably repentant and that we face no opposition. On your signal that all is clear, I will follow with the rest of my men.'

Shit. This was it. This was where Ronan would take his final breath hoisted on a rebel's spear. He would have argued that he was not the right man for the job, but Robert spoke the truth – he had laid claim to being a worthy knight. Now he was being called upon to prove it, curse his flapping tongue.

Ronan's mouth suddenly dried up, and he found it impossible to acknowledge Robert with words. Instead he simply offered a nod, waving his arm for his conrois to follow. Mainard was right behind him as he kicked his horse forward, another half-dozen knights in his wake.

Ahead of them, at the end of the road, the gates to Waruic still lay open.

A handful of men rode forward to take on a whole settlement, and none of them with any idea what they might face. Ronan began to regret his lack of piety. If ever there had been a time when prayers might do him some good then it was now. Gisela had been right – only God knew his fate, but in his heart Ronan was certain this would be his end.

They moved along the road to the gate all too quickly as Ronan's eyes scanned the high parapet for any sign of archers. The way was clear through the entrance, not a single spearman in sight. Surely this had to be a trap? Those Saxon earls would not abase themselves before the might of King William so easily. There had to be some trick to this. He was riding right into the maw of a lion.

But this was his fate. Ronan could do nothing to avert it, and as he rode across the town threshold he gripped his rein and his lance with all the resolve he could muster.

The town was deserted. Every door closed and window shuttered. Not so much as a stray dog barred their path as Ronan led his knights deeper into the settlement. Rising up in the midst of the houses he could see the tower of a church in the distance, and all he could do was follow the main road as it cut through Waruic toward that one edifice. They did not encounter a single soul until Ronan led his men out onto a main market square in front of the church. There, he saw a group waiting to greet him, black robes adorning their thin bodies, hair shorn close to scalps.

God save him from bloody priests. After what Robert had done to every village and hamlet on the way to Waruic, it made sense that they were the only ones brave enough to face the might of King William's army. Did they think themselves immune from harm? Armoured in their faith? Ronan knew only too well that a priest could die as easily as any man. Oftentimes easier.

At his approach, the priests dropped to their knees. Some clenched their hands in prayer, lips moving in silent preachments for salvation. When Ronan's horse drew to within a few yards, the one at their head opened his arms and forced as genuine a smile as he could muster.

'My lords,' he said, voice surprisingly strong for a man in such a vulnerable position. 'Please accept the blessings of our church. We have waited on you with much anticipation. The people of Waruic rejoice at your arrival.'

Ronan glanced around the empty square. 'They have a strange way of showing it, priest.'

The old man struggled to his feet while the rest of his group continued to pray. 'They are fearful of your wrath, my lord. But I assure you their loyalty to the king is without question.'

'If it was without question we wouldn't be here.'

That seemed to fluster the old man somewhat. 'I... er... am sure we can resolve this misunderstanding in a peaceful manner.'

Ronan had heard enough of the priest's bluster. 'Where are Edwin and Morcar?'

'They are here, my lord. But it was thought best if I speak on their behalf before they present themselves.'

So they *were* going to surrender. Ronan felt a strange wave of relief wash over him. Was this truly over? Had he been spared the dire fate he was so sure lay in wait for him?

'Well, you've spoken. I suggest you go and bring them to me. I would hear this offer of submission from their own mouths.'

As the priest and his followers rushed back inside the church, Ronan heard the clap of hooves on the road behind him. Turning, he saw Robert at the head of a column of knights. He trotted across the abandoned marketplace before reining his mount in beside Ronan's.

'I grew tired of the wait,' he said, not bothering to hide his displeasure. 'And heard no sounds of violence once you entered. Today is turning out to be a particular disappointment.'

'I think you'll be pleased with what I've found,' Ronan replied, as the doors to the church opened up.

This time two men appeared, well-dressed in cloaks of scarlet secured with gold clasps. Both held themselves as proudly as they could, but it was obvious they were wary of what awaited them. The first man was tall and fair with a strong jawline and broad shoulders. The second was shorter, stockier and somewhat surlier than the first. Everything Ronan had learned on the battlefield told him the shorter man was the one he should be wary of.

'I am Earl Edwin of Mercia,' said the taller of the two. 'And this is my brother Morcar. We know why you are here, and wanted to offer our assurances—'

'Where is your army, Edwin?' Robert interrupted. 'Your loyal housecarls? Have they abandoned you to your fate?'

'There is no army,' Edwin replied, and that much was obvious, unless they were crammed inside every hut and hovel in Waruic.

'Of course not. Most likely ran away at the first sign of

the king's might. You are lucky William is a merciful ruler. If it was up to me I'd raze this place to the ground and hang your heads from the burning timbers.'

Edwin took another step closer, lowering his voice. 'I know news of rebellion reached the king's ears, but I can assure you—'

'You *can* assure me,' said Robert. 'You can both assure me by kneeling, right here, right now, and pledging your allegiance to the rightful king of England.'

That brought a wry smile to Edwin's face. Morcar seemed much less amused by the prospect.

'Very well,' Edwin said, dropping to one knee.

Morcar stood defiantly in the silence for as long as his nerve would allow, before he too lowered himself down beside his brother. Together they pledged their fealty, though Ronan knew it was only words. These treacherous English dogs would switch their loyalties with the changing of the wind if it served them to do so.

'Take them,' Robert ordered, once the Saxon nobles had finished. 'They have a long journey to the capital ahead of them. Make sure they're treated just as they deserve.'

Robert's men came forward and bundled the two brothers away. Ronan watched them go, unable to stop himself from smiling at his good fortune. On seeing Robert's glum expression, the smile fell from his mouth.

'Are you not pleased?' he asked. 'We've managed to take the town without losing a single man.'

Robert shrugged. 'I have to admit, I would have preferred them to put up at least the notion of a fight. But I guess there is one consolation.'

'What's that?'

'I was right, Ronan. You questioned my methods in burning every town between here and the capital, but I was right. Now the merest whisper that I am coming will see cities fall to their knees and beg for mercy. That's how we take this country. And that's how we keep it.'

Ronan was forced to concede, Robert had a point.

'I should never have doubted you,' he replied. The words tasted bitter on his tongue.

Robert laughed. 'No, you should have kept faith. But no matter. Your work here is done, cripple. Now you can run back to Earl Brian and tell him how well you've served the king. I'm sure he will shower you with riches for your service.'

Ronan hadn't even considered what he might do once this business was over with. Now it seemed he was free to pursue his own ends once again, though being showered with riches was most certainly an enticing prospect.

'Thank you, my lord. It has been... an education.'

Robert waved him off with indifference, and Ronan turned to Mainard. 'Get back to the camp and inform the rest of the men we leave at dawn.'

As Mainard and the rest of the conrois rode along the path from the city, Ronan swung his leg over the saddle and dismounted. He winced at the sudden jolt of pain in his crippled leg, but instantly dismissed it. Perhaps it would do him good to walk awhile. Take in some air, now this whole sorry affair was behind him.

Leading his horse along the deserted street, he began to think that Robert was indeed right. Perhaps now, this time of rebellion was truly over. The fearsome reputation of King William's forces would only be elevated by the easy fall of Waruic. Surely his reign would continue uncontested?

A smirk crossed Ronan's face as he thought back to his recent malady. How stupid of him to believe in omens. In portents that might never come true. Only an idiot would heed such things as ill luck.

'For King Harold!'

The cry cut the quiet air like a clarion call.

At first Ronan had no idea where it had come from, but as he turned the realisation dawned on him too late – it was right behind him.

He barely had time to register the furious face of the madman, or the glint of the steel in his hand. Hardly felt the pointed tip of the blade puncture his byrnie and the hauberk beneath. Ronan didn't even feel the pain as that dagger slipped between his ribs up to the hilt.

All strength fled his limbs before he had a chance to reach for the sword at his side. There was no time to defend himself before he collapsed to the muddy street, hand gripping the hilt of the knife still stuck in his side.

There was time to consider, as he lay on his back, the bright sun bathing his face, that he was wrong. He truly did have the shittiest luck.

20

Tantone, England, July 1068

He sat in a cage of oak. Thick branches had been whittled to solid stems, intertwined to create a pen as strong as iron. A carpenter had taken pride in this work, crafting it to a fine finish. Styrkar thought it might have been made to cage a hunting hound or a captured wolf, but the longer he sat within the cramped confines, the more he knew it had been made for a man. There was little room to stand or even lay down, and no way he could escape. This was his prison. A gaol for the Red Wolf.

His stomach growled, but hunger had become a close companion in recent days. As the daylight began to fade he wondered if he would be given food before night came. Water or ale would have been a decent enough substitute, but Styrkar had come to accept he was in no position to hope for mercy, not from captors such as these. To them, the Red Wolf was no one special. He was but one prisoner among many.

Through the wooden bars he could see others in the

shadow of a barn a few yards away. They were bound together at the neck, perhaps a score chained in a sullen row. The once proud Norse now looked pathetic as they hunkered together, some still wounded, their injuries festering, others moaning their sorrows to deaf ears, begging to be put out of their misery.

Styrkar had no pity. Even compared with his own sorry condition, they were a wretched bunch. What hypocrites these mercenaries were. Men who had come to slaughter, following a proud creed, now on their knees pleading for clemency. The best they could hope for was to die with sword in hand but now, captured and brought low, they begged like lepers to be sent to their end. Styrkar had seen it before – how the Norse thought themselves invincible warriors, courageous and fierce, but when they were defeated they still cried for death like any other men.

For himself, Styrkar did not yearn for such release. This was his punishment and he would endure it. Accept whatever was coming.

Two men approached, carrying buckets of slop between them. It stirred some excitement among the Norse prisoners as they anticipated the meagre fare. For his part, Styrkar reclined in his cage. No amount of begging would see him fed, and he would not have asked even if it had.

The two men poured their slop on the bare earth in front of the prisoners who crawled forward, snuffling at the ground like pigs at a trough. Some fought for the juiciest morsels, tearing bones from the hands of their fellows.

Styrkar could only watch, wondering if he too would have fought for morsels. Fought to survive. Deep inside he knew he no longer had the will. He was too stricken with grief and loss to care anymore. Magnus had died in his arms. His brother in all but blood, breathing his last at the end of a battle. A battle that could have been avoided if only Styrkar had tried harder. If only he had persuaded Godwin of the folly in all this then Magnus would still be alive. His only solace was that Godwin may well have survived. Hopefully he had fled with his men to their ships and made the crossing back to Éire. With luck he would realise the crown of England could never be his, and decide not to return.

Though he had received no word of Godwin, other news had reached his cage. The loose lips of their guards had revealed that Eadnoth the Staller had died in the battle. It was the noble end the constable of Tantone would have wanted, and Styrkar could only imagine the feasting done in his name. But with the death of Eadnoth, Styrkar's fate hung in the balance. Now who would he explain himself to? Who would judge this traitor's fate now the local lord was dead? Would it be a swift execution? Would he be paraded as the betrayer he was before a slow demise? Was he to rot in a cage or be gifted to the Franks?

And what would happen to Gisela if he was to meet the axe? Styrkar could only hope she would be spared. That his part in turning back Godwin's raid had earned her a reprieve. Surely word had reached Ronan that the sons of King Harold had been defeated. That Styrkar had kept his side of the bargain. Even that Frankish bastard must have honour enough to see he had done his part and Gisela should be allowed her freedom.

He tried to put thoughts of Gisela from his mind. It would not do to dwell on such things, not now he had so many problems of his own. His stomach rumbled again as he watched the Norsemen eat. They consumed their scraps ravenously. It was a grim slop they ate with such appetite, and Styrkar could only envy them the feast.

Something banged against the cage, making Styrkar flinch. As he recoiled from the noise, clinging to the side of the cage, he heard men laughing.

'The fucking caged wolf,' someone spat.

Styrkar glared through the bars, seeing a man ogling at him. How he would have loved to wipe that leering grin from his face, but from inside his prison there was nothing he could do. Any defiance would only have been met with contempt, but when he saw a wolf-head torc about the man's neck it only made his anger grow deeper.

'Do you like my new trinket?' the man said, fingers teasing the iron torc. A precious gift Styrkar had now lost, along with so much else. 'It is a fine bauble. I thank you for it.'

Styrkar gripped the bars of his cage, desperate to quell his ire. He would have called the man a thief, demanded he give back what he had not earned, but he knew what the answer would be. Such begging would only make Styrkar look more the fool.

'Fucking traitor,' said another voice. 'We should just kill him and have done with it.'

More men approached, surrounding the cage, glaring at him with hate. Styrkar could understand their loathing, he had betrayed them after all. But then he had betrayed so many others along with them. If they wanted their vengeance they would just have to fall in line.

'Bring me a spear,' someone said. 'We'll put this bastard out of his misery.'

There were grumbles of assent from the others. Helpless in his cage there was nothing Styrkar could do to stop them. He would be stuck like a pig. An ignominious end, but perhaps the one that he deserved.

'Enough.' Another voice. Those men moved aside as Harding pushed his way through the press and approached the cage. 'None of you have the right to execute this dog. I am the one in command now.' When no one moved Harding shoved one of them, almost knocking him to the ground. 'Fuck off and do as you're told,' he growled. 'There is work to be done.'

Their sport finished with, the rest of the men slunk off into the dark to go about their business, leaving Styrkar and Harding alone.

The son of the Staller regarded Styrkar through the wooden bars. There was no hatred in his eyes, but no pity either. He looked curious, as though Styrkar were some exotic bird in its cage.

'I have heard many stories of you,' Harding said eventually. 'I heard you're a man to be admired. Loyal as a hunting hound, they say. My father would talk fondly of Harold back in the day, and fearfully of the Red Wolf. The scourge of the Welsh, and now bane of the Norse. And yet you betrayed him in the end.'

'I owed Eadnoth nothing,' Styrkar replied. 'He fought for the Franks. For the Bastard King. You are all traitors to Harold.'

'Harold is dead, Red Wolf. And yet here we stand.' Harding's expression turned to one of disdain. 'And there you sit. The great housecarl cowering in his cage. Survivor of Senlac. A man who stood alone against a conqueror, now nothing more than a tethered beast. How did it come to this?'

Styrkar thought on those words. Thought on what he had been, and what he had become. There was no use in trying to explain. He barely understood himself.

'It is of no matter,' Styrkar replied.

Harding nodded knowingly at his answer, but there was no way he could understand.

'We have buried my father,' Harding continued. 'He died with honour and was laid to his rest in a manner befitting. I now hold sway here.' He glanced over towards the Norsemen who had finished their meagre feast, and a grim smile rose on one side of his face. 'I might ransom some of those men back to the King of Éire. Others I may sell as slaves, if it suits me.'

He looked back at Styrkar. The implication was obvious. Styrkar was at this man's mercy and he could be bought and sold at Harding's whim. The prospect of a life in chains was not one he relished. He had fought all his life to free himself from such shackles, but if that was his fate then he would accept it.

'You're probably wondering what I have in store for you?' Harding said. 'What will happen to the great Red Wolf? Should I just give you back to the Franks? They would pay me handsomely for such a renowned outlaw. Maybe I should just execute you myself? Take up my father's axe and strike the head from your shoulders in celebration of his sacrifice. A pagan rite, in honour of the ancient ways of Sumersete. The old man would have liked that.'

As Styrkar thought on it, he considered that perhaps the

axe might make a much better fate than to be sold into slavery once again. But Harding shook his head.

'No. I have much better plans for you, my friend. There are greater things than chains in store for the Red Wolf.'

With that, he left Styrkar to his cage. All he could do now was think on those final words. A starving animal cowering in the dark, with nothing left but to ponder its final days.

21

Waruic, England, July 1068

He lay on a straw mattress, dying and forgotten. Gisela sat watching as Ronan mumbled feverishly. How he had survived this long, she had no idea. The wound in his side had become infected, disease spreading through his body, and he should have perished days ago. But here he was, this crippled knight, clinging to life.

Wealdberg leaned forward to mop his brow, for all the good it would do him. Stanhilde stood back, framed in the light of a flickering candle, biting her nails.

'How long do you think he has left?' the girl asked.

Gisela shook her head. 'Not long if the fever does not lift.'

Wealdberg took a step away from him, then shook her head again. 'I don't know how he's lived this long. Maybe it would be best if someone put him out of his misery.'

How many times had Gisela wished for Ronan's death? How many times had she thought about praying for it, though surely asking God to kill a man would have been the greatest of sins. Besides, she had to keep him alive, if not for her sake, then for the child inside her. Their lives depended on Ronan and he had to live, at least until Styrkar came back for her.

But would her lover ever be coming back? Was he even still alive?

Before she could worry further whether he would ever return to her, the flap of the tent was wrenched back. Lord Robert strolled into the dark confines, ignoring the women as he approached Ronan on his deathbed. Stanhilde and Wealdberg bowed their heads, moving from his path, but Gisela stood taller showing she was not afraid of this brute.

In Robert's wake came the smaller figure of Mainard. Was he Ronan's squire? Or a fully ordained knight? Gisela had never worked it out, but he was most certainly loyal to the man now stricken with fever. It seemed he was Ronan's only friend in the world.

Robert regarded Ronan for some moments with hands on his hips. He appeared little concerned with the knight's plight, as though this were a sick animal rather than a loyal follower.

'Any change?' Robert asked still staring at Ronan's clammy body.

Neither of the women wanted to answer, and kept their eyes on the ground.

'No, my lord,' Gisela replied. 'There has been no change. He requires the attention of a healer. If we were to call for a—'

Robert dismissed her comment with a wave of his hand, appearing more disappointed than concerned.

'If there is nothing to be done then why are so many of

you at his bedside?' He glared at the women. 'You two, I'm sure there are other things to be done in the camp.'

Stanhilde and Wealdberg went scurrying out of the tent as quickly as they could. Gisela should have followed them, but she'd be damned if she would jump at the word of such a wretch.

Robert turned his head, looking her up and down, displaying little emotion. At first Gisela thought he might speak, might send her off after the other two women to make herself useful. Instead he glanced down at her ripe belly, and without another word turned to leave the tent.

'Is that it?' Gisela asked before he could go.

Robert stopped. She could see him clench his fists before he turned that brutal gaze on her. 'And what do you suggest I do?'

'Ronan is one of your men. He was wounded in your service. You should at least see that he is cared for—'

'He was wounded in service to the king. Not me. And his fate is in God's hands now. If you want any more help, then I suggest you pray for it, handmaid.'

With that he turned and left the tent. Gisela could only grit her teeth and hold back her anger. An anger she would happily have spit in Robert's wake, but there was no way she would challenge him. Not now her only protector lay dying.

Mainard took a step closer, looking at Ronan with concern, and shifting his weight uncomfortably from one foot to the other. He looked like he was scared to touch his friend. As though he too might be afflicted with the fever that was wracking Ronan's body.

'What should we do?' he asked.

What *should* they do? Ronan continued writhing in his bed. He was in the grip of infection, and if it did not pass it would kill him as surely as any knife.

'We must keep him cool to help him fight the fever,' she answered. 'Bring me water and rags.'

'Should we not bleed him?' Mainard asked. 'Or use leeches? I've heard that helps with—'

'Just get me the water,' Gisela snapped, half expecting him to chastise her for her sharp tongue. Instead Mainard nodded before he too left the tent.

She was alone at last, with the object of her hatred helpless and at her mercy. But now he seemed so pathetic, so small. This man who had threatened her with death, threatened her unborn child, was now nothing but a corpse-in-waiting.

She could easily have picked up a knife and cut his throat. Watched him bleed out onto the bed, like a pig for the butcher's block. Gisela's eyes flitted across the tent looking for a weapon before she even realised that could never happen. She was no murderess.

So what was she? A slave? A thrall at the behest of the brutes surrounding her? Gisela's hand drifted to her swollen belly. As she touched it she felt the baby kick. No, she was not a slave. She was free to go wherever the road took her, and soon she would be a—

'Mother?'

The word cut through the silence of the tent. Ronan tried to sit up in the bed, clawing at the sodden sheet that covered him. His eyes were open, glaring wretchedly, before they closed again and he began to mumble in his fever dream. Gisela took a step closer, feeling guilt and pity begin to overwhelm her in equal measure.

'Ronan?' she said, wondering if he was on the brink of consciousness. Wondering if she might finally be able to speak with him.

'Mother,' he called again, this time holding out his hand.

It was a gesture of desperation, as though he were lost in the dark and needed someone, anyone, to guide him back to safety. Could she just abandon him to such a fate?

Gisela moved to his bedside, taking his clammy hand in hers. It seemed to calm him for a moment and his feverish ranting died down. She raised a hand, feeling the perspiration on his forehead. Her touch calmed him yet further and Ronan quieted, succumbing to a deep slumber.

Despite his even breathing he still held tight to her hand. There she sat for some time watching this man teeter on the edge of death. Her one protector. The only one who could keep her and her child safe in this wicked country. But could he keep her safe? No, only Styrkar could do that, but he was not here. There truly was no one left to protect her now.

As Ronan slept she began to wonder what was keeping Mainard. Gently she let go of his hand, before standing and slipping out of the tent. In the light of day she could see the encampment was busy, knights and camp followers going about their daily business like any other. To the north stood the city of Waruic, quiet and unmolested. Lord Robert had decided to spare its people and not burn it to the ground after they had shown such rebellious spirit; a rare show of mercy on his part.

As Gisela made her way through the camp she was

ignored, but for the odd glance from now-familiar faces. The further she walked the more she realised she wasn't a slave. She was as free as anyone else here. If she wanted, she could carry on walking right out of the camp boundary, but then where would she go? Who would take in a lone woman and her unborn infant?

As she thought on what to do, Gisela felt something in her hand. She had absently placed it inside her kirtle, and closed her fingers around the carving of the wolf Ronan had given her. She took it out and looked at the tiny figurine, her only reminder of the lover who had left her.

But he had not left her. He had been sent away on a mission to betray his brothers so that she might live. And what would he think of her now? Would Styrkar have wanted her to run? Would he have wanted her to take their unborn child as far from this place and these tyrants as she could? Or would he have wanted her to remain here, in relative safety?

Before she could consider that further, a song began to rise from within the boundary of the city. She could not make out what was being sung, but the Frankish knights in the camp began to stir, wondering what was happening.

To the north she could see others in the encampment talking to each other in agitated tones. Their delight soon became obvious and it wasn't long before they struck up songs of their own. Songs of victory.

Before Gisela could enquire as to what was happening, she saw Stanhilde running across the camp in her bare feet. She almost stumbled as she approached, before stopping in front of Gisela, heaving breath into her lungs.

'Have you heard?' the girl asked. 'Have you heard the news?'

Gisela shook her head. 'Heard what? What is happening?'

'There has been battle done at Bledone,' the girl replied. 'The sons of King Harold have been driven back across the sea.'

'By the king?' Gisela asked.

Stanhilde shook her head still trying to get her breath back. 'No, it was an army of Sumersete. The brothers came with a mighty Norse host, but they were stopped in their tracks and routed.'

The dread implications began to well up in Gisela's gut. Was Styrkar with them? Had he betrayed Ronan and joined the sons of Harold in their raid? The notion that he may have condemned her, and their child, by his actions began to grow. Not that Ronan could exact any kind of reprisal from his sickbed.

There was no point asking the girl any news of Styrkar or whether he had been killed or captured. He would have been one more raider in a field of thousands. But if he was not involved in the battle then surely he would have come for her by now. Would have raced across the fields of England to free her from bondage. Only death would stop him.

Gisela gritted her teeth at the sudden rush of grief. Surely he had perished along with the rest. It was the only reason he would not be here.

As Stanhilde ran off to spread news of the victory, Gisela looked down once more at the carving of the wolf. All that she had left of Styrkar.

But not all.

She placed her other hand to her belly, feeling the child she would soon birth stir within her.

Turning her head back toward Ronan's tent, she knew now there was only one person who could protect them now. But only if she could first save his life.

22

There wasn't a cloud in the sky, though the air had grown unseasonably crisp. From his cage, Styrkar watched the comings and goings, seeing the Norse being fed, waiting for his own morsels to be flung through the bars. It was a day like any other, but a sense of tension was rising. A palpable disquiet Styrkar couldn't quite understand. Until it began.

Harding's housecarls came for some of the Norse when the sun reached its zenith, unshackling them from their fellows and leading them off through the town. Some time passed as distant shouts echoed across the roofs of Tantone, the sense of dread rising when none of those Norse were returned to their shackles. Then it was Styrkar's turn.

Six men surrounded his cage, unbolting the door and urging him out at spearpoint. His neck was tethered, the rope pulled tight at his throat. It was a familiar feeling, one he should have raged against, but weak as he was he offered little resistance. Two men held the tether on either side as he was led away from the compound and through the winding pathways of the settlement. Few people were on the road as he was driven past like a beast. Styrkar spied one woman pull her infant behind her skirts rather than let him witness the captured animal in their midst, but there were few others to watch his humiliation.

A raucous noise caught his attention from beyond the town's boundary. It might have filled any other man with terror as it rose above the rooftops before dying out like a doused fire, but for Styrkar it held no fear. Whatever fate lay in wait he would face it, no matter how weak he felt.

The road led to a clearing just beyond the town. A crowd had gathered, all warriors, baying and jeering into a pit dug deep and wide. Styrkar was held back some yards away to watch the spectacle. None of his captors spoke, but he knew what this was – his fate was to be sealed in butchery.

To one side of the pit he could see Harding surrounded by his housecarls. Though the rest of the crowd were frenzied by what they witnessed, Harding stood expressionless, unmoved by the grim show.

Though he could not see into that pit, Styrkar knew what this was. A battle to the death for the entertainment of others. Coins were being exchanged, even hides and chickens, as these men who thought themselves warriors watched their prisoners die for sport. But men had died for less. Styrkar had killed them for less. Perhaps this might be the most fitting end for him after all.

A sudden cheer erupted from the crowd. More coins passed hands as some men looked inconsolable at their loss, others elated at their win. A corpse was dragged from the pit, perhaps a once proud warrior, now nothing but meat. After him came crawling another of the Norsemen, his hair hanging limp, his body riven with cuts and filth. Styrkar caught a look of desperation on his face. He had won his battle, been spared the journey to Valhöll, but for how long?

As the Norseman was led away, Styrkar was prodded in the back by the butt of a spear and urged forward to take his turn. The fates of other men left his thoughts, and the crowd turned to see what was next, their loathing immediate and obvious. Faces that had moments before been filled with elation twisted to hatred, and some spat on the ground in front of him. It seemed as though every man here wanted him to share the fate of the corpse they had dragged from that pit. For the Red Wolf to become one more butchered animal on the pile. Grumblings of discontent worked their way through the gathering, and Styrkar wondered if he would even have the chance to fight for his life before someone drew a blade and struck him down.

Harding stepped forward, and the noisome crowd fell silent. His men tugged on the tether and drew Styrkar short, as their fledgling lord regarded his prize.

'This is an auspicious day,' Harding said, loud enough for all to hear. 'Standing before us is the fearsome Red Wolf.' That brought mirth from some of the crowd and Styrkar was made keenly aware he looked anything but fearsome. 'The man who survived Senlac Hill. Who fought the Franks at Hereford. Look at him – see how far he has fallen. He betrayed my father, Eadnoth, who you all knew. Betrayed our new king, who's favour we now hold dear. But perhaps even a traitor has a chance at redemption.'

With a gesture, Harding had his men take the rope from Styrkar's neck. At spearpoint he was then urged forward to the lip of the pit. He had a chance to glance into its dark confines before a kick to the back propelled him forward.

Styrkar fell into the hole, landing heavily in the muck. It stank of filth and blood, a familiar stench only a veteran of the battlefield would recognise. As he stood to the growling cheers of the crowd, someone else was bundled toward the edge of the pit.

To yet more cheers another of the Norsemen was thrown in. As this one rose to his feet, Styrkar could see he was barely a man at all; more a boy, his blond hair matted, his face desperate and fearful. Upon seeing his opponent, the boy's face twisted in anger and he unleashed a howl of fury. It was obvious he was trying to instil as much courage in himself as he could, a sign that he was afraid, but Styrkar could have no pity for this frightened boy, not if he was to live out the day.

One of the housecarls threw two swords into the pit and they landed between the fighters. There was no order for them to begin. No herald to tell them what to do, and the boy rushed forward to grasp one of the weapons. Styrkar was faster. Everything was instinct now, the roar of the crowd forgotten as he dashed to the centre of the pit and closed a hand on one of the swords. The boy barely had a chance to reach his own weapon, before Styrkar had raised the blade and hacked him down. His opponent fell face-first in the slop, his neck hacked to the spine, head lolling awkwardly. He gave out a gurgling breath in the filth before lying still. A boy who had travelled here with dreams of the riches he might pillage, now dead in the dirt.

Silence filled the pit as Styrkar took a step back from the corpse. He looked up, seeing every eye on him, their disdain clearly writ. Their sport had been ruined. This was not the contest they had been brought here to witness.

Harding glared his displeasure into the hole. It was obvious he would be the one blamed for this poor spectacle.

'Again,' he bellowed. 'Bring two.'

Styrkar could only stand and wait as two more of the Norse were bundled through the crowd by burly housecarls. These two were far from children – one bearing the old scars of battle on his face, the other heavy about the shoulders despite days imprisoned at Harding's displeasure.

Without further urging from their captors, both dropped into the pit, accepting what they had to do. Styrkar took a breath, forgetting his fatigue, knowing that he would need all the Red Wolf's rage if he was to survive.

Two shields were thrown to the Norse along with a sword each. No sooner had the battle-scarred veteran taken up his arms than Styrkar darted forward. The Norseman barely had a chance to bring his shield to bear as he was forced back under the weight of Styrkar's attack, slipping on the boggy earth and falling to one knee. Before Styrkar could finish him, he remembered this man was not the only threat.

Instinct made him turn, made him raise his sword in time to parry an overhead strike from the second warrior. Their weapons rang, the blow heavy, but Styrkar met it with all his strength, then he darted aside as the other Norseman rose to his feet.

Styrkar backed to the edge of the pit as his enemies stood side by side, locking their shields in the mockery of a shield wall. It was the only tactic they could rely on in the narrow confines of the pit, but at least they could not flank him.

As he backed away he almost stumbled over the corpse of the boy he had killed. The lad's sword still lay untouched, and Styrkar bent to pick it up. A weapon in both hands might not give him much of an edge against two warriors, but by Fenrir's teeth it made him feel better.

The warriors glared from beyond their shields as the crowd snarled its hunger into the pit. Both men seemed reluctant to attack, biding their time. Perhaps they had heard of Styrkar's reputation. Perhaps they thought it easier to defend themselves than attack, and that behind their shields they were at an advantage. The Red Wolf would have to prove them wrong about that.

Styrkar's lips curled back from his teeth and he snarled a challenge before charging forward. Both warriors braced their shields as he unleashed the baresark, filling himself with animal fury and smashing the wooden shields with his swords, one then the other, unrelenting, offering neither man the chance to strike back.

The sound of the steel on wood was drowned by the roar from above, spurring him to greater effort. One shield cracked, splinters flying. Then at the next blow it split, and Styrkar's blade hacked in, slicing open the defender's arm. He bellowed, the one with the scarred face, staggering back as Styrkar stabbed in with his other sword, taking him in the throat. The blade was buried deep in him, and it was wrenched from Styrkar's grip as he fell, but there was no time to gloat over his triumph.

In fury, the second Norseman battered Styrkar with his shield, driving him back to the wall of the pit. They both spat and hissed their rage; at such close quarters neither could bring a weapon to bear. Styrkar roared, his voice rising above that of the fevered crowd, and he shoved against the shield with all his might, giving himself room to strike. Again he battered at the Norseman, again and again. The broad-shouldered warrior looked desperate, finding space to swing his blade desperately, but Styrkar ducked the steel, grasping his own sword with both hands.

Then he went at that shield as though felling a tree. Splinter by flying splinter the shield was whittled to tinder until the Norseman was driven to his knees. Heaving in air, Styrkar staggered back. The warrior realised he was beaten, holding little more than wooden shards and a useless blade in his battered hands. He knew there was nothing he could do in the face of such berserk fury and his eyes spoke a plea for mercy.

But the Red Wolf was not sated. He had to be fed.

With a roar, he struck his final blow, cleaving open the Norseman's skull to the tumultuous bellow of the gathered crowd.

When the man slumped to the mud, Styrkar stared up, heaving in breath, seeing the approval on the faces of men who a short time ago had wanted nothing but his murder. Among them he saw the face of Harding, a smile stretched across it.

The sword in Styrkar's grip felt heavy, but he was sure he had the strength to make at least one more corpse if he had to. But that opportunity would have to wait. Two housecarls jumped into the pit, spears levelled as they snarled at Styrkar to drop the sword. It slipped from his fingers, his yearning for death abating as the Red Wolf left him, nothing but a weak and tired man.

As he had done once before that day, he allowed them to

tie him about the neck and push him out of the pit. Styrkar was almost throttled as they dragged him up with that rope, and hauled him across the ground like the worthless meat they had pulled out earlier.

The hysteria of the crowd had been replaced by mirth, and though some of them still looked at him with hatred, others nodded with approval, satisfied with the display he had given.

'The shield breaker,' someone shouted, to the amusement of some. But for others it was a name they approved of.

As Styrkar rose on trembling legs and was dragged back towards the compound of prisoners, someone struck up a chant, and in his wake the name *Shield Breaker* was sung in a bellowed chorus.

A glance back, and he saw Harding glaring at him. That confident smile was gone now, replaced by contempt. Perhaps he had not envisioned the crowd turning Styrkar from prisoner to hero. Maybe all he really wanted was to honour the memory of his father with yet more death.

Well, he would have to wait. For now, at least, the Red Wolf lived.

23

He yearned for sleep, to fall back into the quiet comfort of oblivion, but his mouth was too dry, his thirst too unquenchable to allow it.

When Ronan lifted his head, a feat of tremendous effort, he could see the flap of the tent blowing gently in the breeze. He tried to call out, to summon aid, but couldn't even manage the most pitiful of croaks. His eyes wandered in delirium until they fell on the jug and cup that sat next to his pallet bed. He stretched out an arm withered by inaction, fingers falling inches short of the cup. When he tried to move his body closer, pain lanced through his side as though he had been stabbed. Again.

Ronan let himself roll back, feeling a tear run down the side of his face, unable to wipe it away. At least there was no one here to see him weep. That was one mercy at least.

Memories flooded back as he lay there like some feeble old man, thoughts of how he had allowed himself to be attacked. And by who? Some peasant waiting in the shadows? A pig herder not fit to clean his boots?

And what had happened since then? As much as Ronan tried, he could not piece that time together. Days and nights melted into one, faces came and went, but where were those faces now? Had he been abandoned? Left to die here in some quiet corner of this misbegotten land?

He gritted his teeth, trying to swallow, but could conjure no spit in his mouth. Turning his head he focused on the jug once more. This time when he moved he snorted in defiance of the pain, growled till it hurt his throat. His fingers stretched, almost there, the cup just within his reach. Probing fingertips almost grasped it, but instead flipped the cup from the small table to spill its contents on the ground. Anger seethed up in his broken body – he would not be defeated. Ronan moaned, a pitiful mewling as he stretched further, ignoring the agony that wracked his body as he grabbed the jug. Damn it was heavy, but he managed to lift it, grasping it in two hands as he poured its contents into his mouth.

After swallowing down all he could, he collapsed again. Heaving in breath, feeling the cool water run down his face, forcing a smile at his one tiny victory, but he could not just lay here forever hoping for rescue.

There was daylight beyond the opening of the tent. He swallowed, leaned forward, then called, 'Is anyone there?' His voice sounded as broken as his body felt. A plea no one could have heard. Ronan fell back to his bed defeated.

How long had he been here? There was a chill to the air that told him much time had passed since they had taken the town of Waruic. Had it been days? Weeks? Had Robert moved on and left him here to be tended by idiots with no aptitude for the task?

Movement as someone entered the tent. Ronan lifted his head, feeling a spark of hope ignite. When he saw who had entered, he realised his notion of being left with 'idiots' had not been far off the mark. Still, when Mainard approached his bed, Ronan could not help but feel some relief at seeing a familiar face.

'By Christ, but you look pale as a corpse,' Mainard said. 'I can't believe you're alive.'

'My thanks for your reassuring words,' Ronan breathed. 'Why don't you just dig my fucking grave now?'

Mainard bowed his head in shame. For all his discomfort, Ronan couldn't help but feel guilty for his ingratitude.

'My apologies,' Mainard replied.

'No. You have my thanks for keeping me alive. I owe you a great debt.'

Mainard shook his head. 'I wasn't the one who tended you. I just did as I was told, and brought water, dressings and such.'

'Then who?' Ronan asked.

Mainard looked awkward, as though he was reluctant to reveal who Ronan's saviour was. 'The woman. Gisela. She has not left your bedside for days. She treated you with utmost care, as though you were kin. Without her you would be...' He was reluctant to mention the fate they both knew was obvious.

Ronan wondered if Mainard was mistaken, or just making it up from some notion of modesty. But no, Mainard was anything but modest. Still, Ronan found it hard to believe this woman, who he had treated as nothing more than leverage for his own ends, would care for him like one of her own.

'Gisela? Where is she now? I must thank her.'

This time Mainard looked even more uncomfortable and chewed his lip as though trying to stop the words.

'Speak man,' Ronan demanded, pushing himself up on his bed and regretting it as the tent span around him.

'She is birthing her child,' Mainard said, as though it was a concept he understood little of.

'And?'

'The labour is… difficult. She has suffered for two days with it.'

It was not an unusual thing. Though Ronan's knowledge of midwifery was scant, he had known women take an age to give birth. 'What are you not telling me?'

'They say it is unlikely she or the child will live.'

Ronan had no idea who 'they' might be, but he could only trust Mainard was telling the truth of it. The idea that Gisela had saved him, despite all he had done, and now might perish sat ill in his gut. Perhaps it was his weakness of spirit, or his gratitude at being spared, but Ronan knew he could not just lie in a torpor while this woman suffered.

'Get me up. I have to see her.'

Mainard shook his head, raising a hand to ease Ronan back in his bed. 'No, you have to rest.'

'Fuck rest,' Ronan snapped, so violently it hurt his parched throat. 'Get me out of this stinking pit and take me to her.'

Mainard offered no further word of protest, and eased Ronan from the pallet bed. All Ronan wore was a linen undershirt to hide his modesty. It was filthy and damp, but his pride mattered little now.

He squinted in the bright daylight as they left the tent, and Mainard took his weight on one shoulder. Cold air hit him in a rush, causing his head to spin, but still he pressed on, his legs almost giving way at every step. Through his spinning vision Ronan saw the camp had been all but broken. Only a few remnants remained, tattered embers abandoned for the wolves. He truly had been left behind to rot, but what could he expect from a man like Robert of Comines? That he would assign a priest to Ronan's bedside all hours of the day and night?

A scream brought Ronan out of his self-indulgent reverie. It was a pained cry like an animal in a trap. One that would have curdled his blood was it not already frozen by the afternoon chill.

'That's her,' Mainard said as they struggled toward another tent in the distance.

'No shit,' snarled Ronan, all his effort concentrated on putting one foot in front of the other. 'I'm wounded not bloody deaf.'

They moved with more urgency, Ronan doing his best to limp closer to the anguished cries. It felt as though both his legs were crippled now, but still he closed the distance to the tent before pausing outside. Another scream froze him to the spot.

'We don't have to do this,' Mainard said, fearfully.

But he did have to do this. He owed Gisela at least as much care as she had granted him.

'Take me inside,' Ronan ordered, and they both struggled into the confines of the tent.

He was hit by the stench of sweat and blood as soon as he entered. Candles lit the dank interior, and Ronan could see two women ministering to Gisela as she lay on her back in the corner. She was naked, belly swollen, and one of the women was kneeling between her legs.

Ronan suddenly felt ashamed, as though he were desecrating the sanctity of some holy place. He shouldn't be in here, no man should, but he knew he could not run away. Not now.

'What's going on?' he said above the sound of Gisela's feverish moaning.

The woman between her legs turned, a thunderous frown creasing her brow. When she recognised him, her expression changed to one of shock.

'She is in breech, my lord,' she said, as though apologising for the inconvenience. 'We've tried to turn it but the bairn won't move.'

Ronan turned to the other woman, this one younger but just as ugly. 'You, go get the bloody priest.'

'We've already tried, my lord,' the girl replied. 'But he says he's no midwife. And he will not say prayers for a woman whose child is to be birthed out of wedlock.'

Ronan ground his teeth at the impertinence. The arrogance. Damn the fucking priest and all his pious kind.

'Go and find that shithouse priest,' Ronan snarled. 'Remind him that the king himself was one such bastard, and that if he wants to keep his hands attached to his wrists he should do as he's fucking bid.'

The girl nodded, rushing from the tent. Gisela gave another agonised cry, and for an instant Ronan caught sight of blood and piss that made him feel all the fainter. Mainard held tight to him as he swayed, desperate to take control of his wits before they fled him altogether.

'I need help,' the older woman snarled from between Gisela's legs.

Help? Ronan wasn't sure what he was supposed to do. Even had he been in good health he had no experience in birthing children.

'Do as she says,' he said to Mainard, urged on by another agonised groan from Gisela.

Mainard looked at him, then at the women struggling on the floor, before shaking his head. 'I... I can't,' he replied, stepping back from Ronan then fleeing the tent altogether.

Ronan would have called after him, cursed him for a coward, but it was all he could do to stop himself following in Mainard's wake.

'You'll have to bloody do then,' the woman said, fixing Ronan with a determined look.

'We could wait for the priest,' Ronan said desperately.

'What's he gonna do? Pray this baby into the world? Get over here and help me.'

Ronan was unused to being barked at by a woman, but then he was unused to all of this. He limped forward as best he could, before dropping to his knees by Gisela's side. He winced at the sudden pain in his legs, in his side, in his bloody head, but as Gisela reached out he forgot his own suffering. He grasped her hand in his, not knowing what to say, what to do, hoping that just by being here it would be enough.

A squeal of pain and terror escaping her throat before she fixed him with a pleading look. Her grip grew tighter, and Ronan could see the torment in her eyes. He half expected her to curse him, to beg for anyone else to hold her hand but Ronan of Dol-Combourg, but she didn't. They just held onto one another in that moment, as though they were all that might save one another in the storm.

'It's coming,' the woman said. 'Now or never.'

Gisela screamed.

Ronan tightened his grip as she squeezed. He placed his other hand on her sodden brow, willing her to have the strength to survive this. She had saved him. He owed her this much at least – to be here for better or ill.

As the woman ministered between Gisela's legs he heard her begin to whisper some kind of incantation. It was in no language he had ever heard, no foreign tongue he recognised. When Gisela screamed again the woman's voice rose in pitch, those words seeming more curse than blessing.

Was this some kind of witchcraft? Some pagan rite? Or was it just a strange kind of wort-cunning known only to the primitive bastards who inhabited this blighted land?

Fuck this place and fuck its savage people. How had he ever ended up here? He had come to conquer, not help a dying woman birth her doomed child. But here he was, and here he would stay for as long as Gisela needed him.

'Here it comes,' the woman said. 'Nearly there, my love.'

Another scream as Gisela convulsed. Ronan held on tight. He would have spoken words to soothe her ordeal, but what words would calm this? He had watched men die from their wounds, screaming in pain, but it had never been so discomfiting as what he witnessed now.

With one last tortuous effort, Gisela's child was pulled into the world as she bellowed from the depths of her lungs. Ronan glanced down, in time to see the woman holding that pile of blood-soaked flesh. Gisela fell back, becalmed, her breath shallow, the last of her strength fled.

'You are brave, girl,' Ronan found himself saying. 'Braver than any man I have known.' Whether that was true or not, Ronan wasn't sure but it seemed the right thing to say.

'Does it live?' Gisela whispered meekly. 'Does my child live?'

Ronan turned to see the woman had wrapped the newborn in a blanket. It was silent as she frantically rubbed warmth into its limbs.

'Well?' Ronan demanded.

The woman ignored him as she ministered to the infant. Ronan considered whether to threaten her, tell her if she did not save the babe he would have her head cut from her shoulders. But why? Was that the only way he knew how to help?

Before he could even begin to feel shame for his thoughts, the child coughed, a phlegmy herald to the piercing wail it then emitted.

'Your daughter lives,' the woman said, rising to her feet and bringing the babe to Gisela. She laid the child in her mother's arms and took a step back.

'Thank you,' Gisela whispered. 'Both of you.'

Once more, Ronan had the overwhelming sense that he was intruding on something sacred. That he did not belong. With some effort, he struggled to his feet. After limping toward the open flap of the tent, he offered the midwife a quick glance. So what if she were some hedge-witch. She had saved that child, and with luck Gisela too. Besides, Ronan was too weak to question any of this.

Outside Mainard was waiting pensively, and on seeing

Ronan he moved forward in time to catch him as he stumbled. He should have rebuked the man as a coward, but right now it seemed somewhat pointless. Besides, there was only one thing in the world he needed right now.

'Get me back to bed,' Ronan pleaded.

PART TWO

THE AETHELING

24

The baby was quiet now as she fed. A short moment of peace between the howling. Gisela had never heard such a thunderous voice, and she had met enough newborns in her time. She'd slept little in the past few days, but suffered it gladly for the gift she now held in her arms.

Flame-red hair already covered the child's head, though it gave her more the look of a squirrel than a fierce Dane warrior. But those eyes. Those ice-blue eyes were every bit her father's. Gisela could have wept at the thought of him, but she had to be stronger than that. It was what Styrkar would have wanted.

She had to concentrate on the things she could be thankful for. A roof over her head was one. Being allowed inside the boundary of Waruic, within the safety of its walls, was a privilege she had accepted with grace, despite the fact she still felt like a prisoner. There was no doubt this was Ronan's doing, but the thought of thanking him for it sat ill with her. Instead, she would have to settle for thanking God.

A knock at her door. The baby stopped feeding for a moment, looking around as though she might answer herself. The thought almost made Gisela laugh. Almost. Fact was, it could be anyone who had come to her humble dwelling, and perhaps not with the best of intentions.

She wrapped the baby tighter and stood up from her little stool. Unbolting the door she opened it a crack, though she might as well have flung it wide – if someone was here to do her harm they could just as easily have kicked it in. When she saw the two women on the other side she allowed herself a smile.

'Here she is,' said Stanhilde in that high voice she reserved for babies and animals.

Gisela took a step back allowing her to step inside, with Wealdberg close behind her.

'Can I?' Stanhilde asked, holding out her arms for the infant.

Gisela handed her over. 'She's just had a feed, so you might end up with a surprise all over your kirtle.'

Stanhilde shrugged. 'I've had worse than vomit over it.'

Gisela shared a knowing look with Wealdberg. They both knew exactly what she was talking about.

'You are looking better,' Wealdberg said. 'I brought you a few things.'

She laid a sack on the table, most likely vegetables for a pottage. Gisela nodded her thanks.

'Much better,' Stanhilde said as she fussed the baby. 'I'm sure those bags under your eyes will be gone soon enough.'

Another glance at Wealdberg, who raised a knowing

eyebrow at Stanhilde's insensitivity. It was something they'd both had to grow used to.

'I have nothing to offer in return,' Gisela said. 'The last of the ale is gone.'

'Not to worry,' Wealdberg replied. 'There's mead in there for you. That'll help keep your strength up.'

'Thank you,' Gisela replied.

Stanhilde began to coo at the infant. Despite her youth and her reputation around the town, Gisela could only appreciate how well she took to motherhood.

'She's gonna have some crop of hair, I reckon,' the girl said. 'And those eyes. She'll turn the head of every man in England. Her father must have been a handsome beast.' She stopped, realising what she'd said before looking at Gisela. 'I'm sorry, I didn't—'

Gisela smiled and shook her head. 'It's all right. He was handsome, there's no mistake in that.'

Another stern look from Wealdberg, but this one had an edge of sympathy to it.

'Still no word from the west, then?' the older woman asked.

Gisela shook her head. 'None.'

It had become obvious that Styrkar was not coming back. Whether he had been killed or not was anyone's guess, but if he could have returned he would have done it by now. He was as good as dead either way.

'Maybe you need to think about leaving this place. Getting as far from here as you can and starting again.'

'And where would I go?' Gisela asked. It seemed an impossible idea, especially now she had another mouth to feed.

'Don't you have family in Flanders? There must be someone there who can take you in, if we could work out how to secure your passage...'

'There's no one,' Gisela replied.

She had not been back home for a decade. In that time word from her father and brothers had ceased, and she had considered the FitzScrobs her family. Now all that was gone too. Even if she returned to the castle at Hereford there was no way they would take in a fallen woman with her bastard child. A child she had to find some way to care for. A glance at Stanhilde and she was reminded of how few options there were. But allowing herself to be pawed over by someone so she could live under a roof seemed a more desperate act than she'd be able to bear.

'Then you've only got one option,' Wealdberg said.

'What do you mean?'

'Don't you remember Ronan at your side when you were birthing?'

Gisela thought back to that day. She had been in a delirium, barely conscious as her child was born. But yes, when she thought on it she could remember his face marred with concern, his hand gripping hers.

'And he's put this roof over your head,' Stanhilde added between fussing the baby, who now seemed to want nothing else but sleep.

Wealdberg took a step toward her, leaning in as though to impart some great wisdom. 'I know it won't be easy for you, love. But now might be the time to rely on the help you already have. Rather than put your hopes on someone coming back from the dead to save you.'

Gisela's gaze drifted from Wealdberg to the baby in

Stanhilde's arms. Had she been holding onto a ghost all this time? Hoping that he would come for her in the night and take her off, back to their home by the sea? She had to accept Styrkar was gone, but at least she would always have a reminder of him, that red hair and those ice-blue eyes would always be with her.

Then again, could she really give herself to Ronan? He was the architect of all her ills. He had torn her from the arms of the man she loved and forced him to betray his brothers. Could she ever trust such a fiend? Rely on him to keep his word? Perhaps she should take her chances and get as far from him as she could.

'I will speak to him,' Gisela replied.

'Just you be careful,' Wealdberg said.

Gisela reached out and Stanhilde handed over the baby. She would have told Wealdberg that she was always careful, but the evidence in her arms spoke differently.

'I'm not afraid of Ronan.' And she wasn't. At least not anymore. 'If he wishes me to stay under his protection all the better. But there is also no need for him to keep me prisoner. Especially not now I am a fallen woman.'

Stanhilde sniggered at that, but Wealdberg retained that serious look on her serious face. With a nod of thanks to both women she made for the door.

Once she had left the relative safety of her hut and walked towards Ronan's dwelling, unease began to grow. Ronan was her captor, and now she was to ask if he might protect her. It was a deep betrayal of Styrkar, of all they had shared, but would he not have wanted her to do all she could to protect their child?

Best not think on that. Best just to learn the lay of the

land. Surely that was the most sensible approach. How a strategist might have done it. But Gisela was no war leader and this no war. She had no weapon with which to fight, nor gold with which to bargain. Nevertheless, when she finally reached the hut Ronan had requisitioned for himself, it felt as though she were about to go into battle.

She knocked at his door, and waited as she heard shuffling inside. The door opened, and she half expected to see the squire Mainard, but instead it was Ronan's face that greeted her. He looked much better than the last time she had seen him. Then he had been pale as snow, a man on the brink of death. Now there was colour back in his cheeks, though from the look of it a few grey hairs were appearing through the blond on his head.

'Gisela,' he said, sounding genuinely pleased to see her. 'Please, come in.'

Ronan moved away from the door. He walked with a staff, using it to help him shuffle on his crippled leg, and she followed him in, closing the door behind her. A fire burned in the hearth and her baby mewled comfortably in the welcome heat.

He sat down, patting the stick with one hand. 'As you can see, I am still afflicted. Only now my ailment is even worse than before.'

'I'm sure you will recover,' she said. There seemed something changed about him. An aspect to his face that made him look like a different man to the one she had known. It took her a moment before she realised it was his smile – now open and friendly, in contrast to the cruel smirk he had always worn.

'You are more confident than I,' he replied, and his

gaze drifted toward the fire. The pleasure with which he had greeted her suddenly sloughed away to be replaced by glumness. As he sat in dour silence, Gisela found herself feeling sorry for him. Not in her wildest imaginings could she ever have seen that coming.

'You have survived a great test. God has spared your life. That in itself is a reason to rejoice.'

Ronan snorted a little as he smiled, glancing at her before his eyes fell to the child she held in her arms. There they lingered as he watched the baby struggle in her mother's arms, fighting sleep but succumbing to it nonetheless.

A thought began to manifest in Gisela's head. A mad thought she should have snuffed out like a candle, but it continued to burn with the light of hope.

'Would you like to hold her?' Gisela asked.

As soon as she said the words she regretted them. What was she even thinking? But then, she knew exactly what she was thinking. If Ronan was to gain some affection for her baby, perhaps he would want to protect them both.

'No,' Ronan replied, glancing back to the fire. 'I'm afraid paternal instinct has never been my—'

'Here,' Gisela said before he could refuse, crossing the room and gently placing the baby in his arms.

At first he seemed surprised and uncomfortable holding the swaddled child, as most men were when first faced with it. But in moments the smile was back on his face, his finger touching the baby's hand until she gripped it as she slept.

'What will you call her?' Ronan asked eventually.

Gisela had not given it much thought, so preoccupied had she been with feeding, changing, washing, sleeping. For a moment she considered Styrkarsdottr might be the most appropriate. Then she dismissed the notion. It would only serve to mark her daughter as more of an outsider if she was given so obvious a Danish name.

'I don't know,' she replied. 'Perhaps something Frankish?'

Ronan nodded his approval. 'In the circumstances, I think that would be a good idea.'

In the circumstances? Because the conquerors were Franks of course. Because it showed a loyalty, and acceptance. Would that make Ronan trust her? Could she ever really trust him? There was only one way to find out.

'So, what now?' she asked.

He glanced up at her. She could not read the look in his eyes and for a moment thought perhaps he had seen through her subterfuge. Her attempts to manipulate him. But then he shrugged.

'Anything you wish, Gisela. You may leave if you want to. Take your child wherever you like.'

'And where do you think I should go?'

He looked back down at the baby, and she thought perhaps he had no answer. Maybe he simply didn't care.

'You are also welcome to stay here, should you wish it. Under my protection, of course.'

She could have dropped to her knees and kissed his feet, but held herself back from such abasement. He had spared her, and for that she was grateful, but he would always be her captor in a sense.

'And what about you?' she asked. 'What next for Ronan of Dol-Combourg?'

He turned to the fire again, a little shake of his head, almost imperceptible.

'I have no idea. Robert has struck north. My friend, Earl

Brian, resides in the south. And here I am between, no use to either. More a cripple than I ever was.'

She took a step toward him, looking down at the sad figure before her. In the past he had terrified her, abused her, kidnapped her, condemned her lover. Now he just looked pitiful. But this pitiful figure was all that stood between her daughter and destitution. If their destinies were entwined, they would have to make the best of it.

'You will grow strong again,' she said, more an order than a prediction. 'I will see to that.'

When he looked up at her, she could see his eyes wet with tears. 'You have gone through an ordeal, Gisela. And I have played my part in that. Perhaps you should think on your child and forget—'

'I won't hear of it,' she said, taking her baby from his arms. 'We are stuck together now, Ronan. For good or ill.'

That smile slowly crept its way up the side of his mouth once more.

'For good or ill,' he said.

25

He sucked the cold marrow from the bone, not even caring about the noisome sound he made as he did so. It was all he might eat for a day, maybe two, and his body was already a shrivelled husk.

Snow dusted the ground, and he hunkered within the wolfskin pelt he'd been given. It served as cloak and blanket within his cage, and he doubted it would see him through the winter. He might eventually freeze in his prison, if he didn't starve first, but Styrkar knew it was more likely he would die in that pit before cold or hunger got him.

There were no Norse left. He'd killed them, or they'd killed each other over the weeks since that first fight. They'd left their scars on him too, some healed, some left to fester. Now all that remained in the compound was a cage with its wolf, alongside Harding's hunting dogs, sulking in their pens. Glancing over, Styrkar could see they looked even less enthused by the coming winter than he was.

It reminded him of years ago, back in Ánslo, and the last time he'd been made to sleep with dogs. They had fussed him then, crowded around him, kept him warm all that long night. Now though, he was just another animal, caged alongside the rest and fighting for scraps.

One of the hounds sniffed the air from its pen. Styrkar had seen it many times, the leader of the pack, the one with the keenest nose. It rose to its feet and barked at the entrance to their little compound, before the rest joined in.

Someone was coming. It was obvious who.

Harding led a group of his housecarls into the wooden confines of the compound. He didn't offer Styrkar so much as a second glance as he went to the dog pen to fuss his favourite hound. The animal whined as it sniffed its master's hand, then licked his fingers. The rest of his men waited patiently, leaning on their spears, chatting idly. Not one of them had a care in the world, nor deigned to acknowledge the wolf in its cage.

Styrkar had finished with the bone and flung it through the bars. Months ago he might have felt some shame that he'd been seen sucking on that marrowbone like a cur. Now he bore no such thing as pride, but then a man's priorities changed when he was forced to live in a cage, before he died in a pit.

Finally, after Harding had finished greeting the last of his hounds, he turned his attention to Styrkar. It left no one in doubt as to who was at the bottom of the pecking order.

Harding strolled up all casual, like they were old friends, leaning on the cage as though they might be talking about the weather or crops over a neighbouring fence.

'Today could be the day,' Harding said, as though he

were looking forward to some festival or other. 'One you've been waiting for all your life, Red Wolf.'

The day he'd die? Styrkar hadn't been waiting on it with any particular anticipation, but he supposed Harding was right in his way – everyone was waiting to die eventually.

'But no one lives forever,' Harding continued, as though reading Styrkar's thoughts. 'It's been good knowing you.' That brought chuckles from his men. For his part, Styrkar remained silent. 'Word is the new king does not care for the keeping of slaves. Word is he finds it... distasteful. Word is, he'll soon be levelling a stipend for their ownership that goes straight into his coffers. So obviously, word is there'll soon be no more slaves. None worth the keeping, anyway.'

With that, Harding turned and made his way back toward the town. It was a signal for his men to get to work, and there was a frantic beavering at the cage as they opened the door and tied a rope around Styrkar's neck. He was pulled through the snow, wolf cloak lost, half naked and shivering. Styrkar expected to be taken the route he'd been driven so many times already. So many times he'd lost count. The long walk to that deep pit, but this time was different.

He recognised Eadnoth's feast hall as it rose at the end of the road ahead, though he supposed it was Harding's hall now. The fledgling lord made his way through those huge open doors, the people who were spilling out of the doorway moving aside to let him in. By the time Styrkar reached it he could hear a racket echoing from inside, those voices filled with excitement and anticipation. It reminded him of the witan at Berchastede, where a gaggle of useless lords had gathered to elect a child king. This time though, he doubted anyone was going to be given a throne. This time the only reward would be death.

When the men had dragged him inside, jostling the crowd for room till they got to the middle of the hall, Styrkar could only feel grateful for the warmth. A fire was burning in its pit, and with so many bodies crammed inside the air was stifling. As soon as he was brought forth, the crowd quieted. All eyes were on him as he stood, surrounded by eager faces. Across the flames of the fire he could see Harding sitting in his father's chair, though much like the feast hall, it was his now. The young warrior did a better job of filling it than his father had, but still he lacked the authority of Eadnoth.

The ropes at Styrkar's neck were untied, and he was left to stand amid the grumbling crowd. The Red Wolf set free in a pen full of sheep. The thought of escaping crossed his mind, of grabbing a sword or a spear and fighting till he was free, or dead, whichever happened first. But no. There was to be violence here, he was sure of it, and after so many weeks he had grown used to being part of the spectacle. At least he'd get to die in the warm.

As he waited, the crowd on the other side of the fire parted. They weren't even jostled aside, just made a gap to let someone through. A big someone. No one had to tell Styrkar this was who he'd been brought to fight, he could tell by the look in that warrior's eyes. He stared across the fire like he wanted nothing but murder. A brute of a man, better fed than Styrkar. Hardly seemed fair. But none of this was fair. If the Red Wolf had wanted fairness he was in the wrong bloody place.

One of Harding's housecarls put a sword in Styrkar's hand. He glanced down, seeing it was rusted, poorly balanced, almost like they were setting him up to die. Across the firepit, the brute of a warrior hefted his own blade. One that looked freshly forged for the kill.

The noise around them had died down now. A hundred witnesses holding their breath. Were they waiting for Harding to order the fight to begin? There was no need, Styrkar knew what this was, and had performed it a dozen times. From the look on that face glaring at him over the fire, his opponent did too. They were like a pair of obedient hounds, taught nothing but to hate one another. Taught nothing but to fight one another. No one needed to say a word.

They started to circle, keeping that fire between them. From the look of the warrior he was a wild one – part of his nose missing and his body bore as many scars as Styrkar. Still, he approached with caution, a seasoned fighter. Maybe not so wild after all.

Styrkar stopped, done with the circling. They'd sized one another up enough. Best get this done with.

The brute took a swing as soon as he was close enough. Styrkar ducked as the blade swooped an inch short of its mark. Then he swung his own rusted sword, opponent leaning back just out of range. Before Styrkar could bring his weapon to bear once more, the warrior dashed forward. It was all Styrkar could do to raise his blade and parry, a clash of metal echoing through the feast hall, the gasps of the crowd drowning out the noise.

Swords locked for an instant. Before Styrkar could back away the warrior struck with his head between the crossed blades, catching Styrkar full in the face. He reeled, eyes filling with tears, the heat of the fire singeing his arm as he swung wildly. The tip of his sword caught his opponent's blade, and he heard a ring of steel. When he managed to regain his senses he could see the end of his sword had snapped off an inch from the tip. No good for stabbing now, not that it mattered as the warrior came barging forward.

The brute was too close to take a swing at, his own sword forgotten as he shouldered Styrkar in the chest. Both their weapons fell clattering to the floor. Any other time Styrkar would have reacted quickly, would have grabbed his enemy and rung his neck, but weak as he was he couldn't stop the warrior grabbing him around the waist.

He was lifted, raised high above the watching crowd, before being slammed to the wooden boards. A cheer rose to the rafters, leaving no doubt who the crowd was rooting for. Styrkar grappled with the warrior, feeling how powerful he was, a rabbit in the jaws of a hunting hound, desperation almost overwhelming him. The wolf inside grew angrier as they wrestled amid the straw.

On they fought, neither one getting an edge until the warrior clamped his broken teeth on Styrkar's shoulder. He roared. A howl to silence the crowd, a feral cry of pain and frustration. Of hate.

His fist entwined in the bastard's hair, unable to wrench the jaws from his flesh. Instead he punched out with his other fist, again and again. He was weak, but he would still have wagered on his own strength over most other men. The jaws slackened as he punched again, hearing a grunt, not knowing if it was him or the man he was wrestling. With a howl he punched one final time, hearing the crack of bone as the jaw clamped to his shoulder broke.

The warrior rolled away, moaning in pain. They were

both desperate now, glaring at one another in the firelight. Slowly they rose, breathing heavy, blood and sweat dripping.

'Kill him,' snarled a woman's voice from the crowd. Styrkar had no idea who she was talking to. Most likely she didn't care. Most likely she just wanted murder.

Both men sucked in the cloying air of the feast hall, eyes locked on one another. Beasts fighting over scraps. Two wolves in a pit.

For a fleeting moment, Styrkar thought how alike they could have been. That perhaps in a different place at a different time they might have been as brothers, fighting side by side on the battlefield. But he could not let that thought unman him. They were not brothers, and one of them had to die.

With a growl he darted forward. The warrior grabbed him, but Styrkar attacked low, grabbing those meaty thighs, and this time he was the one to lift his enemy above the crowd. His muscles screamed in protest as he slammed the man down, hearing a satisfying thud as he hit the floor.

The Red Wolf fell on him like a wounded beast. He could see the warrior's eyes rolling in a daze, but there could be no mercy. Not now. Not for either of them.

He grasped a fistful of hair again, slamming that scarred head to the ground. Punching with his numb fist. As he did so he began to growl his feral growl. An animal on the attack.

Blood spurted from the man's mouth, as he was unable to close it with his jaw broken. Another punch, more smashed teeth, before Styrkar regained his sense. The heat of the fight subsiding, to be replaced by cold focus. This had to end.

Three sharp strikes to the warrior's throat and the man's

eyes bulged. He choked, clapping hands to his neck, unable to breath. He would have writhed on the ground but with the weight of the Red Wolf upon him he couldn't move. Vainly he tried to suck air through his broken throat, gagging his last, until eventually he stopped moving.

Styrkar glared around, as much as he could glare in such a daze. All eyes were on him as silence fell over the feast hall.

He crawled off the dead man, intending to stand, intending to howl his victory in their stunned faces. Instead he collapsed to the hard wood. Scrabbling in the straw beside the fire- pit.

A murmur began to spread, rising to chatter. No one cheered, clearly they had all wagered against him. Their misfortune almost made him laugh, but as he crawled he felt something beneath his hand that removed all mirth.

Metal under his palm. The tip of a rusted sword.

As he heard footsteps approach, he lifted his hand, stuffing the rusted metal in his mouth. Then he was dragged, exhausted, to his feet.

They bundled him out, through the crowd, into the cold. Styrkar managed one last look toward Harding, sitting on his father's throne. The displeasure on that face almost made Styrkar laugh. What would Harding do, now he had a slave he could not rid himself of. Perhaps another pit, but this time he would just fill in the hole after throwing in his troublesome thrall.

Styrkar tried not to think on it as he was dragged through the snow, the cold gripping his bones, numbing the ache in his limbs. The cage was waiting for him, door yawning open, welcoming him home.

They shut him in with little fuss. He was too broken to resist. Despite the numbing cold, the bite on his shoulder was starting to sting, but he did his best to ignore it. With any luck the wound would close. There would be no infection. Not that luck had been on his side in recent weeks.

'Congratulations on another victory,' said a voice.

Styrkar looked up to see one of the housecarls had stayed behind, to gloat most likely. When he recognised his wolf-head torc about the man's neck he knew it was a certainty.

He ignored the man, merely hunkering in the cage, glaring at the cold ground. At his silence, the man spat. It caught one of the bars of the cage, but Styrkar still felt the spatter.

'How long do you think you're gonna live?' the man asked, seeming to take pleasure in the speaking of every word. 'Even the fiercest wolf can't fight forever.'

It was no struggle to ignore the man. Styrkar had ignored much in his time here. The cold, the hunger, the pain. What were words to ignore but more empty air?

'Nothing to say?' the man asked. 'Of course you haven't. If I had as little time left as you, I'd keep my peace. Save my breath.'

Styrkar would have had plenty to say had there been anyone worth saying it to. As the man grew bored and left him alone, he could only think he had the right idea though. There might not be many breaths left for him to take.

When finally he was alone, he reached up and took the rusted sword tip from his mouth. It was true, he could not fight forever. And it was also true that Harding needed rid of his bothersome slave. Perhaps it was time to do Harding one last favour.

26

Waruic, England, December 1068

He took a step, and managed it without feeling the searing pain he'd grown used to enduring for so long. Perhaps this was the day he could truly say he'd recovered. Though survived might have been a better description. It was certainly the first time he'd been able to make it across the room without that damnable stick. When he put weight on his other leg, the crippled leg, he felt the old pain, but at least that was pain he was familiar with. In a strange type of way it was comforting, but then familiar things usually were.

'Well done,' Gisela said from across the room.

She smiled at him, cradling the baby to her breast. Ronan smiled back his appreciation. A few months ago he would have chided her scornfully. Demanded she not patronise him, but now all that had changed.

In recent days he had learned to accept her help, without complaint. It had not been easy, but it was doubtful he would have been on his feet so quickly if not for her tending to him.

All his life he had been in battle, with himself, with the judging looks of others, with their whispered comments. *There goes the cripple, that untrustworthy shit. The Bastard of Dol-Combourg.* They had been comments he had fed off, lived up to, and fought against all his life. But with Gisela, there was no longer any need to fight.

As he watched her gently caring for her daughter, it made him realise how much time he had wasted on spite. Made him regret all those years of struggle.

Ronan gently lowered himself into the chair nearest the fire. The room was warm, the winter had not been a hard one so far, but still they were thankful for their lodgings. It kept the cold out at least, and he could only be thankful for that, along with the respite from fighting, only for other men to grow wealthy off the back of it. Ronan began to think a man might easily stay here forever had he a mind to.

When he glanced again across the room, he knew there was little chance of that. Gisela had chosen to remain at his side while she nursed her child, but there had been no affection. No desire. This was expediency, cold and cruel as it was.

Perhaps he should have tried to woo her. To make her his own. Then again he had tried that in Hereford, and to his shame he had failed. Though failure was not the only source of that shame. Ronan had behaved like a brute, and he knew it. But brute was what he was, and a clumsy advance on a vulnerable girl was the least of his sins. Some might even call him a monster. He was abhorrent by his actions, as well as in his body. Crippled inside and out. A woman like Gisela would certainly never see past that.

Or would she? From the kindly looks he had received from her, she could not possibly consider him a monster. Had he also seen some affection in those blue eyes of hers? Could he hope...

Of course not. He was her enemy. The man who had condemned the father of her child, and how could he ever compare to the towering giant she had taken as her lover? But then, Styrkar was dead, and Ronan was very much alive.

'We have a decision to make,' Ronan said, feeling his heart beat the faster as he said it.

Gisela looked up from fussing the child – the one she still hadn't named yet – her brow furrowing. 'We?'

'Yes. This concerns you as well as I.'

'What is it?'

Ronan found himself ringing his hands. Why was he so nervous? Was he worried she would have her own ideas about her future? Worried she would want to leave him?

'We cannot stay here in Waruic forever. Though we have a roof for now there is still rebellion in the air. There could be further uprisings, and the garrison ordered to move on. And so I've decided we should probably leave. The three of us... if you'll come with me.'

'And go where?' Gisela asked.

'My friend Brian has an Earldom to the south in Cornualge. The safest place is there, and I belong by his side. You could come with me. No one has to know who the father of the child is. You could pretend—'

The door opened with no warning. Ronan almost jerked

to his feet, but on seeing Mainard rush in out of the cold he settled back into the chair.

'Your presence is required,' Mainard said. He had a serious look to him. A worried look.

'By whom?' Ronan replied.

'Someone's here. Someone who's asked for you by name.'

Ronan rose unsteadily to his feet. 'Damn it, Mainard, are you going to make me bloody guess?'

'It's Guillam Mallet.'

That was enough to freeze Ronan where he sat. Of all the knights who had fought at Senlac, Mallet was the one who had distinguished himself the most. Some said it was he who had cut down King Harold himself, though there had been a number of claimants on that score. Whatever the truth of it, Guillam Mallet was not a man to keep waiting when he asked for you by name.

Ronan limped to grab his cloak from the mantle and swung it about his shoulders. Gisela looked concerned as he made for the door, but all he could offer was a half-smile of reassurance.

When he had closed the door behind him and made his way out into the cold streets of Waruic, he could barely match Mainard's pace.

'What's he doing here?' Ronan asked.

'I don't know, but he's brought an army with him.'

'So what does he want me for?' Damn his leg ached in the cold.

'I assume with Robert gone north, he wants to know what the lay of the land is.'

Lay of the land? Ronan had no more idea of that than any other peasant in their hovel. The further they walked along the frozen road, the more he felt a tightening in his gut, until it was twisted almost as painfully as that knife had in his side. To add insult, by the time they reached the market square the snow had begun to drift down from the sky. The scene that greeted Ronan was the last he'd expected.

Two young knights sparred in the centre of the square. Chairs had been placed around the periphery so that onlookers could watch. And in the largest of those chairs sat the Lord of Graville.

Guillam Mallet must have been a man well past his middling years but he looked little older than Ronan. His hair was thick, shaved at the sides in the knightly manner, and he wore a moustache that was neatly trimmed down to his chin. A host of serfs and attendants milled around as though they were seeing to a spring festival, and not an abandoned market in the dead of winter. The standard of Graville was held by a stern knight standing behind Guillam, bearing the three-buckle crest of his family.

At Guillam's side sat the woman who could only be his wife, though Ronan had no idea of her name. She too barely looked her age, and Ronan found himself quite taken. She was certainly too well-dressed to merely be a consort, though her head was bare despite the snow, her brown hair flowing across her fur-bedecked shoulders.

At Ronan's approach a smile crossed Guillam's face and he opened his arms as though they were old friends. Surprising in itself, as they had never been formally introduced.

'Dol-Combourg, welcome,' Guillam said in a boisterous tone, as though this were his manor and Ronan the guest. He spoke his words in English, but then hardly a surprise from a man born and bred here, though there was no question of who held his loyalty.

'My Lord Guillam,' Ronan said with a bow. It was an effort, but best he make it than test the ire of the most renowned warrior at Senlac. 'To what do we owe the pleasure?'

'Ah, I am merely stopping off on my way north. I am to join Lord Robert at Yorke. The question is, what are you doing here, Dol-Combourg?'

Was that the question? Ronan hadn't realised his presence was the one that needed to be justified.

'I was tragically wounded in the campaign against the sons of Aelfgar. My recovery has been slow, but I shall be returning to Cornualge very shortly to serve its new earl.'

Guillam smiled, his attention suddenly taken by the men sparring in the square. His wife leaned in as though to whisper, but her voice was loud enough for all to hear when she said, 'I heard he was stabbed by a peasant.'

Ronan suppressed the sudden feeling of humiliation. At least no one deigned to laugh at the comment, though from the sideways looks he could tell everyone had heard.

There was a clash of blades and Guillam yelled his approval before clapping the combatants. He then turned his attention back to Ronan.

'There is nothing to interest you in the south, Dol-Combourg. You should accompany me north. We'll need a man like you there. Rough country, so I'm told. Plenty to keep you occupied.'

Rough country was the last thing Ronan needed, and the reputation of the northern extents of this land preceded themselves. But how to refuse and not lose face?

'That is a most tempting offer, Lord Guillam, but I'm afraid I have been away from Earl Brian for quite long enough. I serve in his conrois—'

'Nonsense. It's common knowledge you've been romping around the countryside for months trying to secure fugitives from the king's justice. A most noble endeavour, I'm sure, but now you're needed elsewhere. *I* need you. No one knows more than I how important it is to have men close who know the language. Know the people. And I require every knight I can lay my hands on. I am bound for Yorke to take on the position of sheriff and I require a man with experience. And who is more experienced than you?'

Ronan could feel the situation getting away from him. All eyes were on him now, and he began to feel like the spitted pig at a feast.

'Believe me, my lord, I understand the difficulty of the task that lies ahead, but I am sure—'

'I was also of the understanding that you were serving at the pleasure of Lord Robert.'

Pleasure was most definitely overstating it. 'That is true, but—'

'And has Lord Robert sent word that such commitment was carried out to his satisfaction?'

Only to the degree that Ronan almost died. 'After the fall of Waruic he did mention that I should return to Cornualge.'

'Did he indeed? I assume you have a decree stating such?'

'No, I just—'

'Then it's settled.' Guillam smiled at him as though they'd just reached some kind of accord, and Ronan hadn't just been bullied into submission. 'The northerners are proving difficult to subdue. Robert is being sent to curb them.

We both require someone with knowledge of their ways. Someone cunning. Is that you, Ronan?'

Was this flattery now? Ronan was finding it hard to parse the situation, but it looked like his options were limited whichever way he looked at it.

'It would certainly appear that way, my lord.'

'Good,' Guillam bellowed. 'Then we are agreed. We strike north at first light.'

And it seemed that was it. All attention went back to the sparring pair, now heaving thick mist from their lungs as they fought in the snow. Ronan was all but ignored as he slunk from the market square like a fox from the coop. To add insult, the snowfall grew heavier with every step, and his crippled leg ached like he was being tortured.

'Looks like we're heading north then,' Mainard said as they trogged back in the cold.

'Just make the damned arrangements,' Ronan replied.

The warmth of his dwelling was most welcome as he made his way back inside, but Ronan couldn't shift the cold feeling in his gut. Gisela sat by the baby as she slept in her crib, offering a smile as he entered. Ronan took his seat by the fire, dropping his cloak to the floor.

'Is all well?' she asked, though he could tell from her tone she knew it wasn't.

'Certainly,' Ronan replied. 'Lord Guillam Mallet is everything I'd expected and more.'

The fire crackled a hospitable tune. One that wouldn't last.

'We're not going to Cornualge are we?' Gisela asked.

'No. I am going north.'

'No,' she said determinedly. '*We* are going north.'

He turned, seeing a stern set to her eyes. He'd discovered how stubborn she could be in recent days. It had pleased him at times, but now he wasn't sure it would serve her well.

'It's no place for a woman and her child. We might be surrounded by rebels and you'll be joining a determined army. There might be as much danger from those you're travelling with—'

'Is this Lord Guillam taking his family?'

Ronan thought back to the woman seated next to him. To her self-assured arrogance.

'Unfortunately so.'

'Then how bad could it be?'

Ronan thought on all the ways it could be very bad indeed, and then dispelled them in an instant. If Gisela was with him, it would at least relieve his own burden, and he would do his utmost to protect her and the child. It might well be safer than leaving her here.

'Very well. If you're not to be dissuaded, we'll go together.'

27

Grimeshou, England, December 1068

Wealdberg kept singing her little song as the wagon rolled on ever northwards. Gisela would have found it annoying by now, but it seemed to soothe the baby to sleep well enough, and it took her mind off the sodding cold. Stanhilde had decided to stay in Waruic and make her own way, so now it was just the two of them following an army north.

Ronan had ridden ahead with the rest of the army, their horses leaving the road little more than a slick river of mud. The camp followers were left to trundle on in their filthy wake, wagon after wagon rolling along like a trail of slugs following a swarm of ants.

She gazed down at the child. Still unnamed. Gisela was unsure of what name would be best to help the child fit into this ever-changing country. With luck the answer would present itself soon enough.

'What the bloody hell is that?' Wealdberg said.

Gisela looked up, seeing the smoke rising ahead. She knew

240

exactly what it was, and there was little doubt Wealdberg did too.

'Nothing stands in their way, does it,' Gisela said.

'Nothing that survives,' Wealdberg replied.

The older woman's song fell silent as they made their way further along the mud-strewn road, until they reached the source of the smoke.

It was a tiny hamlet, its low palisade nothing but ash, flames still rising from one of the thatched roofs. As she clutched her baby, Gisela began to feel the anger growing, the knowledge that she was helpless to do anything about this only making that pain all the sharper.

She had agreed to come. Had insisted on it. Now all she could think was that perhaps it had been a mistake. But mistakes were all she had left, and all she could do was find a way to deal with them.

'Stop the cart,' she said.

Wealdberg gave her a confused look. 'What?'

'Stop the bloody cart!'

At her insistence, Wealdberg drew the cart to a halt, the horse snorting in protest.

Gisela climbed down, waving an apology to the carts behind that had been forced to stop in their wake.

'What are you doing, girl?' Wealdberg asked. 'It's bloody freezing, and there's nought you can do for anyone now.'

'I have to see.' Gisela gazed at the fallen palisade and the burning huts within.

'What for?'

Gisela turned back to her, to those hard eyes in that hard face. 'I'll catch up.'

With that she turned and made her way toward the

hamlet, hearing the wagons begin to trundle on up the road. There was no way she could explain to Wealdberg what she was doing. She barely understood herself. Something inside was urging her to witness this horror. To see everything this army had done. To take in all their butchery, if not for herself then for those they had ravaged on their journey north.

The fires had melted the snow surrounding the hamlet, and she crossed the threshold where the gate had been, now smashed to little more than firewood. Had the people of this town thought it would keep them safe? Had they not heard what the Franks had done in the south to so many other places? Had they even resisted?

The hamlet wasn't big, and it didn't take her long to reach the centre of it. As she passed the burned-out dwellings, the corpses, she tried not to look at the horror, but her eyes were drawn to it. Even the livestock was dead, a pig here, a sheep there, gutted and left to rot in the snow. But why? Wouldn't the Franks have at least taken them away and added them to their own stock? This was just waste. A whole town gutted and slaughtered and left in the wake of the rampaging Franks. A message perhaps? But to who? Gisela could have spent the rest of her life trying to work that out and not come up with an answer.

Or maybe the answer was plain. Five hundred men had come through here leaving nought but devastation behind. Consuming this land like a plague. Domination was all they knew, the only method to this madness. Gisela had heard just how savage these northerners were supposed to be, but they had been met by savagery much worse.

A shrill cry went up from somewhere near. It was muffled,

maybe someone trapped in one of those burning buildings, and before Gisela knew it her feet were tramping across the ashen ground to find them.

She clutched her baby tight to her chest, feeling her begin to mewl. The scream went up again, this time quieter, but oh so close. Gisela turned to see a house standing at the edge of the town, stone and thatch still intact. The door was ajar, and in the murky shadows she could make out movement inside.

Closer, and she heard voices – men's voices. Movement in the dark, someone struggling. A Frankish knight stumbled from the house just as she ran up to it. There was a gap-toothed grin on his wide face, his dark surcoat bearing a proud eagle. It was the only noble thing about him.

Inside the house was more movement, more violence. Gisela knew what was going on. Knew someone was being defiled beyond that threshold. She should have run, but the fear would not come. Only the red rage of anger.

'Let that woman go,' she spat, just as the knight noticed her advance.

His brow twisted – confusion, mirth, annoyance. 'On your way, bitch. Or you'll be next.'

Gisela was shaking. Her daughter had begun to squirm, sensing the discomfort, the ire. 'I said, let her go.'

The knight leaned in, his grin widening. 'Fuck off, or you'll be next. And your whining spawn'll come after.'

'This is the child of Ronan of Dol-Combourg,' she snarled back at that ugly face. 'You dare to threaten us?'

The knight's leer wavered. Good fortune that he recognised the name and the reputation that went along with it. The doubt didn't last long, before his expression changed to one of indifference.

'Why would I care what the cripple's whore demands? Be on your way before you feel my boot up your arse.'

'Let that woman go,' Gisela demanded. She was standing her ground as best she could, but her stubbornness was waning. To add to her doubts, the baby gave a wail.

The knight glanced over his shoulder, then turned back with a more steely look to him. 'You might be Ronan's bitch, but the cripple holds no sway here. We follow Lord Robert.'

'You'll release that girl, if I have to come in there—'

The shock of his mailed hand striking her cheek rocked her backwards. One step, two, her feet barely keeping purchase on the frozen earth.

'Piss off, whore. And take your bastard with you.'

She barely heard the words through the ringing in her ears as she stumbled to one side, then the other. Blood trickled from the corner of her mouth. Her eyes had filled with tears as the baby shrieked from the bottom of her lungs in time to the breathy sobs and laughter from inside that house.

Oh that Styrkar were here. He would have wreaked such vengeance. Would have slaughtered every man here for laying a hand on her. But her lover was not here. He was dead and gone, and she would never see his face again.

Even as she began to run north she felt the shame of leaving that woman to her fate, but she was impotent, unable to raise a hand to help. Not even Ronan's reputation had forced doubt upon those bastards, and now she was running as though wolves were on her scent.

She took the muddy road, following the wagon tracks north, and before long had lost a shoe in the bog. Not long after the other was lost along with it and she was tramping bare foot, mud slick on her legs and cloak, gripping tight to her squalling child. By the time she reached the camp she was half frozen. Tents had already been erected, pennants flying, the crests of every knight fluttering proudly.

How dare they display themselves with such pomposity. They had nothing to be proud of, these curs.

Still enrapt in the haze of her fury, she saw Wealdberg making her way across the camp. Gisela tramped up to her, forgetting her numb toes and the blood dried to her lips.

'Where is Ronan?' she demanded.

Wealdberg looked astonished to see her, those hard eyes narrowing as she saw the blood.

'What's happened to—'

'Where in hell is Ronan?' she repeated.

Wealdberg motioned to the far end of the camp where the pennants of Mallet and Comines flew. 'He's over there. But I wouldn't go disturbing him, they're talking about—'

'Take her,' Gisela said, bundling the baby into Wealdberg's arms. 'See she's kept warm, she must be freezing.'

No sooner had Wealdberg taken the child than Gisela stalked across the camp toward the largest tent. There was no one to stop her as she grabbed the flap and wrenched it aside, heedless of the men talking within, determined to find a target for her ire. Ronan turned immediately at her interruption, his eyes widening as he saw the state of her face and her shoeless, muddy feet. Robert turned more slowly, measured, regarding her with a raised eyebrow, as though a bird had just shit on his jerkin.

'Monster,' Gisela gasped, suddenly finding herself breathless.

Robert glanced about as though she might have been talking to someone else, before offering a shrug. She knew her opinion mattered less than that of the fur rug that lay on the ground between them, and it only served to anger her further.

'Gisela, you need to leave,' Ronan said, taking a faltering step toward her.

'Bastard,' she shouted, finding her breath at last. 'You think you will conquer this land by razing every village? As long as you let your men murder innocent people you will never hold sway here. You will only enflame yet more rebellion against you.'

She saw Ronan close his eyes, expecting Robert's inevitable tirade, but instead a smile crept up the brute's face.

'I don't often discuss matters of strategy with women,' he replied. 'But just this once I'll break my own rule.' He took a step toward her. When she didn't retreat he stopped, his smile wavering for the briefest moment before changing to a grin. 'I intend to stamp my authority on the north. I intend to speak the only language these people truly understand. For years they have been at one another's throats. Village against village. Kingdom against kingdom. Their leaders are petty and mean and vicious, and will only obey when they are under the heel of a mightier warlord. I intend to be that warlord. And I will stamp my heel with all the authority of my king.'

'Your king?' she said, voice calmer now. 'Do you think he would approve of what you have allowed your men to do?'

'The king is well aware of my methods. Why else would he have sent *me* to do the deed?'

'Does he know he has sent a coward? A pig who orders the rape of women, the murder of children?'

Robert took another step forward. Gisela glanced at Ronan but he looked powerless to interfere. It was clear she was on her own.

'He knows. And neither does he care. The northern scum of this country live and die at my pleasure.' He leaned in so close she could smell his stinking breath. 'And so do you.'

'I think that will do,' said Ronan, stumbling forward, grasping her arm and all but dragging her from the tent.

She could hear Robert begin to chuckle, amused at their encounter, where she was just further incensed. Ronan had not led her more than twenty yards before she snatched her arm away from his, watching as he struggled to maintain his balance on the hard earth.

'You haven't changed have you?' she snarled. He looked a little hurt, a little confused at that, but she carried on regardless. 'I thought you might have. I thought I had managed to tease some good out of you, but you're just the same. Just as cruel.'

He held up a hand as though to appease her. 'I don't have any choice, Gisela.'

'Of course you have a choice.'

His shoulders slumped in defeat. If he'd had any notion of reasoning with her it was gone now. 'I don't. But you do. You're free to leave, if this is too much. Take your infant and go where you wish.'

'I may just do that,' she snapped.

'But there's just one problem. Where would you go now?'

Gisela realised her teeth were clenched. The words she had been so eager to share with the most dangerous

Frankish knight in the north had fled her, and now Ronan had asked her the most difficult question of all.

With no answer, she turned and made her way back across the camp. Her baby needed her, and it seemed she was powerless to help anyone else.

28

Tantone, England, December 1068

The days were cold, the nights colder still, bringing a chill that not even three wolfskins could keep out of Styrkar's bones.

He watched from the cage as the hound keeper went about his nightly business by the light of a torch. The man was old, stooped by his years, but from his proud bearing it was likely he'd been a warrior once. Perhaps one of the fyrd, maybe even a housecarl. He performed his duties as though he'd been born to it, treating those dogs with an unusual affection. Perhaps too much affection. From what Styrkar knew the last thing you wanted were hounds eating from your hand, especially if they were to be any use in the hunt. They had to be vicious. Lean. Hungry for the kill. But here was an old man treating them like a bunch of eager children, and he their kindly uncle.

When he'd finished he threw his sack of bones over his shoulder and turned to leave, before reconsidering. Almost as an afterthought, he fished in that sack, took a step toward

Styrkar's cage and flung one of his bones. He paused then, regarding Styrkar with some sorrow.

'Won't be much longer,' he mumbled in the same voice he'd used to soothe his dogs. 'There's a cold front coming. It's not likely you'll make it through the rest of winter, lad. Should be a mercy.'

With that, he turned and walked away, taking his torchlight with him.

Styrkar sat looking at that bone in the moonlight. Any other night he'd have reached for it, coveted it, gnawed at it till his teeth ached. This time he reached out through the bars of his cage, picked up the bone and flung it toward the hounds. They strained on their leashes, whining hungrily at the bone that lay just out of reach.

Fuck his hunger. There was more to do than feast on scraps.

He sat for a while, waiting for all to go quiet, making sure he was alone with the dogs. Since he'd killed the warrior in the feast hall he'd been all but forgotten, a corpse-in-waiting, left on the outskirts of town. When he was sure there'd be no one stumbling by to see, he scrabbled in the mud at the corner of the cage, unearthing the rusted tip of the sword, though now it was blunted, most of that rust scraped off. It still had a bit of an edge, though. Enough of an edge for what he needed.

Styrkar pulled one of the wolfskins tight about his shoulder as he crouched low and continued to work at the wooden bar. Over the past few days he'd whittled away at that wood and he was almost through. Almost free. It was solid oak, and he only had a tiny piece of metal to use as a saw, but given enough time a man could work through anything.

He barely perceived the cold, barely noticed it creeping at him, chilling him, clawing with its freezing fingers as he sawed and sawed. So frantic was he that his fingers began to bleed, but pain was no stranger and easy enough to ignore. Eagerness turned to desperation. He'd promised himself he would not spend another night caged. This had to happen now.

The wooden bar in his hand began to loosen, spurring him to greater heights of exertion. With a final frantic effort it broke with a crack. Styrkar pulled it free, glaring through the breach in the bars. It was a slim gap to freedom. A few months ago he would have struggled to fit between the opening, but now he found himself squeezing through with little trouble.

As he made his way from the compound he paused. Each of the hounds was staring at him, some inclining their heads in confusion, others panting, tongues lolling. Not one of them barked in alarm. He could only guess they envied him his new-found release, glad that one of their number had found his freedom.

Styrkar clung to the shadows as he crept into the town. The road through its centre was empty, everyone kept in their homes by the cold. He should have run, should have leapt over the palisade and put as much distance between himself and Tantone as he could.

But the Red Wolf would not allow him.

It thirsted. And there was only one way that thirst could be slaked. Harding was somewhere close by, and until the

Red Wolf had drunk of his blood there would be no freedom for Styrkar the Dane.

His cloth-bound feet crunched through a dusting of snow as he made his way toward the centre of the town, clinging to the shadows. Across the road he caught sight of the huge building that resembled a forge, but this was no blacksmith's dwelling. The mint of Tantone had been built for the forging of coins, the centre of the south's wealth. Even now, in the dead of night, men sat guarding it, warming themselves over a firepit. Styrkar should have struck forward and murdered them. Should have burned down that symbol of the king's power, but that would only have resulted in his death. And he had to live, if only long enough to see Harding perish.

Leaving the mint behind, he struck forward through the dark. Harding's lodge was not much further, and he could just see it towering over the surrounding buildings. When Styrkar had first been here there had been a trail of men making pilgrimage to pledge themselves to Eadnoth. Now its doors were shut to the cold night, but they would not keep out the Red Wolf.

All was quiet. For a moment he considered beating at those doors, calling on Harding to answer for his deeds, demanding that he face him in combat. But the coward Harding would never answer such a call. Styrkar's death would come at the end of a dozen spears and he would never have a chance to see himself avenged.

Instead he slipped into the shadows, moving around the side of the great hall. There had to be an open window, perhaps a door at the rear for the comings and goings of thralls.

Before he made it around the perimeter of the lodge, he saw firelight casting flickering shadows from the rear of the building. There was no noise but the whispering breeze and the crackle of burning wood. Styrkar crept to the corner of the great hall and peered around it.

Sitting by the fire was the old hound master, huddled in a fur cloak. His knobbly fingers worked at the fletching of an arrow as he tied a feather to the shaft. He gazed down the length through one eye, making sure it was straight, before tightening the twine, then another look before more tightening.

Should Styrkar have stolen forward and fallen on the man from the shadows?

It's not likely you'll make it through the rest of winter, lad. Those had been his words. Spoken with some sympathy, if Styrkar hadn't missed his intent. Did a man like that deserve to be murdered in the cold and the dark? What would it make him if he killed a man who had shown pity to a beast such as the Red Wolf?

He walked from the shadows to stand by the light of the fire. Its warmth enveloped him like a welcome from an old friend, and Styrkar thought he might have stood in that heat for the rest of his days and damn the consequence. Instead he sat on a stool not far from the hound keeper's. As he did so, the old man made no move to stop him, nor reach for a weapon, nor open his mouth to call out. He just lowered that arrow, his eyes fixed on his savage guest.

Styrkar was aware of what he must look like – all wild and bedraggled, half-starved and desperate – but the old man just looked on him as though he were any one of the townsfolk come to pass the time.

'It is a cold night to be sitting outside,' Styrkar said. All the while he could feel the Red Wolf rumbling inside, still thirsting for blood, still wary of danger.

The old man placed his half-finished arrow down. 'I am old and I prefer my own company these days. The cold don't bother me the way is does most folk, and being locked inside just makes the winter nights last longer. I have little need for the comforts of indoors. I'll be plenty comfortable when I'm dead, I reckon.'

It sounded a good enough explanation. 'Does Harding sleep within?' Styrkar gestured to the lodge that held them both in its shadow.

The old man glanced over his shoulder as though he only just noticed the feast hall he sat beside, then looked back in the fire. Was he weighing up whether to be loyal, or whether to answer truthfully? Whichever, he finally decided on honesty.

'My lord rests in his longhouse. But you'll be dead three times over before you reach him.'

'That's as maybe. But I have no choice but to try.'

The man shook his head. 'Even were you twice the man you used to be, it's a foolish idea, lad. You're free now. Take the road from Tantone and don't look back. It's the only way you'll live.'

They were encouraging words, but even as he spoke them, Styrkar saw the old man's wrinkled hand move toward the knife at his belt.

'Even if Styrkar the Dane thought it a wise choice, the Red Wolf would not,' Styrkar said, holding the old man's gaze. 'And in the end, the wolf always wins.'

'We all have a choice.' His hand still moved, ever so slow, toward the blade.

'No. Most often we don't.'

Styrkar cleared the gap between them before the old man could slide the blade from its sheath. He clamped one hand on his withered wrist, tightening the other about his throat as they both fell to the frozen earth. Despite days of malnourishment, Styrkar was still more than a match for the hound keeper, but he could tell he had once been strong.

He squeezed the old man's wrist, tightening his grip until the knife fell from his hand. Releasing his throat he reached for the weapon but the man managed to grab his hair, letting out a yell – a desperate cry that echoed up from the side of the lodge, above the town and into the cold night air.

Styrkar raised the knife, teeth gritted, and for a moment he paused. This old man had done him no real harm. If anything he'd been the only one who'd treated him as anything more than an animal. Styrkar would have spared him for that, at least. The Red Wolf would not.

His blade plunged into the man's chest, between the ribs and into the meat like he was carving the tenderest cut. The hound keeper's bellow turned to a sigh, and he breathed his last right into Styrkar's face.

He stood gingerly, feeling the ache in his limbs, still holding the knife tight in his fist. Damn that old man. Dead in the night, when he should have been lying safe in his bed. If he had forgotten his loyalty to Harding there would have been no need for him to die. But Styrkar knew better than anyone how deep the seed of loyalty could be planted.

A shout from somewhere close wrenched him from his

regret. Clattering within the longhouse, the sound of feet on the wooden floor. Along the passage between the lodge and its adjacent huts he saw the shadows of warriors appear at the far end.

Any thought of vengeance was gone. Any chance of stealing inside and finding Harding was now burned to ash. Styrkar dashed for the safety of the shadows, the knife still in his grip.

He stumbled blindly, feet like blocks of ice as they pounded the hard ground. The snow was starting to fall; with any luck it would help conceal him as he fled.

In the distant light of a torch, he saw the palisade. A ladder of rickety stairs led up to the parapet, and he almost tripped as he reached the bottom. He gripped the knife in his teeth as he scrambled up the ladder, reaching the top just as more voices rose in a crescendo behind him.

The wind struck him as he reached the summit, blowing hard over the edge of the wooden wall. Beyond it was blackness, the open wilds concealed under a blanket of shadow.

Gripping the edge of the palisade, Styrkar flung himself out into the night. He sucked in a breath, the knife falling from his mouth, the cold air freezing his lungs as he was thrust into the void. Then the earth hit him like a boulder, and he gasped out the lungful of air in a long wheeze.

Quickly he scrambled to his feet, veiled in the dark, pulling his threadbare cloak of fur about him before stumbling into the night toward his freedom. He had taken no more than a dozen steps before a bell rang in his wake, rising from within Tantone, reminding him as he fled that he was far from free yet.

29

Yorke, England, December 1068

The cathedral looked like it was on fire. Or perhaps it was just wreathed in smoke from the other buildings; it was difficult to tell with such a black fog swirling around the city. A burning stink hung in the air, coarse and sharp in Ronan's throat. Almost as sharp as the screams ringing out like a knell over those rooftops.

He was glad to be in the tower atop its hill, secluded from the raping and the looting. Such things gave him no more pleasure, if indeed they ever had. All his previous butchery had merely been a means to an end. Ronan was no sadist. Or so he kept telling himself. Still trying to act the good man, despite all evidence to the contrary.

Still, those cries of woe struck him as discordant, a dirge that offended his ears. For the two men he shared the tower with, it seemed more a jubilant tune to which they might dance a jig, had they a mind to.

Robert and Guillam stood side by side, gazing from the wide window, surveying their handiwork. The contrast between the two men struck Ronan as he observed them. Guillam towered, tall and handsome, his hair combed neatly, moustache trimmed. Beside him, Robert struck a much more brutal figure – squat, bald, hulking about the shoulders. Despite their physical differences though, they were very much of the same mind, and shared the same methods.

'To your success in the north,' Guillam said, raising his cup.

'And to your new appointment, sheriff,' Robert replied, clacking his cup against Guillam's so hard that wine sloshed over the brim.

It was true that Mallet now stood as High Sheriff of Yorke, but he seemed distinctly unconcerned that the city from which he would govern was now in flames, and several hundred knights still ran rampant through its streets.

Behind them, Ronan could only watch, his stomach churning with revulsion. Was it just the smoke? Or was it disgust at what he was being forced to endure? Either way, his bloody leg screamed as he was forced to stand and celebrate. Perhaps he should have made his excuses and left. Did either of these men even know he was present? It was doubtful they would care either way.

He turned, stumbling on his crippled leg, using the wall to keep him on his feet. A scream pealed out, and Ronan felt himself shudder at the noise as he left the room and limped along the passage. The flash of a memory ignited in his field of vision. A memory long buried. The flames as a house burned, the screams of so many people. Men, women and children locked inside on his order.

Ronan squeezed his eyes shut at the thought of it, but

it remained there, burning into his eyelids. The sound torturing him with its resolute timbre.

What the fuck was wrong with him? This was not how it was supposed to be. Those people were beneath him, worthless peasants all. He had never cared about the consequences of his actions, but since that knife in his side, since those days and weeks teetering on the brink, he had grown... what was it? A conscience?

He shook his head to clear the memories, casting them off as best he could before all but falling down the stairs to the ground floor of the tower. He stumbled to the room set aside for his use, opening the door and shutting it behind him, shutting out the memories.

Gisela sat in a chair holding her child close, staring through the narrow slit of a window. There wasn't much to see, but the sound of butchery still drifted in. The smell of it permeating the air. She did not speak, but he could feel the fire coming from her, blazing brighter than the flames that now consumed Yorke.

'This will not last,' Ronan breathed. 'Once this business is done, we can leave. We can find somewhere new far from all this, just the three of us.'

She shook her head, still staring through that narrow gap. 'You are a fool, Ronan.' Her voice was quiet but he could still hear the steel in it. The disdain. 'This will never be over. The Franks burn and murder, and the English will rise up in response. Then your people will purge their rebellion, and on and on and on.'

'Then we'll leave this cursed country. All of us. I will take you to Frankia. To Flanders—'

She laughed. It was shrill, on the verge of hysterics, as

though he had told her the wittiest of tales. Slowly she turned her head, and he could see that her eyes were misted with tears.

'I was going to go back there with Styrkar. We were both going to escape, but we stayed in that old villa on the coast. A new life for the both of us. Until you came.'

Gisela stood, placing the sleeping child in a crib he had found for her. It had not been easy to locate, but Ronan had thought it only fitting and made the effort anyway. Every child should have somewhere safe to sleep, but as he heard one more distant cry from the city, he knew that there would be dozens of other children sleeping on the streets tonight.

'I was... I was hoping we—'

Gisela turned, a tear running down her cheek. 'Hoping what? That we would run away together? Start a new life? Fall in love? Marry beneath an old willow and live out our days as a family? Are you mad? Or just so deluded, Ronan, that you would think that was possible?'

She stared, gritting her teeth, clenching her fists. He thought she might rush forward and beat him with her balled hands, but instead she stood still as the city burned around her, and he had never seen such a look of hate.

There was a time when Ronan would have grown angry at such a rebuttal. Would have forced her to do his bidding, to see things his way. Now he only felt as though his heart were being squeezed in a fist. His only desire was to lie down and wait for the world to end while he wept.

The door swung open, a cold breeze blowing through the room, bringing a stronger stink of smoke with it. Ronan turned to chastise the intruder but stopped when he saw the man's face.

'What's this?' Robert asked, cup still held in one hand. 'A lover's squabble?'

The ache in Ronan's chest moved down to his gut. He took a painful step toward the crib, an absent gesture of protection. One he found hard to understand, but accepted nonetheless. Gisela stood in silence, glancing toward Ronan, toward her baby. He could see the struggle in her tear-filled eyes, her fear and anger fighting one another as she tried to subdue both emotions.

Robert stepped into the room. He stank of wine and wore the boorish cloak of a drunkard. Casually he regarded the crib, raising an eyebrow before also raising his cup in a mock toast.

'A blessing,' he said. 'It warms the heart, truly it does. I have not seen my own spawn for the longest time. Did you know I had children of my own?'

Ronan found it hard to believe a man who would show such wanton disregard for the offspring of others could be a father. Not one of much worth anyway. He glanced to Gisela, seeing that her anger was waning, overtaken by fear, before looking back to Robert and shaking his head.

Robert took another step forward, gazing into that crib, to the child that lay sleeping within. 'She's a beauty and no mistake. Look at the red of her hair, never seen anything like it.'

Ronan forced a smile. 'You are right, Lord Robert, we are truly blessed.'

Robert regarded him with those watery eyes, his lips turning up into a sneer before he barked his contempt. 'Fuck off, Dol-Combourg. As if that child's yours. That's a Saxon bastard if ever I laid eyes on one.'

Gisela moved toward Robert as though she might strike him, but managed to stay her hand. Her fear was gone now. Only hate remained.

'The only bastard here is you,' she spat. 'You're nothing but a butcher.'

The silence that followed filled Ronan with a dread he had never felt before. He had feared for his own life more than once; on the field at Senlac, in a half-dozen battles before it, and many since. But now he knew all was lost. The axe was falling, and he could not think of a way to stop it.

Robert regarded her with his amused expression before draining his cup and tossing it aside to rattle against the stone floor. Ronan expected his rage, but it did not come. Instead he shrugged, as though agreeing wholeheartedly with her assessment of him.

'Perhaps you're right,' he said, almost on the brink of slurring, but not quite. 'These are times of great upheaval. They bring out the worst in all of us. And I am a man who has, in the past, profited from such times. Some might call that a sin. Only God can be the judge.'

As he turned back toward the door, Ronan felt his shoulders sag, the tension momentarily lifted. Robert pulled the knife from his belt so casually Ronan barely noticed. He thrust it into Gisela's belly with such practised precision it seemed the most natural thing in the world.

Ronan staggered forward as she fell with a gasp. He managed to catch her, ignoring the pain in his cursed leg, grasping her head, clamping his other hand to the wound. She lay in his arms for a moment, before he felt her hand cover his. Was this the first time she had touched him since he had been wounded and lay in his deathbed? So many days he had yearned for that touch, and now it was to stem the tide of blood that seeped through both their fingers.

She gazed at him, those tearful eyes drunkenly searching for something as her mouth moved but no words came. A trickle of blood escaped the side of her lips.

Robert stopped as he reached the door, turning with a look of sympathy as he wiped his knife clean on one sleeve. 'Don't feel too bad, Dol-Combourg. I doubt it would have worked out between you anyway.'

Gisela's eyes drifted toward the crib, her hand reaching out. The baby began to squall, but there was nothing to be done. No one to calm her as her mother lay dying.

The door squeaked on its hinge as Robert opened it. 'I ride for Dun Holm in the morning. I won't be needing you to join me.' Ronan glared up at him, feeling his impotent rage simmering inside. Knowing he was powerless to do anything about what had just happened. 'Perhaps you should go back to your friend Brian. The north is clearly not the right place for you. It's obvious you don't have the stomach for it.'

With that he walked out of the room.

Ronan felt Gisela press something into his hand. Her breathing was shallow and she looked tired, as though she were about to fall asleep. He looked down to see the carving of the wooden wolf in his bloodstained palm. A last gift from her one love. And now she had given it to him.

Ronan would have told her he didn't deserve it. That she should not think to give a man such as him anything so precious. His words would have been wasted. Gisela stared toward the crib, but the last breath in her body had already fled.

As Ronan held her, to the sound of distant cries mixing with the stink of smoke and blood, the child wailed for her mother.

30

Glestingaburg, England, December 1068

He loped across snow-covered hills, the landscape rolling on ahead of him through a perpetual white haze. The Red Wolf's breath came in short gasps, blowing out a stream of mist before he clutched at another lungful of air like a man drowning. He dared a look over his shoulder, seeing nothing through the white curtain, but he knew they were following, relentless in pursuit of their quarry.

How he would have loved to stop, to wait for them to come racing at him, to challenge them, and then die engaged in one last act of savagery. But survival was all he could think on.

The hill ran down to woodland, and he almost lost his footing as he raced toward it. His feet felt like stumps, chilled to numbness by the cold. As he entered the trees, the relief he felt beneath those sheltering boughs was short-lived. Above the wind, the keening howl of hounds shattered the peace of the woodland.

He paused, taking a breath as he leaned against the

frozen trunk of an oak. It would not be long before they caught up. Not long before he felt the jaws of those hounds tear at his clothes, at his flesh. Perhaps he should choose to stand here, to at least conserve his energy for the fight. But no. It would be an ignominious end, to be torn apart like some fallow deer at the end of a hunt. Better to carry on, better to expend his last reserves in flight. Who knew what salvation might lie ahead?

Gritting his teeth against the cold and fatigue he ploughed on once more through the trees. With every step it felt as though the sound of those hounds was growing nearer, plaguing him with the constant threat of capture. The treeline came out at the brow of a hill, and he stumbled, losing his footing on the uneven earth before tumbling down and down to the bank of a stream.

No time to think, no time to assess. The Red Wolf scrambled to his feet, enduring the icy waters as he waded knee-deep, hoping against hope that the stream would hide his scent. Knowing that it would not.

A hill at the far bank and he was scrambling for purchase, ignoring the chill infesting his bones. At the brow he stopped. The barking of hounds was close. From the summit of the hill he could see for miles around. There was woodland not far to the north but he would never reach it before those dogs came. It seemed there would be no salvation.

His laugh started as a low rumble, carried on a wheezing breath. It turned to a bellow, roaring from the depths of his gut, echoing to the white desolate land.

'Enough running,' he whispered to the winter air, turning to face his fate.

The first of the hounds was already splashing through

the stream, its coat slick with wet. It mounted the bank on the other side and paused only long enough to shake the water from its fur, before bounding toward the hill. The rest weren't far behind, half a dozen of them, barking their excitement now their prey was in sight.

As soon as the first hound reached the top it stopped, hackles raised, teeth bared in a snarl. After such a long pursuit it was panting heavily, steam issuing from that growling maw. Now it had found its prey it paused, unsure of whether it should attack without the help of the pack.

The Red Wolf stood, staring down that hound, waiting on the rest to appear. Should he take the initiative? Grasp the beast about the neck and throttle it before the others came? Before he could decide the answer it was too late either way.

Without a sound the rest of the hounds mounted the crest of the hill. Their barking had stopped, the hunt over with. They circled him, unsure of what to do, and with that glimmer of doubt, the Red Wolf thought that perhaps he had a chance after all.

He recognised every one of these dogs, he had been caged with them for weeks, shared food with them, shared the cold with them. But for the bars of his cage to separate them, the Red Wolf might have been accepted as a member of this pack. Perhaps it was not too late.

Slowly he knelt, keeping his eye on that lead dog. As he did so its snarling stopped, its muscles untensing as it reconsidered its instinctive urge to pounce, to rip and tear. With a grunt he beckoned the beast closer. As though heeding its master, the hound padded forward, the rest of the pack looking on curiously as it came to sit before the

Red Wolf. He reached out a hand feeling the damp fur, ruffling its neck as it shivered with him in the cold.

When the leader showed no aggression to their prey, so the rest of the pack sat calmly, watching on as their breath misted. There would be no kill today. For now the hunt was over.

As Styrkar rose to his feet at the top of the hill he could see movement at the treeline. Men in heavy cloaks just visible as they left the woods. Time to run once more. Only now as he made his way down from the hill there was no barking in his wake – no sound at all as he ran across open fields and into the welcoming embrace of the forest.

There was a fire in the distance, barely visible through the trees. It beckoned to him, tempting him with the promise of warmth, but still he lurked in the darkness. Watching, waiting for his moment.

He could smell meat cooking on that fire. Rabbit most likely. Taunting him till drool threatened to run down his chin. Still, he had to wait. These men were awake, their blood up from the chase. But they could not stay awake all night.

One eye he kept closed to preserve his night vision. The other stared longingly as he hunkered in the dark outside the clearing. Those hounds were tethered now, lying next to the fire, as their masters talked in the dark. The Red Wolf moved closer that he might better hear their words. He could only hope an opportunity to attack came soon before he froze to death in the shadows.

'Never seen hounds act that way,' said one of the men.

He was just visible through the treeline, leering at those dogs with disdain.

'Maybe they just lost his scent,' said another.

'What is he, a bloody ghost? Dogs don't just lose scent of what they're hunting at the top of a bloody hill.'

'This whole thing's a fool's errand,' said a third. 'If Harding wants that bastard so badly why isn't he out here freezing his arse off?'

'You don't have a dog and bark yourself, I suppose,' said a fourth hunter, sounding more mournful than the rest put together.

Silence, until one of them stood, pulling the furs tighter about his shoulders. 'I'm away for a piss. Make sure that fire's still burning when I get back.'

The Red Wolf tensed in the dark, every muscle poised. Perhaps he would not wait till they all slept. This was an opportunity he could not let go.

As the man blundered into the woods, making a racket as he fought his way through the foliage, the Red Wolf moved in silence. He paused behind the man as he undrew his cock. Poised to strike as he heard the piss patter against the frozen ground. No sooner had the hunter finished than he pounced.

The man struggled, grabbing the arm that was locked around his throat, wrenching him back. They both fell, legs kicking desperately for purchase, but the Red Wolf held his prey firm. He squeezed, tighter, harder, teeth gnashing, hoping against hope that the sound of their struggle did not bring anyone from the camp. A laugh echoed through the trees, long and loud, and as the man in his arms went limp, the Red Wolf breathed a sigh.

He rolled the body over, stripping off the cloak, resisting the temptation to wrap it around his shoulders and feel the latent warmth of the man's body. Then slowly he slid the sword from the dead man's scabbard. Now it was the Red Wolf's turn to hunt.

The three men around the fire laughed again as he stalked the perimeter of their camp. He could see them clearly through the sparse treeline, one of his eyes still shut, the other glaring with hate. Kneeling, he waited, trying his best to ignore the remains of a charred coney on its skewer over the fire, hoping his stomach would not rumble too loudly from the dark.

When more time had passed one of the hunters stood, looking curiously into the wood.

'Alwin?' he shouted.

When there was no answer the hunters looked to one another with growing concern.

'Where the frigging hell is he?' one asked, the youngest of their number by the look of him.

Another of them drew his blade. 'Can't have gone far,' he breathed, but his eyes were locked on the trees. He knew something was afoot.

'Alwin?' they shouted again.

More silence.

All three of them were on their feet. The light from the fire was dimming, the encroaching shadows of the forest closing in on them. The Red Wolf could almost smell the stink of their fear.

He stooped, picking up a stone, then flung it at the edge of the trees on the far side of the camp. Every one of the three flinched, one of them darting forward, hefting his sword threateningly. They all had their backs to him now, and he moved forward, holding the fur cloak in his hand. With a sweep of his arm he stifled the winnowing flames with the cloak, plunging the clearing into blackness. In that instant, he opened his other eye, the one still accustomed to the dark.

The first of them turned, but the Red Wolf was already moving, leaping over the cloak, sword raised. He brought it down with all his might, cleaving the man's forehead, cracking the skull. As the corpse fell, a second hunter staggered back, blinded in the dark, reeling in terror.

A thrust of his blade and the man's neck was laid open. He gurgled as the Red Wolf wrenched the sword free, looking to the last man, ready to end him before he could think to retaliate.

As he darted forward to cast that final blow, the man turned tail and fled into the woods. The dogs were barking now, raising their voices to the moon at the first sign of violence. It was deafening, but only served to spur the Red Wolf on. He bolted in pursuit of the final hunter, sprinting through the woods to the sound of barking dogs. To his ear it was as though they were urging him on to hunt, to chase down his quarry and feast.

The pursuit was brief. Through dark shadows he could see the man stumbling, half blind and stricken with panic. As he reached a clearing, moonlight streaming in through a gap in the canopy, the man turned his ankle on a tree root. His gasp of pain was high pitched, the sound of his fall heavy on the hard winter ground. The sword had fallen from his grip and as he floundered, the Red Wolf took his time.

'Please,' the hunter said, as he saw his doom approaching. Saw the hate in those eyes. Saw the intent. 'We were just doing as Harding told us. I've got no quarrel with you.'

A moment of pause. The Red Wolf looked down at the man, pathetic as he was. Perhaps it was the cold and the hunger, but for a moment he thought of leaving him be. Of showing at least a little mercy. Then he saw what the man had about his throat.

An iron band. The head of a wolf at each end.

'That's mine,' the Red Wolf breathed as he pointed his sword.

The hunter nodded. 'Take it,' he replied, trying his best to pull it free, but he couldn't loosen it enough to take it off. He began to sob as he struggled, pulling desperately but it seemed his neck had grown too fat for the torc.

A sweep of the sword, and the Red Wolf loosened his head from his shoulders.

Picking up the bloodied torc, he turned and made his way back through the trees. By the time he reached the camp, he saw the fur cloak had caught aflame, the fire burning anew in the middle of the clearing. There, the Red Wolf sat amid the corpses, eating his fill of their abandoned meal with no one but hounds for company. Later, he would don their clothes and take their weapons, but for now he had to rest awhile.

31

Hagenesse, England, January 1069

They rode east, heads bowed against the frigid cold. Every mile it felt as though the air grew that much chiller, the wind blowing in from the sea and threatening to freeze them in their saddles. Ronan glanced back, seeing Mainard hunkered atop his horse, hood pulled low over his face. Perhaps he should have felt thankful he had at least one man still loyal to him in this godforsaken country. Whether Mainard was loyal, or fulfilling his duty for his own ends, was still in question. Right now, Ronan had a duty of his own to think on.

He peered into his cloak, at the bundle secured there safe against the cold. The nameless child was sleeping, untroubled by the inclement weather. Ronan felt a pang of jealousy at that. She was still innocent, unaware of what had happened to the land she was born to. Probably for the best. Let her slumber in her ignorance, it was not her fault she had been birthed into such a riotous age.

'This fucking country will be the death of me,' Mainard snapped above the sound of the wind.

The baby stirred at the sudden outburst, and Ronan rocked her gently, easing her disquiet. He would have chided Mainard for disturbing her slumber, but for the fact he may well have been right. This country might still be the death of them all.

'We should have heeded Guillam's warning,' Mainard continued, his mouth loosened by the cold and the worry. 'He told us not to leave Yorke. That this was a bloody fool's errand. We could still be there, warm by a fire, with mead and a comely Danish whore for company.'

'Fuck Guillam,' Ronan replied, still rocking the child, in no mood to hear her wail.

Mainard shrugged. 'I don't like him any more than you do. Nor bloody Robert. But defying them is folly. They are beasts in human form and I wouldn't want to be the object of their ire for all the gold in England.'

Ronan could well understand Mainard's concern, but he was well past fearing for his own life. He should have killed Robert for what he'd done. Should have drawn his blade and cut the bastard down, and to hell with the consequences. But he hadn't. He had done nothing but hold Gisela till the last drop of lifeblood had spilled from her corpse. Then he'd buried her in a pauper's grave and bought the only stone he could afford to mark her passing.

He gazed down at the child, fast asleep once more. She held little resemblance to her mother. To Ronan's eye she looked more like Styrkar. It should have angered him to see such a resemblance to his hated enemy, but instead it only served to remind him of what he owed. As he thought on that, he began to doubt whether he was doing the right thing. Would Gisela have wanted this? Or would she have wanted Ronan to take care of her child himself? He almost laughed at that, but the cold had already frozen his mouth into a rictus snarl. What would he do with an orphan child? He was a knight in service to a conqueror, not a wet nurse. This was the best thing to do for her, there was no other option. Gisela's daughter had to be hidden as far from his countrymen as Ronan could get her.

As he saw the priory at the end of the road ahead, he realised it was too late to doubt himself anyway. There looked to be nothing remarkable about the place considering it was such a holy site. Just one more crumbling tower in this country filled with ruins.

'Is this the right place?' Mainard asked, screwing up his nose.

'Can you see any other buildings in this blasted land? What other place could it be?'

Ronan had asked the hedge-witch who helped Gisela give birth where was best for the child now the mother had passed. He had expected her to offer to take the infant, but instead she had told him of this priory, and how it took in orphans from across the country. It had seemed a sensible choice at the time, but now he began to have his doubts. The building was virtually a ruin, but nevertheless, they were here now. Perhaps it was warm and welcoming inside at least.

They rode their horses into what passed for the priory's courtyard, little more than a muddy yard. Ronan paused as he gazed at the rundown building. Maybe he should just leave the child on the doorstep, give the nuns inside little option but to care for her. But as he gazed down at the infant, he knew he owed her more than that. The least he could do was ensure she was placed in good hands.

He slid his leg over the saddle, struggling to the ground, feeling the pain in his cursed foot. Gritting his teeth he limped toward the door, holding the precious bundle tight to his chest. The wood was rotten just under the lintel and when he knocked sharply the door rattled in its frame. This looked a cold harsh place, well suited to this cold harsh land, and Ronan's doubts only intensified the longer he regarded it. As the silence wore on he considered giving up on the idea altogether, but before he could turn and make his way back to the waiting steed, he heard the sound of bolts being slid back.

The door opened a crack, an old and weary face peering out at him. The woman wore her nun's habit close over her brow. Her wrinkled face peered out from the dank interior as though she had been disturbed a dozen times that morning and was growing irritated by the constant intrusions.

'Who disrupts the sanctity of the Priory of Saint Begu?' the old woman asked. Her voice was more forceful than her withered frame could have suggested.

'I would speak to the prioress,' Ronan demanded, ignoring the old woman's discourtesy.

The nun shook her head. 'She is not receiving visitors at this time. Come back when—'

Ronan shoved the door, forcing the old woman to stumble back out of his path.

'This is consecrated ground,' she shrieked. 'You shall not desecrate this holy place.'

He ignored her, slamming the door shut behind him, though it did little to stifle the chill in the air. The interior smelled musty, the walls filthy, corridor dimly lit by flickering torches. It was more a sepulchre than a priory.

'Are you deaf?' the old nun demanded.

Ronan was about to turn on her, to teach her the meaning of respect, when another nun appeared in the corridor.

'That will be all, Golda,' the woman said.

As the old nun scurried away, Ronan could see that this second woman was more officious, more confident. And a handsome one despite her modest garb.

'I am Beyhilde,' she said. 'The prioress of this house of saints. And you are one of the Frankish arrivals, unless I have missed my guess.'

'Ronan of Dol-Combourg.' He bowed with a smile. 'And no, you have not missed your guess.'

Beyhilde raised an expectant brow. 'And what can we do for a servant of the new king?'

Ronan would have thought that obvious from the bundle he was holding, but clearly the prioress was determined to make him say it.

'I am of the understanding this priory takes in orphans. It just so happens I have one.'

Beyhilde lowered her eyes to regard the child. Her stern visage was unmoved by the sight of the infant. 'I doubt you are aware of the number of orphans we are asked to provide succour for.'

Ronan shrugged. 'I can imagine it's a lot.'

A flicker of amusement on Beyhilde's lips. 'A lot more in recent months. No thanks to your king.'

She turned to make her way back along the corridor, and

Ronan limped after her. He hadn't exactly expected a warm reception, but this was becoming ridiculous.

'This is an ancient and revered priory, Ronan,' she said without deigning to look at him. 'As you can see, we are blessed with a large number of girls brought to us from across these lands.'

The corridor came out into a wide nave. One of the sisters was lighting candles as they passed, and through an open door Ronan spied the cloister, where children knelt before another nun, reciting some scripture or other.

'And I'm sure you do an excellent job of teaching them God's word.'

Beyhilde stopped at the foot of a wooden staircase before turning to him. 'Oh, we do.'

She led him up the stairs to another corridor. Several dormitories led off it, row upon row of wooden pallets lining their floors. Too many for him to count.

'Each of these beds has been taken by the daughter of a Saxon lord. Daughters sent by their dispossessed families, no longer able to take care of them. With their fathers dead, no thanks to your king, there is nowhere else for them to go. Here they are cared for and educated under the eyes of God.'

Her voice had gained a disdainful edge, and Ronan was beginning to develop a sinking feeling in his gut.

'And I am sure King William is grateful to you for that.'

They had reached the end of the corridor now. A tall window stood shuttered against the cold, but Ronan could still feel the wind creeping in through the slats.

Beyhilde turned to him, hands clasped together, lips pursed. 'And I am sure he would understand that we are in no position to take in every waif abandoned by its father. *You* must understand that this is no place for the bastard of a Frankish invader.'

Ronan nodded. 'I understand perfectly.'

And he did. He could have explained the child was not his, that she had as much right to be sheltered here as any other. Then again, he was already tired of the place, and there were some ways to explain things that were quicker than others.

Ronan laid the child down atop a cabinet that sat next to one of the open doors. She stirred for a moment before settling down once more.

'I am pleased we both appreciate where we stand,' he said as he began unbolting the shutters, opening the window wide, feeling the sudden chill cut him almost to the bone.

Beyhilde took a step closer. 'What are you—?'

He grabbed her habit, feeling his fist close around the hair bunched beneath. She let out a shocked breath as he thrust her toward the open window, letting her dangle there for a moment so she could take a look at the cold earth thirty feet below.

'Here's where we stand,' Ronan snarled. 'You on the precipice. Me keeping you from falling. Now listen closely – I couldn't give a frozen shit about the stinking Saxon spawn you bring up in this cesspit of a priory. I don't care how ancient or respected it is. King William owns this place now, and every orphaned bastard in its walls. As his valued *servant*, I can do whatever I wish to this place and everyone in it. And when I make a request, I expect it to be obeyed. Am I fucking clear?'

'Yes,' Beyhilde spat. 'Yes, I understand.'

He dragged her back inside. 'Now pick up the child, she is your responsibility from this moment on.'

Her hands shaking, the prioress picked up the baby, holding it to her breast as though it were her own infant. For her part, Gisela's daughter barely stirred.

'From time to time, I may return,' Ronan said, voice calm and even so she would hear every word. 'I expect this child to be well cared for. If I come back here and find she has been abused in any way, I'll burn this shithole to the ground, and your saint along with it.'

Beyhilde nodded, her habit askew, wisps of hair poking out making her look almost laughable. Ronan didn't laugh.

Instead he turned, leaving the prioress and the child behind him, making his way through the cold and austere building until he was outside once more. As he closed the door behind him he felt a strange kind of relief.

Mainard was still waiting atop his horse, cloak pulled tight about him.

'Took your time,' he said, when Ronan began to climb atop his own mount.

'Just had to make sure we'd reached an agreement on the conditions,' he replied, reining the horse around and urging it out of the courtyard.

'Maybe we should have asked for shelter overnight. It's a long road back to Yorke and this weather's freezing my bloody bones.'

'Fuck Yorke. And Fuck Guillam. We're done with that.'

'So where are we bound for?' Mainard looked worried about the prospect of yet more uncertainty.

'South I guess,' Ronan replied, pulling his cloak tighter about him. 'But wherever we go, it'll be miles from here.'

32

Waruic, England, January 1069

Hunted had become hunter. The cold in his bones only served to fuel him as he moved ever northwards, chilling his heart to the task ahead. Those men he had killed in the forest had slaked his thirst momentarily, but now that delight was waning. The Red Wolf needed new prey, and the blood of only one man would satisfy. Ronan was hidden somewhere in this country, and with him would be Gisela. But how to find one man?

Word of rebellion had reached his ears. In the villages and hamlets he passed through, farmers and traders would talk of it in hushed tones as he listened from the shadows. Edwin and Morcar had only now chosen to rise up against the king – too little too late it seemed – but where there was rebellion the Franks would follow, ready to quash any resistance to the new order. Waruic was said to have been subdued with little resistance from the errant earls. No surprise that they had failed once more, but more important was who had been sent to quell them.

There was no guarantee that Ronan would be among the Frankish numbers, but it was the only clue he had to follow. So, with the distant scent of his prey on the air, the Red Wolf had pursued it.

It was morning when he spied the town in the distance, hunkering squat against the snow-covered landscape. Even at such an early hour there was much activity, and already he could spy Franks milling about the place like rats on a corpse.

Perhaps he should have shown caution, but his eagerness could not be sated. Besides, he was but one more traveller on a road of many. What reason would the Franks have to stop him?

As he approached the open gate he passed an overturned cart on the road, its wheel broken, its payload spilled across the path. Half a dozen men struggled to right the cart and repair the wheel as a man sat atop his horse nearby, barking orders. The rider wielded a stick, railing at these men, his thralls or servants, but this was no Frank. Just one more Saxon abusing what authority he had left.

The Red Wolf paid him no heed as he made his way through the gate. The sword he had stripped from one of the dead men was at his side but he kept his hand well away from it. Best he drew as little attention as he could, pulling the hood tight about his head to ward off the cold. He needn't have concerned himself, as the Frankish guards at the gate seemed too enrapt in their own conversation to offer him so much as a second glance.

Within the boundary of Waruic he felt some relief that his guise as an ordinary traveller had worked. After so long trapped in a cage, then travelling the wilds, he had thought that perhaps his visage had changed, that he might be terrifying to behold, but it seemed those fears were unfounded.

The streets were busy, filled with the usual chatter and verve. At one corner a man sat hunkered in thick furs playing a bone flute, as his neighbour banged a drum in time to the tune. A woman called out loudly for someone to buy her milk and cheese and a dog barked nearby trying to drown out the sounds of all three of them.

When he'd heard there was rebellion here, the Red Wolf had expected to be greeted by burned buildings and corpses when he arrived. Clearly Waruic had been spared such ravages where so many other burhs had not.

His attention was drawn to the town's church rising above the other low dwellings. Perhaps if he was to track his quarry such a place of worship might be a good start. For what man of God did not know the comings and goings of their own flock?

The door stood ajar when he reached it, and when he pushed it open the warmth greeted him in a welcome embrace. There was music here too as a monk sat in one corner playing a low melody on his pibgorn.

A smattering of worshippers sat among the pews, heads bent in prayer. Others sat wrapped in their cloaks, most likely just sheltering from the cold.

The Red Wolf took his seat, waiting silently, appreciating the chance to rest in such a place of sanctity. As he sat, he could only wonder what prayers these people might be making. Were they grateful to have been spared the ravages of conquest so many others had suffered? Or were they even now beseeching their Lord God for deliverance from the hated Franks?

Had more of them answered the call of King Harold they would need no such deliverance. They would have pushed the foreigners back across the sea and be living free under Harold's laws. Prayers would not save them now.

One by one, the scant congregation began to thin out, their morning prayers finished. Even the monk on his pibgorn ceased his tune and made his way from the church, leaving the Red Wolf alone.

The door closed behind him and he heard footsteps approaching. He pulled his hood further over his head as a white-robed priest came to stand at his side.

'Is there anything I can help you with, my son?' the priest asked.

From beneath his hood, the Red Wolf could see this priest was young, his face open and smiling. Perhaps a good man, if that could be said of any holy men in this land.

Years before, when he had travelled the country with his master, Styrkar had met many priests across the length and breadth of England. For the most part they had been base men, more concerned with their own status than the wellbeing of their flock. But some had preached their word with benevolence. Perhaps this was one such priest, but it would not see him spared from the Red Wolf's wrath if he refused to reveal what he knew.

He rose, towering over the young man before pulling back his hood. The smile on the priest's face wavered as he took in the grim visage before him. A flicker of fear in his eyes. Good.

'You can help me,' said the Red Wolf. His voice sounded strange to his own ear, he had not heard it for so long. More a growl than words. 'I have come for information. I would know the whereabouts of a Frankish knight.'

The priest took a tentative step backward. The Red Wolf moved forward until the priest was backed against a pew.

'I– I don't know any of the Franks. I don't know anything.'

His lip quivered as the Red Wolf glared. Eyes widening as he saw the glint of steel in the Red Wolf's hand. He hadn't even realised he was drawing the knife until he felt the handle, cold and reassuring in his grip.

'You must have offered blessings on those Frankish heads. Must have given succour to them while they were here. I seek one of them – a man crippled in the foot. Arrogant. Wicked.'

'Y– Yes I prayed with some of those men but I do not know the one you speak of.'

'Then I urge you to think, before it is too late. Before you get to meet your god face to face.'

'Please,' he sobbed. 'I am just a man. Weak of flesh. Nothing but a servant of Christ, and I swear I do not know the man you describe.' His eyes widened again, as though he were suddenly realising the danger he was in. 'Are you a devil? Come to punish me for my alacrity?'

'I am worse than any devil. I am vengeance. Come to seek a man named Ronan. A crippled knight. He would be travelling with a woman. A beautiful maid. You must have seen them.'

A tear rolled down the priest's face. He stifled a sob as he slowly shook his head. 'I don't know of whom you speak. I swear by almighty God. Show mercy on me, I beg you.'

'If you do not know, then who would?'

The priest shook his head again, this time more desperately. 'I know not. The Franks were here in numbers to face the earls Morcar and Edwin, but they surrendered without a drop of blood shed. The bulk of their host has gone, but I know not where.'

The urge to plunge that knife into the bright white vestments was almost too much to bear. Just one motion and he could bury that blade deep. But as he looked on this pathetic man in his hallowed house, something of the Red Wolf sloughed away, and Styrkar returned once again.

He staggered back, shocked at what he was doing. Disgusted by the animal he had become. Styrkar had been brutalised for so long, treated like a beast, forced to fight, starved, beaten, hunted, that he had forgotten the man he used to be. The man Gisela had fallen in love with.

As he turned his back on the priest and stumbled away, the knife fell from his hand to clatter on the ground. The winter cold struck him as he pushed open the door to the church and stepped out. Slamming it closed behind him, he sucked in a chill breath, feeling it purge him of the wolf within.

In the distance he could hear the man on his bone pipe still kept in time by his companion on the drum. He walked from the church, head down, keen to rid himself of Waruic and its mundanity. The gate stood open ahead of him, the release of the wilds just beyond it, beckoning him ever closer.

A woman moved to block his path. Styrkar stopped, glaring down at her, unsure of what to do as she stared up at him in disbelief.

'You're him,' the woman said. She was young, but he could tell by her eyes she had seen much hardship in her few years.

'Leave me be, woman,' he replied, stepping aside to get past her, but she moved to block his path again.

'Styrkar,' she said.

He stopped, brow creasing in confusion. He had never seen this woman before, he was sure of it. Yet here she was, picking him out from the crowd in a town he did not know.

'How do you know me?'

Her eyes opened wider, as though she were revelling in the look of him. Hard to believe when his visage had struck such fear in the priest.

'I've heard stories about you. Of the warrior with ice for eyes and flames for hair. Of his bravery. Of the gentle nature he is always at pains to hide. Must say, I expected you to be handsomer though.'

It certainly sounded like him, though why she might think him gentle was a mystery. 'And who has told you of me?'

'Why, Gisela of course.'

Styrkar felt the ice around his heart crack a little at the mention of her name. Hope began to warm that place in his chest that had remained frozen for so long.

'Where is she?' he asked, almost pleading.

'Gone north with the Franks,' she replied as though it were obvious. 'To Yorke.'

'Was she well? Was she safe?'

The woman shrugged. 'As well as she could be for a woman who'd just birthed a child.'

He stared, barely comprehending the words. 'A child?'

'Yes. A daughter. Yours, without no doubt from how much she looks like you. Gisela never stopped talking about—'

He pushed past her, eyes focusing on the gate ahead, reeling from the news. Gisela and his daughter were waiting for him somewhere in the north. He had to find them, had to reach Yorke with all haste.

'If you find her,' the woman shouted in his wake. 'Tell her Stanhilde wishes her well.'

Styrkar barely heard the words as he marched out through the gate, past the Franks, eyes fixed on the road to the north. Before he could begin to walk it, he stopped. The overturned cart had been righted, but the man atop his horse was still yelling, cursing his thralls for the slovenly bastards they were.

He was waving his stick as Styrkar approached, cowing his men, who bowed their heads in subjugation. As he drew closer, the man stared down at him with a disdainful look.

'What the bleeding hell do you—?'

Styrkar grabbed his arm, dragging him from the saddle, throwing him head first to the ground. There was a crunch as his head hit the frozen earth, but Styrkar was already climbing atop the steed. He heard shouts from the Franks at the gate as he reined the horse northward. Their cries faded to nothing as he kicked the horse into a gallop and raced to unite with his family.

33

Berewyke, England, January 1069

They had found an estate not too far to the southwest of Yorke. Ronan had planned to forge on through the snow and wind till they reached Brian's fortress in Dunheved, but that had become impossible. Instead they had presented themselves to the local lord, a Saxon too fearful of the king's wrath to turn them away.

The place was modest compared to the great castles of Bretagne but they had been made comfortable, given a place of honour. The lord had even offered Ronan his own chamber to rest out the storm, and who was he to refuse such hospitality?

Still, it was difficult to know whether they were being offered such luxury out of fear or respect. Then again, was there much of a difference? He was one of the victors, and to him came the spoils of conquest.

This place may have been modest but its history was obvious. The keep stood on an ancient motte, the bailey lying within the walls of a fortress said to be thousands of years old. It bore an esteemed heritage and here he was, a bastard son with a crippled leg, being treated like a visiting king.

As he thought on it, he knew it was most definitely fear that had made the Saxon lord so keen to please, but who cared for respect when this was the reward? Ronan could only smile as he warmed himself by the fire, thinking about how high he had risen, but also how much further he had to go. He could well understand how men such as Robert of Comines were held in such regard, men who brokered in fear, men who seized what they wanted no matter the number of innocents left crushed and broken in their wake. But Robert was nothing but a memory now, gone north to claim his earldom in Dun Holm. Gone to spread more violence and mayhem until the northerners were brought to heel, and William's kingdom was at peace once more.

As he reclined in his chair, he realised how little he cared for all that now. How long he had been serving other men's goals. How much he hated this conquest, and what it had cost him. A brief memory of Gisela, of her smiling face, flashed across his vision, but he dismissed it. He had become good at forgetting, but for a man who had as many dark deeds to his name as Ronan, it was a valuable talent. There was meat in his belly and ale by his side. Better to think on the here and now, and be thankful for what he had.

The sound of splashing water came from the next room, and Ronan glanced toward it. Mainard was in there now, bathing himself, albeit in the water Ronan had already used. He had been grateful nonetheless.

'This is the life, eh, Mainard?' Ronan called.

There was no answer, but he did not need one. Let

Mainard enjoy his repose. Ronan had enjoyed his all right. The warmth of that water had soothed his leg, which seemed to plague him more and more the further north they travelled. Now as he sat by the fire it was reduced to a dull ache. One more thing to be thankful for. Unlike the tepid ale, but Ronan had never considered himself a complainer. Who could say whether in time he might grow used to it? When he raised the tankard to his mouth and tasted the sourness of it, he realised that no amount of time would ever accustom his palate to such bitter slop.

'I look forward to the wine we will drink when our journey south is done,' Ronan called.

The only answer was yet more sloshing of water in the next chamber. He imagined the floor would be sodden with it by now. He had never known a man enjoy the confines of a wooden bath quite like Mainard. And enough to ignore someone when they tried to make conversation. Perhaps he should have chided Mainard for that, reminded him who's service he was in, but what would that prove? It was a long road to Dunheved and they would have to take their pleasures where they could find them.

An errant draft blew through the room, agitating the flames in the hearth, before disappearing. The fire winnowed, and Ronan felt the sudden chill keenly. He struggled to his feet, limping to the hearth and bending to grab another log. A noise from the next room stopped him, more splashing water and the sound of something bouncing on the floor.

Ronan stood, frowning at the open doorway. 'What are you doing in there?'

No answer for a third time of asking. Had Mainard fallen asleep?

'Do you need—?'

Something was flung from out of the darkness of the chamber to bounce a few feet in front of Ronan. It rolled across the floor, coming to a stop by Ronan's foot, and he took a moment to comprehend the reality of it.

Mainard's severed head looked up at him with sleepy eyes, blood pooling from the stump of his neck.

'Fuck!'

Ronan staggered back, away from the head, stumbling on his cursed leg and knocking over his chair. A silhouette filled the doorway, a devil from the darkness.

'No,' Ronan snarled, anger fighting his terror. 'You're dead. You're bloody dead.'

But he wasn't dead. The giant that filled the doorway, hood drawn up and face hidden in shadow, could only be one man. And there was no doubting his intent.

Ronan turned, limping to the door as fast as his crippled leg would allow. His hand fumbled at the handle, sliding back the stiff bolt before wrenching it open with fear-numbed fingers. The cold wind struck him as he all but fell out into the night, plunging into two feet of snow as the storm gusted about him.

Immediately the cold dread he felt in his bones was overtaken by the harshness of the elements. Ronan shouted for help, his breath instantly torn away and lost on the wind. He hadn't covered half a dozen yards before his foot caught on something hidden in the snow and he went tumbling.

For a moment he thrashed helplessly before his eyes fell on a corpse lying buried in the drift. One of the keep's guards, his throat hacked open, the blood already frozen to his neck like a crimson collar.

Ronan looked back, seeing that shadow hulking in the doorframe of the keep. All he could do was stare through the squall, waiting for the wolf to pounce. His teeth gnashed as that figure just stood, watching from beneath his hood, savouring the moment and taking pleasure from his fear. The bastard.

With a growl, Ronan dragged himself to his unsteady feet, and battled on through the snow. The gate stood open and he stumbled down the scarp, gripping onto the frozen rope to stop himself falling. The wood of the flying bridge clattered beneath his feet, and when he was at the bailey he screamed for help again. No one came.

The snort of a horse alerted him to the stables nearby. Ronan plunged on, limping as best he could, squinting through the heavy snowfall. He passed another corpse as he reached the stable door and pulled it open. No sooner had he stepped inside than he was shoved in the back and sent sprawling into the muck.

He turned in time to the whinny of a horse. Another steed trembled in the sudden cold, its muscles spasming, but all Ronan cared about was the giant bearing down on him. Styrkar stepped into the stable, towering over his quarry. Ronan crawled through the straw and the shit, but he knew there was no escape.

The Red Wolf stopped. His hands were empty, but sword and axe were strapped at his hips. He raised both hands and pulled back the hood. His hair hung in lank strands around a gaunt face. Ronan was staggered at the transformation – this once handsome warrior now a spectre of his former self, eyes sunk deep into their sockets, flesh pulled tight about his skull. It would have been shocking to behold had Ronan not already been gripped by the sheer terror of him.

'Where is she?' Styrkar hissed.

Ronan worked his mouth, trying to say the words but they would not come. If he spoke the truth of Gisela's fate, surely it would seal his doom.

At his silence, Styrkar stooped, grasping him in those huge hands and lifting him from the ground. With a grunt, Ronan was flung across the stable to crash into a wooden partition. A bucket rolled from beneath him, spreading rank water across the ground as a horse stamped its foot in panic just by his head.

He started to crawl, desperate to escape, but it was a useless gesture. He felt that steel grip take hold of his collar, hauling him up once more.

'Where is she?'

This time the growl was close to his ear, heralding the sound of an axe being pulled from a belt. Ronan could see its glint from the corner of his eye. He thought desperately on what words might see him spared a grisly fate, but he knew there were none. All that was left was the truth.

'She was murdered,' he managed to say, in a voice just short of a scream.

Styrkar stopped, holding Ronan there in his grip. All he could do was wait for the fall of the axe, but it did not come. Instead Styrkar let go of him, and he fell to the ground with a thump. The wind howled outside, rattling the stable rafters, and as he lay there, Ronan spied yet another corpse lying in one of the nearby stalls.

'Who... where?' Styrkar asked finally.

Ronan struggled on the ground, managing to lean his back against a post. Styrkar looked down at nothing, the fury and hate on his face now faded, but Ronan knew it could return at any moment.

'She was killed in Yorke. By a man named Robert of Comines. I did all I could to protect her, but he is a more savage killer than you. He has gone north to claim his earldom in Dun Holm.'

'And my daughter?'

So he knew. Perhaps that would serve in Ronan's favour.

'Gone to a priory. The safest place I could find.'

Styrkar looked down at Ronan and nodded his understanding. 'Then we are done.'

As he raised the axe, Ronan screamed, 'Wait,' but he already knew it would not stop the inevitable. His hand fumbled in his jerkin, fingers closing on the tiny keepsake he could not bring himself to part with.

'Gisela gave me this,' he held up the tiny carving of the wolf. It was enough to stay Styrkar's hand. 'She saved me, and I her. We trusted one another, even at the end. I was the one who took your daughter to the priory. Only I know her location.' And it was true, now that Mainard had been parted from his head.

Styrkar grasped him by the collar again, pressing the blade of the axe to Ronan's cheek. He could feel its keenness, so sharp he could have shaved with it.

'Where is this priory?'

'And then you kill me?' Ronan said as calmly as he could manage. 'I think not.'

Styrkar growled, raising the axe high, his frustration winning over his sense. 'Tell me or die!'

'Kill me if you want. Torture me. Drag me out into the winter to freeze. I will not tell you, Red Wolf. And you've already slain the only other man who knows.'

Styrkar lowered the axe. 'Very well. Tell me, and I will spare your worthless life.'

Ronan couldn't help but bark a laugh, despite his nearness to death. 'You don't mean that, Styrkar. And it hurts that you'd think I would fall for such a ruse. I tell you and I die, that much is certain. But if you swear, on the memory of your precious King Harold, and all the pagan gods you hold so dear, then I will take you to where she is.'

Styrkar sighed, the fire in his eyes waning before he nodded. 'All right, I swear it. On Odin and Fenrir and the trickster god Loki, I will do you no harm.'

He took a step back, and with some difficulty Ronan struggled to his feet. He began to brush himself down, but he was so crusted with filth it seemed pointless to make the effort.

'We should wait out the storm and travel in the morning. The priory is at least two day's ride from here.'

'No,' Styrkar replied. 'The priory can wait. You said yourself my daughter is safe.'

'Then where?'

'First we ride north to Dun Holm. You will show me to this Robert and he will say Gisela's name before I add his head to my tally.'

'Then we had best rest,' Ronan replied. 'Dun Holm is a long way north.'

Another shake of the Red Wolf's head. 'Saddle the horses now. I will wait for no storm.'

With little choice, Ronan turned to the whickering steeds and began preparing them for the journey. So much for home comforts.

34

Middeltun, England, January 1069

He had lived through deep winters before, been forced to suffer the biting cold with nothing but a thin cloak to keep him from freezing, but Styrkar had faced nothing like this. Even with furs drawn tight about him he felt as though he might never be warm again. Still, he would not be stopped as their horses trudged ever northward through the snow.

At first he had thought his fortunes changed – that the gods were looking over him with benevolence after what he had suffered. On his journey north, word had reached him by chance that a crippled Frank was sheltering in a nearby manor, the casual prattling of patrons at an inn directing him to Ronan's location. But on finding his quarry he learned the worst of all tidings. Gisela was gone. Murdered. Styrkar now new, beyond all doubt, that the gods had truly abandoned him.

Ronan was beside him, bound at wrist and neck, his mount tied to Styrkar's. A heavy cloak was draped around him – more mercy than he deserved, but it would at least keep him alive long enough for them to reach their goal. For them to find this warlord Robert in Dun Holm. That was if both of them did not freeze to their saddles first.

Nevertheless, he could not turn back, despite the storm that threatened to kill them. Gisela had to be avenged. He owed it to her and the daughter she would never see again. But was it what she would have wanted? She had been a gentle soul, loving, nurturing, offering Styrkar so much more than anyone else ever had. More than he had deserved. In turn he had betrayed his brothers for her, and turned his back on his countrymen so that she might be saved. It had all been for nothing.

Should he turn his back on this one last task? Have Ronan take him to his daughter so that he could flee this cursed isle with her? Find somewhere new as he should have done with Gisela?

No. That was a dream for another man. That Styrkar was gone and only the Red Wolf remained. The hunter moving ever north, and he would have his reckoning before he died on a Frankish blade.

The sky was darkening as the road dipped into a valley, and he saw yet more evidence that they were on the right path. Another village devastated by the passing Franks. Ronan had told him this Robert of Comines was a vicious butcher. If there had been any doubt of that it had quickly been expelled. This was not the first place left blackened and burned by the passage of the Franks as they made their way north to claim their seat in Dun Holm. It seemed Robert was eager to carry on the example of his king and leave the north as blasted a waste as his master had the south.

As they passed close to the shattered palisade, now nothing more than fallen logs, he realised they would have to find shelter soon. There was no way they could travel through the night in this, if not for their own welfare but that of the horses.

Tugging on the rope tied to the bridle of Ronan's steed, he led them from the road and toward the devastated hamlet. Riding through the smashed gate there was little sign of life. He could only imagine the bodies buried beneath the snow, the livestock slaughtered and wasted. It would have angered him, but there was no more rage to draw on. He had locked it away in his heart, and when finally he faced this Frankish lord he would unleash it like a torrent.

They had almost reached the far end of the burh by the time he saw a building intact enough to provide shelter. It was most likely a store hut, its door swinging in the wind to bang discordantly against the neighbouring fence. Styrkar dismounted, reaching up and dragging Ronan from his saddle. The cripple put up little resistance as he was bundled inside the dark confines of the hut. It took little coaxing to get the horses inside, and after tethering them to a post he took the rope around Ronan's neck and tied it tight to one of the rafters, leaving him enough slack to sit.

He secured the door, shutting them in against the storm. A little moonlight beamed in through the roof, and by it he could see Ronan sitting, his face sullen though he was doubtless relieved to be out of the snow.

Wrapping himself tighter in his cloak, Styrkar sat on a bundle of straw at the far end of the shack. All he could do was stare, quelling the hate, resisting the temptation to string the bastard up from that rafter and watch him dangle.

Ronan slowly raised his gaze and they regarded one another in the dark. Then the cripple smiled. Was he trying to provoke Styrkar's ire? Did this bastard want to fucking die?

'What's so funny, cripple?' he demanded.

Ronan shrugged, then pulled his cloak tighter about his shoulders. 'I just find it amusing how our situations have changed. At one time it was you who was tied to a post and me the captor. Now...'

'It would serve you well to remain silent.' Styrkar's hand strayed to the axe at his side.

'Come now. Do not forget the oath you have made. If you ever want to see that daughter of yours you need me alive.'

Absently, Styrkar's hand went to the pouch at his belt. In it were a few coins taken from the corpses he had left in the south, along with the wooden carving he had made so many months ago, when he was a different man, leading a different life. He remembered well that vow he had made. Curse him, but the man was right.

Ronan leaned forward, the mirth gone from his face now. 'Believe me when I say, I cared for that woman. She was special. Through all this, despite what she had seen, and what I had done to her, she still nursed me back to health when no other cared. And for that I did my best to see her safe. You should be thanking me, not treating me like a dog.'

'Were that true, she would still be alive. And neither of us would be here in this storm.'

Ronan sat back with a despondent sigh. 'I did everything in my power. But there are some things no one can be protected from.'

'Why should I believe that? The word of a man who has done nothing but cheat and lie. For all I know you were the one who murdered her.'

Ronan's brow creased in anger, his hands clenching into fists. 'I would never have done anything to harm Gisela. Even had she not saved my life I still saw the goodness inside her. She was the one decent thing I found in this whole godforsaken land. But she did save me, and I owed her. I may be no saint, but I always pay my debts, Red Wolf. That is why I saw her daughter to safety.'

Now it was time for a smile to cross Styrkar's face. 'You think that makes amends for all the evil you have done, Ronan? One good deed to wash away all the blood you and yours have spilled across this country? All those murdered. Raped. Had their farms burned and their children made orphans?'

'And are your hands clean?' Ronan spat. 'Were the men you killed at that keep not a night ago guilty of some sin against you? I don't think so. They were just in the wrong place at the wrong time when the Red Wolf set his eye on them. What about the orphans you have made? How many more corpses will lie in your wake until your lust for death is satisfied? How many men have yet to fall to your axe and sword, Styrkar?'

The wind rattled the hut, to match the fury of Ronan's outburst. When it was quiet again, Styrkar knew it was a simple question to answer.

'Only one,' he replied. 'Now, I suggest you try and get some sleep before morning. The road north is still long and may hold much danger for the both of us.'

If Ronan had more to say, he did not feel the compulsion to say it. Instead he wrapped himself tighter in that cloak and hunkered down to rest. Styrkar reclined on the bed of straw, covering himself to try and stifle the cold, not that it did much good. His sleep was fitful, plagued by the howl of the wind. When he did manage to dream that howl turned to screams, as faces leered at him from the dark before his blade cut them down. When morning came it brought merciful silence and clear skies with it.

As Styrkar sat up, his muscles aching, he saw Ronan was already awake, still propped against the post, staring at him blankly. They spoke no more as he untied his prisoner and led the horses out into the crisp morning air. There was no need to tarry as they left the shattered village behind them and struck out north once more, the road barely visible beneath a blanket of snow.

The day remained clear as they rode, but the cold still brought a shiver to Styrkar every now and again. At this rate he would be good for little by the time they reached Dun Holm. How he expected to track this Robert and exact his justice he had no idea, but the Red Wolf would find a way. Even if he had to carve his way through an army, he would see Gisela and his daughter avenged.

As the midday sun reached its zenith, and ominous storm clouds roiled on the distant horizon, Styrkar spied riders on the path ahead. From such distance he could not tell if they were friend or foe, though in reality he knew there would be few friends in such blighted country. The northern regions were wild and intemperate, and the chances of finding any allies here were slim.

'What should we do?' Ronan asked. Styrkar turned to see him glaring at the riders ahead. 'Should we get off the road?'

It was obvious he had the same thought – that these riders were more than likely foes to the both of them.

'We wait,' Styrkar replied.

'We what? Are you mad? Not even the Red Wolf could take on half a dozen armed men. Even if they are Englishmen they may still only seek to rob you. If they are my countrymen then all the better, but you? The best you can hope for is to be my prisoner once more.'

'I will be no one's prisoner. If they are Franks they will have to kill me.'

'And if they're not? If they're just bandits on the road, what about your vengeance then?'

Styrkar took the axe from his belt and hid it beneath his cloak, keeping his eyes fixed on the approaching riders. There were half a dozen of them, all in furs. Some held spears but it was impossible to tell if they were Franks or not.

The closer they came, the more he could see Ronan shifting uncomfortably in his saddle. It was obvious his only desire was to run and hide, but the Red Wolf was done with running. He had fled for days from Tantone, and been hunted like an animal. Today he would stand his ground no matter the odds.

When they were within a dozen yards the riders reined in, seven of them, all keen-eyed beneath their hoods. Every one of them had a beard, and even before the first one spoke, Styrkar knew they were English.

'Long way north,' said the one at the front. 'Dangerous road for a couple as weary looking as you.'

'Perhaps we're dangerous men,' Styrkar replied.

The man laughed as his eyes fell on Ronan shivering atop his scrawny steed.

'You maybe, but not that one. What business have you in such country as this?'

There was no need for a lie. It didn't seem to matter if this man knew the truth of it or not. 'I seek a Frankish lord named Robert.'

That seemed to cause some disquiet among the riders, their leader raising an eyebrow as he leaned forward in his saddle. 'And what would you be seeking him for?'

Styrkar let the cloak slip a little, showing the axe he held in one hand. 'Because I would have his head.'

A smile crawled up the leader's bearded face before he let out a laugh that some of his men echoed. 'Then lucky for you we're after the same thing. He is bound for Dun Holm, intending on becoming its ealdorman, and we serve someone who intends to stop that from happening.'

'Then we are of the same mind,' Styrkar replied.

The rider's eye turned on Ronan, his gaze narrowing. 'And who the fuck is this?'

Ronan glanced at Styrkar, who could only offer a shrug in return. 'This is a Frank who was showing me the way.'

'That so? Well, we know the way, so I suppose you don't need him no more.'

For a moment, Styrkar was inclined to agree, and took some pleasure from Ronan's sudden panicked expression. 'I'm not done with him yet.'

The rider shrugged. 'Suit yourself. Best you come with us. Our lord is not too far north of here. I imagine he'll appreciate all the help he can get when he takes Dun Holm and shows those Franks the error of their ways.'

'What is the name of this lord who thinks he can defy the might of the Bastard King?'

'His name is Edgar, named the Aetheling. The rightful king of England. Does that suit you, traveller?'

Styrkar remembered the witan at Berchastede. Remembered how the thegns of England had decreed a boy should be their new king. Remembered how it had never come to pass.

'Aye. I suppose it does,' he replied. 'Lead the way.'

35

Segerston Heugh, England, January 1069

Night was falling by the time they reached the small burh just north of Dun Holm. The road they had taken allowed them to avoid the advancing Franks, and they had seen neither hide nor hair of the enemy. They had skirted the city, watching that unwary place, its populace ignorant of what was about to strike. Robert was still on his way north, ready to fall on Dun Holm and bring it to heel. With any luck, there would be more than just unwary townsfolk awaiting him.

Those ominous clouds had rolled in and snow was falling heavily as they rode through the gate of the burh. Styrkar had not been sure what to expect. The last time he had joined a company of rebels they had been a ragtag bunch of outlaws hiding in the forest. What waited at the burh was anything but.

Men mustered for war. The sights and sounds of warriors checking armour, shields and spears brought back a rush of memories. Of standing by the side of his king, watching the grim faces fixed in resolve, knowing their final day might soon be upon them. Despite the cold, this army looked keen for battle, hungry for it, lustful for it. But many of them were young, filled with bluster as they prepared for their first battle. They would soon learn just how hungry for war they were when the killing started. When they saw their friends hacked down, when their brothers lay screaming, grasping onto their innards as they died.

The riders reined their steeds in at the centre of the burh. Barely anyone paid them any heed, too enrapt in their own preparations. Styrkar recognised their mood, he had borne it many times. The quiet before the tempest. A time to reflect on what was to come. On what you might lose.

As he swung his leg over his horse and slid to the hard ground he heard someone shout, 'Styrkar?'

Turning, he saw a grizzled thegn approaching. He bore a grim visage amid a head of blond hair and beard, a jagged scar from brow to chin. Every inch of him spoke of his Danish descent, but Styrkar knew him to be as English as King Harold.

'Maerlswein?' Styrkar said.

The big man had a face of thunder as he approached, but still he gripped Styrkar like an old friend, laughing from his belly like they were long-lost brothers.

'I was sure you were dead,' Maerlswein said, looking Styrkar up and down as though he were a ghost back from the grave.

'And I you,' he replied.

Maerlswein had been a sheriff during the time of King Edward and the steward of Harold's fyrd after he had been crowned. It was obvious since the invasion that he had fallen far, as had so many others.

'What brings the Red Wolf north? Are you to join our merry band?'

'I seek a Frankish lord named Robert of Comines.'

Maerlswein's left eyebrow rose, the right one with the scar no longer able to move. 'My guess is you do not wish to congratulate him on his appointment as ealdorman.'

'You guess right, my friend.'

Maerlswein clapped Styrkar on the shoulder. 'Then you have come at an opportune time, Red Wolf. We plan to greet that very man ourselves.' He glanced up at Ronan, who still sat atop his horse. 'Who the fuck is this sorry bastard?'

Styrkar glanced up, seeing the sullen look on Ronan's face. Though he took no pleasure in his prisoner's discomfort, neither did it concern him. 'This is my captive. A Frankish knight of some renown.'

'You intend to ransom him?' Maerlswein asked.

Styrkar shook his head. 'I need him. He knows the whereabouts of someone dear to me. We have a bargain that I will spare his life in return for him showing me where they are.'

'Then we should make sure he is comfortable,' Maerlswein replied, gesturing to his men. 'Put this Frankish bastard somewhere safe. The pig pen should do it. He'll be warm there in the shit overnight.'

Obediently, the riders who had brought them north dragged Ronan from his horse. He was powerless to resist as they bustled him along the snowy ground.

'There is someone you must meet,' Maerlswein said.

'Someone who will be grateful you have arrived. We need every sword we can get if we are to take our pleasure with the new ealdorman.'

He led the way through the burh toward the longhall. It wasn't much of a building, its thatch wearing thin and stonework crumbling, but Styrkar still felt grateful to shelter from the cold. When they drew closer he could hear the sound of raised voices from within. It almost reminded him of the witan at Berchastede, those raucous calls for attention bellowing out, desperate to be heard.

Maerlswein pushed the door open, the sound of those voices growing louder. Styrkar followed him inside, feeling the warmth of the fire, sighing in relief as it began to relieve the chill in his bones.

His eyes first settled on a figure in the shadows of the hall. The man leaned against the wall, his face hidden as he watched the two other men arguing. He was tall and lean, hand resting on the jewelled hilt of a sword.

'We need prisoners,' growled one of the men at the centre of the hall. The outline of his wiry frame danced in the shadows cast by the fire. His eyes were wide in fury, hair thinning atop a large head, beard so wispy it was a wonder why he had tried to grow it at all. 'We can ransom them in exchange for land. We need something to bargain with.'

Opposite him was a younger man, broader at the shoulders with a fuller head of brown hair and a beard thick and braided. Despite their differences though, they bore an uncanny resemblance to one another.

'We need to wipe those bastards out,' he replied. 'To show strength. Write our intentions plain and simple in their blood.' The younger warrior punctuated his last word by slamming a fist into his palm.

Both men went silent when they realised they had an audience. They turned to glare at the pair who had disturbed their quarrel, and Maerlswein stepped forward.

'An ally has come to join us. A good friend to King Harold. This is Styrkar, known as the Red Wolf. A man whose name is feared by the Franks in the south.'

Movement from the shadows as the figure with his jewelled sword took a step into the light. Styrkar recognised him instantly, though he was much changed from the timid child he had seen at Berchastede. Edgar the Aetheling had been a boy then, cowed by the occasion when surrounded by so many magnates of England. He had been proclaimed a king, but looked anything but. Now he was visibly broader at the shoulder and keener in the eye. Though he was still young, a crown atop his head would not have looked out of place.

'Styrkar,' Edgar said, stepping forward to offer his hand. When they shook, Styrkar could feel the strength in that grip. 'We are honoured. Your reputation precedes you. Any servant of King Harold is welcome among our number. Would that I had been of an age to fight by your side at Senlac.'

'You would most likely have died along with so many others,' Styrkar replied, but then there was no other way to say it.

Edgar nodded at the truth of his words. 'But I am not dead, Red Wolf. And neither do I intend to return to dust any time soon. Not until I have claimed the crown that was stolen from me, and driven every last one of the Bastard's followers back across the sea. We are about to take that first step. Dun Holm lies not far to the south, and one of the king's puppets is about to take up residence. He will find it an uncomfortable seat to sit upon.' He turned to the two men who had been arguing most vocally. 'Only we are undecided as to how much discomfort to bring.'

The one with the thinning hair stepped forward, raising his chin in a lordly manner, though he looked anything but a lord. 'I still urge caution, my lord Edgar.'

'This is Gospatric,' said the Aetheling. 'It is his earldom who Robert of Comines comes to claim. Naturally he is not of a mind to provoke the king too much.'

'And I am Waltheof,' said the second man, before anyone could speak for him.

Edgar smiled at his boldness. 'Gospatric's cousin. An educated man if you believe it, though he seems to have abandoned reason in favour of slaughter.'

'We can show no mercy,' Waltheof repeated. 'And there is no more time to discuss the matter. The bishop has already left to warn Robert of what awaits. Our next move must be swift and decisive.'

'Ethelwin has fled?' asked Maerlswein.

Edgar raised his hands helplessly. 'What were we to do? Imprison a man of the cross?'

'Bloody coward,' Maerlswein growled.

'Coward or not, Ethelwin sees things clearly,' said Gospatric. 'We cannot just solve this with a massacre. If we allow the Franks to surrender, to ransom them back to their king, we effectively control the north. He will give us back our seats as ealdormen.'

Waltheof stepped closer to his cousin. 'Give back *your* seat you mean?'

Edgar held his hands up for both men to cease their argument. Surprisingly, the older pair went quiet. It seemed that the authority Edgar had lacked at the witan had developed greatly in the years since.

'As you can see,' said the Aetheling. 'We have still not reached an accord.'

Styrkar regarded the young king-in-waiting closely, thinking on how wise he had seemingly become. He was happy to sit in the shadows while his followers discussed tactics, listening, learning, but there would come a time when all leaders had to make their decisions.

'And what do you think, Aetheling?' he asked. 'Fight or bargain?'

Slowly a smile crept up one side of Edgar's mouth and he regarded Styrkar slyly. 'Negotiation will earn me no earldoms, Red Wolf. And I have greater ambition than a few acres of land. I seek to sit on the throne of England. Only slaughter will see it mine.'

Styrkar found himself smiling at the young lord's response. 'That is the grit you will need if you are to become a king. I am with you.'

'This is foolish,' Gospatric snapped. 'Slaughter will only provoke the king's ire. If we show we are men of reason then William will give us what we demand. If we annihilate his men it will only enrage him. He will strike north himself to wipe us all out.'

Styrkar took a step toward the dispossessed earl, glaring down at him. He was glad to see the man's resolve waver slightly, his left eye twitching in a tiny display of fear.

'That's what I am counting on,' he whispered, before turning to the rest of the gathering. 'But first we must greet Robert of Comines and show him the hospitality of the north.'

Gospatric shook his head in frustration. 'This will just—'

'Styrkar is right,' Edgar interrupted. 'We have talked around in circles for long enough. Gospatric, you paid off William once before and he betrayed your faith in him. Even if he gives you what you want, he will only cheat you again. You're a fool if you can't see it. There are no more bargains to be struck with the usurper. The Red Wolf and I are of the same mind. The Franks will not leave Dun Holm alive.'

'About fucking time,' Maerlswein snarled.

Waltheof barked a laugh of feral delight. 'I will gather the men. We march before sunrise.'

With that they left, leaving Styrkar by the fire of the longhall. He raised his hands to the flames, hoping to warm them through before he was thrust out in the cold once more. The next time they might be warm again, it would be with the freshly spilled blood of dead Franks.

36

Snow fell within the walls of Dun Holm, dusting every rooftop with white. A trail through the centre of the town had been lit by torches. Styrkar thought it a beautiful sight as he glanced about the deserted streets.

The populace of Dun Holm had been told to stay within their dwellings for their own safety. Danger was approaching from the south. A malevolent shadow, armed and armoured, that threatened to consume this place. To rape and burn and pillage. It would be stopped here. This lonely thoroughfare in the northernmost extent of the kingdom was where they would make their stand.

Styrkar glanced over his shoulder. Somewhere through the dark was Ronan. He had thought it better to bring the wretch rather than leave him north. The closer he was the better, lest the cripple escape and he never see his daughter again. Some of the younger fyrd held him bound and at spearpoint, told not to let him out of their sight. Told not to listen to any entreaties he might make. Styrkar knew only too well how treacherous a bastard he was. They had been told if the battle did not go to plan to slit his throat and leave him to bleed in the snow. It was a pleasure Styrkar would have gladly indulged in himself, but there were more pressing matters to attend with. Grim matters of vengeance that could not wait. Absently he squeezed the shaft of his axe as he thought on those matters. Anticipated the kill. If it ever came.

There were only a few of them waiting in the open. A score of men, furs draped over their mail, shields held to the ready. Edgar stood at their fore, wearing no helm, chin raised proudly as he defied the cold. His hand rested on that bejewelled hilt, and for a moment Styrkar wondered if he could wield it with any skill. Undoubtedly they would find out soon enough.

Flanking Edgar was Waltheof, as ready for battle as Styrkar had ever seen a man. He was broad and looked capable enough. Most likely he would be a man that could be relied upon when the fighting started. His cousin Gospatric, on the other hand, looked anything but ready. He shifted his weight from foot to foot, checking his sword was loose in its scabbard, adjusting his grip on his shield as though it were the first time he had ever held one. How he had been appointed an ealdorman was beyond Styrkar's ken, but he had seen poor leaders elevated to positions beyond their ability before. Doubtless he would see it again… if he lived long enough.

When he saw movement along the road, all thoughts of who was watching his back drifted away. Styrkar's eyes narrowed as he focused on the distant gate. Two hundred yards away horses were slowly plodding their way across the town's threshold, carrying their own torches. Once they rode into the light, those torches were thrown into the snow.

Around him, men began shuffling nervously as those riders drew closer. They started to breath faster, snorting clouds of vapour in the chill air as they prepared themselves for what was coming. More and more riders funnelled through the gate. A hundred. Two hundred. Frankish knight after Frankish knight, until the road was packed with more than they could count. And here they stood, twenty men facing an army.

A warrior rode at their head, helmed and armoured, the fur of a wolf draped across his shoulders. Styrkar felt his teeth grind as he guessed this must be Robert of Comines. At his side rode a priest, the bishop Ethelwin most likely. A standard fluttered behind them, every man holding a lance. They were ready for conquest, the bishop doubtless having warned them of what to expect.

Gospatric leaned into Edgar. 'It's not too late to change your mind. We can bargain with them. Make a deal. This doesn't have to end in bloodshed.'

Edgar offered no reply as he watched the riders approaching, listened to the crunch of their horses' hooves in the snow, heard the jangle of their barding.

Robert reined his horse to a halt before the gathered warriors. It was all Styrkar could do to hold himself in check, to resist the urge to race forward and take on this army alone. Instead he watched as Edgar walked slowly forward, hand still resting on his sword. He carried himself like a man without a care. Gone was the boy, a puppet to be used by bolder men. For the briefest moment, Styrkar recognised a king.

'Edgar,' said Ethelwin. The bishop sat uneasily in his saddle like a man unused to riding. He was slumped, gazing down over his chins and shivering within his robes.

'Ethelwin,' Edgar replied, but his eyes were focused on Robert, who glared back with a look of relish on his broad, hard face.

'This is a mistake, Edgar,' said the bishop. 'You must accept the way of things. The king has sent an army. It cannot be stopped.'

Edgar still held Robert in his gaze. 'There is no mistake. Turn your horses around. Return to your king, and tell him I will see him soon.'

Robert barked a laugh that echoed between the snow-capped buildings. 'You are bold, boy. I'll give you that. But you expect to face me with this sorry gathering?' He gestured to the twenty who stood barring the road. 'I have travelled a long way through this shithole of a country, and I am cold and I am tired. Make way, and you and your men might live out the night.'

'My sorry gathering is more than a match for an army of Frankish scum,' Edgar replied.

If he was trying to provoke Robert it didn't work, as the Frankish lord grinned the wider. 'That was the answer I was hoping for.'

Robert reached for his sword. Ethelwin blurted 'Wait,' to him, but Edgar drew his blade quicker. The jewelled sword rang from the scabbard. Styrkar was already moving as Edgar struck at the throat of Robert's horse. There was a deafening squeal and the horse reared, spraying blood across the snow.

Panicked voices defiled the air, but Styrkar was focused,

racing to reach Edgar as one of Robert's knights kicked his
horse forward, sword already raised. Styrkar wrenched
his own sword free, axe drawn back as he darted into the
knight's path. Their blades clashed as he parried the swing
meant for Edgar's exposed head, his axe cutting down in an
arc. There was a crunch as the axe smashed into the knight's
mailed arm, bone breaking.

Robert's horse collapsed as his men nudged their steeds
forward, hefting their lances, preparing to charge at the
score of warriors braced behind their shields.

Then the snow around them erupted.

For a hundred yards on either side, the fyrd threw off
the snow-covered furs they had been hiding beneath. They
raised their long spears, yelling their rage as they charged
at the hapless knights atop their panicking horses.
Maerlswein's voice rose higher than any other as he charged
into the fray to spear a knight from his saddle and skewer
him in the ground.

Chaos took hold, as Styrkar spied men in the distance,
rolling a cart across the road to block the Frankish retreat.
Warhorses wheeled in confusion, knights desperate to bring
their lances to bear, but the surprise of the attack meant
hardly any of them could single out a target.

In an instant the quiet town of Dun Holm was consumed
in noise and violence. Styrkar dragged one rider from his
horse, axe crashing down again and again, the sound of
ringing metal fuelling him until his victim was still. At his
side he heard Edgar's cry of unfettered rage as he too struck
at a rider, ducking his errant lance and smashing the man's
leg.

Styrkar staggered back, watching from amidst the

carnage as the Aetheling fought. He swung his blade with all the confidence of youth, but also the ferocity of a man driven by untamed wroth. As Edgar hacked down a flailing knight unseated from his horse, he reminded Styrkar of himself, all those years ago, before Harold had tempered his rage and taught him to channel it.

A shout nearby brought him from his reverie. One of the knights had been shoved from his saddle by a long spear, and he dropped at Styrkar's feet. A gift.

The knight looked up, his weapons lost, his face forlorn. He opened his mouth, but the Red Wolf's axe took him before he had a chance to shame himself with pleas for mercy. He should have been grateful he was spared such ignominy.

Styrkar looked up in time to see one of the riders bolt from the fight, desperate to escape. His horse hadn't covered ten yards before the knight was speared from the saddle, lifted high into the air where he screamed in pain. There he hung, impaled on that spear before he fell in a flurry of snow, to be cut down and silenced by a mob of frenzied warriors.

Turning back to the fray, Styrkar scanned the riotous battle. He searched for his prey but Robert had disappeared amid the violence. Instead his eye fell on Edgar, now engaged with a dismounted knight. They traded blows, battering one another's shields, before Edgar slipped on the ground now turned to mud. Still Styrkar did nothing to help, advancing slowly as the battle raged all around, watching as this boy who would be king fought desperately, gasping and growling as he fended off the knight's blows. Though Edgar was young and fit, the knight was clearly the stronger and more experienced. He had Edgar on his back, bearing down on him, smashing sword against shield as though felling a tree with it. The Aetheling gritted his teeth, facing the onslaught with determination, asking no quarter despite his desperate plight. It would be an end worthy of any king.

Styrkar's blow was swift, taking the knight in the neck. His body sagged, collapsing in a heap on top of his floundering foe. With some difficulty, Edgar pushed the dead weight off him.

'On your feet, boy,' Styrkar growled. 'You won't win any crowns sitting on your arse in the mud.'

As he helped Edgar up, he scanned the crowd once more. There, only a few yards away, Robert fought amidst the confusion. He shouted for his men to rally, but his voice was lost amid the din. A few of them had managed to raise their shields in a fractured wall around their lord, but it would not hold the northerners back for long.

'Are you with me, Aetheling?' Styrkar breathed.

Without answering, Edgar bellowed, shouting for his men to attack as he raced at the Frankish shields. Styrkar was not to be outdone, charging after Edgar and smashing into the knights. One of them fell back in the face of the assault, as Styrkar swung his sword again, taking another in the shoulder.

At the sound of Edgar's call, other northerners joined them. Maerlswein at the forefront, his long spear abandoned, to be replaced by a Dane axe that he swung to cave in the helm of one hapless knight. Styrkar had a chance to see Robert flee in a panic, dragging the stumbling Ethelwin with him along a dark path, as his men put up a last attempt to hold back the Saxon fury.

Riderless horses milled around the bloody street, corpses lay steaming in the chill air. A couple of the knights threw down their shields, holding up their hands, begging for mercy in the Frankish tongue.

Styrkar pushed his way through, seeing the trail in the snow Robert and the bishop had left. Edgar called for his men to follow as the rest of the Franks began to surrender. They didn't have to go far before they came to a stone dwelling in the shadow of Dun Holm's cathedral. Robert was already stumbling through the door as Ethelwin fell to his knees.

'The bishop's house,' Edgar breathed, stopping short of crossing the threshold.

'So what?' Styrkar said, taking a step forward.

'This is sacred ground,' Ethelwin blurted, fumbling at the metal cross about his neck and holding it up as though he might set a curse on any who would defy its sanctity. 'I offer sanctuary to Robert of Comines. Any Christian of faith who dares besmirch such a holy dictate will be excommunicated, and his soul damned to the everlasting fires of Hell.'

Edgar and his men had stopped now. Styrkar regarded the bishop, then turned to the Aetheling, who looked powerless to proceed.

'You heard him, Red Wolf,' Edgar said, his face spattered with blood, his lust for further slaughter sated. 'Our fight ends here, for now.'

'Your fight,' Styrkar said.

Edgar frowned. 'What do you mean?'

'You might fear for your soul, Aetheling, but I am no Christian.'

37

Dun Holm, England, January 1069

Ronan had watched as those horses trogged relentlessly through the snow. Saw Robert's standard flying high, saw him riding at the head of his army as it advanced ever closer to the jaws of a Saxon trap. He hated that bastard for what he had done to Gisela, but still he wanted to shout out a warning from the shadows, to yell at his enemy that there was danger here. He even took a faltering step forward as Robert and the bishop reined in their horses, but one of the warriors holding the rope at his neck tugged him back. He almost fell as the rope pulled tight about his throat, but he managed to stay on his feet, a silent witness to the slaughter that was about to take place.

All he could do was watch helplessly as Edgar stepped forward, that upstart boy, as he exchanged words with Robert. Two arrogant bastards in the snow, waving their cocks at one another. Of course Robert had fallen for the ruse, the stupid bastard. His hubris was always going to be the death of him. He'd barely moved as Edgar drew his sword, hacking out the horse's throat. Then the real killing had begun.

Screams consumed the square as the snow erupted alongside the column of horsemen. Robert's men had barely enough time to draw their swords before they were impaled on spears by the score. And as Ronan watched the ambush turn to butchery, all he could think about was how he would soon die.

Watching his only allies in this entire earldom cut down in front of him, made Ronan realise the fragility of his position, if he hadn't already known. When this was over, when Styrkar the Dane took his vengeance on Lord Robert, there would be only one thing keeping him alive. He would be forced to show the Red Wolf the whereabouts of his daughter, and once he had led him to that priory near the sea he would be of no further use. Styrkar would kill him, quickly, slowly, it mattered not which, he would be just as dead either way. Perhaps there might be an opportunity to escape in the coming days, but there was no guarantee of that. His best chance was to act now.

One of the Saxons guarding him stepped forward, gripping sword and shield tightly, watching intently at the battle raging mere yards away. He was clearly eager to rush forward into the melee and add his sword to the slaughter.

The second Saxon held tight to the rope at Ronan's neck. He stood close, and Ronan's eyes were suddenly drawn to a knife hanging loose in the scabbard at his belt.

'You should go, my friend,' he said to the boy, enrapt by the battle. 'They may need your—'

The one holding the rope about his neck punched Ronan hard in the ribs. He grunted, doubling up.

'Shut your fucking mouth, Frankish scum.'

Plain words, that really needn't have been said. As Ronan tried to suck the cold air into his lungs, he reckoned the Saxon's point had been well made. But he was running out of time. If he was kept here for much longer those Franks would die, no matter how valiantly they fought. Then he would be left at the Red Wolf's mercy – fated to become just another corpse in the snow.

'Are you just going to stand there?' Ronan spat at the boy, still watching as the battle raged. 'If you do nothing you will look like a coward. When your brothers later sing their songs of victory, will you hide in the shadows with nothing but your shame?'

Ronan expected another punch to the gut, but as the boy took another tentative step toward the fight, his fellow Saxon said, 'Wait. What are you doing?'

The boy shook his head, still staring at the battle. 'The cripple is right, Scobba. We have to help them.'

Scobba tugged on the leash at Ronan's neck once more, tightening it about his throat. 'We have been ordered to wait here.'

'But look,' said the boy, motioning to the skirmish. 'They need us.'

Scobba cursed at his friend's stubbornness. 'Maerlswein gave us this task himself.'

The boy just shook his head, taking another step. Scobba moved forward, desperate to stop him, and Ronan saw his chance. As the Saxon stepped in front of him he reached out with his bound hands and slipped Scobba's knife from its scabbard. He gripped it tight, realising he would have only one chance.

Before Scobba could grab the boy, Ronan slid the knife into the back of his neck. Scobba spasmed, his legs giving way. Still gripping tight to his only weapon, Ronan fell forward as his victim collapsed. He wrenched the knife from the back of Scobba's neck, reversing his grip, before plunging it into his back for good measure.

The boy hadn't even noticed the murder above the sound of violence raging in front of him, his focus entirely on the fighting. Leaving the knife buried in Scobba, Ronan picked up the dead man's fallen shield, swinging it as best he could. The edge caught the side of the boy's head. Ronan almost stumbled as the boy fell, raising the shield once more and bringing it down again and again until the boy went still.

He gasped in the cold air, glancing up, expecting one of the Saxons to have seen him in the act, and come racing to take his justice. A horse burst from the fray, its rider quickly impaled atop his saddle. There was no one to witness Ronan. No one to stop him fleeing into the night.

After wrenching the knife from Scobba's back, he began to limp through the snow, away from the fighting, toward the relative safety of the shadows. His leg screamed as he squeezed between two close-built huts, feeling elation begin to bloom as the sound of the battle relented behind him.

Dun Holm was all but abandoned but for its main thoroughfare, and Ronan fled unhindered, eyes wide with the thrill of escape. His hands were still bound, and he held the knife tight, but he would have to see to that later. With any luck he would be able to cut the rope free of his wrists and hide somewhere, anywhere. For now he had to put as much distance between him and the fighting as he could manage.

'You there!'

A voice from somewhere behind him. Ronan would have carried on running, but his cursed leg chose that moment to fail him. His foot slipped, raw pain tearing up from ankle to knee before he went sprawling in the snow.

He tried to pick himself up but it was all he could do to stifle the murmur of pain desperate to escape his lips. A glance over one shoulder and he saw someone trotting toward him through the drift. An old man, Saxon, some kind of club in his hand. This was all he needed – to be beaten to death by some peasant bastard miles away from anywhere.

The knife was still in his grip, but on his knees and with his hands tied he'd be useless with it, even against one old man. Slowly he slid it into his belt, covering it with his shirt, as the old man drew closer.

'Who are you?' the man said. 'What are you doing?'

He would have thought that much was obvious – floundering in the snow like a drunkard thrown from an alehouse.

'I... I was a prisoner,' Ronan said, feigning his best English accent, and acting as pitifully as he could manage. It needed little effort. 'Brought by those Frankish bastards, to make an example of me in front of the town. But when the fighting started I just ran.'

'Let me help you,' the man said, taking a surprisingly strong hold of Ronan's arm and pulling him up from the snow.

It was all Ronan could do to stifle a smile. 'My thanks, friend. I was beginning to think I might freeze out here in the snow.'

The old man took a knife from his sheath and began to slice at the rope binding Ronan's wrists. 'Never fear. You can take shelter in my home till all this is over. Those foreign arseholes don't stand a chance. They never should have come this far north.' When he had freed Ronan's hands, the old man clapped him on the shoulder. 'This way.'

He turned to lead Ronan through the snow. A kindly old man, doing his best to help. Doing his best to defend his land from invaders. There was every chance he'd never done anyone any harm in his life.

Ronan took the knife from his belt and cut the man's throat, hacking deep and swift. He let out a gurgle as he died, and Ronan pushed him forward, in no mood to look into those accusing eyes. Blood stained the snowy ground, as Ronan glanced from left to right to make sure no one had witnessed the murder.

'You have my apologies, friend,' Ronan said as he regarded the body. 'And also my gratitude.'

He should have run then, put as much distance between him and his dark deed as possible. Instead he stood for a moment, trying to reconcile the odd feeling that swelled up within.

Any ambitions Ronan might have harboured to be a good man were as dead as the corpse at his feet. They had died with Gisela, he knew that now. All those hopes, the aspiration he could be something other than a brutal servant to a brutal king, were dashed in an instant. Only Ronan remained. Not the man he had hoped to be, but the base monster everyone said he was. With that one, cold realisation it felt as though a great burden had suddenly been lifted. His life making sense once more... the only life he had, and if he didn't get his crippled leg moving, he'd lose it pretty soon.

He stumbled on, the distant noise of the battle growing quieter. The Franks were almost beaten, those savage Saxons having finally taken their revenge.

A horse dashed from the gap in two nearby shacks, snorting in derision. Ronan dodged into the shadows as the rider barely noticed him. He was pursued by half a dozen spearmen, who cornered him against the side of a long, stone feast hall.

Ronan kept to the shadows as he sneaked past, the unarmed rider bellowing in fury, and then pain as he was jabbed a dozen times by the Saxon spears. His screams rose in pitch as he was hoisted from the saddle, but Ronan shut out the horror, his only thoughts now on escape. He had to flee, to leave this madness behind him, but how? Even if he escaped the palisade of Dun Ho_m he would surely succumb to the harsh northern elements.

As the sounds of violence subsided, he finally made it to the wooden wall. Keeping one hanc braced against the palisade for support, he slowly picked his way around the town. His heart was beating a drum in his chest, and he could barely breathe the chill air anymore. Ronan would not allow himself to stop. He had come too far, and suffered too much, to give in now.

Through a blur of tears he saw something move up ahead. He froze, heart sinking like a stone at the prospect of being caught. A snort from the darkness, and Ronan was squinting, wiping away the wet in his eyes. In front of him stood a horse, riderless and alone in the shadow of the palisade. He'd never believed in miracles before now, but he would certainly give them credence if this was real.

'Woah there, you beautiful beast,' he cooed, moving forward slowly lest the steed take flight.

The horse snorted again as he reached out a hand to brush its hide, feeling the muscles tremble at the stallion's neck. His other hand snapped forward, grasping the rein before the horse could bolt. It reared, but Ronan held on fast, dragging its head down by the bridle. In one last desperate motion he leapt for the saddle, gritting his teeth against the pain in his leg. The horse trotted in a circle as he struggled to swing his good leg over its back, finally managing to seat himself. Grasping the reins he kicked heels to flanks, steering the beast toward the wide-open gates.

Trot turned to canter, then to gallop, as he fixed his eyes on the open gates and the dark squall of the storm beyond. From the corner of one eye he saw bearded Saxons rushing to intercept him, but they would never be fast enough. Their cries of rage were lost on the wind as the horse careered through the gate and out into the blustery night.

He was free, and that was all that mattered. Fuck the north. Fuck the Saxons. And fuck the day he had ever heard the name Red fucking Wolf.

38

Dun Holm, England, January 1069

The old bishop looked fearful, but still he clung to the doorframe like Heimdallr guarding the Rainbow Bridge.

'If you value your life, you will move aside, priest,' Styrkar said. His blood rage had passed now. Every action was measured, controlled. This one last kill would be unhurried, and he would savour every intimate moment of it.

Ethelwin shook his head. 'If you value your eternal soul you will turn back from this house of God. You may not pass the threshold—'

Styrkar grasped the priest's robe and lifted him off his feet. He could see the terror in his eyes. So much for faith in his God.

'I do not believe in your White Christ or your Holy Cross, old man. Your curses hold no terror for me.'

'Heathen,' Ethelwin breathed. 'Pagan scum.'

'Words are more worthless than blind faith. Move from my path so that I may have my reckoning, or join the man you have given sanctuary after I send him to meet your God.'

Ethelwin's lip trembled. He was close to tears. It was doubtful his faith had ever been tested as much as this. It was a test he failed.

Styrkar loosened his grip on the bishop, who quickly scrambled out of the way. One push and the door opened. A single torch burned within, shedding scant light on the cross that hung on the wall, the candles unlit on the shelves, icons and symbols of a God that could help no one now the Red Wolf had come to slay his last victim.

Cautiously he stepped over the threshold, expecting Robert to be waiting with sword in hand to defend himself. Instead, he saw a man kneeling next to the blackened hearth, hands clasped, shorn head bowed as he prayed. It was a disappointing sight. Styrkar had heard this Frankish lord was a brute, a warrior of renown, but it seemed his courage had given out at the last moment.

'Your prayers serve no purpose now,' Styrkar said, as the door creaked closed behind him, shutting out the noisome sound of the northern warriors outside.

Robert gazed up with tears in his eyes. Despite clasping his hands tight together they still shook in fright. 'This is a house of God. I am protected by the divine right of sanctuary.'

'Protected? Just as Gisela was protected? But that did not save her.'

Robert frowned in confusion. 'Gisela? I don't know who you're talking about.'

A flicker of anger and the Red Wolf gripped his axe tighter, feeling the wood solid against his palm, aching to use it. 'I do not doubt that. I guess a man such as you would remember few of the lives he has taken. Those you have raped. Butchered.'

'I was only doing my duty to the king,' Robert blurted as Styrkar paced relentlessly toward him. 'If you have a quarrel it is with him, not me. I am just the sword in his hand.'

'Every man is judged by his deeds, no matter the name of his master.'

'But you will gain nothing by murdering me.'

Styrkar towered over the knight, the urge to kill filling his belly like a fire. 'I will gain vengeance.'

'I have gold. The king has gold, coffers brimming with it. I am worth more to you alive than dead. King William would pay handsomely for my life. Think. Think on what you could gain by offering me for ransom. You could have whatever you desired. Wealth. Land—'

'Can you give me back the mother of my child?'

Robert's face changed. His fear drifted as he realised there was nothing he could say that would spare him his fate. That only served to anger Styrkar more. He would have preferred this man to be snivelling, begging, showing himself for the coward he was. But now it seemed he was resigned to what was coming.

'It seems there is nothing I can give you,' Robert said.

'Your head is enough,' Styrkar replied.

Robert closed his eyes, mumbling more prayers to his God. Begging that his soul be spared eternal damnation. Pleading forgiveness. Still Styrkar did not raise the axe.

It should have been so easy, one swift strike to end this. To end the pain. But he could not help but wonder if this was what Gisela would have wanted. More death. Another corpse in the ground alongside so many others. More likely she would have offered mercy. Forgiveness. But then she had the sweetest soul of all. For the Red Wolf there remained only bitterness.

He swung the axe. A single act he had performed countless times in taking the lives of countless men. Sometimes he had raged, crying his fury as he hacked down warriors by the dozen. This time there was only the sound of the blade slicing through that thick neck. Robert's head fell to the floor with a dull thud, the body slumping to one side.

What had he been expecting when the deed was done? Looking down at the corpse, Styrkar felt no sudden release.

He took a step back, leaning against the wall. His legs gave way and he was suddenly crouched on the ground. Exhaustion hung heavy on his shoulders now. He had staved it off for days, a burden he had managed to carry with nothing but his desire for vengeance. With that satisfied he felt as though there was no strength left. His burden was gone. Now all that remained was the desire to find his child.

But should he? That innocent girl might be better off without him. He was the Red Wolf. The bane of the Franks. The Shield Breaker. Could he ever be just a father? The severed head lying in the shadows of a holy man's house suggested otherwise. Those dead eyes glaring from the dark gave him pause. Robert had deserved to die – any man who had lost their lover to such a monster would have done the same. But Styrkar was not just any man. He was as much a beast.

He pushed himself to his feet, taking a laboured step forward before he stooped to pick up the severed head by the ear, since there was no hair to grab it by. The door to the house was swinging open in the breeze, and he used his axe to push it wide, stepping out into the cold night to see an army waiting for him.

The northerners were standing in silence, every face turned toward the door as he walked out. Some looked eager to see what had happened, others breathed heavily from the fight, their faces still spattered with the gore of vanquished Franks. As the Red Wolf raised the head of their dead enemy for all to see, a sudden cheer went up.

Edgar stepped to the fore, to take his place beside Styrkar. 'You see?' he cried. 'The Red Wolf has shown us the way. He has defied the word of a bishop, taken the head of William's servant, and yet here he stands. The Lord God has not struck him down. There is no ominous rumble of thunder. Surely we are blessed by Christ in our mission to retake these lands.'

Edgar's army roared its approval, bashing their weapons against their shields. Among them knelt the captured Franks who had survived the battle. Their hands had been tied behind them, their faces beaten and bloody. Edgar regarded those defeated men with disdain.

'These foreigners have rampaged across England's pastures and forests. They have burned and pillaged every acre. It is our divine right to mete justice upon them before we make our way south.' He took the head of Robert from Styrkar's hand and held it aloft. 'What is this?' he demanded.

There was a lull among the crowd as the Aetheling turned the head so they could all see that dead face. None of them had an answer.

Edgar's mouth widened to a rictus grin before he growled, 'A good first step.'

Maerlswein answered with a feral roar. The steward of the fyrd raised his axe high and brought it down on the exposed head of a Frankish prisoner, splitting it like a log, spewing crimson on the snow. Like hounds on a fox, the rest of the northerners took his lead. Weapons rising and falling. Hacking down their prisoners where they knelt, before any of them could think to plead for mercy.

As they went about their cruel business, Gospatric pushed his way forward. Though he wore helm and shield as though dressed for war, it looked as though he had managed to avoid much of the fighting. There was no mark on him, nor a drop of blood to sully his mail.

'Edgar, this is madness,' he spat, his eyes wide with concern. 'We cannot just slaughter the king's men and expect no reprisals. Do you realise what you've started?'

The Aetheling cast Robert's severed head aside, letting it bounce on the ground to rest in the doorway of the bishop's house. He reached forward and grabbed the collar of Gospatric's jerkin, spinning him around to view the slaughter.

'I know exactly what I've started. This...' He pointed at the last of the Franks as their bodies were pummelled repeatedly by axe and sword. 'This is not about any of us. This is not about reclaiming a title and some spots of land. This is about the crown of England, and ensuring it rests on the head of a worthy king. We are on a road now, Gospatric. A road on which we take no prisoners.'

He shoved the ealdorman aside, glaring at his men before gesturing to the house behind him. 'Burn it to the ground,' he ordered.

With a cheer, torches were lobbed atop the thatch.

One or two men raced forward to fling their burning brands through the open door. As the house took light, Edgar turned to Styrkar. 'Will you walk with me, Red Wolf?'

It seemed a fair request. As the house burned, and the curses of Bishop Ethelwin rose to the sound of crackling flames, Styrkar walked by Edgar's side back toward the marketplace of Dun Holm. The ordinary folk had come out of their houses by the time they reached it, picking over the bodies of the dead Franks like carrion crows.

'Our next move is to push south, and quickly,' Edgar said. 'If we are to gain a foothold in the north, Yorke must be the next city to fall.' He stopped, turning to Styrkar and regarding him with a frown. 'I hope we can gain support on the way, the people of the northern burhs and hamlets, but I will also need capable veterans.'

Styrkar glanced at the townsfolk still tentatively peering from their homes. They were fearful, but the relief in their faces was obvious. They had just been spared the ravages of Lord Robert and his men. Edgar had saved them from their fate, with Styrkar's help. Without doubt it was what Harold would have wanted. And Edith, and Magnus. Even Gisela would have asked him to do all he could to spare these families from the cruelty of the Franks in any way he could. Was it right for him to abandon the rest of the country to its fate for his own selfish ends?

'Yes,' he replied. 'I am with you, Aetheling.'

A smile crossed Edgar's face and he clapped Styrkar on the shoulder. 'Then I am honoured to have the Red Wolf at my side.'

A northern warrior came toward them through the snow.

Styrkar recognised him as one of the fyrd he had set to guard Ronan.

'My lord,' the young man said, bowing his head, unable to look either of them in the eye. 'I am sorry but your prisoner has escaped.' He swallowed, the shame of failure clearly cutting deep. 'He murdered Scobba. Stole a horse. I am sorry my lord…'

Edgar placed a hand on the young warrior's shoulder. 'It is all right. He shall get what he deserves, as will all these invaders.' He looked to Styrkar. 'I am sorry, my friend. I hope this bastard was not too important to you.'

For a moment Styrkar thought about the daughter he had not seen, and now might never. How he had already thought on that being the best outcome. But it seemed now the decision was taken from his hands for good. Though it hurt that his child might never even know her father's name, he knew now it was for the best.

'No,' Styrkar said. 'He was of no importance at all.'

39

The air was biting, the sky overcast as he strode toward the main gate. Before he could enter through the ancient ramparts he felt the tension in the air. A dread pall hung over the entire city, those fortified walls looking as though they'd been erected as much to keep its people in as keep anyone out.

When last he had entered Yorke it had been as victor. They had smashed Sigurdsson's army and driven it back across the northern plains, freeing the country from tyranny, for a short while at least. Now he was nothing more than a lone rebel, and tyranny once more held the north in its cloying grip.

No one tried to stop him as he entered, the ordinary folk carrying on with their business, but there was a keen sense of unease. Frankish guards milled about the gate, given a wide berth by the populace. Most likely they revelled in the power they held over these people. Conquerors regarded with nothing but fear. How far they would fall when the Red Wolf laid them low.

Once inside, Styrkar realised how much the place had changed since last he was here. At Harold's side he had experienced the verve of the place. Seen how the ancestors of both Saxon and Dane had mixed as though they were kin, their differences forgotten. Now the atmosphere was subdued, and the Franks had turned this once vibrant place into little more than a charnel house.

The first sight that greeted him was a row of corpses hung from a gibbet. Four bodies swung gently, left to rot for all to see. Beside them were more heads than he could count skewered upon poles, flies buzzing about them in a frenzied dance, despite the cold. A stark warning of what lay in store for any who defied the new order of things. There would be a reckoning for this – and sooner than the unsuspecting Franks might think.

Styrkar took up a position close to the gate. Nearby a smith rang a tune in his forge. It was the only music on the quiet street, almost the only sound at all. Gone was the chatter of street vendors or the lilting refrain of a minstrel. Only that ring of hammer on anvil – the tolling of a bell to herald the coming storm.

Someone shouted from atop the battlement – a Frankish voice, panicked and shrill. The guards at the gate spoke back with urgency in their sing-song language. Through the arch, they could see what was coming now. Edgar led his army from the woods nearby, a host gathered from all across the north, and the Franks could finally see what price they would pay for their butchery.

Half a dozen of them rushed toward the gate, desperate to bar it against the advancing war host. Without a word, Styrkar grasped the axe beneath his cloak, his measured stride closing the gap to the desperate gate guards. From the opposite side of the street another hooded figure approached, mirroring his advance. Maerlswein had an equally vicious axe in his own hand.

Before he reached the guards, two more of Edgar's fyrd revealed themselves from behind a nearby building, raising bows, nocking, drawing. Styrkar's swing took the first Frank in the neck and he fell without sound. The thrum of bowstrings rang through the air, a yelp of pain before Maerlswein bellowed. Another guard turned, eyes widening before he was greeted by Maerlswein's axe. The violence was brief but bloody, and in a moment the way was clear for the army beyond the gate.

There was a shout behind. Styrkar turned to see one of the Franks yelling in alarm, racing toward the centre of the city, but he was tackled by two men – ordinary folk of the city. In an instant the people of Yorke flocked to their side and began to beat the armoured man where he lay. A woman wrenched the helmet from his head as another began to smash his skull with a rock.

Emboldened by the sudden spark, more of Yorke's peasants began to shout encouragement to one another. It spread through the streets as they took to the ramparts, attacking the hapless Franks atop their battlement. A torch was thrown at the hut next to the gate, its thatch starting to burn, a show of defiance that quickly spread, infesting the streets like a plague of rats.

By the time Edgar reached the gate at the head of his fyrd, more buildings were burning further inside the city, shouts of alarm rising in pitch across the rooftops.

'I only asked you to see the way clear, Red Wolf,' he said, viewing the carnage already spreading in front of him. 'Not set the city aflame.'

'It would seem the people of Yorke are as keen to see an end to their subjugation as you are, Aetheling.'

Edgar grinned. 'Then we had best help fulfil their ambitions.' He raised his sword before yelling, 'Advance!'

The fyrd poured through the gates, men gathered from as far north as Dun Holm, down to the Thrydings of Efor. Styrkar walked at Edgar's shoulder as he led his men through the city, the dung heap smell of the streets now mixing with the stink of burning buildings. When they reached a crossroads, Edgar turned to Gospatric who stood close to his cousin Waltheof.

'Take your men along the western path,' he ordered. 'I will meet you at the cathedral.'

Both men nodded their assent. They had once been magnates in their own right, but each one now followed the word of the Aetheling as though he were their thegn.

Styrkar could see the huge cathedral rising above the rooftops. To left and right the alleyways and passages were in turmoil as the city-folk hunted down their persecutors and dispensed swift justice. He felt the excitement build, his blood coursing as they came out onto the wide open field that lay at the foot of the huge church.

Here the Franks had chosen to make their stand. Hundreds of them, shields braced, spears made ready. A few had managed to mount their warhorses, the beasts snorting and stamping in anticipation of the battle to come.

Edgar roared, his lust for battle overtaking his sense. His men took up their weapons, sensing what was coming, yearning to strike back at the heart of the enemy as they had done at Dun Holm. Styrkar might have urged caution but he too was caught up in the reverie, throwing off his cloak and charging along with him.

They had not covered ten yards before the folly of their zeal was revealed.

Flanking them on both sides were crossbowmen, hidden in buildings that overlooked the field. Edgar had fallen into as devious a trap as he had set in Dun Holm.

Bolts strafed their flanks. Men fell screaming as the air hummed with the sound of bow fire. Styrkar barely had a chance to raise his shield before it was struck by a volley. Over its brim he could see the Frankish archers shooting from the right, their elevated position giving them a perfect view of the open ground.

'Form a wall,' Edgar cried above the din of dying men.

The fyrd crowded together in their hundreds, raising their shields high. Sudden darkness consumed them as they shielded themselves from the relentless volley. Through a gap in their defences, Styrkar could see some men cut down as they were too slow to join the defenders. Some had already fled in panic, others too stubborn or enraged to defend themselves, charged at the Frankish line to be run through by a spear and cut down by knights on horseback.

'What do we do?' yelled a panicked voice.

'Hold your bloody nerve,' growled Maerlswein close by.

Someone screamed next to Styrkar, falling forward and opening a gap in the shield wall. His body exposed, he was struck by another bolt, then another, before the gap in the shields was plugged.

The Franks were bellowing at one another, riling themselves up in preparation for a charge. Styrkar risked a glance through the shields, seeing the horsemen gathering, ready to make their attack as they had done so many times on Senlac Hill. Before they could begin, there were shouts of alarm from the flank.

'Look,' someone shouted. 'Their crossbows.'

Flames were licking at one of the buildings housing Frankish archers, the men inside already shouting in panic. Before Styrkar could wonder who had come to their aid, a roar echoed from across the field as Gospatric and Waltheof led their fyrd to attack the enemy flank.

Edgar stood up from the shield wall, raising that jewelled sword. 'On me, men of the north!'

Maerlswein roared, punching the sky with his axe, his eyes fierce in the face of the hated Franks. Styrkar bolted forward, in no mood to be left behind as the Saxons raced across the open ground at their foe.

A thousand warriors battered the Frankish shield wall. Some of their warhorses bolted, those organised groups now scattering in disarray. Styrkar's axe rose and fell a dozen times as he battered at the shields of his enemy, crushing their will, forcing them back. Though he was filled with hate, and frenzied by the work, he began to feel fatigue creep into his bones.

The cries of dying men plagued his ears where before he would have revelled in the song of battle. A thrusting spear barely missed his face, a barking knight gave him pause, forcing him to take a step back in the face of his attack.

A memory flashed in front of his eyes – a dying man in a pit, starved and desperate, begging for mercy. Styrkar shook his head to rid himself of the thought but he was unmanned, and staggered wearily among the fray.

Was this what fear felt like? Was this how a coward faced his end on the battlefield?

More bodies poured onto the open plain before the cathedral. The townsfolk of Yorke had come to heed Edgar's call, and they began to pelt the Frankish lines with stones, harrying their defences as the northern fyrd took advantage and pushed them back to the walls of the great church.

Through the confusion, Styrkar spied one of the Franks picking his way through the melee, his shield raised, desperate to flee. He recognised that frightened face, feeling urgency grip his innards. Ronan.

Styrkar leapt forward with renewed vigour, yelling as he raised his axe. Ronan's eyes widened at his approach, his shield not coming up fast enough to stop the axe before it caved in his forehead.

The Red Wolf's bellow of victory tore at his throat, only to be cut short when he realised this was not Ronan at all, but just another corpse on the field. Another Frank come to rape and steal, with only ash and blood as his reward.

What was happening? Were his senses betraying him? His eyes were filled with fog, his veins pumping hot tar through his body. Styrkar staggered back, losing his footing on another corpse, just as something hit him in the head.

He fell, feeling the warm sensation of blood running down his cheek. The axe was gone from his grip, the confusion of battle raging around him in a tumult. He tried to move but his limbs would not obey. The world around him span, and he shook his head, desperate to clear it.

Gradually he managed to focus, seeing a figure in white approaching through the maelstrom. She stepped across the battlefield unsullied by the violence that raged around her. Gisela's face was serene among the violence, her eyes focused only on him. Styrkar had to stand, to help her, to hold her again, but he was too weak to move. He tried to call out but his voice was lost on the cloying air.

Gisela held out a hand to him across the battle, and Styrkar felt his strength ebb. Tears filled his eyes as he swallowed down a sob. He had already lost her once, and as her image faded he felt the keen dread of knowing he might never see that face again.

Hooves pounded the ground, the rhythm of their beat drawing nearer. Styrkar's eyes focused in time to see a knight charging, his warhorse a black silhouette against the roiling crowd, lance levelled at his heart.

He tried to stand, to face this bastard like a warrior, but the days and weeks of fighting in a pit, of being starved and beaten, had finally taken their toll. He could do nothing to avoid the fate racing toward him.

Someone screamed in rage. A deafening cry of defiance in his periphery that heralded the throw of a spear.

The knight was impaled in his saddle, pitched backwards as his steed carried on its charge, galloping past Styrkar and away into the city. As he reeled from the prospect of death, he managed to look up, seeing the bloodied figure of Edgar standing over him.

He gratefully took Edgar's outstretched hand, painfully

rising to his feet. The battle was subsiding, the remaining Franks fleeing for their lives only to run into the furious grip of Yorke's abused and battered people.

'I owe you my life, Aetheling,' Styrkar whispered.

'You owe me nothing, Red Wolf,' Edgar replied. 'You have helped gift me the north.'

And as the sound of battle subsided, the bells of Yorke's cathedral began to ring across the city. Styrkar watched as Edgar made his way across the field, walking among both corpse and victor, his name called out in unison by his men – *Edgar, Edgar, Edgar*.

It wasn't long before the ordinary folk of Yorke began to join in with their chant, heralding the man they would have raised as their new king. For Styrkar there was no elation. His voice was the only one silent among a chorus of thousands, as though he alone realised this was far from over.

40

F our men were tied to stakes, clothes torn, faces
displaying varying degrees of bruising, from purple
welts to pounded meat. Surrounding them was a hushed
crowd. It looked as though the whole of Yorke had come
to see justice done, and brought their children with them
for good measure. Though they were silent, Styrkar could
still sense their hate, simmering like a pot about to boil
over.

Edgar paced before the prisoners, drawing out the
moment, allowing the tension to build. His own anger
was obvious, his face a solemn mask of contempt. Was he
doubting his current actions? Considering mercy? Was this
a line he was reluctant to cross? He had been but a boy two
years ago. Now he was judge and executioner. A war leader.
He had the stomach for battle, no one could doubt that, but
did he have the stomach for this?

Those prisoners surely thought so. Styrkar could see
more than one of them had already soiled his leggings, the

348

stink of shit and fear wafted from where they knelt, bound and waiting to die.

As though his mind had suddenly been made, Edgar turned to the crowd, raising his chin and pointing an arm at the kneeling wretch in the centre of the group.

'This man,' he proclaimed, voice strong and steady. A good start. 'This man came here to subjugate you all. To take your city. To persecute you. To steal your freedom as well as your lives.'

Disquiet spread throughout the gathering. Murmurs of assent. A hiss of contempt.

The man on his knees glared about the crowd in terror from the one eye that hadn't been battered to a swollen lump. As pitiful as the sight was, Styrkar felt little sympathy, but neither did he share the bloodthirsty fervour of the crowd. He could well imagine how the man felt. Not so long ago it had been Styrkar who was beaten and bound. Not a good position for anyone – especially a man who had come to conquer.

'The rest of these bastards chose to throw in their lot with a tyrant,' Edgar continued, glaring at the other men lashed to their posts. 'Chose to turn their backs on their own kinsmen. People they had known and who trusted them.'

Now the crowd was more animated, reserving the bulk of their ire for those they felt had betrayed them. The other men on their knees had been stewards and officials of Saxon and Danish blood, tempted by the power King William had dangled before their eyes. They had gambled on the wrong man.

'Every one of these curs will ultimately be judged by

God.' Edgar pointed a finger at the grey sky, his eyes wide with fury. 'But first, they will be judged by us all.'

As the crowd raised their voices in a cheer, the prisoner at the front began to babble desperately in the Frankish tongue. It was doubtful he could speak the language of the English, but even he must have seen what was coming. Styrkar had no idea what he was saying, but it was clear Edgar understood every word.

Their exchange was brief, an entreaty for mercy that Edgar listened to without emotion before he leaned in close to the steward and spoke one word, 'Non.'

Easy enough to understand, even for a man who could not speak the language of Frankia.

Edgar turned to the crowd. 'I leave it to the folk of Yorke to bring their justice to the north. A justice that has—'

Before he could finish the first stone was thrown. It hit one of the kneeling English in the shoulder and he grunted. After that first stone came more, in ones and twos as though the city folk were reluctant to discharge their fury. But after one of those stones hit the steward in the head, and he wailed like a lost child, the crowd was emboldened.

Hail fell on the prisoners, as Edgar moved to the side, watching with a grim expression. Styrkar had seen enough violence in recent days. Though these men deserved their fate he took no relish in it.

He turned toward the edge of the square, where his eye was caught by something waving in the breeze. Among the distant onlookers was a white-garbed woman. Styrkar squinted, barely able to make out her features in the distance.

Gisela?

He almost spoke the name, but stopped himself when he realised the folly of that hope. Gritting his teeth against his grief, he turned back to see Edgar beside him.

'Come,' said the Aetheling. 'Our work is finished here, but there is much more yet to do.'

With the sound of men being stoned into their graves behind, Styrkar followed Edgar away from the execution. The rest of the city was quiet now, a far cry from the day they had arrived. Still, it felt as though the folk of Yorke still feared to leave their homes and carry on their lives in freedom. Perhaps they knew, as Styrkar did, that they were far from freed yet.

'The Sheriff of Efor fled south as soon as our attack began,' said Edgar, hand resting on that jewelled hilt. If he was affected by condemning those men to death he did not show it. Perhaps demonstrating just the stoicism he would need if he was to be king. 'Maerlswein and his fyrd pursue him even now, but I doubt their chances of catching him.'

Styrkar shrugged. 'Whether Maerlswein catches him or not, news of your victory will reach William's ears soon enough. You have defied him. He will strike back with all the fury the Franks can muster.'

A nod from Edgar. 'That is inevitable. Even though we now hold a bastion in the north, William still holds the south.'

'So we must shore up our defences. Ensure the walls are strong enough to repel him.'

'I am not sure even the strongest fortifications can hold William back forever. He has a formidable army at his command. And we have... one city.'

They had reached the bridge over the Ouse. The river

flowed wide beneath its solid structure. From its midpoint they could see across the whole of Yorke.

'The walls of this city have stood for centuries,' Styrkar said.

Edgar gestured along the great river. 'And yet there is a way into the city along the Ouse from east and west. Yorke's ramparts may be ancient but much of them are crumbling and in disrepair.'

'They cannot bring their steeds into the city by water. William will want his knights at the fore to trample us to dust. We should look to our walls and build them high.'

Before Edgar could answer they saw Gospatric and Waltheof approaching from the other side of the river. Both men looked troubled, their twin frowns making the cousins look more alike than ever, despite the differences in their bearing.

'The city is ours, Edgar,' Gospatric said. 'Our intentions are made clear now that we hold the north. So I would ask again that we send word to King William. We now have a position of strength from which to bargain.'

Edgar clenched his fists, darkness descending over his youthful features. 'Again Gospatric?' he snarled, so furiously it even made Styrkar balk. 'After we have seized yet another victory you would choose to bargain with the Bastard? You are right, we hold Yorke and the north along with it. I am not about to just hand it back to William in return for empty promises.'

Surprisingly, Gospatric was not cowed by Edgar's response. 'You think we can hold this city forever? Word will reach him soon and he will make his way here with fire and steel.'

Instead of raging, Edgar turned to gaze out over the river, before spitting a gob over the side of the bridge. 'And I will be waiting with men gathered from across the northern Thrydings. Men determined to take a stand against the usurper.' He turned back to Gospatric. 'Are you too scared to join us, ealdorman?'

Gospatric bristled at the suggestion he was craven, but he had no answer. Instead, Waltheof stepped forward beside his cousin.

'We admire your courage, Aetheling. Your bravery has inspired the whole of the north. Many men will flock to your banner with the promise of freedom, but it is no good to them if they are dead.'

Edgar sighed. 'I hear you, Waltheof. Believe me, I do. But I was chosen at the witan to rule this country, and I would see its people freed.' He turned to Styrkar. 'What say you, Red Wolf? Do I at least have your support?'

Edgar already knew the answer to that, but it was clear he wanted Styrkar to say it in front of his skittish allies.

'I am done running,' Styrkar answered. 'I have waited many moons for another chance to face the Bastard in battle. I can think of no better place than here. No better time than now. And I would have no other man at my shoulder, Aetheling.'

'This is madness,' said Gospatric, throwing up his arms in frustration. 'We cannot hope to prevail on the field against William and his army. He and his allies have proven themselves at Senlac. In Exonia, in Waruic, in every part of the bloody south. How do you hope to stop him here in this crumbling relic of a city?'

Now it was Styrkar's turn to step forward. He towered

over Gospatric who, to his credit, did not take a step back. 'The walls of Yorke are not strong. There are breaches in every rampart. But all we have to do is stop his horses running rampant through the streets. Stop his mounted knights and we can defend this city for as long as we need.'

Gospatric shook his head in frustration. 'We have neither the army nor the supplies to wait out a siege. We will starve before he gives in.'

Edgar placed a hand on both their shoulders, perhaps sensing this might end in more than just a disagreement on tactics. 'My friends, perhaps we won't have to.' He was smiling, all his doubt now faded away. 'All we need do is bait the trap, and draw in his mounted warriors as we did at Dun Holm. Give them a glimpse of victory before we strike back and slaughter them.'

'Wasn't that William's own tactic at Senlac?' Waltheof asked. 'To bait the fyrd into breaking the shield wall?'

'It was,' said Styrkar, remembering well their despair when the fyrd who had raced down the hill were cut to pieces in a counter charge.

'Then he has proven it works,' snapped Edgar. 'And it will be the last thing he would expect, for his own ruse to be used against him. I realise you all have your doubts, but I will not abandon Yorke. Flee if you want to. Run and hide in the forests, but know this... the north is watching. If you hope to rule here again, your deeds over the next few days will decide whether the people of the north will follow you, or judge you as cowards.'

Before either of the cousins could protest, the hulking figure of Maerlswein made his way along the bridge, with some of his fyrd close behind. His beard looked unkempt, his garb dishevelled from the road.

'My lord Edgar,' he said with a nod. 'We pursued the sheriff for as long as our steeds would allow, but he escaped.'

Edgar clapped Maerlswein on the shoulder. 'No matter, my friend. You did well.' Then, turning to the others, 'It seems our time has run out. The decision has to be made. Gospatric, Waltheof, if you are with me, gather your men, prepare the walls for a siege.'

Silence. Then Waltheof let out a long breath of resignation. 'Looks like we have no bloody choice at all, Aetheling. We are with you.'

With that, the cousins, along with Maerlswein, made off to prepare the city of Yorke for the storm that was coming. Edgar turned to Styrkar when they were finally left alone.

'One more battle, Red Wolf? Do you have it in you?'

Styrkar turned to look at the distant ramparts, realising how much work was to be done before the battle to come. 'I am with you, Aetheling.'

'Who knows, perhaps you will have your chance to face King William himself.'

Styrkar's eye was caught by the billowing of a white dress below the southern gate, but he turned his head before he could see who might be wearing it.

'That's what I'm counting on.'

41

A rook cawed its annoyance, breaking the silence within the wall. Two hundred men stood staring to the south, through the open breach known as the Myglagata – the Great Gate – built by the Danes as a main thoroughfare to the south. It was meant to funnel trade right into the city. Today it would only funnel an army intent on bloodshed.

Styrkar thought it fitting that he would die here, in the shadow of a gate built by his ancestral countrymen. It gave him some small comfort. For the rest of these men he guessed they would have to find solace in their own way as they faced the relentless tide making its way north.

He glanced over at the ramparts surrounding them, regretting it as he did so. She was there, standing atop that battlement, face a mask of serenity, white dress flowing in the gentle winter breeze. Had she come to take him to Valhöll so he might live forever in the Dread Hall?

Styrkar shook his head, dismissing the image, trying to focus on the here and now. On what was coming. The

Myglagata was the only entrance to Yorke south of the River Ouse. It would be William's only way to take the city. They had reinforced the walls as best they could, but there were still breaches. To the east, the way was guarded by Waltheof and his fyrd, and to the west, Gospatric stood watch. With no way to cross the river, the Franks would be forced to attack the only opening available to them. And the Red Wolf would be waiting.

In the mouth of the gate a wagon had been turned on its side, sacks full of dirt piled around it. With luck, it would be too tempting an entrance for the Franks to ignore. If they could defend the pass just fiercely enough, it would draw the enemy into a funnel, and give them the impression that Yorke was held by little more than a disjointed rabble of peasants. Then they would lead the king's army into a killing field where Edgar's archers were waiting.

The Aetheling stood at Styrkar's side. He too was focused on the road that ran south from the gate, a curious smile upon his lips. It was as though this king-in-waiting relished his chance to finally face William in battle – to prove he was no untested boy, but a man worthy of a crown. Styrkar could only think it was foolish for him to endanger his life this way, but then he knew all too well that a man could not prove himself a king without risking himself alongside his army. No one would follow a coward, and Edgar had already proven himself far from craven.

'You should not be here,' Styrkar whispered. 'You should wait back with the others. There is no need for you to stand at the vanguard.'

A smirk on Edgar's face as he continued to stare to the far distance. 'My place is here, Red Wolf, by your side. My days of hiding behind other men are over. I am not so naïve to realise that I have been used for the betterment of other men in the past. That time is at an end.' He turned to look Styrkar in the eye. 'It is *my* time now.'

Styrkar felt a swell of pride, and not a little hope rise within him. It did not last as he looked back to the road.

Horses and men marched from the south, a host that swelled to fill the horizon. Someone needlessly shouted a word of warning from atop the rampart, but they could all hear what was coming. The distant sound of a horn blowing, a drum banging, the relentless tramp of hooves.

Styrkar squinted in the sun, taking a step forward, straining to see if the king had joined his host, but there was no sign of William's standard among the myriad fluttering pennants. It mattered little. Soon, Styrkar would once again have the chance to whet his axe in Frankish blood. For now that would be enough.

They watched in silence as the conquering army arrayed itself in front of the walls. There was no herald to demand surrender, just a row of shields and a forest of spears. Knights atop their horses arranged themselves in their groups, shouting words of encouragement to one another.

Edgar took a step forward, turning to the hundreds who had come to defend Yorke.

'We hold this gate for as long as we can,' he cried. 'And when I give my order, we withdraw to the city. Are you with me?'

Half the men cheered their assent, but it was not enough for Edgar.

'Are you bloody with me?' he bellowed.

A cacophony of voices roared their agreement as they

moved forward to defend the scant barricade. Styrkar took his place at the front, gripping tight to his axe, watching the Franks march ever closer. He could see archers to the fore, remembering the storm of arrows he had faced at Senlac. The baresark tormented him, yearning to be unleashed, the hairs bristling on the back of his neck.

That marching row of shield men stopped forty yards from the gate. A pipe blew its shrill note, and Styrkar knew instinctively what was coming.

'Get down,' he growled.

The noise of a hundred bowstrings thrummed from beyond the wall. Styrkar ducked beneath the wagon as the men behind the barricade raised shields and dashed for cover. A relentless tirade of arrows struck the wagon. More still soared over the wall, striking shields and anyone not fast enough to find shelter. The screaming started as wounded men crawled across the dirt, begging for help.

No sooner was the first volley let fly than another struck, and another. All they could do was hunker down against the arrow storm as the Franks kept them pinned. A grim memory of Senlac Hill struck Styrkar as he remembered the way the invaders had tried to quell the Saxon numbers. It had been a black day, but with luck this time would be different.

Styrkar risked a glance beneath the cart. He could see the tramping feet of William's knights as they advanced on the gate under the cover of their archers. They were almost upon them.

All at once the arrows stopped. Every shield in Saxon hands was skewered by a dozen shafts, and many men cowered, unwilling to face what was coming. If they did not stand and fight they would all be slaughtered before they could think to lead the Franks into a trap.

Styrkar stood, raising his axe, bellowing at the defenders – a raw cry of feral hate – before he leapt up onto the wagon. The first of the Franks was already there, glaring up in surprise at the enemy he faced. Styrkar swung his axe like a headsman at the block, smashing into that conical helm and hacking a divot in its midst.

No sooner had he slain his first victim than Edgar leapt up by his side, hacking down with his jewelled blade.

'For the Aetheling,' someone cried, before they were joined by more men, batting aside the Frankish spears with their shields and smashing into the attackers with a ferocity born of hate.

Styrkar spat curses as he slew, and others leapt to their aid, heedlessly joining the fray. More and more men raced forward, desperate to add their weapons to the defence, even though the gate could never hold off such a mighty host. But that had never been their intention.

The stink of pitch hit Styrkar's nostrils as he hacked down another foe. Before he could look to the next, torches were thrown at the base of the wagon, and flames began to lick at their feet.

'Back!' Edgar yelled, and the men at the barricade retreated to within the shadow of the gate.

The fire took quickly, engulfing the wagon along with the rest of the debris they had piled in the breach. Styrkar watched, with Edgar at his side, as their only defence burned with intensity. The flames licked high, the heat becoming so strong they had to step back. Soon, all that would stand barring the way were a few determined men with nothing but their shields and their courage.

Beyond the flames, the horsemen had mustered. Those knights looked pitiless atop their mounts, lances held high, shields proudly bearing their heraldry. They shouted at one another in their foreign tongue, stirring themselves into a battle ardour as they prepared to charge.

'Wait,' Edgar urged his skittish fyrd. Styrkar could see they were ready to flee, but the trap had to be baited well if it was to work.

The heat of the flames had died now, the wagon reduced to blackened wood, the sacks burned down to nothing but ash.

'Hold your nerve, lads,' Edgar said through gritted teeth.

A single cry, and those warhorses bolted. They burst through the winnowing flames, trampling the fallen barricade beneath their hooves.

'Retreat!' Edgar yelled.

His men needed no further encouragement. As much as Styrkar yearned to face the enemy he too turned tail and fled with the rest, racing along the thoroughfare between rows of tightly packed dwellings.

The alleyways to left and right had been blocked by piles of stone and wood, allowing no other way to escape but straight down the road ahead. Hundreds of men ran in the path of the galloping horsemen, straight toward the distant bridge that spanned the river.

Styrkar could hear the clapping hooves gaining in his wake, at any moment expecting a Frankish lance to skewer his exposed back. He and Edgar were at the rear, all thought of battle gone now – flight was their only desire.

Just as the knights were about to trample them beneath their steeds, they crossed the threshold to the main square. More fyrd were waiting, along with a heavy wagon loaded with rocks.

'Heave!' bellowed a group of them as they pushed the wagon across the entrance to the square.

Styrkar heard the shriek of horses, as the knights at the forefront tugged on reins to halt their charge. No sooner had the way been blocked than Edgar's archers went about their task, aiming volley after volley of arrows down on the mounted men. Over the top of the wagon Styrkar could see those steeds wheeling in panic, the Frankish knights yelling at one another, cursing now the tables had been turned and it was they who were on the receiving end of a deluge.

The fyrd began to cheer as Edgar stepped forward, raising his sword at the hapless knights.

'Send them back to Hell,' he snarled, as more arrows rained on the knights. The horses squealed, one of them rearing before it fell, crushing the rider beneath. Others tried to bolt from the killing field, but were shot down before they'd made twenty yards.

A horn pealed out from the west, a long low lament that silenced the fyrd where they stood. Edgar lowered his sword, glaring toward the rampart from which the sound had echoed.

'Shit,' he spat, eyes filled with fury. 'Gospatric's position has been overrun.' He turned to Styrkar. 'Do we fight?'

Styrkar could already hear the sounds of battle coming from beyond the rooftops to the west, along with the distant snort of horses. The prospect of battling the Franks burned within him like a hunger, but he had seen their numbers. If Edgar fell here all hope of casting down the usurper would be lost.

'We cannot hold this square if the flank is breached. We must withdraw to the other side of the bridge.'

Edgar needed no further urging, yelling at his men to retreat deeper into the city. The fyrd obeyed, racing north toward the river and away from the marketplace. Again, Styrkar was at Edgar's shoulder as they followed their men, but before they could clear the square, a clap of hooves resounded from nearby.

The first horseman burst into view, lance piercing the side of a fleeing Saxon before he could escape. More knights followed, as panic began to spread through the ranks of Edgar's army.

Styrkar raced forward, axe already swinging as he battered a Frankish shield, pitching the rider from his saddle, before finishing him on the ground.

Glancing up he saw Edgar falter, losing his footing as he raced to join his men, and sent sprawling. A Frankish knight had the Aetheling in his sights, tip of his lance glittering in the afternoon sunlight. Styrkar would never reach him in time.

He grasped the axe with both hands, hefting it back over his head before flinging it. The axe span, end over end, to hit the knight full in the head, sending him toppling from his steed.

By the time Styrkar reached Edgar, he had already found his feet. Styrkar grasped the shaft of the axe and wrenched it from the knight's corpse.

'It seems that debt you owe me is paid, Red Wolf,' Edgar said.

Styrkar turned to see the knights riding rampant atop their steeds, making ready to pursue the stragglers desperate to escape the square.

'If we don't cross the bridge, debts won't matter either way, Aetheling,' he replied.

With a nod, Edgar led the way, the rampaging Franks close behind them.

42

Yorke, England, March 1069

A frenzied storm of chaos was descending over the city. Men fled in all directions, panicked by the sight and sound of Frankish knights. Their steeds ran rampant, lances flashing to spear anyone not swift enough to flee.

Ahead, Styrkar could see a flood of men crossing the bridge. On the nearside stood Maerlswein bellowing at them to keep moving, urging them on north of the river where they might be able to hold back the Frankish tide. A glimpse over his shoulder and Styrkar knew that was folly.

The Franks had reached the square now. Their spears and shields visible between the row of dwellings to either side of the thoroughfare. It would not be long before they rallied their forces and pressed northward.

Before he could reach the bridge he felt the swift whip of an arrow pass his head. As he drew closer to Maerlswein he realised there was a row of archers holding the bridge. One last line of defence against an entire army.

'We must withdraw,' Edgar said to Maerlswein as they

reached his side. 'The Franks have taken the southern half of the city.'

'But we can hold them here,' insisted Maerlswein, his lust for battle not yet sated. 'The crossing is narrow enough to defend with but a hundred men. I will not—'

Styrkar ducked as he heard the rush of air pass his ear. When he turned, he saw Maerlswein had been struck in the shoulder by a crossbow bolt. The warrior grunted, grasping the shaft, his teeth gritted more in anger than in pain. For a moment it looked as though he might wrench the bolt out with one hand, but his eyes suddenly rolled back in his head. Styrkar grasped him before he could fall.

'Retreat,' Edgar barked at the archers.

Together the remaining Saxon archers began to make their way across the river. Styrkar all but dragged Maerlswein with him until they reached a row of spearmen defending the apex of the bridge. Behind them the noise was almost deafening as the Franks yelled and banged their drums in preparation for the coming charge. Styrkar could smell the bitter stink of the pitch that covered the bridge. Their last line of defence.

'Where is Gospatric?' Edgar demanded, as three of Maerlswein's fyrd came forward to aid their wounded steward. 'Where is Waltheof?'

'Fled, my lord,' one of the fyrd replied. 'Already gone north with their men to escape the city.'

Edgar clenched his fists as Styrkar looked on. They had intended to hold Yorke for as long as they could, but it seemed those plans had blown away like so much ash on the breeze. Glancing back at the advancing Franks, their shields locked as they marched inexorably, Styrkar could see no way they could win the day.

'We cannot hold the bridge,' Edgar said, a despondent edge to his voice. 'All of you, withdraw to the north. We will rally at Haxebi. You…' He gestured to a man with a fearful look in his eye, holding a lit brand, '…hand me that flame.'

The man did as he was ordered, before fleeing across the bridge. Edgar turned toward the south, as Styrkar stood by his side with the half-dozen spear-carrying fyrd brave enough to remain. The Franks had marched almost to the edge of the river now, and there looked to be nothing that could stop them.

Edgar drew his arm back before flinging the flaming torch. It spun end over end before landing ten yards along the bridge. At first the torch simply sputtered, before the pitch suddenly caught. The wood of the bridge was wreathed in a halo of fire, flames licking across the causeway to block the Frankish advance. But as Styrkar watched, he knew it would not be enough to stop those knights atop their steeds.

'Fuck,' Edgar spat, seeing the same thing. 'That will not hold them for long.'

Through the flickering flame, Styrkar could see more horsemen arriving, carrying their banners with them. Billowing in the breeze, he caught sight of a pennant he recognised, one he had seen two years before. The gold cross on white. The king had come.

Styrkar stepped forward, his thirst for vengeance quashing the urgency to flee. And as he watched, he saw the man he had spent years waiting to face.

William sat atop his horse. He looked every inch the warrior king, his brow dark in its lust to conquer. To crush these upstarts and remove any challenge to his claim on the throne.

'We must go, Red Wolf,' Edgar said close behind him. 'There is no glory in dying here.'

But the Red Wolf did not seek glory. He sought revenge, and it was but yards away through the flames.

Before he could think to charge through the fire, a knight at the other side galloped forward. His fellows shouted at him in warning, but it seemed he saw glory for himself in trampling down these last rebels on the bridge.

His horse whinnied as it leapt the fire, hooves tramping down on the wood of the bridge. Styrkar planted his feet, bracing himself against the charge, but before he could bring his axe to bear, Edgar's spearmen rushed forward.

The warhorse reared in the face of those spearheads, its terror at the flames, the fast- flowing water beneath throwing it into a panic. The rider raised his lance, but as a spear was thrust into the side of the horse, it clattered toward the edge of the bridge.

The railing cracked, wood splintering under the horse's weight. Styrkar heard the yell of the knight atop his steed as he realised all that awaited him was the inglorious depths of the River Ouse. Styrkar did not even watch as both horse and rider were pitched into the water with a resounding splash. He was already searching for his next enemy.

'You should take your men and run,' Styrkar growled, as stray crossbow bolts streaked overhead.

'No. Not without you. I need you alive, Red Wolf.'

Slowly, Styrkar turned to face the young man he had followed down from the north. His jaw was set, his visage imperious, every inch a rightful king. A man to be followed when he gave a command. But not this day.

'I would have placed the crown of England upon your head myself, Aetheling. But now, my fate lies along a different path.'

Edgar opened his mouth to speak, most likely to demand Styrkar do as he commanded, that he was of lordly birth and should be obeyed. But as he glared there was a sudden realisation in his eyes. Edgar knew that the Red Wolf would never obey – not even the word of a king.

'Then I bid you farewell, Styrkar the Dane. May you finally find what you're searching for.' With that he turned, leading his remaining men north across the bridge to safety.

Styrkar turned to face the Franks once again. The fire still burned, smoke drifting so densely across the bridge he could hardly see, but on the far side he could still make out ranks of men in mail, awaiting the order to advance.

He buried the blade of his axe in the wooden parapet of the bridge, before unbuckling his mail. He wrenched the heavy armour over his head, feeling the immediate relief from its constraints. As soon as he did so, he saw her approaching through the billowing smoke.

She walked towards him, untroubled by the heat of the flames or the cloying black cloud that drifted on the breeze. Her face was just as he remembered – the most beautiful thing he had ever set eyes upon.

Gisela regarded him with deep sadness in her eyes. Did she yearn for him as he did for her? Was such a thing even possible? In that moment he felt his heart begin to crack. A heart beaten to solid iron, now breaking asunder in his chest.

'I should have listened to you, so long ago in our house by

the sea,' he whispered. 'Should have left this cursed land and lived the life of a normal man. Lived in peace. I could have just been yours, and you mine, and nothing else would have mattered.' He squeezed his eyes shut lest the tears run down his face. When he opened them again she was gone.

He was alone, the only thing defending a bridge against an unstoppable army. And in that moment he forgot Styrkar. Forgot the daughter he would never see, the friends he had lost, the life he would never lead. All that remained was the Red Wolf.

The haft of the Dane axe was in his hand, and he wrenched it from the wood of the bridge. It felt so familiar in his grip. So alive. As though it too thirsted to spill Frankish blood. And there was so much blood yet to shed.

Beneath him the bridge began to vibrate with the weight of tramping feet. They were coming. Through that choking mist of woodsmoke they would charge, but the Red Wolf could not wait.

A snarl issued from his lips as he raced into the black, choking fog, feeling the heat of the flames overwhelm him in a rush. He just caught sight of a coned helm, his axe swinging. The resounding clang rose above the crackle of flames, the jolt in his arm serving to embolden him as he swung again blindly. He struck a shield, knocking one of the Franks back, hearing his cry of dismay.

They began to panic, calling out in fear and confusion as he battered his way forward, smashing his shoulder into the shields before him. A sudden gust stifled the flames and through the roiling of smoke he caught sight of the king atop his steed.

Stone-hard rage filled his blood and the Red Wolf roared.

The axe swung, right to left, knocking over a knight before he could think to raise his spear. Another had sword drawn, but the axe cleaved him from neck to ribcage, the impetus of the stroke shearing through his mail. As his enemy fell back dead, Styrkar lost his grip on the axe. Before he could recover it, he was surrounded by shields, feeling the head of a spear slice his arm.

Desperately the Franks pushed back the mad berserker in their midst, through the smoke and the flames, and back onto the bridge.

He grabbed one of them by the throat, lifting him into the air as another grasped him around the waist. More rushed forward into the miasma, heedless of the danger, but their bravery mattered little to Styrkar.

'Do you know who you face?' he roared, his grip tightening around the neck of the hapless knight. 'I am the Red Wolf. Shield Breaker. Bane of the Franks. And I will seal your doom.'

They battered him back to the edge of the bridge, the wood smacking into Styrkar's side and cracking a rib. He growled in rage, the weight of the press causing the wood to give beneath his weight, the singed timbers threatening to split completely.

'Come,' he cried, smashing a fist into a nearby helm. 'Let us face our end together.' The wood behind him cracked, the rail splitting under the weight of violence. 'We shall enter the Dread Hall together, and fight forever in—'

The side of the bridge gave way.

Styrkar plunged over the edge, still grasping his enemies, still smashing them till his fists were raw and he was consumed by the chill arms of the river.

At first there was only the black and choking waters as he sank beneath the weight of a dozen armoured men. Then, through the dark, he saw a face serene against the inky shadows.

Then nothing.

43

The fire roared in its pit, the flames threatening to set light to the thatch above, but no matter how much wood he threw in Ronan still couldn't get warm. For days now his damnable leg had been numb, and no matter how much he tried to rub back some feeling it still felt like a necrotic lump below the knee. His toes hadn't blackened from the freezing weather, but it would have been no surprise for him to take off the wrappings to find they had dropped off.

He had thrown three blankets over his shoulders, but it felt like all the furs in the north would bring him no relief from the accursed cold. His teeth were clamped together lest they chatter free of his gums, fists bunched, two blocks of ice stuck to the end of his wrists.

When he had fled Dun Holm, blind elation had kept him warm in the thick squall of snow. It hadn't lasted long. He had ridden blindly for what seemed like hours through the storm, the daylight bringing neither solace, nor relief from the elements. Then his stolen steed had collapsed beneath him. Ronan had barely survived the fall, bruising his shoulder and cracking his cheek on the frozen earth. It was only the start of his woes, as he had been forced to limp miles through the snow, shivering and cursing his ill luck for yard after woeful yard.

The first night he had found shelter in a pig pen, ignoring the stink of shit and taking comfort from the warmth of the surrounding swine. On the second he had found an abandoned shack, though the fire he had managed to build had done little to stifle the grip of winter. On he had wandered, starving in the wild, until by some miracle he had been found by his countrymen. They had laughed. Fucking laughed as he moaned and shivered, but still he had been grateful when they brought him to this place.

It was a staging point for the retaking of Yorke. An army had gathered here under the purview of the king himself. Every peasant in their shithole of a village had been cast to the wilds as this quiet rural idyll became a garrison from which they would launch their attack. Ronan had taken little interest in the plans to subdue the upstart northerners – his only concern was staying alive. And now here he was, alone in this cesspit but for one idiot squire who could find him not a drop of ale or cider to warm over the fire.

'Where the fucking hell are you?' Ronan raged, unable to quell his discontent any longer.

No answer from the squire. Ronan's anger simmered so much he would have beaten the boy for his lack of initiative, but he doubted even that would thaw the blood in his veins. For now he would have to sit and shiver, and hope that once he managed to make it back to the south there'd be more appropriate accommodations waiting.

Still, the misery he experienced in this ramshackle dump of a house was much better than what had been visited on the people of Yorke. Before the sun had set, Ronan was able to see the smoke rising from the distant cathedral. He could only imagine how those peasants were suffering for their defiance. King William had clearly not been remiss in the demonstration of his ire.

'Where's my bloody cider, squire?' Ronan bellowed again, as loud as his hoarse throat would allow.

As though in answer, the door to the chamber opened, letting in a chilling breath of air.

'About time,' Ronan said, still staring into the flames. 'A man could die of thirst waiting for you, lazy bastard.'

'That's hardly any way to greet a conquering hero,' said a deep, refined voice.

Ronan turned to see Guillam Mallet closing the door against the cold. At first he was shocked – embarrassed that he had mistaken a man of such high status for a lowly squire. The next thing he thought was how rich it was of him to suggest he was in any way a hero, after fleeing the city of Yorke at the first sign of danger some days ago.

'Apologies, my lord,' Ronan said. 'I thought you were someone else.'

Guillam's consequent smile was radiant as ever. 'No harm done. Don't get up, Ronan, I merely came to apprise you of our victory.'

That seemed an odd excuse. It was obvious their victory had been secured when the burning started. And for a man like Guillam to come here himself seemed at odds with his position.

'I am sure the king is relieved that the murder of Lord

Robert is avenged, and the north is once again under his gracious stewardship.'

Guillam smirked at that notion as he stood by the fire, warming his hands in the light of the flames. 'Gracious? You're a funny man, Ronan. You know as well as I do that even now he takes his revenge on those defiant northern bastards. Every Saxon and Dane in the north will know the consequences of defying their king. Robert's soul can rest easy knowing the king has spread his justice.'

He let that final word hang in the air for a moment. So long that Ronan shivered again. If by 'justice' Guillam meant burning their hovels and raping their women, then he was certainly right.

'I for one am glad of it,' Ronan said finally. 'I've had more than my fill of this place. Now it is secure, I can't return to the south quickly enough.'

Guillam winced in disappointment. 'About that... As much as I'm sure Earl Brian would welcome you with open arms, I am afraid the north is not done with you yet, Dol-Combourg.'

Ronan swallowed, feeling the sense of dread dilute the cold that still infested his every fibre. 'I... I'm not sure what you mean. The northerners are quelled. What happens now in this region is none of my affair.'

Guillam gazed at him, raising an eyebrow and smiling. 'Oh, but it is. In fact I have discussed this very matter with the king himself. Though we have sealed a victory at Yorke, the north is far from subdued. And you, Ronan, have proven yourself a resourceful man. A survivor. You escaped kidnap and imprisonment at the hands of these

Saxon rebels. Survived so deftly in the wilds, even when surrounded by enemies at every quarter.'

As much as he appreciated Guillam's praise, it might have been more accurate to say he had more often been surrounded by pig shit.

'I think I understand what you're saying, but—'

'Then it is decided,' Guillam said with a shrug, picking up the iron poker and stoking the flames of the fire. 'You will stay here, at Yorke, until the deed is done.'

This was getting out of hand, and Ronan could feel the panic loosening his insides. The only way to quell it was by rising unsteadily to his feet to fix Guillam with as determined a stare as he could muster.

'Listen to me. I appreciate how complimentary you're being, but I am done with this place. I am done with its people. I am done with the cold, and the danger. I have done *enough*.'

Guillam nodded his understanding. He had always appeared a congenial man. A man of breeding, who understood the needs of the men around him. For a moment, Ronan even thought he might have done enough to press his point, until Guillam stabbed the end of the poker in his chest.

Ronan squealed, losing his balance and falling back into the chair. The heat of the poker had burned a hole in his shirt, and he could feel the sting of it against his chest.

'Perhaps you misunderstand me, cripple,' Guillam snarled. All amiability was gone now. His furious eyes bored into Ronan as though he might raise that poker again and spill his brains onto the straw-covered floor. 'This is not a request. The Saxons of the north are double-dealing scum. They will stab us between the shoulder blades as soon as our backs are turned. If I am to maintain order here I need someone equally as untrustworthy. If it makes you feel better, pretend I said cunning. Would that be more *complimentary?*'

Before Ronan could think of an answer the door opened again. In walked the squire, heralded by more cold air, carrying a tankard upon his tray. He gazed in surprise at Guillam before offering Ronan the cup.

'Your cider, my lord,' he said nervously.

'My thanks,' Guillam replied, taking the tankard. 'I am a little thirsty.' He took a swig as the squire made himself scarce. Then he licked his lips before finishing the whole cupful. 'Surprisingly good. Anyway, I appreciate having the chance to talk with you. And I look forward to seeing you at Yorke tomorrow.'

He smiled and nodded his goodbye, before tossing the tankard into the fire and leaving Ronan alone.

The burn in his chest did nothing to alleviate the cold in his bones. As he reached down for the blankets that had fallen to the floor, he felt a sudden twinge of pain down his leg, in his shoulder, down his back. He wanted to weep but gritted his teeth against it. Ronan would not accept the pain, would not accept this weakness. By God, he already had so many other things he was forced to accept.

He was now little more than a thrall to a madman. And just when he had been so close to escape. He had managed to run from men determined to murder him, into the hands of someone who wanted to throw him right back into the fucking wolf pit.

Eventually he managed to sit upright, to grab those blankets, to rub a little warmth into his limbs. And as he stared into the fire, he began to calm. Self-pity would get him nowhere. Surely there was something he could salvage from this.

For the briefest of times he had considered following the path of a good man. That had been snatched away from him as surely as Yorke had been snatched from those bastard rebels. If that taught him one lesson it was plain – *good men get nothing.*

If Guillam was right about one thing, it was that Ronan was cunning. He would find some way for this to pay. Sift through the ashes and discover gold somewhere, no matter who he had to trample to do it. If any man could, then it was Ronan of Dol-Combourg, the bastard cripple.

With a smile he raised his eyes to the roof and bellowed, 'Bring me more fucking cider!'

44

*T*he sun brightened the interior of the old villa, lancing in through gaps in the wooden roof. A fur hide hanging over one of the windows billowed in the breeze, as the sea air blew fresh and crisp. He breathed in the comforting feel of it, trying to remember a time now lost. A time when he had been happy.

Reaching forward he pulled the fur aside, allowing the light to bathe him as he squinted toward the sea. It was calm, its surface shining like the polished edge of an axe glinting in firelight.

This was all so familiar, but at the same time distant, as though at any moment it might slip through his fingers, this whole scene a reflection of something he had lost so long ago.

'Come.'

He heard that single word as a breath of scented wind on the air. No sweeter sound had ever been spoken, and he turned his head to see her there. In her arms she held an infant, quiet in its slumber, hand gripping one of her braided locks.

For a moment he stood, drinking in the sight of them. Letting it wash over him before he could stand it no longer.

He stepped toward the pair, embracing them both in his arms, holding them gently to his chest as though he might never let them go. In that moment he had never felt such joy, a sensation denied for so long, but now pouring over him like the water from a mountain spring.

The house shook with a sudden gust of wind, rattling the beams above them, resounding through the floor of the villa. He ignored it, too enrapt in this feeling, unable to let go lest he lose what he had yearned to hold all the tortured years of his life.

'Am I done now?' he whispered. 'Can I rest here with you both in my arms?'

There was yearning in his voice, a need to make amends for so many mistakes. He desired only to plant the roots of his life in this place, with this woman and the child they shared. Once, in a past he could barely remember, he had left her to seek a final reckoning when he should have gathered her up and fled. Now he had one last chance to redress that mistake.

She gazed up at him. Her face was filled with sorrow and a single tear rolled from the corner of her eye. 'No,' she whispered back. 'You are not done yet.'

His eyes opened to the bright sun. Breath came ragged as he raised a weary arm to shield himself from the glare. Styrkar could barely move, but he made the effort as he was rocked and buffeted as though on a ship at sea.

A cough broke free of his throat and he felt his ribs ache at the effort. As his eyes focused he could see he had been laid in the back of a cart. The sound of it trundling along the road made him wince. He cringed further when a voice shouted, 'By God, he's awake.'

Styrkar realised he wasn't alone in the back of that wagon. He pulled aside the fur blanket covering him and shifted his weight to lean his back against the side of the cart. Opposite him sat a hulking figure, and his eyes quickly focused on a face he recognised.

Maerlswein sat bare chested as he grinned through his bushy beard. His shoulder was heavily bandaged and in one fist he gripped tight to a tankard.

'For a while there I didn't think you were going to make it, Red Wolf,' he said with a laugh, before quaffing down more of whatever was in his tankard. 'We fished you out of the Ouse about a mile downstream of Yorke. You and a few other dead fish. Everyone else thought you were done for, but the Aetheling wasn't about to give in to a little thing like death.'

'And I am grateful for it,' Styrkar tried to say, but it came out as little more than a dry croak.

Maerlswein moved forward gingerly, offering Styrkar a swig from the tankard. He accepted gratefully, swallowing down the bitter ale. He was managing to breath more easily now, though his body ached from the effort.

'How is your wound?' Styrkar asked, gesturing to Maerlswein's bandaged arm.

The warrior grinned again. 'Just another hole to be plugged, my friend.' He raised the tankard as though in a toast. 'I'll just have to keep drinking and make sure it's stopped leaking.' With that he laughed again, before swigging down the rest of the ale.

Styrkar turned his head at the sound of approaching

hooves. He saw Edgar atop a horse, riding proudly despite the ignominy of their recent defeat. The Aetheling reined in beside the trundling cart and smiled in relief.

'I knew you would not die so easily, Styrkar the Dane. You must have fought as though battling your way out of Hell itself.'

Styrkar shook his head. 'I do not remember,' he replied. The memory of it was intertwined with a recent dream. A dream now fading from his mind. 'Where are we heading to?'

Edgar gestured along the road. Styrkar could see fyrd and peasant alike walking the muddy trail. 'We have allies north, in Alba. They will take us in, allow us to lick our wounds. Then, when we are rested and ready for the fight once more, we shall return to England and prove to the usurper that the men of the north are not so easily defeated. Are you still with us?'

Though he was encouraged by Edgar's words, Styrkar was not so sure it would be as simple as he described. He felt weak as a newborn foal, his lust for Frankish blood all but spent.

'I'll be honest, Aetheling, I am not so sure. I am burned and bruised. All I feel good for is to dig a hole and crawl inside it.'

Edgar nodded. 'I understand, my friend. No one has done more to defy our enemy than you. But let me ask you one thing... when you said you would have put the crown of England on my head, did you mean it?'

Styrkar thought on the words, the memory of what he had said on that burning bridge coming back to him in a flood. He remembered his hate, the heat of his blood, the unquenchable thirst that could only be sated by the death of the Franks and their king.

'First tell me, Aetheling, if I help you take this crown, will I have another chance to kill the king?'

Edgar's smile widened. 'That is one promise I am sure I can keep.'

Styrkar fixed him with as firm a glare as he could manage. 'Then I will give you the crown, and the usurper's head along with it.'

'I believe you, Red Wolf,' Edgar replied. 'Only a fool would bet against it.'

With that he pulled on the rein of his horse, and rode on further up the line of rebels.

Maerlswein was already laughing from his place in the cart. 'Even though you're half drowned and bloodied,' he said, 'I'm still thankful we're on the same side.'

Styrkar shivered in the northern chill, and pulled the fur back over his shoulders as he hunkered down in the cart. He was weak, beaten, but he knew that would not last. He had survived worse, and learned lessons from it that no one could forget. That a man's word meant little when his life and love were in peril. That to lose that love could twist him into a monster. But most of all, Styrkar had learned that love was powerful, but also fragile. It could be snatched away with the single thrust of a knife. But hate... hate endured. Hate could not be killed with even the most keenly tempered blade, and it could only be silenced by one thing... vengeance.

Glossary

Baresark – Legendary Norse warriors who fought without armour.

Byrnie – A coat of mail worn by Frankish knights.

Conrois – A group of between five and ten Frankish knights, who fought together as a unit.

Fyrd – A civilian army consisting of freemen drawn from the shires.

Heimdallr – A god in Viking myth.

Housecarl – A nobleman's personal bodyguard.

Pibgorn – An ancient wind instrument.

Seax – A single-bladed Saxon weapon, used as a knife or short sword.

Thegn – A noble given lands by the king in return for service during times of war.

Thrydings – Equivalent to modern counties (Ridings).

Torc – A ring of metal worn about the neck.

Valhöll – The Hall of the Fallen in Viking myth.

Witan – Or 'Witenagemot', a meeting or council of senior Saxon nobles.

About the Author

RICHARD CULLEN originally hails from Leeds in the heartland of Yorkshire. As well as being a writer of historical adventure, he has also written a number of epic fantasy series as R.S. Ford. If you'd like to learn more about his books, and read FREE exclusive content, you can visit his website at wordhog.co.uk, follow him on Twitter at @rich4ord, or join him on Instagram @thewordhog.